WITH EVERY HEARTBEAT

LINDA KAGE

With Every Heartbeat

Contact Information : linda@lindakage.com

Publishing History
Linda Kage, March 2015
Print ISBN: 1507598750
Print ISBN-13: 978-1507598757

Credits
Cover Artist: Kage Covers
Editor: Stephanie Parent
Proofreader: Shelley at *2 Book Lovers Reviews*

Published in the United States of America

DEDICATION

I'M DEDICATING this story to Ada Frost, awesome friend, amazing critique partner, personal hero and one of my favorite authors! She's the first person to claim one of my book heroes as her own and threaten to cut a bitch for looking at him wrong. So for the safety all you other readers out there, be careful what you say when making any claims about Quinn. I'm telling you this woman will get stabby for her book boyfriends. She wanted me to write a shy hero and shy heroine, and what my Ada wants, my Ada gets!

So, this one's for you, Ada. Thank you for your friendship. Thank you for your advice. Thank you for your support. Thank you for being you. Love your heart!

ONE

ZOEY

THE PARTY WAS completely out of control. Thumping loud music, alcohol in every hand, topless girls in the hot tub outside, and more of them booty-grinding on the coffee table indoors. If I'd been wearing pearls, I would've clutched those bad boys for dear life as I stood in the doorway, gaping at the sight before me.

This was my first college kegger...and on Shark Week, no less. I couldn't believe Cora wanted me to meet her *here*.

"Out of the way!" a voice bellowed behind me. "Coming through."

I turned just in time to see a silver keg barreling directly for me. With a squeak, I dove to the side and fully into the frat house, barely saving my piggies hanging out the front of my sandals from being smashed. The pair of drunk guys pushing the beer inside on a dolly leered at me, offering me a drink if I agreed to flash them. I respectfully declined, and they shrugged, moving on and disappearing into the rowdy horde.

Clutching my imaginary pearls, I gulped heavily. What the heck was I doing? After living eighteen years under the strict dictatorship of my father, I'd never seen anyone drinking spirits before, much less getting wasted from them, as pretty much everyone around me was. Heck, we even took grape juice during Communion at the church we attended because wine was forbidden in my little world.

I was so out of my element; I wanted to run and hide. But I didn't have anywhere to run *to*. Arriving three days early, I was literally locked out of my new apartment until I found my roommate.

After I'd called her from the track phone she'd sent me and told her I was in town, Cora had instructed me to meet her at this address. And I was sure it was this address; I'd double, triple and quadruple checked.

I'd texted her from outside moments ago, telling her I was here, hoping she'd come out to me, but all she'd replied was: **Come on in. I'm in the back.**

The back. She might as well have told me to meet her at the end of a dark, creepy alley of a ghetto where homeless bums were scurrying through trash and thugs were dealing drugs, and oh, Holy Hosanna, was that guy smoking a joint? I didn't know the difference between a real cigarette and...well, what-ever that thin, short thing was hanging out of his mouth, but it certainly didn't smell like regular nicotine tobacco wafting my way.

Telling Cora no way, that she needed to hike her skinny little tush outside to meet me, would only ex-press how much of a loser I was. So I bolstered myself, squared my shoulders and drew in a deep breath.

Welcome to college, Zoey.

Had I mentioned I was so out of my freaking element?

Grabbing a piece of my blonde hair and trying not to appear as awkward and scared as I felt, I wound the comforting lock around my finger and step-ped forward, determined to do this. But a startling cheer from the crowd as a guy jumped onto the coffee table to dance with the topless girls had me hunching my shoulders and bolting toward the first doorway I saw, hoping it led to "the back."

My heart pounded, and I felt so inept because everyone around me was having fun. No one was scared out of their mind, no one looked as if they could burst into tears any second just because they were here, and no one seemed to be on the verge of hyper-ventilating. The jealousy bug nipped hard. I kind of wished I could be as uninhibited and free-spirited as all these people.

Why was it so hard for me to walk through a crowd of drunk strangers? To mix and mingle? To socialize? Growing up as isolated as I had was no excuse. Cora had grown up in the same environment, and she *was* here, wasn't she?

She'd *better* be here.

Focusing on the anger I felt at myself for being such coward, I used the heat behind that to propel myself forward. I could do this.

I *would* do this.

The next room I entered was thankfully mellower than the first. No dancing, no music, no nakedness. But it was still just as crowded, if not more so. Lots of people clumped into groups, talking. Most of them were male, which brought up another irrational trepidation I had. After being homeschooled through the first eight grades, I hadn't been around much of the opposite gender, at least not many who were my age. My father had made sure to keep me away from boys. So seeing this many of them, everywhere I turned, was a little unnerving. My limbs heated and face flushed. I was certainly going to be attending college with a lot of hotties.

Already knowing I wasn't going to find Cora in this room, I started to turn but stopped cold when I did recognize one face, like the supreme hottie of all hotties.

Cora was an avid Facebooker. She posted pictures and updates constantly. So I was well aware of what her boyfriend looked like. I'd been bowled over the first time I'd seen his snapshot pop up on her page three months ago. Quinn Hamilton was perfect in the looks department—like ridiculously, flawlessly perfect. I couldn't believe my best friend had been able to snag a complete dreamboat like him.

Not that she didn't deserve someone gorgeous or wasn't good enough to catch a hunk. She was beautiful and way more outgoing than me. She could probably get any guy she wanted. But Quinn Hamilton had just seemed like movie-star pretty, completely untouchable to regular non-movie-star citizens like us. Even as he stood among a throng of attractive, drunk college guys and sipped from a red SOLO cup, he managed to shine above them all.

It didn't seem possible, but he was even better looking in person. Grainy pictures online so did not do him justice. I stared a moment longer because, well... art was meant to be appreciated, and he was a masterpiece.

3

After maybe a bit too much appreciation, I finally scanned the faces around him, hoping Cora might be near. But I didn't find her anywhere.

I knew I should approach him since he was the best chance I had of locating my best friend, but going anywhere near such perfection felt utterly forbidden.

I'd have to meet him eventually, sure; he was Cora's boyfriend. But I wasn't ready yet, mostly be·cause he'd just smiled at something someone was telling him. The skin around his eyes crinkled with genuine warmth, his lips lifted into the most attractive demeanor, while his entire complexion just... brightened. And yeah, I couldn't do it.

I turned to find the exit behind me, only to discover it was blocked. Fear and a bit of claustrophobia clutched my throat, making it suddenly hard to breathe. I needed to get out of this house. The sooner I found Cora, the better.

Okay, fine. I'd meet the boyfriend, then. I could do that. Sure.

I started toward Quinn Hamilton just as the guy talking to him pulled up his phone and showed the screen to Quinn. I was only a few feet away now; one more step and I'd be close enough to reach out and tap him on the shoulder—holy Lord, could I actually sum·mon the nerve to touch those thick, amazingly formed shoulders?

But the curious smile lighting his face dropped as soon as he looked at the phone.

I stumbled to a halt as his eyes went flint hard and narrowed on his friend. His lips were tight as he said something in a low growl I couldn't hear. The other guy threw back his head and laughed as if it was the funniest comment in the world. But Quinn dropped his drink—yeah, right on the floor—splattering...what was that—water?—all over his shoes. Then he grabbed two fistfuls of the other man's shirt and propelled him backward, right through a crowd of people until he had his opponent pinned to the wall with the guy's shoes dangling a good foot above the floor.

Holy—

"I said, *delete it*," Quinn roared, loud enough for not just me, but everyone in the room to hear. Maybe everyone in the house. Possibly the city.

The skin pulled taut over his hard jaw as he glared at the man he was holding captive, letting everyone know he wasn't kidding around.

The room went hushed, and every eye turned toward them. I shrank a step back, not sure what to do or where to hide. While all my duck-and-cover instincts flared to life, someone came shoving through people and right past me, hollering, "Hey, hey, hey! What the fuck is going on?"

When the newcomer reached Quinn, he tugged him away from the other guy, who gratefully slid to the floor and made a production of gasping for breath and straightening his shirt.

"Get his phone," Quinn commanded the man who'd so easily been able to pull him out of a fight.

Without question, his friend snatched the phone from the guy who was still patting himself down.

The new guy's face drained of color before he sent Quinn a grimace. "Shit," he muttered. His thumb punched the screen a few times before he shoved it back at its owner.

The owner scowled. "Hey! You deleted it."

"Hey! Douche nozzle," Quinn's friend shot back, imitating the phone owner's insulted tone. "You shouldn't have had it in the first place. Where did you get it, and who the fuck else did you show it to? Did you send it to anyone?"

"Why do you care? Or were you the one banging her?"

"Oh, I'm going to bang you, buddy." This time it was Quinn's friend, not Quinn, who grabbed two handfuls of shirt and shoved the phone owner against the wall. "I'm going to bang your fucking head against this fucking wall if you don't answer my fucking questions."

That was probably more f-bombs than I'd heard in my entire life. To have them assault my stunned ears all in one breath left them ringing. Frozen to the spot, I clutched my own shirt with two handfuls and watched as Quinn gripped his friend's shoulder and tried to tug him back.

"Enough. The picture's gone. It's over."

But his friend wasn't as easy to bring to heel as he'd been. Keeping his stare on the phone owner who was struggling to break loose, he sneered. "The fuck if it's over. Little prick here needs to learn some manners."

"Fuck you," Little Prick answered. Then he spit in his captor's face.

I swallowed, knowing exactly what was going to happen next. And yep, Quinn's friend turned a hot, angry red. "Oh, you're dead." Then he wound back his arm, his hand already balled into a fist. I winced, bracing for the punch, even though it wasn't aimed at me. I knew how much they hurt.

But Quinn intercepted this one, catching it in his palm.

"What the hell?" his friend started as Quinn let go of the fist to wrap a single arm around his waist and lift him off the floor.

Oh, wow. He was strong. His rowdy friend was by no means little, but Quinn didn't even break a sweat as he carried the cursing guy under his arm toward an exit in the back of the room. As soon they disappeared out the door, everyone started gossiping. The spitting phone owner began talking big about how he would've won the fight, while I just stood there, petrified.

I wanted out of this place so bad. And the only person whom I knew could help me find Cora had just walked out the door.

Deciding that staying here a minute longer was more intimidating than Quinn Hamilton, I raced after him. When I found myself in a quiet, dark backyard, I paused, but I heard familiar muttering so I didn't retreat into the house.

"Why the fuck did you stop me, Ham? That little dipshit deserved to get the piss kicked out of him."

I might've only heard him say a few words inside the frat house, but I immediately recognized Quinn's voice as he answered. "Coach said you'd get kicked off the team if you got into another fight."

"Fuck Coach. No, you know what. Fuck *you*. You should've kicked his ass *for* me. Yeah. Coach probably would've eaten that shit up. He'd *love* to see you get a little more aggressive. He probably would've pissed himself if he'd seen you shoving Belcher against that wall." With a laugh, he slugged Quinn in the shoulder. "That was pretty badass. Impressed the fuck out of me. I didn't know you had that shit in you."

I shook my head, amazed by the guy who'd gone from cussing Quinn to complimenting him in one long, run-on sentence. Quinn seemed similarly amused. His back was to me, so I couldn't see his face, but he gave a small laugh and shook his head. "Um...thank you?" he said as if not certain whether he was being praised or insulted.

He had a nice laugh. Nice smile, too. Very nice backside. Not that I was looking...much.

Under his pretty face and intimidatingly hulking

physique, however, I wondered exactly what kind of person my best friend had attached herself to. He'd been so quick to shove that other guy into a wall. I prayed Cora hadn't found a violent man. That was one thing I wouldn't be able to handle.

Then again, he'd been just as quick to settle down, and he'd even stopped his friend from taking the argument to the next level. Actually, he'd seemed more protective than hostile. Made me wonder what kind of picture had been on that phone.

"Can we help you with something, sweetheart?"

I jumped at the question, realizing Quinn's friend had spotted me spying on them. My mouth went dry. It was now or never time.

With a small clearing of my throat, I nodded. "I...I'm sorry. I was just...I was looking for Cora."

Hearing her name, Quinn turned.

And looked directly at me.

His blue-eyed gaze froze me. I felt like the guy he'd shoved against the wall: held captive in his grip and unable to break free. Then he blinked a pair of overly long dark lashes. Every organ inside me seemed to ignite into flames. My skin prickled and my flight-or-fight instinct kicked in, making me think my reaction to him was fear. But I'd never felt a tightening deep in my stomach when I'd been scared before. This was...I don't even know.

My body didn't seem to know what the heck was wrong with me, either, so it rebelled against the overwhelming foreign sensation, making my breath quicken and my fingers and toes tingle.

"I..." Smoothing some hair behind my ear, I gaped back at Quinn Hamilton. "I'm sorry for interrupting. I know you don't know me. But I've seen pictures of you, so I knew who you were, and I thought you could help me. But, I..." I tried to apologize again as I backed toward the doorway, except the words stuck in my throat. "I'm..."

"Zoey," Quinn said softly, as if finishing my sentence for me. And, oh my word. Hearing my name come from his mouth set off all kinds of tingling and tummy tightening inside me.

Yep. I was in big trouble.

"I've seen pictures of you, too." A soft smile lit his face as he started toward me. "Cora's inside."

I tripped in reverse as he came closer, my eyes going wide.

My behavior caused him to jerk to a halt. His mouth opened and apology entered his gaze, but he said nothing. He cleared his throat and pointed toward the back door of the frat house. "I can...I'll show you where she is."

Nodding my compliance, I stayed mute as shame flooded my limbs. The guy had only been trying to be nice and help me out, and I'd been shying away from him as if he were an ax murderer.

Way to make a first impression to Cora's boyfriend, you idiot.

He moved around me, purposely giving me a wide berth, and opened the back door, only to step aside to let me enter first. I drew in a breath and skipped up onto the small back steps, coming close enough to him that I could immediately notice how incredible he smelled. Clean and male with a subtle hint of spice.

"Thank you," I started to say, but his friend broke in, calling after us.

"Hey!" I turned in time to see him waving his hands. "What the hell, man?"

"Oh." From the surprise in Quinn's voice, I think he'd forgotten about the other guy completely. "This is Cora's new roommate. I'm going to help her find Cora." Then he glanced at me. "That's Ten. He's *my* roommate." He let out a small sigh and rolled his eyes before adding, "Unfortunately."

"I heard that," Ten said, setting his hands on his hips. "If you leave now, who's going to talk me out of kicking Belcher's ass?"

Quinn frowned and glanced at me before turning his attention to Ten. "Can't you talk yourself out it?"

"Probably not."

Quinn motioned me with a tip of his head to go ahead and enter the house. "Don't worry. He'll talk himself out of it," he assured me with a sigh.

Two

ꙮ QUINN ꙮ

AFTER I REASSURED Zoey that Ten wouldn't start any fights without me, her lips loosened with a relieved smile. My stomach followed suit, loosening with its own relief.

I had desperately wanted Cora's friend to like me. Cora had told me about Zoey's past, her strict, abusive father, her shielded homeschooled upbringing, her shy demeanor. I had felt like a kindred soul to her the moment I'd learned of her because I could too easily relate to a lot of words Cora had used to describe her. I'd actually been hoping I could maybe, possibly, I don't know...finally *talk* to someone else who under-stood some of the things I'd been through.

But then stupid, idiot Belcher had shown me that picture of my friend Noel's girlfriend topless, and yeah...Zoey Blakeland's first impression of me was shoving him against a wall.

Awesome.

She probably thought I was exactly like her father. She'd certainly shied away from me quickly enough when I'd merely walked toward her. Now I was going to have to work double-time to convince her that was the first time I'd ever shoved anyone anywhere. I was the least violent person I knew. I mean, I had been... until tonight.

My hands were still shaking, surprised by how quickly

I'd manhandled the baseball player. But Noel was one of the few friends I had. I couldn't handle anyone disrespecting his girlfriend by showing off topless pictures of her.

Realizing I was actually capable of such violence messed with my head, though. Made me worry what I might be truly capable of doing.

"So, uh..." I didn't know what to say to Cora's new roommate. The first thing to pop into my mind was that she was early. We weren't planning for her to make it into town until Sunday evening. But I thought mentioning that would make her feel as if I didn't want her here, when the idea of Cora having her best friend on hand was actually nice.

Unprepared for this, I scratched the back of my head. "Cora's this way," I said and started for a back hall I used a lot to avoid running into too many people, but then I wondered if I'd freak her out by taking her into a long, dark hallway alone. So I changed directions, except she'd already been following me to go the other way, and we collided into each other.

"Sorry." I grabbed her shoulders to keep her from toppling over.

She might be tall for a girl, but she was still a dainty thing. I was like a big, bumbling buffoon next to her sleek, willowy frame. Feeling her all soft and pliable under my hands made her seem extra feminine and sweet, which in turn made me more aware of how male I was, which was...awkward.

Really awkward.

She smelled good, too. I caught myself leaning in to catch another whiff so I could figure out what the heck that scent was. I stopped cold when she looked up at me with big sea foam green eyes.

And oh...wow.

I totally didn't mean to freeze, but I was thunder-struck, and I paused for way too long of a second.

Great, now she was going to think I was coming on to her or something. She'd have Cora talked out of dating me within the hour.

My hands jerked off her as if she'd scalded me. My ears burned with humiliation while I cleared my throat. "You okay?" When she nodded, I did too, motioning us back toward the crowded part of the frat house. "We, uh, we should probably take this way."

I was trying too hard. I always flubbed things up whenever I wanted to impress someone. My stress levels rose, I paid too much attention to every little thing I did and said, and I became so self-conscious my stutter usually returned.

Refusing to say a word so I could at least keep that little embarrassment under control, I led Zoey into the next room where noise and the bustling activity of a college party assaulted us. She inched closer to me, which was nice, since it meant she wasn't flat-out afraid of me, but I told myself she did it because the place was cramped; there was honestly nowhere else for her to go.

When some drunkard stumbled backward into her, she gasped and grabbed my wrist, smashing her side into mine. I curled a protective arm around her and used my free hand to nudge the drunk away. She didn't pull away from me, so I kept her flush against me and led her to my girlfriend.

Cora was exactly where I'd last seen her, dancing to some hip-hop song with two guys who were laughing and talking with her above the music between all the Jell-O shots they were downing. Eyes closed, she lifted her hands above her head, swished her hair around her face and rotated her hips in a way that reminded me of the first night we'd met. The night I'd lost my virginity.

"There," I said, pointing her out. I freed Zoey so she could go to Cora. But she didn't leave my side.

Her mouth fell open as she gawked openly, moving her face forward as if she didn't believe her own eyes. "Is..." Her mouth moved a few more times before she looked up at me. "Is she *drunk?*"

I froze, not sure how to answer. But, oh, boy.

Apparently, those two had a lot of catching up to do.

Instead of saying anything, I left her and eased through the dancers to catch Cora's elbow. When she turned and saw me, her face brightened, which al-ways lit me up inside. I couldn't explain how nice it was to be with someone who was always happy to see me.

"Quinn!" she cheered, vaulting herself against me and looping her arms around my neck. "Are you fin-ally going to dance with me?" When she lifted onto her toes to kiss me, I kissed her back.

I liked it better when she was doing shots instead of sucking down beer. Tasted better. Plus the smell of beer haunted me with too many bad memories. As her tongue slid against mine, I decided tonight's Jell-O of choice must've been cherry.

Cora definitely knew how to make cherry my favorite flavor.

"Your friend's here," I said, pulling away to call into her ear above the music and licking the last hint of cherry off my bottom lip.

She frowned up at me, obviously confused. So I pointed out Zoey, who was still hovering in the same spot I'd left her, arms crossed over her chest as if she were cold...or scared out of her mind.

"Oh my God. *Zoey!*" Deserting me, Cora lifted her arms over her head and shook them excitedly as she wove through people to reach her friend. Swooping in, she gave Zoey a huge hug, to which Zoey couldn't really hug her back because Cora had pinned her arms to her sides. "I can't believe you're really here. This is so exciting. We're going to have the best year *ever.*"

When she pulled away, she grabbed Zoey's hand. "Come on. Let's dance."

Zoey's eyes went huge and her head began to swish back and forth. I knew the last thing she wanted to do was dance. In fact, I knew she wanted to get out of this place. Bad. The way she kept glancing around with such apprehension reminded me of how I'd felt a year ago when Noel had invited me to my first party.

He'd been the big star, the first-string quarterback for the football team, and I'd been a lowly freshman nobody. An invitation from him hadn't been some-thing I could turn down. I had wanted to fit in and feel normal, so I'd sucked up all my anxieties and gone.

I'd hated every minute of that loud, overbearing frat house.

And I still hated parties, but my girl loved them, so I kept taking her to them, which made her happy and in turn, made me happy. But that didn't mean I didn't totally sympathize with Zoey. She wanted to leave, so I was going to help her escape.

I caught Cora's shoulder before she could tug Zoey too far away. "She's probably too tired to dance. She had to have driven all day to get here."

Cora paused and glanced back at Zoey, who quickly

bobbed her head up and down. "Do you mind if I just get my key and find the apartment?"

"Of course not." Cora was usually easy to convince of anything when she was drunk. She grinned at Zoey and looped their arms together. "I'll go with you and help you settle in."

Though Zoey looked relieved by the suggestion, I scratched my ear with unease.

"Uh..." I spoke up before I meant to. But I could already see where that offer was headed. Cora could never stay awake during a car ride after she'd been drinking. Besides, we had come here together in her car—hers because she hated having to climb up into my truck when she was wearing a short tight skirt like the one she had on now.

Both women glanced at me, so I thought up something quick to say. "I can follow you guys in Cora's car." And after that, I'd probably help Zoey carry a passed-out Cora up to their apartment.

Cora sent me a big, bright smile. "Sounds great. Let's go."

I was silent as Cora took off, easily gliding through the crowds while she dragged Zoey along. From behind, they could've been sisters. Heck, twins. Their hair was the same pale blonde and roughly the same length. Well, Zoey's was actually up in a ponytail, but it seemed as if it was probably about as long as Cora's. They had the same build and even the same height, though Cora was in heels, which meant Zoey was probably a little taller, placing her around five ten.

Chattering the whole time, Cora steered us through the maze of people before we reached the exit. I drew in a deep breath, glad to be free of that crammed place. Slipping my phone free of my pocket, I texted Ten.

I'm out. Making sure the girls get home okay. Behave yourself.

I should've known he'd have something obnoxious to reply. And he did: **Girls? Plural? You are so the man. Give me every detail tomorrow.**

With a sigh, I declined to respond. He'd probably only come up with something cruder to say. So I pocketed the phone as we came to a brand new, silver Lexus. Zoey unlocked it with her key fob and made the lights flash in welcome. I slowed to a startled stop.

For some reason, when Cora had talked about her best friend, I'd pictured Zoey Blakeland as a little more destitute...like I'd been. Everything else about her childhood has seemed so similar to mine; it had made sense for me to think she was just as poor as I'd been. But Cora had come from a well-to-do home, so it also made sense that her friend might too. It just surprised me to discover she drove something so nice.

As Cora climbed into the passenger seat as if she'd already forgotten about me, Zoey paused and sent me a hesitant glance.

I shifted a step back. "I, uh...Cora's car is just around the corner. I guess I'll see you guys there."

Zoey nodded but waited until I'd backed up a couple more paces before she slid into the driver's seat. I watched, blowing out a long breath. Then I lingered until she'd started the engine and pulled away from the curb before I turned away. My gut roiled uneasily, certain I'd flubbed up my one and only chance to befriend Cora's new roommate.

As the taillights disappeared around the corner, I finally tracked down Cora's Maserati, a little red convertible I felt like an ape driving because I could barely fit behind the wheel. She loved to drive fast, and could zip it around town well, but there was no way I could afford to get it fixed if I ever damaged it, so I never drove it as recklessly as she did.

After safely stowing it in the gated parking garage connected to her high-rise apartment building, I pocketed the keys and glanced around for the silver Lexus.

Zoey looked a little frantic when she waved me over. "Uh..."

"She passed out on the way home?" I guessed. When I got a nod for my answer, I smiled. "No problem. I can carry her."

"Does she do that a lot?" Zoey bit the corner of her lip as she worriedly dogged my heels to the passenger side door. "Is she okay?"

"She's fine. She does this every time we go out." I sent Zoey a smile to reassure her before I undid Cora's seat belt and slid her out into my arms. I was used to the process by now. When her head fell limply on my shoulder, Zoey gaped wide-eyed.

Then she shook her head. "Oh, here. Let me get..." She rushed to shut the door and scurried around me as if to hurry ahead and open the door of the building, but Henry the doorman, beat her to it.

"Evening, Mr. Hamilton. Had another hard night of partying, I see."

While he shook his head with a fatherly kind of disappointment, I offered him a rueful grin. "Hey, Henry." I turned sideways to fit Cora's slumped form through the doorway.

When Zoey followed us in, Henry paused, narrowing his eyes slightly.

I stopped. "This is Zoey Blakeland. She's Cora's new roommate."

"Oh." Relaxing immediately, Henry's face softened into a smile. He made a production of taking Zoey's hand and bowing over it. "It's a pleasure, Miss Blake-land. You ever need anything, you just ask me, you hear?"

Zoey blushed and nodded before slipping her hand free. "Thank you."

She followed me to the elevator, where I pushed the button with my shoulder. Once the three of us were closed inside with Cora quietly snoring on my shoulder, Zoey cleared her throat. "Um...which floor?"

I shook my boggled head. Right. I'd forgotten she didn't know where we were going. "Sorry. Eighth."

As the floor lifted under us, an uncomfortable silence filled the quiet car. I resituated Cora in my arms because it felt as if she were slipping a little, but that still left me with more time than I liked before we arrived at our destination.

Offering Zoey an overly bright smile, I said, "I can help you carry some boxes in tonight if you need."

Her eyes went wide as if I'd suggested something scandalous before she shook her head adamantly. "Oh, no. That's okay. I'll just...I'm going to wait until tomorrow."

Crap, I'd forgotten again. She must be exhausted from all her driving. Once more, I came close to asking her why she'd showed up early. Had her father done something to prompt her into leaving prematurely? Was she okay?

The elevator stopped and the door opened. I cleared my throat, motioning her with my head to go first. "Here we are."

She stepped into the hall and then paused, letting me take the lead and reminding me all over again she had no idea where she was going. I wished Cora hadn't drank so much. She should be the one to show Zoey around and introduce her to the place. Not inept me.

"This is us." I slowed in front of the door marked 8E on a brass plaque.

When I sent her an expectant glance, she shifted from one foot to the other and winced. "Umm, I haven't actually gotten a key yet."

"Oh, right. Sorry." I flushed, knowing I should've realized that. But I hadn't even thought it through.

Why had my brain turned to mush tonight?

Usually, I tucked Cora's keys between my teeth when I had to carry her home. Then I'd just drop them into my hand to unlock her door when we reached her place. Tonight, I'd had it stuck in my head that Zoey could get us in, so I'd—

Oh, no.

My stomach plummeted with doom as I met Zoey's gaze. "Her keys are in my pocket."

Her eyes went wide and lowered to my hip as we both realized the conundrum of our problem.

"I'll just..." I tried to readjust Cora on my shoulder so I could hold her with one hand and release the other long enough to pull the keys free. But as soon as I let one hand go, her limp body began to nosedive, so I quickly grabbed hold of her again with both arms to catch her.

Next, I tried to half prop, half squish her against the wall to free a hand, but that didn't work either. I couldn't pass her over to Zoey—no way would she be able to hold Cora's weight. I was about to just sit Cora on the floor against the wall when Zoey let out a loud sigh.

"This is crazy. Just...which pocket?"

My gaze slid her way, and I froze. I didn't want her hand to go down my pocket...because the very idea affected me. It affected me in ways it totally shouldn't.

And great, I was already reacting. But it'd probably take me more time than I wanted, stuck out here in the hallway with her alone, with nothing but my passed-out girlfriend between us, when it'd only be hand-in, hand-out, door-unlocked, and we were done, if I just let her get the key. So I exposed my left side to her.

"L...left side." My voice was hoarse.

She had to dodge past one of Cora's limp dangling hands. I don't know why I felt so compelled to watch her face, but I did as she bit her lip and gingerly wedged her fingers into my pocket.

Down, down, down...

I wasn't the type to wear tight jeans, or even snug denim, so the keys had fallen all the way to the bottom of my pocket. She had to step in closer before she slid her hand even further...down. The warmth of her fingers immediately soaked through the cloth and heated my thigh. Another certain member of my anatomy took notice of how close she was getting to it and it woke up, twitching with interest, which made me grit my teeth.

The moment Zoey finally wrapped her hand a·round the key, she slid her gaze to mine and froze. Her eyes were so big and green and innocent, I couldn't look away.

It was only for a second that we stared at each other, but it felt like an eternity. It was certainly long enough for my penis to go from merely perking one eye open with interest to springing to full attention and ready for duty.

I was so glad I was holding Cora and hiding everything that was going on down there, because this had to be the worst first impression I was ever having on anyone. And to make matters worse, her smell wafted up between us, making me curious all over again what that scent was.

I closed my eyes, trying to block all the senses in my body that were unwillingly going crazy, and then I held my breath.

Zoey gasped. I don't know if she realized how much she was affecting me, or how much she was dawdling, but she jerked the keys from my pocket, nearly taking a chunk of denim with her in her haste, and then spun away fiddling with key after key until she found the right one.

"The, uh, the light switch is to the right," I said as the door swung open.

Zoey nodded and disappeared inside. A moment of silence followed before Cora's front room flooded with light.

"Oh!" Zoey turned from the switch she'd just flipped on. "That feels...strange there."

"Yeah." I offered her a stiff smile. "That's what I always thought, too." Since the door opened to the left, it would've been much more convenient to have the switch on the left side.

Zoey stayed standing by the closed front door as I headed for the hallway. I glanced back at her to find her looking around uneasily like a stranger in a strange place. Heart going out to her because she seemed so uncertain, I cleared my throat.

"So, this is the front room. The kitchen is down the hallway here." When I turned back and started walking, I heard her hurry after me. "There's a bathroom here, and then another one at the other end of the hall. And Cora has a personal bath." I kept walking, tipping my head toward various doorways. "That one is your room. The next is the office and storage, and across from it is Cora's."

At Cora's room, I backed in, using my shoulder to nudge her door open. Then I dipped to flip on the light switch with my elbow. Cora didn't even stir as I tucked her into bed. I usually put her on top of the bedding first, then made her comfortable before I pulled the sheets out from under her and covered her up. Thinking nothing of it, I slid off her high heels, unbuckling the delicate tiny straps first. Then I worked my way up and began to unbutton the top clasp to her skirt's zipper when a gasp came from the doorway.

I looked up to find a wide-eyed Zoey in the door-way, gaping at me as if I was trying to take advantage of the passed-out drunk chick on the bed.

My face heated as I jerked my hands away from Cora's skirt. "I was just..." I cleared my throat and jammed my fingers into my pockets. "I-I'll let you see to her comfort from there." I glanced one last time at Cora, restraining myself from the need to strip her down to her panties. She hated to sleep in clothes, and I hated knowing she was going to wake up feeling suffocated.

But a pair of appalled, wide green eyes compelled me to step away from her. Zoey scurried out of the doorway as I approached. In the hallway, I paused and ripped a hand out of my pocket to rub it uneasily across the back of my head. "Do you, uh, do you have everything you need for the night?"

I have no idea what I was really asking, but it felt wrong to leave her here like this in a place that was foreign to her without making sure she was okay.

She nodded and glanced into Cora's room. "Is she going to be okay?"

"Oh. Yeah." I grinned sheepishly as I turned back to study Cora. "Sure. She'll sleep for the rest of the night, and probably late into the morning. Usually water, ibuprofen, and a little breakfast makes her feel best after she wakes up."

Instead of looking reassured, Zoey shook her head and frowned. "But she shouldn't be drinking that much. It's not—"

When she broke off directly and squinted at me as if picking apart my brain and seeing what I was thinking, I tipped my head to the side, wondering what she would've said if she'd finished that sentence.

"It's not what?"

Zoey straightened her back and drew in a breath. "Nothing." Her eyes were filled with concern as she glanced in at Cora, though.

I felt as if I was being left out of a secret, but I was usually paranoid about people thinking the worst of me and keeping things from me, so I pushed my qualms aside.

Neither of us spoke for a good thirty seconds, so I blew out a breath. "I'm gonna...yeah." I hooked my thumb over my shoulder and motioned down the hall toward the exit. "I'm going to go then."

"Okay," she said and nodded once more. She was big on nodding. Not so much on talking. But then, I was exactly the same.

I stepped in reverse away from her as I sent her a small smile. With a little farewell wave, I said, "Welcome to Ellamore. It was nice to meet you."

"Thank you. You too." She averted her gaze as color flooded her cheeks.

At first, I empathized. There was nothing I hated more than blushing, which I did more than I wanted to. It was one of those horrifyingly embarrassing reactions that came when you were caught thinking or doing something you knew you shouldn't and making matters worse by letting everyone else around you know it.

But then it struck me that she was thinking something she knew she shouldn't be. All I'd said was that it was nice to meet her. I don't think even Ten could've found a way to turn that into a dirty thought, which meant...her body had just responded in a way she hadn't wanted it to.

Whew. My sympathy turned to relief, glad she was also feeling the unwanted attraction between us. It'd been awful thinking I was experiencing it all one-sided. But to know it was shared was a relief. Except...wait.

Unease finally struck. Oh, no. This was not good. Poor,

innocent Cora was lying mere feet away while her boyfriend and best friend were experiencing *vibes* for each other? How wrong was that? I needed to get out of here...like five minutes ago.

"'Night," I mumbled, stumbling around so I could haul butt for the door.

I hardly ever felt instant attraction to women. I'd grown crushes on girls over the years after getting to know them or watching them for a while, but Cora had been the first to give me an instant punch in the gut the first moment I'd seen her. It didn't seem possible that her best friend would be able to draw the same exact reaction from me.

While I drove home, my fifteen-year-old truck trying to rattle apart around me, I realized one awful fact. As much as I'd been hoping to connect with someone who'd shared a similar past, I wasn't going to be able to make friends with Zoey Blakeland after all. I was going to have to keep my distance from her instead.

THREE

⋅⊱ ZOEY ⊰⋅

THOUGH IT WAS late when I pulled into town the night before, I was up with the sun, unable to stay asleep, unable to calm my nerves.

But I'd done it. I'd really done it. I had escaped the home of Ernest K. Blakeland, bank president of North Heritage National and co-founder of the Ridgeway Gold Country Club.

If I was lucky, he'd never find me. If I was margin·ally fortunate, he wouldn't discover my location until I'd done what I'd come to do. And if God hated me, he'd be downstairs right now demanding to know Cora's room number.

But I wasn't going to think about that possibility. I had plans, and I was going to see them through, no matter what he did.

Cora needed me.

The first thing I did was check on her. She was sleeping so soundly I had to put my fingers by her parted lips to make sure she was still breathing. I still couldn't believe she'd put herself at so much risk last night by drinking.

As soon as she woke up, we were going to have a serious

21

talk.

I let her rest for now, though. She needed all the rest she could get.

My next order of business for the day was to carry my boxes up to my apartment from my car. Henry, from last night, wasn't on duty. The new guy who'd taken his place reminded me so much of the doorman off *Curious George* I almost expected to find a dachshund at his side.

I faltered and fidgeted, not sure how to introduce myself.

"Hi," I finally mumbled. Okay, that was lame. Face heating, I tried again. "I'm Zoey. I just moved in last night."

His grin spread. "Into 8E with Miss Wilder?" When my eyes widened in shock, he grinned. "Henry already told me. I'm Terrance." He bowed. "Welcome to the Chateau Rivera, Miss Blakeland. Is there anything I can do for you on this fine day?"

"No." I ducked my face and shook my head, not used to such respectful treatment. "No thank you. I was just going to carry in my things from my car...if that's okay."

"Well, sure. Let me help you."

I don't know how Cora had managed to find such an amazing apartment building, but I was grateful for Terrance's help, especially five trips to my car later when my back was screaming and weakened leg muscles were shaking from carrying so many boxes. The doorman helped cut the work in half, but it still left me feeling sweaty and gross.

I didn't stop working, though. I was so out of place here, I needed one small touch to make me feel at home. Finding the box I was seeking, I popped off the lid and let out a sigh of relief to find all my three-ring binders tucked neatly inside. I drifted my fingers over the cool, metal coils holding them together and pulled one free to flip open the pages.

The stories I wrote were silly. They were usually about lost little girls who'd strayed from home and found themselves in colorful, magical kingdoms full of new and frightening, yet wonderful things to explore. And there was always a love interest with a happily ever after. But they were everything to me. Writing was my peace, my sanity, and my heart and soul.

I spent the next half hour carefully lining the notebooks up on the bare shelves above my new bed. It was easy to tell which ones were older by their colored, frayed condition so I put them in order from oldest to newest. Then I blew out a relieved breath, feeling better about being here.

Resolved to my new future, I made Cora breakfast. It was way past noon; she needed sustenance, and I was beginning to get hungry for lunch myself.

She still wasn't up when I finished, so I carried a tray into her room and set it on the nightstand, then I sat on the mattress beside her and drew the blonde hair out of her face carefully.

"Cora," I sang softly. "Time to wake up."

She groaned and rolled over onto her stomach, where she buried her head under a pillow. "Why am I wearing clothes?" came the vexed, muffled question.

I blinked, not sure what to say. "Um...because you passed out before you made it all the way home to undress, I guess."

She made a very irritated sound before asking, "Where's Quinn?"

"He went home." I took the pillow away. "I made you breakfast."

She lifted her face, her bloodshot eyes hopeful. "Waffles?"

I shook my head. "Scrambled egg whites. I heard they're good for people on dialysis."

"Ugh." She flopped her face back onto the mattress with a dramatic sigh. "Don't mention that word today. I just want to forget about anything medical for the next twenty-four hours."

It was all I could think about, though, so...no. Forgetting wasn't an option for me. I'd obsessed about her health for the past six weeks, ever since the night I'd received that dreaded phone call from her.

"How about some water and ibuprofen?" I asked, remembering Quinn's instructions from last night.

She sat up, looking cross and still tired. I bit my lip, beyond worried as she silently took the pain reliever.

Her voice was raspy as she said, "Mmm. Warm water, good. The cold water Quinn brings me first thing in the morning always hurts my teeth."

Her morning voice reminded me vaguely of how she'd sounded when she'd been sobbing and hysterical on the phone. "*I've entered the fifth stage of kidney failure. They've started me on dialysis three times a week. This is the end stage, Zoey. If I don't get a transplant, I could die."*

Those four sentences had haunted me every night since hearing them. I didn't want my best friend on earth—my *only* friend—to die. So I'd made a life-altering decision before that dreaded conversation was over.

I'd offered to be a living donor. The problem was, I couldn't tell my father because he'd never agree to it. He'd find a way to keep me from helping her.

But I wasn't going to let that stop me. Instead of preparing to attend the college nearest my hometown where he'd enrolled me, I had secretly applied for admission into ESU, the college Cora attended some six hundred miles away from Ernest K. Blakeland.

The day I'd gotten the acceptance letter from them, my planning had started. I was already pretty good at saving back money. Father had never allowed me to do or get anything, so the monthly allowance from my mother's inheritance trust fund merely sat in the bank, gaining interest. Transferring money over to an account my father knew nothing about was a bit of a challenge, since he happened to be the president of the bank. But I managed to get it done. To be safe, I'd transferred it again, and then once more for good measure, so he wouldn't know which financial institution the money ended up in.

It was my money and I was finally of legal age. I shouldn't have had to hide it from him, but "shouldn't have to" wasn't a term my father knew when it came to me.

After withdrawing a sizable chunk of my interest for cash, I'd taken a bus to a few towns over and bought a car. Then I'd driven it back to my neighbor-hood and parked it down the street behind an abandoned garage where one of our neighbor's summer homes was being foreclosed. Each night, I'd carried one or two boxes down and stored it in the car in preparation for the big escape.

Three days before my planned breakout, Father had attended a benefit charity dinner. Thinking there might not be a better time to leave, I jotted out a quick note, telling him I was leaving and never coming back, and if he'd ever cared for me at all, he wouldn't look for me. And then I'd become free.

I had no idea free was such a scary thing until I was suddenly on my own with no rules to tie me down.

"So what are our plans for the day?" I asked Cora,

nudging her hip with my knee as I scooped up a forkful of scrambled egg whites, hoping she'd give me some guidance to help me with all my freedom anxieties. "Are we going to visit the doctor and tell him I'm going to do the transplant with you?"

When I held out the forkful, she obediently ate the bite, only to choke on it and wave her hand in front of her face, her eyes watering. "Salt," she gasped.

I shook my head. "Too much salt can't be healthy for you."

She pushed my hand away when I held out another bite. "I'm dying. Do you really think I care about eating *healthy* right now?"

The casual way she said that shot an arrow of cold, panicky fear right through the center of my chest. "You are *not* dying. That's why I'm here, remember. And yes, you do need to eat healthy if you want to get better. And probably drink *less*." I lifted my eyebrows to let her know how much I didn't approve of all the drinking I'd seen her doing last night.

She rolled her eyes. "If there's anything I've learned in the last few months it's that life is short, and I'm going to spend it doing whatever the hell I want. So just get off my fucking back about what I eat or drink. Okay?"

I blinked, startled to hear such language. She ignored me as she ripped off her clothes until she was down to a matching bra and panty set. I just sat there, stunned. She'd turned so angry and defiant since the last time I'd seen her. It made my heart ache.

As she crawled off the bed and pulled on a loose top and shorts, I shook my head.

"You've really changed," I murmured. I didn't know the woman before me anymore. What was worse, I didn't know how to help her, either.

Being nine months older than me, she'd left home for college last year, while I'd been stuck there to suffer through my senior year of high school without her. It had been difficult, but we'd always been able to talk online. And through all our messages, I hadn't been able to tell just how much she'd altered.

I was curious if college, her declining health, a mixture of both, or something else entirely was the cause of it.

She sniffed. "Changed for the better." Turning away, she

started for the door. "You go ahead and eat that crap. I'm having Cocoa Pebbles."

I don't know why—maybe it was stress—but I fol·lowed her orders and shoved the bland egg whites into my mouth, chewing robotically, as I trailed her into the kitchen.

"Damn, I wish it was Saturday morning," she grumbled without explaining why.

I stood in the doorway, silently polishing off her eggs while she prepared herself a bowl of cereal and then seated herself at the table and propped her feet up until she could balance the bowl on her knees. Catching sight of me hovering, she rolled her eyes. "Sit."

I sat, upset that I seemed to be such an annoyance to her. After drawing in a deep breath, I asked, "So, are we going to see your doctor today about the kidney transplant?"

She made a disgusted sound, letting me know she still didn't want to discuss any of that. But then she swallowed her mouthful and shook her head. "I have a consultation set up for us on Wednesday. Today is car wash day."

I paused chewing. "Car *what* day?"

A wicked gleam entered her eyes as she laughed. "The football team's annual charity car wash," she explained. "They have it every year on the Friday afternoon before the first day of class. But this year, they're inviting a bunch of girls to help, so we're having a competition of sorts. Girls against the guys to see who can draw in more business. And since you showed up early, you get to go, too. Which means...we have to dress you up sexy."

I swallowed the last piece of egg white wrong. My eyes watered as I pounded on my chest to clear my airway. "Wait...what?"

HALF AN HOUR later, I was fresh from a shower and pulling on my swimsuit with great reservation. My best friend's life was in grave danger, yet we were preparing for a *car wash* as if nothing whatsoever was wrong? This just didn't feel...right.

Thinking I could talk my way out of wearing this thing—unlike the way I'd been unable to talk my way out of attending the car wash with Cora—I marched from my room to hers.

"Cor—"

She wore nothing but a towel around her head and one wrapped around her body, but I could see her patting something onto the inside of her forearm. She whirled around, and we both contorted our faces into horror the moment we saw each other.

"What the hell are you wearing?" she squawked as my gaze widened on all the bruises she was concealing with makeup.

"Wha...where...? Who did this to you? *Quinn*?" I hurried to her and grasped her arm to examine all the ugly purple, blue and green marks trailing up her arm.

Even though Cora tried to pull away, she threw her head back and laughed. "*Quinn*? You think Quinn would hurt me? Oh my God. You are so far off track. *Quinn* wouldn't hurt a freaking ant. Instead of killing spiders in the bathtub, he catches them and sets them free outside. He's the most harmless guy I've ever met."

I bit my lip and gently ran my fingers over her bruises, hoping she was telling the truth. "I saw him push someone against a wall last night."

Cora merely shook her head. "Um, no, honey. There's no way you saw Quinn push anyone any-where. He's not the least bit violent; he's just not *capable* of it."

I decided not to argue that point with her, even though I was a hundred percent certain I *had* seen him doing exactly that. Instead, I focused on her arm. "Then...where did those come from? Cora, if someone is—"

"Oh my God," she groaned, cutting me off. "Just shut up already. It's from the dialysis, okay?"

My eyes widened. "The...? Wow, it really tears you up, doesn't it?"

Cora's jaw tensed as she continued to dab concealer over each bruise. "If you saw how many times they stick things in you, you'd think this was mild."

I winced as I kept watching. "You don't have to hide it," I said quietly. "People will understand." She should be proud of how strong and resilient she was. She was surviving kidney failure, for crying out loud.

But she cut me off with a snarl. "No, they won't. Because no one knows."

I opened my mouth, but wasn't sure what to say. So I

settled for shaking my head. "What?"

She snorted and motioned toward me. "Look at you. You've been here less than a day and you're al·ready mother·henning me to death, trying to spoon·feed me and tell me what's best for me. I don't want the hovering or the dictating with everyone telling me what's best for me. Okay? And I certainly don't want anyone's pity."

Shoulders hunching with guilt, I glanced away. "I'm sorry," I mumbled. I'd been so worried about her that I'd only been thinking of myself, wanting to make me feel better by pampering her, by fixing her. But I should've been thinking about what Cora wanted instead of what I thought I should give.

With a small clearing of my throat, I lifted my face with an apologetic smile. "So...no one else knows? Not even...?"

"Not even Quinn," she said, reading my mind. "And you're not going to tell him. You're not going to tell *anyone*. I don't want to be treated any differently than I would be if I were perfectly healthy."

But she *wasn't* perfectly healthy, and she *needed* to be treated differently.

I held my tongue, though. "I won't tell," I promised, though I felt extremely uneasy about the whole thing.

"Good." Finished with covering the last bruise, she smiled perkily and clasped her hands together. "Now let's talk about what you're really going to wear today, because no way are you leaving this apartment in *that*. I have a reputation to uphold, and if you're going to be my roommate, you can't embarrass me." She shuddered in revulsion as her gaze traveled down my figure.

Instantly self·conscious from showing so much skin, I hugged my arms over my chest. "It's the only suit I have."

"Well, it's hideous. Come on, I think I have something for you." She grasped my elbow and led me to a chest of drawers, where she pulled out the top one. "Damn, I didn't even know they still made one·pieces." She dug inside, pausing every few seconds to toss colored chunks of Lycra, polyester, and nylon over her shoulder and onto the bed.

All Cora had were skimpy bikinis. I waved my hands no at each one she picked up and tried to hold up to my body. Stepping in reverse away from them, I refused to even consider the idea.

Finally, she grew fed up and scowled at me. "Come on,

Zo. You left home and came to me so you could finally live a little."

No, I'd come here to save her life. But I winced with apology anyway, because I hated to disappoint her. "I'm sorry. I just...I can't wear those."

Cora held up a hand. "Okay, fine. It's still too soon for you. I get it."

If she thought I'd ever wear anything that revealing, she was nuts.

I grew worried over just how much she'd changed this last year. Cursing and drinking and skimpy clothes. Those things hadn't been Cora a year ago, and she knew they weren't me now. So what had caused such a transformation? And why was she trying to change me too?

More importantly, what exactly had I gotten myself into by coming here.

29

FOUR

ZOEY

CORA WRANGLED me into one of her tight tees. It was a plain gray V-neck but hugged my breasts like a second skin and was short enough to expose my navel with every other move I made. The shorts were indecently short and just as tight. Then she put me in ankle socks and white sneakers. Compared to the swimsuit she'd put on—a contraption of hot pink dental floss attached to three miniature scraps of cloth—I looked like a nun who was covered from neck to toe, but I still felt majorly exposed.

After slopping my hair into a quick, high pony-tail, Cora stepped back and clapped happily. "Ooh, this might even be better. You look like an adorable virgin, ripe for the plucking."

My jaw fell open as my face heated. "I cannot believe you just said that."

She sighed. "Oh, Zoey, I've forgotten how completely naive you are."

I hated that word, almost as much as I hated *being* that word. And she knew it. Swallowing down my irritation that she would purposely and so coldly use it against me, I shied back and cleared my throat.

"You know, only a year ago you were just as innocent," I said, hoping to make her remember, to draw out the friend I once had. But seriously, what kind of wild experiences had Quinn Hamilton given my best friend?

She laughed in my face. "Isn't it awful how stupid I was? But that feels like a lifetime ago, thank God. Don't you worry about it, hon. A few months here will help draw out your courage."

Courage for *what*, I wondered.

"Goddamn dialysis," Cora muttered as she studied herself in the full-length mirror, turning from side to side. "It's gotten me way too pale."

I thought she looked extra tan, but I had a feeling saying so would annoy her, so I just sat on her bed and waited for her to stop degrading herself.

After another minute of frowning and muttering, she met my gaze in the mirror. "Do you think this will actually look as good once it gets wet?"

I made a face at it, thinking it'd probably disintegrate and fall off the second she got spray back from a water hose.

She read my expression and groaned. "You're right. I should wear the blue one."

As she peeled off the pink top, I glanced at my wristwatch. We really needed to get going; the fund-raiser was starting in five minutes.

"I'll wait for you in the front room," I said just as a knock came at our front door.

I glanced at Cora, not at all feeling as if this was enough my home to be answering any doors yet. But she was too busy wiggling the pink bikini bottoms out of her butt crack.

That wasn't a sight I'd ever be able to un-see, so I motioned toward the doorway. "I'll just...I'll get the door."

She didn't even pretend to hear me, so I hurried down the hall and checked the peek hole.

My stomach instantly knotted with tension. What the heck was Cora's too-gorgeous-to-be-real boyfriend doing here? I'd refused to think about him all day, because just remembering those awkward moments we'd had alone when Cora had been passed out between us made me hot and nervous all in one confusing ball. I swear, my hand still tingled from where I'd had to bury it in his pocket to fetch the apartment key.

God, he'd a really warm, rock hard thigh.

I glanced down the hall toward Cora's room, but she was nowhere in sight. Hesitating, I finally opened the door and peeked out at him. He startled a little when our gazes met, letting me know he'd been expecting her. Once he recovered, his blue eyes warmed with greeting and he smiled, flashing a deep dimple in the left side of his cheek.

Yeah, he just had to have a dimple, didn't he?

"Hi," he said brightly. "You guys ready?"

I blinked. "Ready?"

Worry and indecision clouded his face. He lifted his hand to rub at the back of his neck. "You're both still going to the car wash, right?"

"Yes," I answered slowly.

That seemed to fluster him even more. He jabbed his hands into his pockets, which made his shoulders more defined and muscled than they'd been a second before. Then he nervously kicked out a foot over the toe of his other shoe. "And you knew you were riding there with me? Right?"

I shook my head dumbly, flushed and flustered to learn that part. I already felt überly self-conscious going out, dressed like this. But knowing he would be there to witness it made it that much more unnerving. I was aware of every molecule of my body, from the irrational tick of my pulse in my throat to the cool wash of the air conditioner blowing a slight breeze against the backs of my legs. It made my breasts prickle, and my arms coat with goose bumps.

"Oh," I said stupidly. "I...no, I didn't know that. Sorry."

He bit his bottom lip. Watching his perfect teeth sink into that perfect pink flesh set off the fireworks in my chest. I prayed my bra was doing its job and hiding any embarrassing bumps beading out the front of my shirt.

"No, I'm sorry," he started. "I thought Cora would've told you."

I wasn't sure why he was apologizing. He hadn't done anything wrong, but it was endearing that he was so willing to take culpability for something. My father had never owned up to any of his mistakes. He'd just blamed other people, usually me, and then I'd get punished for his embarrassments.

Realizing Quinn was still standing in the hallway, waiting for me to respond, I finally opened the door wider. "It's fine. You can come in and wait, I guess. I thought Cora was ready, but..." I paused, wondering if he'd get mad if he knew she was changing at the last second, making us late.

He merely grinned as he entered the apartment. "She had to change," he guessed correctly as if he was used to such behavior. He turned to me, showing off that dimple again, and making my stomach do somersaults when our gazes met. "Yeah, I've started telling her things are half an hour earlier than they really are to give her time for her last-minute changes."

I nodded, but my mind drifted elsewhere, because really, it didn't seem humanly possible for a person to be so beautiful.

Heat traveled up my toes, zipping along the insides of my thighs, embarrassing me with all the places it flamed the hottest. What was worse, the cool air from the overhead vents was still making my arms prickle and the tips of my breasts harden.

How utterly mortifying.

Trying to act as if nothing earth-shattering was going on inside me, I forced a smile at his explanation, though I was relieved to learn we still had time and weren't running late. I couldn't stand being late for anything.

"So this happens a lot?"

His grin really was infectious as he smiled. "Every time." He started to say something else but he finally noticed what I was wearing. And I mean, like, *really* noticed. His grin froze as his gaze dropped down my body, pausing at my breasts, midriff, and finally my legs.

As I glanced down to make sure my nipples weren't poking through the T-shirt, I tugged at the hemline, hoping I wasn't showing off any of my stomach as well. The bra was doing its job, thank good-ness, and the tug seemed to alert Quinn to what he was doing.

His gaze immediately zipped up to my face and his eyes widened with guilt and apology. "Y-y-you...I mean, did you get unpacked okay?"

I wrapped my arms over my chest because I couldn't fight the impulse a second longer. After tucking a long piece of bangs that hadn't made it into my ponytail behind my ear, I cleared my throat. "Yeah, I'm all moved in."

Quinn nodded and rocked back onto the heels of his shoes as if he were nervous. "Good. I was going to offer to help carry stuff in for you today, but the coach kept us late at practice this morning, doing drills. Then I had already volunteered to help set out all the hoses and buckets and stuff for the car wash. And now, well...I guess it's too late now. Sorry, I—"

"You don't have to apologize," I rushed out, startled he even felt he had to...again. "I didn't expect you to...I mean, it's fine. Really."

Strange. Quinn Hamilton wasn't like anything I thought he'd be. From all the pictures I'd seen of him wrapped around Cora at all these parties, I had assumed he'd be an arrogant, full of himself, outgoing jock. So far, jock was the only thing I'd gotten right, but actually he still didn't strut around with tight muscle shirts and net shorts, to reveal all his athletic perks. Today, he sported a pair of blue jeans and a loose gray shirt, advertising ESU.

An awkward silence bloomed between us. Quinn shifted his weight from one foot to the other. Then he gestured toward the couch and television. "Do you mind if I...?"

"Oh! Yeah, sure. Go right ahead."

Yes, best idea ever. I'd latch onto anything to wipe away the uncomfortable tension between us. And the television was a perfect outlet. I wished I'd thought of it and offered it first.

"Great, thanks. I've been itching to catch up on *Psych*."

I followed him into the living room area, curious. "*Psych*?"

He tossed an engaging grin at me over his shoulder. "It's this hilarious detective show I found on Netflix. We don't get Netflix at my apartment, so I can only watch it here. And Cora can't stand it, so I sneak it in when I'm waiting for her to..." He made air quotes as he grinned at me, "change."

I couldn't help it. I grinned back.

He flopped down on the couch and made himself at home, flipping up the middle cushion to reveal a center console nook hiding a handful of remote con·trols. Taking one out, he turned on the television and pushed another series of buttons to get into the show and the very episode he wanted. When he clicked on an option that said "resume playing," I realized how much more he was familiar with my new apartment than I was.

It must've been incredibly strange for him to wait in

the hallway until I'd given him permission to enter. And then he'd even had to ask to sit down. My face heated; I felt like a moron. He was Cora's boyfriend; of course he knew his way around. He'd demonstrated that last night when he'd told me where everything was.

Once again, I felt completely out of my element.

The show popped on, and the two guys on the screen instantly captured my attention as they argued about something completely inconsequential over the body of some dead guy.

Captivated, I inched further into the room and slid tentatively down into a side chair. Within seconds, I was giggling. I slapped my hand over my mouth just as Quinn grinned at me as if happy to see me enjoying his show.

Two more people arrived at the scene. They looked like detectives. "That's Jules and Lassiter," Quinn explained. "Shawn, the main guy there, has had a major crush on Jules since the beginning. I think they're going to get together." Then he sent me a rueful grin. "At least they better get together."

I smiled back, completely charmed. But, aww, he was a romantic. I loved that.

We kept watching, totally engrossed in the show. I asked question after question. Quinn was currently working his way through season four, but seemed happy to explain everything he knew and catch me up to speed.

We were both laughing over something Gus was saying to Shawn's dad when Cora strolled into the room, wearing a tiny pair of shorts that were unbelievably shorter than my own, and no shirt over her skimpy bikini top. She looked suntanned and flaw-less—not at all like she was suffering from kidney failure—as she artfully tossed a beach towel over her shoulder.

"Everybody ready?" she asked before focusing on the television and making a face. "Oh God. Please don't tell me you're pushing that dumb show on Zoey now?"

Quinn just grinned at her. "She's laughing," he argued, still smiling up at Cora as she sauntered across the living room to crawl into his lap.

My face heated at her bold move, and I shifted, uncomfortable to watch such intimacy. Facing him and straddling his lap, Cora grabbed onto the back of the couch on either side of him, caging him in. Quinn set his hands on her hips and gazed into her eyes as she tsked and shook her head.

"If you weren't so cute, I'd have to reevaluate our relationship. Because dating someone who actually likes this show..." She sighed as if he was hopeless.

Still grinning, Quinn framed her face in his hands. "You look really pretty today."

Cora threw back her head and laughed, her gorgeous blonde hair spilling down her spine. "Of course, your being a total sweetheart helps your case considerably." Then she leaned in to kiss him.

My skin buzzed with awareness as I quickly glanced away to give them a measure of privacy. But I'd already seen enough for my core temperature to skyrocket. The way Quinn had closed his eyes, his too long lashes resting against the tops of his cheeks, was like art. His hands continued to cup Cora's face as if he treasured her. And his mouth. The way it moved against hers compelled me to cop another peek.

I glanced over again just as he pulled away. But the adoration in his eyes as he simply gazed at Cora seemed just as, if not more, intimate than the kiss they'd shared. He really liked her. It was a shock to the system to see such affection between two people. My father had certainly never looked at any of the women he dated this way.

I was held captive as Quinn teasingly scolded, "You finally ready to go now?"

I loved the easy playfulness between them. They seemed to click together. And yet it made a painful regret clench deep in my stomach. I'd be lying if I said I hadn't dreamt of coming to Ellamore this year and finding someone to fall in love with and adore the same way Cora had blathered on about Quinn in all her emails to me. But sharing this kind of connection with another human being seemed out of my scope of reality. Someone as shy, reserved and closed off as I was could never manage to open herself to that kind of intimacy.

As if he could feel my jealousy over the bond they shared oozing out through my pores like a noxious gas, Quinn glanced over. He immediately shifted un-der Cora and set his hands on her hips to lift her off his lap. "We should get going before we're late."

Cora laughed as she climbed off the couch. "I hate to

break it to you, baby, but we're already late."

Quinn glanced at me, his eyes crinkling in amusement as if to share an inside joke. It made everything inside me heat with glee. Then he took Cora's hand and linked his fingers with hers. "Then I guess we don't want to be any later than we already are."

$\mathcal{F}$IVE

QUINN

"HOLD THE motherfucking phone." Ten stopped next to me and set a hand on my shoulder, squeezing to get my attention as he stared across the parking lot towards the girls' side where they were getting almost as much business as we were.

The car wash was going good, automobiles were lined up to the street, and so far, the competition between the genders was neck and neck.

"Who is *she*?"

"Who?" I asked as Ten kept drooling.

He pointed, and I followed the direction of his finger with my gaze as he said, "The only one *not* in a bikini."

I instantly scowled, not liking his attention as I took in the girl he was ogling. She was scrubbing a soapy sponge over a sleek black truck with her back to us.

When she bent over to dip the sponge into the bucket by her feet and soaped it up again, Ten groaned and set a hand over his chest.

"Damn, and the ass is just as sweet as those long, lean legs."

I shrugged his hand off my shoulder and glared at him. "That's *Zoey*," I told him, my pointed glare demanding he

38

back off.

He blinked, the name making him wrench away. "*Who?*"

I sighed and rolled my eyes toward the sky. Really? I'd only told him a dozen times that Cora's friend from her hometown was moving in this week-end. "I introduced you two. You met her last night."

He shook his head. "No, we most certainly did not. I would remember those legs."

"She was wearing jeans," I said dryly.

"Hmm." Ten scratched the stubble growing at his jaw. "Still don't remember her."

I shoved him in the shoulder, unable to control my irritation. "Stop staring."

"Huh?" Ten blinked and finally tore his gaze a-way to arch an eyebrow my way. "Why?"

"*Because.*" I ground my teeth together. "She... she's Cora's friend."

My clueless roommate shrugged. "So? I've boned all of Cora's friends. Which means..." His gaze heated with even more interest as he turned back to stare across the parking lot again. "It's pretty much required for me to get into *her* panties, too."

"No," I ordered, grabbing his arm and physically turning him away so he could face the car we were supposed to be washing. "Not this one. She's a good girl."

Way too good to go anywhere near his man-whore ways.

As if being sprayed with ice-cold water, the lust faded from his eyes. "Good girl?" he echoed in horror. "Eww. Way to waste a perfectly hot body. But..." He sent one last longing glance toward Zoey, "the moment she turns slutty, I'm warning you, I'm going to be all over that, no matter what you say. Because, dayum, those legs..." He sucked in a breath. "I'm even digging the clothes. Covered up like that, she makes a guy wonder what she's hiding under all those layers. Makes you just want to tear off the wrapping and unveil the surprise inside. You know what I mean?"

When he grinned and jabbed his elbow at me, I scowled hard in return.

I didn't want to agree with Ten, but he did have a point. Zoey looked good in that outfit. But ogling Cora's roommate felt all kinds of wrong. With a sigh, I shook my head and turned away. "Just get back to work."

He did, but he didn't shut up. Picking up the water hose to rinse off what I'd just cleaned, Ten kept talking, irritating me even more. "And she's blonde too. I've been craving blondes lately something fierce." Just as he spoke though, his gaze caught on some-thing in an entirely different direction than where the girls were working. "Shit," he hissed.

I glanced over and saw another blonde co-ed walking our way. Like Zoey, she was also wearing a shirt and shorts, no bikini in sight. It was the guy walking next to her that had my stomach tightening into knots.

I looked up to the quarterback of our team more than any guy I'd ever known. But today, I wished he was anywhere but here.

Spinning toward Ten, I lowered my voice, "You're not going to tell him about the picture of Aspen on Belcher's phone, are you?"

Ten glanced at me incredulously. "Fuck, you think I'm insane? Gamble would flip his shit if he knew people were spreading around topless snapshots of his woman."

Noel spotted us, and he—along with the girl beside him—veered our way.

"So who's winning so far?" he asked, obviously clueless about the picture Ten and I had deleted from the baseball player's phone last night, "Women or men?"

I expected Ten to answer because he was always so willing to talk, but he was too busy staring at the blonde next to Noel, while trying to make it look like he wasn't. So I cleared my throat. "I, uh, I think it's a dead heat so far. Hi, Caroline." I tried to offer a pleasant greeting to Noel's sister since Ten was being no help at all. He'd gone radio silent. "Are you here to help the competition?"

She smiled back briefly. "I guess so." Then she shot Noel a brief scowl as if he'd forced her to come with him.

"Which means, I should probably stop talking to the enemy and I head over to Team Girl." Slapping at her brother's elbow, she added, "Hope you aren't a sore loser."

Noel cracked a grin. "Oh, you're going down, little girl."

"Cora's over there," I told her helpfully as she started off. "She can help you get set up."

"Thanks, Quinn." She smiled at me, glanced briefly at Ten, and then kept going.

The three of us stared after her before Noel grab-bed Ten's arm and whirled him away, back toward the car we were cleaning. "Seriously, we need to work on your staring problem."

"I can't believe you brought your *sister*," Ten said, sneaking another peek at her.

Noel snorted. "Well, we were supposed to invite a girl to help compete on the female side, and Aspen wouldn't be caught dead at a campus event. Besides, I wouldn't let her come. All you assholes would never be able to take your eyes off her legs, and we'd definitely lose to girls, then."

As if on command, Ten's gaze went straight to Caroline's legs as he snorted. "I didn't invite a chick."

Noel muttered a curse and pushed Ten about a foot backward. "Eyes in your head, fucker."

"What?" Ten cried, stumbling along behind Noel. "Why'd you bring her if you didn't want anyone looking at her?"

I flushed because I'd been looking too, but Noel didn't scold me. He must've known I wasn't having any dirty thoughts about his sister.

"I brought her because she needed to get out of the house. She closeted herself up all summer long and with classes starting Monday, I was hoping she'd make a friend or two over in girl camp."

Glancing after Caroline again, I hoped that Cora took her in and befriended her. I wasn't sure what had happened to Noel's sister to cause him to uproot her and his two younger brothers from their hometown and move them all to Ellamore at the end of the last school year, but Ten knew about it. I'd caught him and Noel discussing her, worried about how she was healing. The few times I'd met her, she'd seemed fairly quiet and reserved, except I don't think that was her usual behavior. I think something had beaten her down, and she was still working through whatever haunted her.

When I saw her approach Cora, I smiled. My girl was bright and bubbly. She'd take care of Noel's sister, no problem.

I got back to work, and Noel joined Ten and me at our station. Other members of the team would float over to greet him, and sometimes Ten. I would occasionally get a head nod or brief, "Hey," but no one said much else to me except maybe how good Cora looked in her bikini, which perplexed me. Why were they telling me, like I owned her or something? They should tell her if they thought she looked nice. And if they wanted to make me jealous, they were wasting their time. I wasn't the jealous type.

But I nodded at their praise and kept on in my silent way. I'm pretty sure my quietness skeeved people out. Noel and Ten seemed to be about the only two members on the team who didn't care that I rarely talked.

Actually, we worked well together on the field *and* off, since we all three worked at the same night-club as bartenders. Noel had actually been the one to get me the job there, for which I'd be eternally grateful. I'd been living in the dorms my freshmen year, but I hated dorm life. I was so not the communal resident type. So many people, crammed into one building, parties all night long, no privacy—it'd been hard for me to handle.

But with the money I made at my new job, I'd been able to rent an apartment off campus as soon as the semester had ended. This summer had been nice, having my own space to myself. It didn't even matter that Ten had invited himself over and moved in with me a few months ago when he'd given up his apartment with Noel, after Noel had moved himself and his siblings in with Aspen at her place. Ten was loud, obnoxious, and annoying, but he wasn't a bad roommate. He respected my privacy, didn't mess the place any more than I did, and he didn't treat me like a freak. He was actually a pretty great friend, and had a way of making me feel like a normal person whenever I was around him.

Happy that I'd been able to form such a good relationship with both Noel and Ten, I glanced toward both of them working on the opposite side of a little red car as me. I had more than just friendship and a place to live to thank them for. If it hadn't been for Noel getting me my job, I probably never would've met Cora. And I'd no doubt still be a hopelessly shy virgin to this day.

"Shit," Ten muttered, glancing across the car lot. "The chicks are getting more business than us."

I looked up and yep, the line on their side was growing. "We need to step it up, boys," Ten called as he made a show of slowly peeling his shirt off over his head and tossing it aside before shaking out his damp hair.

One car full of women waiting in line with their windows rolled down hooted in approval. Noel followed suit and lost his shirt, but Ten took it to extremes by not so accidentally getting soap suds on his chest and blatantly staring at the women as he wiped them clean. "Oops. I'm such a mess. Oh, damn. There I go again."

Then he made sure to flatten his entire front against their window as he reached across the roof of their car to wipe it down. They got right back in line to get their car re-cleaned as soon as we were finished with them.

"Come on, Ham," Ten called to me. "Lose some clothes. Help us out here, man."

I just smiled and shook my head no. So Ten felt compelled to give me a "wetter look," as he called it, right before he sprayed me with water.

The cold water actually felt good in this heat, but I scowled and told him he was dead. Cheers of approval rang out as I charged after him so I could wrestle the hose away and spray him back. The girls waiting for their cars to be washed urged us on. In moments, the line on our side of the lot had doubled.

Soaking wet, we eventually returned to business. When we were at our busiest, Noel's cell phone rang. He checked the screen and moved off, saying it was from home.

As he stepped to the side to answer it, Ten called for more help at our car. So another player on the team, K.C. Jennings, stepped over.

"So either of you know who the new chick is over there?" He picked up a sponge and started scrubbing. "That blonde? The sweet tall drink of water?"

Ten gave a low whistle. "You better not be talking about Gamble's little sister or he'll skin you bald, man. And I'm not talking about the hair on your head."

K.C. shuttered and pointed. "No shit. *That's* Noel's little sister? Damn, she's hot."

Ten glanced over as well before his eyebrows shot up. He sent me a mischievous grin before patting K.C. on the shoulder. "Actually, no, not that one, but apparently you need Ham's approval before even looking at *her.*"

My gut tightened when I realized they were referring to Zoey. I refused to respond, or look, or even acknowledge that I heard them, but K.C. whirled toward me, lifting his eyebrows up into his hairline. "No shit. You already traded

Cora in for a newer model? Sweet, man."

As Ten burst out laughing, I scowled and straightened. "What! *No.* I didn't. That's Cora's new roommate."

"Cora's new roommate whom you warned *me* to stay away from," Ten was a little too gleeful to add.

I sent him a murderous scowl. "Only because she's not like that."

A grin spread over K.C.'s face. "Well, hell. I can make her 'like that' if you need her broken in."

I just stared at him with the sudden urge to break in his face. How dare he speak about Zoey that way? How dare he even look at her? She'd done nothing to garner that kind of talk. She hadn't even dressed provocatively. All she was doing was innocently cleaning cars, and the horny guys were panting after her like freaking dogs in heat. Couldn't they look at all the other girls over there, with their boobs hanging out and butt cheeks on display? Those ladies actually *wanted* guys ogling them. Not Zoey.

"Just look at those perky tits," K.C. went on, staring some more. "I bet they'd fill a palm to perfection."

I cracked my knuckles without meaning to, imagining how they'd feel against his jaw.

Ten took notice and bumped his elbow into K.C.'s. "Dude, if you value your life, you might want to shut up right about now."

"What? Why? Oh, fuck yeah. Looks like she's headed to the storage shed for fresh water. I think I'll go accidentally bump into her and...introduce myself." When he went to reach for Ten and my soap water bucket, I went to reach for *him.*

Over my dead body would he be introducing himself to Zoey.

But Ten intervened.

"Hey, sorry, Jennings, but Ham already volunteered to do that job." Ten snagged the bucket from K.C. and shoved it into my chest. My mouth opened to argue with him. I didn't want K.C. to trap her alone anywhere for any reason, but I didn't want to get caught alone with her either. The feelings she'd made me experience last night were still too fresh in my head.

"I don't mind doing it for you," K.C. offered, reaching to retrieve the bucket from me. But I held it away.

Like hell, buddy.

I'd rather suffer through another encounter alone with her than let K.C. get anywhere near her. I was half tempted to send Ten. Except, God, I didn't trust *him* around her either. I gritted my teeth.

I guess I was stuck heading toward the shed where I knew Zoey was inside. Alone.

Six

⁊ ZOEY ⁊

As SOON AS WE arrived at the car wash, Cora was immediately surrounded by a horde of other girls. I hung back, not sure what to do. In high school, we'd been loners together, outcasts who'd made a club of two and become inseparable because her parents had been almost as strict with her as my father had been with me.

Watching her now, I guessed she hadn't been quite as lonely without me this past year as I'd been without her. Cora had moved on. Realizing that made my heart ache, made me feel abandoned and pathetic for hanging on to the only friendship I'd ever had. But then I reminded myself she hadn't told anyone else about her kidneys. She only trusted me with that information.

I knew it was a selfish thought, but it still made me feel better.

The gossiping commenced around her, each girl more eager to dish the most recent events with my best friend. They treated her like the queen bee of the group. It took her a minute of gasping about so-and-so being caught cheating on what's-her-face before she remembered me.

As our gazes clashed, her eyes widened. "Oh, you guys

totally have to meet Zoey." Peeling herself away from her friends, she grinned at me and hooked her arm through mine. Tugging me forward, she beamed proudly. "This is my new roomie. Isn't she just the sweetest thing ever?"

"Ohmigod, I just love your hair color. Who do you have dye it?"

"Look at that tan. Which salon do you use?"

Cora laughed. "Save it, guys. This," she displayed a hand over me, "is all natural."

More gasps followed, making me blush.

"No way."

"Oh, honey. You are blessed."

"Bitch, I hate you," another teased, and everyone laughed.

I smiled uneasily, wondering if it'd really be this easy to make friends. But a microsecond later, one of the girls remembered another piece of hot gossip she wanted to tell Cora...in private. As she dragged my best friend away, the other girls wandered off too, leaving me standing there like an idiot. I guess I could've followed, but I knew I just would've felt more awkward and left out if I tried to fit in.

So, when I spotted all the supplies piled up for the car wash with a list of instructions, I got to work, hooking up the hoses and filling all the buckets with soapy water. There was a small warehouse storage building shed close by that had given us permission to use their hot water for the soap buckets. It took five trips, but by the time I had everything set up, cars driving by caught on that we were open for business.

The girls who'd had shirts on suddenly lost them, and I discovered I was the only female in the parking lot sans bikini. Half of Cora's crew took up the promotional end of the sale, standing out by the highway and waving signs at the passing traffic.

On the other side of the huge parking lot, the guys had set up camp as well. But more of them were cleaning cars than actually trying to lure in customers.

I spotted Quinn along with his roommate he'd introduced to me last night. The two of them had teamed up together on cleaning until a third guy arrived to work with them. And that's when the new girl joined our ranks.

She went to Cora for instruction, but Cora didn't have a clue what was going on. She was busy being one of the sign holders.

When no one was very forthright about giving her any duties, I hesitantly called, "You can help me."

She turned, and I was bowled over by how pretty she was. Her hair was a tad bit darker than mine, but it looked, I don't know, *better*. Shinier. It had this natural wave that curled perfectly around her heart-shaped face. And her eyes were a bright jewel blue while mine were more washed-out green. But she grinned at me as if I could be her new best friend.

"It looks like the guys over there are teaming up and having two or three people clean each car," I said.

"Sounds like a good plan to me." She bounded forward and grabbed the hose. "I can rinse."

"That'd be great. Thanks."

We easily set up a workflow, and before long, we were able to talk and clean at the same time. She moved closer to scrub on the same side of a bright orange SUV as me when I couldn't keep up, and spoke low as she leaned in to ask, "So, are we the only two who didn't get the memo that we were supposed to wear bikinis to this thing?"

I blushed. "Actually, I did kind of get that memo. But I refused, so my roommate settled for stuffing me into this."

I wished I were wearing something more like her outfit. Her shirt was oversized with a hole in one sleeve and the shorts were long and paint splattered. She looked so comfortable I was envious.

"Well, thank God you didn't listen to her, or I'd be feeling totally out of my element right now. Though, I swear, those aren't swimming suits they're wearing. Seriously, who would actually swim in one of those things without worrying the first wave to come along would rip it right off you?"

I giggled, totally agreeing.

"And that thing that blonde in the blue is wearing?" she went on, shaking her head with horror. "No. Just...no."

I grinned but felt compelled to say, "She's my roommate."

The blonde flushed hard, her eyes growing wide. "Oh my God. I'm so sorry."

With a laugh, I waved her apology aside. "No, it's okay. I love her to death, but I totally agree with you on the outfit. Not over my dead body."

She set her hand over her heart and blew out a breath. "Whew. Thanks, but I still feel crappy for talking about them all behind their backs." Then she cleared her throat as she picked up the hose to rinse. "So, you're Cora's roommate? You must know Quinn, then?"

My heart sped up at the mention of his name. Keeping my eyes on a bird dropping I was trying to rub off the paint, I murmured, "Yeah, I...I met him last night."

"He's such a sweetheart," Caroline assured me. "Cora has herself the best right there. He's friends with my brother Noel. They're on the football team together and they both also work at Forbidden."

I wasn't sure what Forbidden was, but I nodded politely. "I've only met one other member on the team. Ten, I think his name was."

My new friend nodded as a strange look lit her eyes. "Yeah. I've met him too."

When she didn't go on, I cleared my throat. "I haven't actually been here long. I arrived last night, in fact. I'm going to be a freshman at ESU this year, so Cora's taking me under her wing."

"Really?" Her face lit up. "I'm going to be a freshmen too." Suddenly, she slapped her hand to her forehead and laughed. "Crap, I forgot. I'm Caroline, by the way. Caroline Gamble."

I laughed because I also hadn't realized we hadn't introduced ourselves yet. "Zoey Blakeland."

"It's so nice to meet you."

We both burst out grinning at her dramatically formal greeting as she stuck out her hand and bowed to me. In seconds, the grins turned into laughter. I'm not really sure why we were laughing, but it felt nice.

Business picked up. With Caroline and me working together, we whipped through each car and started getting busier than the guys' side, which made Cora and her band of sign wavers cheer and hoot, calling out insults to them.

But soon, a bunch of the men ripped off their shirts and sprayed each other down. When Ten and Quinn got into a laughing tussle over the water hose, both Caroline and I had to pause and gape. Quinn kept his shirt on, but he was still absolute perfection. Together, the two guys made the game look like erotic water play.

When a third guy burst in, soaking them both down

and breaking them apart, Caroline snorted in disgust. "Noel, you moron," she said to herself. "Way to ruin a perfectly yummy view."

I smiled at the tone she used. "I'm going to guess that one's your brother."

"Yes," she muttered with a roll of her eyes, "the one flicking suds at Oren?"

I shook my head. "Oren?"

Her cheeks grew red. "Sorry. Ten. His name's really Oren Tenning, but everyone calls him Ten." She tilted her head to the side thoughtfully. "I might be the only person I know who actually uses his first name."

I nodded. "Oh." Her brother was one of the better-looking guys. Not as tall and wide as Quinn, or quite as pretty, but he was definitely striking.

"Ugh." Caroline wrinkled her nose and dropped her washrag into the bucket. "Our bucket of soapy water's getting gross."

"I can get a new batch. I know where to get more warm water."

"Good idea. Warm water would clean much better. Thanks."

After I dumped the used batch, I lugged the empty bucket back into the storage building.

Inside, it was eerily quiet, sending out a new host of echoes with each step I took. I hurried to the sink in the far corner, ready to get out of there as fast as possible.

Just when I turned off the faucet, the back door opened and crashed sound throughout the entire metal shelf-filled room. I really didn't want to meet anyone here, especially all by myself. So I ducked out of sight, hoping the newcomer didn't catch me or linger long so I could escape as soon as they were gone. Crouching, I hid at the end of a tall shelf where the boxes stacked on it kept me hidden.

When Quinn came around the corner, toting a bucket, my breath stalled in my chest.

Pausing when he saw the sink, he turned and glanced toward the doorway, looking confused. After a moment, he shook his head and turned on the water. He held his hand under the stream until it must've been warm enough for him to fill his bucket. And I suddenly felt stupid for hiding. I'm sure no one would've come through the doorway with nefarious plans. But I'd just been so freaked out.

Yeah, I'd definitely lived with my father far too long.

I couldn't pop out of hiding now, though, or Quinn would wonder what the heck I was doing, and it was too mortifying to explain what a silly, scared idiot I was.

Just as he finished filling his bucket and lifted it out of the sink, his impressive muscles bunching and pulling under his shirt and making my mouth go dry over the sight, the door to the supply room came open again.

Groaning silently, I rolled my eyes and prayed the misery would end soon. I just wanted to stop hiding and return to the car wash, where I could once again try to act like a normal girl.

Cora skipped inside, which caused Quinn to halt. "What're *you* doing in here?"

She sashayed toward him, twisting her hair around her hand and holding it up off the back of her neck. "I saw my incredibly sexy man headed this way, so I had to follow for a quick...snuggle."

When she reached him, she popped up onto her tiptoes and wrapped her arms around his neck, pressing her mouth fully against his. Quinn bent his head to meet her lips, but he seemed a little uncertain over what to do with the bucket of water he was holding as some splashed out over the sides and soaked his pant leg.

Keeping his lips attached to hers, he bent just enough to lower the bucket to the ground before he used his newly freed hand to sweep around her waist and pull her up off her feet.

As he smashed them together and I wondered what it'd feel like for a guy to draw me to him like that, Cora squealed. "Oh my God. You're so wet." She pushed against his chest, desperate to escape.

He chuckled and set her back down. "What I can't figure out is how you're so dry. We're at a car wash. Everyone should be wet."

"It's a talent," she said as she reached out and grabbed a handful of his shirt. "But what *I* can't figure out is why you're still wearing this dumb ol' shirt. Most of the other guys took theirs off hours ago. And I know for a fact that you have a better chest than all of them out there. What gives, my big man?"

When she tried to pull his shirt over his head, he gave a nervous laugh and tugged it out of her hands to keep it on.

"You know it's not my chest that's the problem."

I wondered what he meant by that when Cora groaned. "Oh, you're seriously not going to let a couple scars on your back keep all my friends from seeing the yumminess that is your front, are you?"

Scars? Something warm and sympathetic rushed through me. What had happened to his back to scar it?

Ducking his head, Quinn mumbled, "It's just easier to keep them covered. I never know what to say when people ask questions."

"You don't have to say anything, baby. It's obvious someone beat you with a belt."

I swallowed hard. Oh, my...I...I didn't even know how to process that. I'd felt the lash of my father's belt more than once. But he'd never hit me so hard that I still had a scar from any of those experiences, except for the one on the back of my leg where he'd forgotten and used the other end. The metal clasp had caught my skin and ripped the flesh open. That had felt bad enough. I couldn't imagine how much it must have hurt to make lasting scars all over my back.

Grabbing his shirt again, Cora used it to tug Quinn closer. "Now give me another kiss before *I* start beating you with a belt."

I frowned at such an insensitive line but was sucked back into eavesdropping when she smashed her mouth to his. Then I leaned a little further out to watch.

I know it was wrong. But watching the way he kissed her was...I wasn't even sure how to describe it. He carried honest caring and affection for her. I'd been worried after reading so many of Cora's emails about him. She'd gushed over how perfect and gorgeous and sweet he was, and I had hoped she wasn't blinded by lust and being used or manipulated by some jerk.

But Quinn seemed to reciprocate her adoration. I was relieved and glad Cora had found a relationship like this, even though I hadn't known they honestly existed. It made my envy spark until a tiny part of me resented her...just a little bit for finding something so amazing.

She'd always had the nice family, a mother who annoyed her by how much she wanted to be involved in Cora's life and a father who was one of the gentlest men I'd ever met. And I'd had a widowed father who'd hit me for things like overcooking his fried eggs.

It didn't seem fair that Cora had gotten the perfect, dedicated boyfriend too. Which only made me choke on my guilt because here I was feeling jealous of the only person who'd ever befriended me while I was perfectly healthy and she was...not.

Oh, man. I was the worst friend in the world.

Quinn was the first to break away from the kiss. His breathing was accelerated, which made his voice sound huskier and in turn made *me* feel tinglier.

"I should get back," he said. "The guys are waiting for their soapy water."

"The guys can just keep waiting," Cora argued as she kissed her way down his neck. "You need to satisfy your woman."

He made a groaning sound, letting me know just how tempted he was, even as he set a hand on her hip to nudge her away. "I'll make it up to you tonight. How about that?"

Cora pulled back and stuck out a fake sulky bot-tom lip. "Promise?"

He kissed her forehead. "We'd better get going before we're caught in here together like this."

"Don't be such a prude, baby. We're not doing anything wrong. We still have all our clothes on."

Quinn just shook his head as he bent to pick up his bucket.

"Okay, fine." Still in pout mode, Cora set her hands on her hips and spun away to flounce toward the door. "Be a fuddy duddy then. You better make it up to me *twice* tonight."

Quinn began to follow her, but glanced over for some reason. I wasn't expecting him to look my way, but when his gaze latched onto mine, I was caught.

I hunched back deeper into my hiding spot, but he froze and his mouth fell open, letting me know good and well he saw me.

I expected a hailstorm of questions and cringed even more under his gaze, already trying to think up an excuse for why I was here...and why I hadn't made my presence known.

But he shocked me when his eyes filled with sympathy. Glancing after Cora as if to check if she was paying attention or not, he turned back. Then he pointed at me and mouthed the question, "*You okay?*"

I blinked.

He wasn't going to expose me or demand answers? Why wasn't he going to expose me?

Heart thumping hard, I nodded.

So he pointed after his departing girlfriend and mouthed, "*Do you need Cora?*"

I smiled a little, charmed that he was so concerned and yet grateful he was keeping my presence private.

When I shook my head, he smiled. After sending me a thumbs-up sign, he followed Cora from the ware-house.

I stayed there another minute, trying to rein in my scattered emotions. I was still mortified about being caught, even though Quinn had been so cool about it. It made me feel like an idiot for hiding in the first place. But most of all, I was ashamed.

Cora was my one and only friend. She'd been the only person to talk to me and introduce herself on my first day of public school after my father finally agreed I could stop using the tutors he paid to homeschool me. She'd been my rock and support every time after he'd punished me. I worshiped the ground she walked on. And now she was hurting, suffering from a debilitating disease. She deserved all the happiness she could get. What the heck was I doing, feeling *jealous?*

I was still pretty mad at myself by the time I re-turned to Caroline. But she looked worried out of her mind until she spotted me. Rushing forward, she asked, "Are you okay? I was about to send search and rescue in for you."

"Oh, I...I...I'm sorry." I glanced across the parking lot, only to find Quinn watching us.

When he caught sight of me looking back, he turned away. I wondered what was going through his head, what kind of freak he must think I was. I turned to Caroline, slightly sick to my stomach.

"I kind of got stuck in there when Quinn and Cora slipped inside to make out. I guess I should've cleared my throat or something to let them know I was there, but—"

Caroline held up a hand and rolled her eyes. "Say no more. I totally get it. I'd hide out for a while too. My brother catches his girlfriend Aspen around the house, all the time, thinking they're 'alone,' and I never know if I should tell them I'm right there or what?"

I let out a silent breath of relief, glad I wasn't the only person who'd ever gone through that kind of dilemma. "What do you usually do?"

She grinned mischievously. "I usually wait until they're going really hot and heavy before I make a loud noise and scare the hell out of them."

With a laugh, I shook my head. "You're kind of devious, aren't you?"

Her smile faded. Turning away to focus on scrubbing the last car of the day, waiting on us to clean it, she murmured, "I used to be, I guess."

Realizing I'd hit some kind of trigger, I sobered and silently got to work rinsing what she'd just cleaned.

But great. Now I had another reason to feel crappy. I'd somehow offended the only person I'd really connected with since moving here.

SEVEN

⌘ QUINN ⌘

THE GUYS ENDED up winning over the girls, washing
eight more cars than they had.

Ten led some bizarre victory dance, but I was too busy
glancing across the parking lot and checking on Zoey to join
in...not that I would've anyway. Dancing was not my thing.

It still bothered me that she'd been hiding in the
warehouse. Had something scared her? Someone bothered
her? I didn't like remembering how lost and alone she'd
looked.

She'd been away from her abusive father for barely a
full day. Maybe it had been too soon for Cora to start
dragging her around to social events.

Except she looked okay now.

She actually smiled at something Noel's sister was
saying to her and brushed a stray piece of hair out of her
face when the wind blew it into her eyes. Her hands
motioned as she answered, and Caroline threw her head
back before letting out a belly laugh.

Noel straightened at the sound and glanced across the
lot to watch them. "Holy shit," he murmured, stopping at
my side. "That's Caroline. She's... God, she's *laughing*." The

concept seemed completely unheard of to him. Turning to me, he looked utterly amazed as he murmured, "I can't believe she's laughing. I haven't seen her laugh all summer."

His lips twitched into a relieved kind of smile. "Whoever that blonde talking to her is, I freaking love her."

I sucked in a breath, startled by how much I wanted to hurt Noel Gamble, my biggest idol on the planet, in that moment.

Ten chuckled and patted Noel's shoulder. "Watch what you say, Gam, or Hamilton's likely to knock your teeth out. Blondie's here with him today."

Noel wrinkled his brow before he did a double take, glancing from me to Zoey and back to me again. "Wait. What?"

With a sigh, I sent a brief glare Ten's way before answering. "Her name's Zoey. She's Cora's new roommate."

"Really?" Noel brightened. "So, she really did come here with you today?"

I nodded warily, wondering where he was going with this. I knew he hadn't been literal when he'd said he loved her. But hearing those words come from his mouth while he was looking at her had not struck me the right way.

"Great." Noel clasped his hands together, grinning madly. "You guys should come get some pizza with us for supper."

I faltered, not wanting Zoey near him for some reason I couldn't explain.

As if reading the indecision on my face, he stepped closer. "This is the most alive I've seen my sister in *months*. She'd holed herself up in her room since she moved here. I am not about to let her lose out on her first attempt at making a friend. Please, man. Just see if your Zoey girl can spend a little more time with Caroline."

"Okay." I sighed, wondering for the millionth time what had happened to Caroline Gamble. It must've really messed her up. And I probably should've told Noel not to call her *my* Zoey, but I didn't. "I'll ask Cora and Zoey if that's okay with them."

"Hey." Ten wormed his way between us, scowling. "Where's my golden invitation to eat pizza with you?"

Noel sniffed and sent him a short frown, throwing Ten's arm off his shoulder. "I didn't see you bringing anyone around to befriend my sister."

"Well...*I* could befriend her," Ten started, putting on an offended front as he pressed his hand to his chest.

Noel threw back his head and laughed.

"What?" Ten muttered, folding his arms over his chest and glaring. "I make a fucking awesome friend."

Noel's chuckle settled before he seemed to realize Ten was serious. His smile dropped flat. Pointing at Ten's nose, he growled. "Stay the fuck away from my sister."

Ten sent him a bland glance. "Why do you feel the need to say that to me in that exact tone every time you see me?"

"Probably because you're a horny little ass who can't keep it in his pants and hits on anything and everything with tits and a vagina."

"Have you ever *seen* me hit on her?" When Noel didn't readily answer, Ten sniffed and shook his head. "That's what I thought, fucker. I do have *some* sense of honor, you know." Spinning away, he stalked off.

As I stared after my ticked-off roommate, Noel scratched his head. "What the hell is his problem?"

I glanced at Noel. If he seriously didn't notice how obviously out-of-character Ten acted whenever Caroline was around, then I wasn't going to be the person to clue him in. I just hoped to God Ten hadn't been lying when he'd said he had more sense than to hit on Caroline, because if he ever did, the outcome with his and Noel's friendship would not be pretty.

"I'm going to go ask Zoey and Cora if pizza's okay with them," I said instead, moving away before a scowling Noel could question me further.

EATING WITH THE Gambles turned out to be more than okay with Cora...and Caroline too. I don't think Zoey had much choice in the matter.

As soon as I mentioned the invite to them, Cora's eyes had gone huge. "You mean, Noel Gamble, the *quarterback*, wants us to eat with him?"

I blinked, wondering why she was so impressed. She knew Noel and I were friends, but...hmmm. Maybe she just didn't realize how close we were.

Maybe I needed to talk a little more about myself around her.

Caroline had still been talking to Zoey when I'd mentioned it to her. Before Zoey could answer, Caroline gripped her arm and started jumping up and down. "Oh, you have to. It'll be so much fun. Please, please, please."

With a laugh, Zoey nodded. "Okay, I guess. I'd love to."

So we ended up following Noel to the nearest pizza parlor. On the way, Cora bragged to Zoey about how fortunate we were to spend the evening in Noel Gamble's company.

"He's, like, *the* football icon around here. Hell, the entire university might as well pin his face up as their new logo because he's such a legendary quarter-back. We haven't seen talent like his in...well, a long time."

My eyebrows furrowed as she kept gushing. Yeah, Noel was good. But he wasn't the entire team. If Ten wasn't such a great receiver, Noel never would've made as many awesome passes as he had. If the entire defensive line hadn't held back our opponents as much as they had, Noel wouldn't even have time on the field to make impressive plays. And—

"What position do *you* play?" Zoey asked from the backseat.

It took me a second to realize she was talking to me. I lifted my face to the rearview mirror, and a shock of awareness spread through me when our gazes met.

Seriously. Why did she have to have such pretty eyes?

Cora laughed and waved a hand. "Oh, Quinn's only a third-string quarterback."

I glanced at her sharply. She was still chuckling over her dismissive reply. "I'm also a *first*-string tight end," I felt the need to add. And a *sophomore* first-string tight end at that. There were seniors who still hadn't made a first-string position yet. I'd been kind of proud of how well I'd risen in the ranks.

My girlfriend rolled her eyes. "Yeah, but the only position that matters is quarterback."

I didn't even know how to respond to that. But learning my own girlfriend thought the main position I played was meaningless didn't make me feel all warm and fuzzy inside.

Why had I never heard her say anything like this

before?

"If the other players were useless, then wouldn't it just be a game of one-on-one out on the field?" Zoey asked thoughtfully.

I shot her a grateful glance in the rearview mirror, but yeah, looking at her was still a bit too overwhelming, so I quickly returned my attention to the road and pulled into the pizza place's parking lot.

"Well, thank God there's more," Cora went on. "Watching a *bunch* of hot men in tight pants is a lot more fun than just watching two." Nudging her elbow into mine, she grinned across the car and wiggled her eyebrows.

I sent her a tight smile, trying not to let her see how much her words hurt...and ticked me off. But didn't she realize how much she was belittling me? Did she really see me as so insignificant? As I found a parking spot, I blew out a long, steadying breath, telling myself not to obsess over her thoughtless words. My grandmother had always told me it only hurt *me*—no one else—when I kept a grudge against someone for an unintentional hurt they'd caused.

"*Keeping a grudge is like swallowing poison and hoping somebody else dies from it*," she'd always told me.

But still...my stung pride continued to smart as I killed the engine. What was worse than realizing my girlfriend thought so lowly of me was that Zoey was there to witness it.

I cast her a quick glance as we got out of the car. She darted an apologetic smile to me before looking away, and I wondered what she was so sorry about. She'd actually defended me. Or maybe she was trying to apologize for Cora's sake, since Cora obviously had no idea what she was putting me through.

I shook my head. It didn't matter. I wasn't going to let a careless slight get me down.

Straightening my spine, I followed the girls to the front entrance where Noel and his sister met us at the door. He paused to hold it open and let us go in first, and I couldn't help but frown at the way Cora tittered and thanked him for his courtesy. I didn't like knowing she'd placed one of my friends on a higher pedestal than she'd placed me.

"Aspen and my brothers are on their way too," Noel told me as I was the last to enter. "Hope you don't mind."

I shook my head. "Not at all. That's fine with me."

As Caroline dragged Zoey in first, Cora caught my arm and murmured into my ear. "Who's Aspen?"

I froze, not certain how to answer. In respect to Noel, I hadn't told Cora about his and Aspen's relationship. I wasn't sure if he wanted it spread around. But if he didn't mind eating here with her in public, with Cora present, I guess it was okay to tell her now.

But instead of going into details, I just said, "She's Noel's girlfriend."

Cora frowned slightly. "I didn't know he was seeing anyone."

I nodded and grasped her hand to escort her to our seats, only to pause when I caught sight of Ten already sitting at two tables that had been pushed together.

"Hey," he called with a big grin, waving us over. "What a surprise to see you guys. You all want to sit with me? There's plenty of room."

Noel slowed to a stop, scowling, but Caroline merely steered Zoey toward him. So Cora and I headed that way too.

Cora's eyes narrowed as they settled on my room·mate. "You didn't tell me *he* was going to be here."

It bothered me that Ten and Cora so openly did not get along. Even from the very beginning, when I first started dating her, he refused to be polite to her, and she'd been just as eager to hiss and spit at him. He never, not even once, let her stay overnight at our place.

I knew women usually got off on a bad foot with him, but he'd at least been decent to all our friends' girlfriends. Why couldn't he have attempted civility with Cora?

Noel reluctantly joined us, but I think he hated the seating arrangement. Caroline ended up directly next to Ten. He smiled at her as she sat, and then he went and politely nodded to Zoey, telling her it was nice to see her again. Then, instead of calling Cora a dirty name, which he usually did, he simply ignored her.

Yeah, it was strange when he was on his best behavior. Kind of gave me the willies, so I could only imagine what it did to Noel.

I was unnerved to end up sitting on the other side of Zoey. My elbow accidently brushed past hers as I sat, which somehow made that mysterious smell of hers invade my nostrils. They flared, trying to figure it out until Cora sat beside me, and her vanilla perfume drowned it out.

The waitress came and took drink requests, but Noel told her we were waiting for three more to join us before we ordered our meals.

Noel and Ten started discussing the first up-coming game of the season and trying to decide how much of a challenge it was going to be to win when Cora gasped and clutched my arm.

"Oh my God. Isn't that the teacher who was fired last semester for having sex with a student?"

As I squeezed her hand in warning under the table, Noel swung his head her way and narrowed his eyes. "What did you just say?"

Crap. I definitely should've warned Cora, but she hadn't taken any of Aspen's classes last year; I didn't think she'd even *know* who Aspen was.

But she did. She pointed. "Look. She's right there."

We all twisted in our seats to look, even though I'm sure most of us knew exactly who we'd see. And sure enough, Aspen had just entered the pizza parlor with Noel's two younger brothers, Colton and Brandt.

"Cor—" I started, hoping to quiet her, but she just kept talking. "Did you not see the naked picture of her that baseball player was showing everyone on his phone last night?"

I winced and lifted my hand to stop her, but Noel was already slowly turning around to pierce Cora with a hard stare. "What picture?"

She started to answer, but I quickly put my hand over her mouth, muffling her.

Noel swiveled his attention to me. "Hamilton?" His voice was low and deadly.

I glanced toward Ten, not sure what to say.

"Don't worry about it." Ten patted Noel's shoulder in way too nonchalant of a way. "We took care of damage control."

"Damage control?" Noel swiped Ten's hand off him and stood up, fisting his hands down at his sides. "What the fuck, man? Someone's spreading around pictures of my woman and you don't feel the need to tell me? Whose phone was it on? Was it the same picture the coach posted on the locker room wall or was it a new one?" When no one responded, he kicked the table leg. "Damn it. Somebody answer me."

Caroline snaked out a hand to catch the napkin basket as it started to topple over while a wide-eyed Zoey moved back in her chair, looking petrified.

Though I was still using one hand to cover Cora's mouth, I set the other on Zoey's arm, trying to calm her. "*It's okay*," I mouthed the words, but her eyes were wide with panic and fear.

"Noel?" A concerned Aspen touched his arm as she reached the table. "What's wrong?"

He spun to her and pulled her into his arms, crushing her to his chest. "I'm sorry. I'm so sorry."

Cora ripped my hand off her mouth. "Oh, *snap*." Her mouth fell open as she watched Noel and Aspen hug. "Noel *Gamble* was the student who got her fired?"

"Say *what?*" Caroline shouted as Noel and Aspen broke apart.

Ten stood up and glared at Cora as if he was going to strangle her.

I rushed to my feet, intervening, and grabbed my girlfriend's hand to pull her up after me. "Come with me."

I think it was past time to get my girlfriend up to speed.

ϵIGHT

⌁ ZOEY ⌁

I DIDN'T KNOW exactly what was going on around me, but it wasn't taking me long to catch up. Caro·line's brother, the star quarterback, had started dating one of his teachers and gotten her fired for having a relationship with her. And they were still obviously together.

Got it.

And now I also knew what had been on that cell phone last night that had set Quinn off.

As he dragged Cora away from the table, I gaped after them, not sure what I was supposed to do. Follow them, or just stay here? I didn't want to stick a·round because it looked as if Caroline's brother was about to blow a gasket. But getting up and leaving now didn't feel right either. Plus, Caroline reached out and grabbed my hand hard, letting me know she needed some serious moral support.

Watching Cora and Quinn disappear down a hall, Noel's girlfriend pulled out of the hug and smiled sadly up at Noel. "I'm guessing someone just let the cat out of the bag, huh?"

"Oh my God." A pale Caroline let go of me and stumbled to her feet, her gaze darting between Noel and

Aspen. She covered her mouth. "Oh my God. So that...what she just said...it's *true?*"

Noel winced as he kissed Aspen on the forehead. "Care."

When his voice cracked with apology, her eyes bulged with horror. "Holy shit." She backed away. "Oh, holy shit." Whirling away from them, she stumbled over me and my chair in her haste to escape.

Okay, now I really felt uncomfortable for sitting through all this.

Aspen—who actually looked younger than her ex-student—turned worried eyes up to Noel. "We really should've told her."

"Told her what?" the youngest boy with Aspen asked.

"Nothing," Noel growled as he grasped Aspen's elbow to steer her toward the exit. "Come on. We're leaving."

"But I want to stay," the older boy said. He had dark hair and looked like a younger Noel. "I'm freaking starving."

"Me too," the younger brother whined. He looked more like Caroline, with her fair hair and similarly shaped face. "I want pizza."

"We'll get it delivered." Noel's tone brooked no room for argument. When his fierce gaze landed on me, I moved back in my seat and held my breath, ready for him to start making threats to ensure my silence. But instead, he asked, "Can you make sure my sister gets a ride home?"

I was so startled to hear that question, I fumbled at first. "Uh...yeah, sure." I bobbed my head, glad to help in any way. "Of course."

His shoulders eased fractionally. Then he sent me a respectful nod. "Thanks."

As he ushered Aspen and the two boys from the pizza parlor, I stared after them, dazed by what had just happened.

I turned toward Ten, who'd slumped into his seat and rested his forehead in his hand.

What now? I asked him the silent question.

He met my gaze, lifted a brow, and then blew out a breath. "Well...fuck."

Without saying another word to me, he stood up and walked off.

I remained seated, letting everything soak in. I didn't stay long, just long enough for the waitress to return with a tray full of drinks. When she found just little ol' me left hovering at the two tables, she paused and glanced around.

"Um..." I sent her a weak smile. "Everyone else had to...go."

She didn't seem to know what to do with the drinks. "What do I do with all these, then?"

"Oh!" I popped to my feet and grabbed my purse. "I can pay for them. I'm so sorry for your trouble."

Still confused, she continued to hesitate. "So...you just want me to take them back?"

I bit my lip. Seeing as everyone had left, *yeah*, I pretty much wanted her to take them back. But I didn't know how to say that without sounding condescending. "Well..." I glanced around. No one from my group was in sight anywhere. "I don't think they're coming back."

They definitely were not coming back.

"That's just lovely." Huffing out a moody breath, she spun away and stalked off, returning the tray full of cups to the kitchen. When she came back, I was standing at the counter, waiting to pay.

She couldn't seem to stop glaring and sighing out her disgust, so I apologized again, but she just blew me off.

Once the bill was taken care of, I clutched my purse to my chest and glanced around, wondering how I was going to find anyone. I glanced down a hall that led to the bathrooms and didn't spot anyone there, so I pushed my way out the back exit. When I saw Ten's back as he rounded a corner, I hurried after him. No idea why I followed *him*. But he was the only person here I somewhat knew, and I was kind of stuck here until I found a ride home, plus I needed to find Caro·line. So I darted after him, only to realize he'd just found her.

I was going to approach, but after the tender way he touched her back to get her attention...I don't know...I held back.

"Hey." His voice was soft. "You okay?"

Caroline spun around and looked up at him a good ten seconds before she nodded. The tears filling her eyes probably told him she really wasn't okay, though.

"I just..." She wiped at her cheeks and sniffed. "I knew she was a teacher, and I knew she was looking for a job, but I...I had no idea she was *his* teacher, or that she'd gotten fired because...oh my God. She never let on that anything like that had happened. Neither did he. They just...they've been so supportive and strong, helping Colton, Brandt, and me settle in and adjust. I didn't even...I had no idea. She doesn't look old enough to be a university professor." Her wet eyes looked extra blue and pleading as she stared up at him. "Why didn't they tell me?"

Ten shook his head slowly. "I'm sure they didn't want to worry you with it. You—"

When he reached for her cheek, she jerked back and gritted her teeth. "But I'm going to be going to that school on *Monday*. I'll be attending the same college where they..." She gulped. "What if I heard some rumor, or...I don't know. Why wouldn't they want me to be prepared for that? What—"

"Hey. Shh." Ten caught her arm and hauled her in for a hard hug. "Your brother wasn't expecting you to hear any rumors. You might hear about an English teacher losing her job, maybe even speculation of why, but very, very few of us know it's actually because of Noel."

She sniffed and burrowed deeper into his chest. "You'd think he'd know he didn't have to protect me like that anymore. I'm eighteen."

Ten smiled. "Doesn't matter how old you get. You'll always be his little sister. He'll always want to protect you."

"And I'm sure I'll always want to knock his head off for it, too."

With a soft chuckle, Ten began to stroke her hair. "I bet." When he closed his eyes and buried his nose in it as if he was smelling her, something tight wrapped around my chest. He liked her. I mean, he *really*, really liked her. I slunk an inch in reverse, feeling like a voyeur. But I didn't know where else to go. So, I just...stayed and watched.

"Is there really a naked picture of Aspen going around?" Caroline asked, lifting her face.

Ten stopped moving his fingers through her hair as his gaze touched hers. "Yeah," he said. "It's what got her fired."

Caroline shook her head. "That doesn't make sense. How could a naked picture of just her get her fired?"

"It had Noel's arm in it."

This time, I shook my head, confused, though no one saw me doing so from my hiding spot. Geesh, I was doing a lot of hiding and eavesdropping on couples today.

"I still don't get it," Caroline spoke my thoughts aloud.

"If all they saw was his arm, then how did they know who she was with? It might not have been a student at all—"

Ten lifted his forearm to point out something I couldn't see from where I was standing. "About a dozen of us football players got this very same tattoo last year. It did end up in the picture of her, so the university knew it had to be a current ESU football player she was with."

Caroline studied the tattoo and slowly ran her finger over it. I don't think she noticed how doing that made Ten close his eyes briefly and then slowly reopen them.

She finally looked up. "So, for all they know, it could've been *you* who'd been with Aspen."

His lips spread with amusement. "It wasn't me."

Her fingers kept lingering on his tattoo while her gaze stayed fastened to his. "I can't believe they've been going through all this, and I didn't even have a clue."

Ten shook his head. "You had plenty else to worry about."

Caroline opened her mouth, but then she shut it before speaking. It took another moment for her eyes to widen with horror. "Oh God. You *know*. About me."

She tried to pull away, but he caught her shoulder and tugged her back. "Wait. Where are you going?"

"I don't know." Keeping her back to his chest, she lifted a hand in a helpless gesture. "To crawl under a rock and die of humiliation."

"You have nothing to be humiliated about." Taking her elbow, he turned her back around to face him.

"How do you know?" she asked. "Did Noel tell you?"

"No. I was there when you told *him*, remember? It was kind of impossible not to hear every word through those thin walls."

Her face drained of color. Shaking her head, she once again turned away, but he held her waist and pressed her back to his chest again as she bent slightly at the waist.

"No. Caroline...don't do that. Don't turn away." He closed his eyes and pressed his forehead to the side of her neck.

More tears trickled down her cheeks. "You must think I'm a—"

"I don't," he cut in intently, spinning her around and forcing her to look at him, cupping her cheeks in his palms. "I absolutely don't think anything bad of you at all."

She blinked and one last wet drop slid from her lashes. Ten caught it with his thumb and wiped it away. Caroline's chest heaved as she drew in a breath. The entire time they continued to stare into each other's eyes, I held my breath as I waited for what would come next.

Caroline was the first to move. She lifted her chin and arched up onto her toes to kiss him.

But he stepped back, turning his face aside. "Don't." His voice was low and strained.

Covering my mouth with both hands, I could actually feel Caroline's rejection pierce my own chest. And, ouch, that had to have stung. She slowly moved back, then curled her shoulder in before whirling away.

As she ran off, Ten stared after her, gripping his hair. Torment creased his face as he closed his eyes and mouthed something I didn't catch.

When he opened up, he stepped forward as if he wanted to follow her, but he caught sight of me instead and skidded to a halt.

His eyes narrowed. I cowered a step back and clutched my purse close. "Uh..." I tried to explain my eavesdropping presence, but yeah, nothing came out.

He sauntered toward me, giving off a lethal kind of vibe. "Well, look who's nothing but eyes and ears tonight. You learn a lot in the past hour, Blondie?"

I took a step back and shook my head intently as I gulped. "I didn't—"

"See anything?" he asked with an arched eyebrow. "Hear anything?"

"No, I...I didn't see *or* hear anything," I agreed.

"No," he murmured softly as he studied me a moment longer. "You didn't, did you? Because you're not a loud-mouthed cow like your bitch of a roommate, are you?"

My mouth fell open. I couldn't believe he'd just said that about Cora. Cora was everything bright and bubbly. Why would anyone call her a—

He hitched his chin to the right. "Why don't you go find Caroline and make sure she gets home safe and sound?"

He sounded so concerned about her; it gave me the courage to ask, "Are you going to apologize to her?"

Ten snorted. "Fuck no." Gritting his teeth, he scowled at me. "In fact, I'm going to have to change up my game around her so she *never* forgives me."

69

Spinning away, he stalked off without explaining himself.

I stood there a moment longer. This was definite·ly turning out to be one of the strangest days of my life. But for some reason, I felt exhilarated. It was so far and beyond anything my father would approve of. I secretly relished having been a minor part in it.

I turned in the direction Caroline had run, but no sooner did I get a few steps than Cora, hand·in·hand with Quinn, veered around the corner.

"Zoey?" Cora asked in surprise. "What're *you* doing out here?"

Concern knit Quinn's brow. "Everything okay?"

I nodded, though I had no idea if anything was okay at all. I motioned vaguely toward the entrance of the pizzeria. "Everyone left. Except Caroline. She ran that way, upset, and Noel asked if we could make sure she got home."

While Cora scowled at the idea, Quinn immediately nodded. "Sure. No problem."

"*What?*" Cora glowered at him. "I don't want to babysit *Noel Gamble's* little sister." As she sniffed in disgust, both Quinn and I gaped at her.

"Cora!" he scolded, as I gasped out, "We can't just leave her here by herself."

She scowled between the two of us. When she must've realized she was outnumbered, she sniffed. "Whatever." Folding her arms over her chest, Cora spun away and started off. "I'm going to wait in the car."

I stared after her, wondering where all the attitude had come from and why she'd been so snotty. The Cora I knew never acted that way.

"She's mad at me because I didn't tell her about Noel and Aspen before," Quinn said, answering my silent question.

I looked up at him and instantly felt awful. He looked guilty and crushed. So I shook my head. "It wasn't your secret to tell."

Just as it wasn't my secret to tell him what was happening to his girlfriend...even if I thought he should know.

He shook his head as if brushing aside his issues with his girlfriend and lifted his gaze, his blue eyes full of pain. "Do we know where Caroline is?"

I made a face. "Kind of. She ran that way after she tried to kiss Ten."

When Quinn's eyes widened, I slapped my hand over my mouth. "Oh, no! I can't believe I told you that. I promised Ten I wouldn't tell anyone what I saw."

I blinked, but he waved his hand. "It's okay. I won't let him know you told me." Then he winced "Did he kiss her back?"

"No. He stepped back, warding her off, and said, 'don't,' so she ran away, crying."

He blew out a breath and ran his fingers through his hair. "Wow. I can't believe he restrained himself. That's so...not like him. But it's good that he had some self-control. Noel's warned him away from Caro-line more times than I can count." He released his hair and glanced around. "What a mess."

When I nodded in agreement, he sent me a small smile. "How about I go this way, looking for her, and you go that way?"

I agreed and we set off in our different directions. I found Caroline a few minutes later, sitting on a bench across the street from the pizza parlor under a streetlight. She didn't say anything or acknowledge me as I approached, but I knew she knew I was there. Silently, I sat beside her and waited.

She stopped hugging her knees and set her feet slowly back on the ground. "I tried to kiss Oren, but he pushed me away."

I swallowed, almost wishing I wasn't her confidante because I wasn't sure just how many secrets I could contain for other people. "I saw," I said.

She glanced at me. "You did? Does *he* know that?"

I nodded. "Yeah. He didn't want me to tell anyone about it."

"Well...I guess that was nice of him to help me keep my mortification private." Tucking her hands under her thighs until she was sitting on them, she waited another few seconds before she looked at me again. "You probably think I'm pretty pathetic, huh?"

With a shake of my head, I said, "No. Not at all. I...actually, I thought you were really brave." Across the street, I caught sight of Quinn as he spotted us. Instead of crossing the street to us, though, he slowed to a stop and respectfully let me have a moment alone with Caroline. "Having the courage to go after something you want...I've never had that kind of strength before. I'd think it'd be amazing, though."

She sniffed as tears filled her eyes. "I'm pretty messed up right now, is what I am."

I smiled. "Then I guess I'm pretty pathetic, be-cause I was just wishing I could be more like you."

Her laugh was self-derisive. "Trust me, you don't want to be like me."

Shrugging, I tucked a piece of my hair behind my ear. "I guess we'll have to agree to disagree on that."

She didn't answer for a while. Then she blew out a breath and said, "Or maybe we're just messed up together."

A grin tugged at my lips. "Maybe." I pushed to my feet. "Come on. I think our ride's waiting."

Brows furrowing, she looked up at me. "Ride?"

I hitched my chin toward Quinn and explained how her brother had already taken the rest of her family home. She nodded in resignation and followed me back across the street. But before we reached him, she tugged me back a step to say into my ear, "Hey. Thank you."

I hadn't done anything very life altering, but I nodded and grabbed her hand, squeezing it warmly before letting go.

Quinn didn't appear annoyed about having to wait on us. He remained low key, his hands in his pockets but worry in his eyes. "Ready to go?" was all he said.

His reaction was so unlike what my father would've done, it was kind of startling how cool he was about the entire situation.

I nodded, answering for both Caroline and myself as I ignored the strange urge to step toward him and hug him. His body was huge and bulky and looked really hard, but I had a feeling a hug from him would be comfortable and safe. Maybe it was because I knew he smelled so good, or because his T-shirt looked so soft and well worn, or maybe it was because he exuded a protective aura I just wanted to burrow into. In either case, it freaked me out how close I wanted to get to him. So I made sure to keep Caroline between him and me as the three of us walked quietly back to Cora's car.

The trip home was quiet and tense, mostly be-cause an angry silence radiated from Cora throughout the car. In the backseat, Caroline and I didn't talk either. All she whispered to me was, "Good luck," after Quinn pulled into her drive to let her out. There was nothing I needed luck for, but I appreciated her concern, anyway.

As soon as we parked in the parking garage to the high rise, Cora shoved the door open and marched off, slamming it behind her. Quinn breathed out a long, loud sigh as he watched her go.

"She'll be fine," I felt compelled to say. "Cora never stays mad long."

He twisted in his seat just enough to glance back at me. A small smile lifted his lips. "Yeah," he agreed, but he still looked miserable as his gaze slid back to his girlfriend who was being let inside by Henry.

Suddenly, Quinn glanced back at me again. "Hey, thanks for everything you did for Caroline."

I blushed, stumped by his gratitude. "I didn't..." I shook my head.

"Noel said he hadn't seen her laugh all summer. When he saw you talking to her at the car wash, making her laugh...that's why he wanted you to eat pizza with them. He was so grateful for what you'd done."

A surprised laugh left me. "But I didn't do any·thing."

Quinn gave a slight shake of his head. "You included her," he said, reminding me of what Cora had done for me that first day I'd met her. She'd asked me to sit on the bench next to her, and then she'd just...talked to me as if I was someone. She'd included me in her life. And now here I was, ready to give up a kidney for her.

"Sometimes, it's the little things we do that mean the most to others," Quinn murmured, echoing my thoughts.

I don't know what changed in that very moment, but the last remaining bit of uncomfortable tension I'd felt around him the first night we met kind of just...melted away. I smiled as my chest eased.

Bringing his knuckles to his mouth, Quinn noticed nothing of my situation. He returned his attention to the entrance of our building. Cora was long gone inside, but he kept staring at the door before he asked, "Mind if I follow you up? Try one last time tonight to mend fences with her?"

"Sure," I said.

The elevator ride up was quiet, but it didn't feel as weird as it had the night before. Quinn was lost in his own thoughts, and I was still digesting all the things that had happened during and after the car wash. After I unlocked the door and let him in, he nodded his thanks and walked back to Cora's closed bedroom door. He knocked once, then let himself in and quietly shut the door behind him.

I drifted back to my own room. My stomach grumbled from the supper we'd never gotten to eat, but it felt weird to wander around the apartment while Cora and her boyfriend talked in her room. So I curled up on my bed and wrote a short story about a girl who tried to kiss a boy but was shot down. In the end, they got back together and lived happily ever after.

I never heard any yelling from down the hall. I didn't hear anything, actually. I didn't even hear Quinn leave by the time I got ready for bed and fell a·sleep. I wondered if he'd convinced Cora to forgive him, but I had a feeling he had. If I'd been his girl·friend, I don't guess I'd be able to stay mad at him very long. Honestly, if I were his girlfriend, I doubt I'd be able to get mad at him in the first place.

But thinking thoughts like that made me uncomfortably warm. Quinn Hamilton really needed to stop being so nice and pleasant to me. It gave my poor, pathetic heart thoughts it shouldn't be having.

From here on out, I decided, I was going to keep myself as distant from him as possible, because guys like that were just too potent for girls like me.

$\mathcal{N}$INE

⊶ QUINN ⊷

CORA WAS SLEEPING soundly on the other side of the mattress when I woke. She liked to sleep in a lot. I swear, she'd sleep till noon every day if she could.

I turned my head and watched her breathe, relieved she'd forgiven me last night.

I knew I'd messed up. I was awful at talking a·bout myself or my friends. I was awful at talking, period. But she'd been so mad at me. Her accusing words still haunted my ears.

"*You made me look like a clueless idiot, Quinn.*"

"*No,*" I'd tried to tell her. "*You didn't look like an idiot. You—*"

"*Looked like an idiot,*" she snapped.

So I attempted to explain why everything had to be kept a secret. Just because there were a few rumors floating around campus about the reason Aspen had been fired didn't mean people actually knew the truth. But if the truth got out, her entire future could be compromised. She might never find another teaching job again. And Noel would be crushed.

But Cora hadn't cared about any of that. She'd just cared that I hadn't felt the need to tell her such juicy gossip.

75

It would've been bad of me to point out how much she and her friends like to spread rumors, whether they were true or not. Telling Cora anything confidential was usually too risky. So I just kept apologizing and promising I'd never keep anything from her again. And finally, she'd loosened up and given in.

After a quick kiss to her cheek while she continued to sleep, I crawled out of bed and pulled on my clothes from last night.

Foregoing my socks and shoes, I padded through the quiet apartment. After a quick freshening up in the bathroom, I headed toward the kitchen. I found the griddle under the sink where I'd cleaned and left it last Saturday. After plugging it in to heat, I hunted up some eggs, vegetable oil, and milk. The pancake mix was right where I'd last left it, too.

I had the batter whipped up and was about to pour my special happy faces when I heard someone enter the kitchen behind me. The startled gasp let me know it wasn't Cora.

Every short hair on the back of my neck stood at immediate attention.

I whirled around. "Hi. Good morning," I rushed out the greeting. "Hungry?"

Zoey jerked to a halt, gaping badly. She had her hair down. This was the first time I'd seen it down. It was still tousled and uncombed, fresh from bed. It made me uncomfortable, as did the rest of her outfit. Sure, her shirt was a lot looser than the one she'd worn last night to the car wash, but it was so large the sleeve on one side had slipped down and fallen off one smooth, creamy shoulder. Her shorts were once again short enough to expose plenty of her slim, toned legs.

Not good. I really had to stop looking at her legs.

So, I did, forcing my attention to her face. Except her green eyes were so bright and innocent today. They caused a catch in my throat.

She tucked a piece of hair behind her ear as she took her attention away from me to study the mess I'd made of the counters.

"Don't worry," I said, motioning to everything. "I'll clean all this up."

It still seemed to take her a minute to soak in what I was actually doing, though. Her gaze finally slid back to me.

"You're cooking."

"I...yeah." I shifted my weight from one foot to the other, feeling majorly awkward. "It's kind of my Saturday morning thing. I...is this okay? I can stop if you want."

Her eyes grew wide. She obviously wasn't used to being asked for permission.

"No, it's fine," she said. Her gaze drifted over the griddle again before moving back to me. "Do...do you have a key to the apartment, then?"

"A key? No." Where the heck had that question come from? Then it hit me.

Oh, no.

Cora hadn't asked her if she minded if I stayed over on some nights, had she?

Since Ten had made it explicitly clear that Cora was not allowed to stay at our apartment, I'd been worried at first when Cora had told me she was going to get a roommate. What if her roommate didn't want me sleeping in *their* apartment? We'd never get to stay together overnight again.

But Cora had assured me Zoey was cool with it. As I stared at Zoey, though, I knew Cora had never bothered to even ask her.

"I...uh...I was...already here," I admitted, flushing hard.

When Zoey turned a bright tomato red as well, I lifted my hands. "Is that okay? If you don't want me here after a certain time, I totally understand. I'm so sorry. I thought Cora had cleared it with you. She told me you were okay with me staying over some nights."

"No." She started to shake her head before she blushed again. "I mean, no, Cora hasn't talked to me about it yet." A frown creased her brow as she glanced away. "She must've forgotten."

"Oh," I said dumbly, still not sure what she thought of me being here.

The griddle popped behind me, making me jump and reminding me it was heated and ready to cook pancakes.

Zoey glanced at the griddle and then back to me before she self-consciously shoved her sleeve up to cover her exposed shoulder. "You know, it's Cora's apartment. Whatever she wants is—"

"No, it's your apartment too," I argued, not wanting

her to think she didn't have a say about what happened here. I really wished Cora had just talked to her about it. "You pay half the rent. You have just as much say-so about what happens here as she does."

Zoey made a face of disagreement. "But she was here first and took care of setting everything up."

"That doesn't matter. You still have just as much—"

"*You can stay the night, okay,*" she burst out, letting me know she didn't want to argue about this. Then her face turned scarlet as she realized what she'd blurted out.

I wanted to apologize for being an idiot and arguing with her over such a silly issue.

"Okay." Ducking my head, I cleared my throat and turned back to my batter. I kept my back to her as I asked, "Want some pancakes?"

I knew she didn't want me there, but I had a feeling if I'd left right then, it would've made her even more uncomfortable.

When she murmured, "No thank you," a muscle jumped in my jaw. I hadn't realized how much I'd wanted to impress her with my Saturday morning special until the disappointment over her rejection ran thick through my veins.

But I said, "Okay. No problem," as if it didn't matter.

Behind me, she cleared her throat discreetly. "So, I guess Cora forgave you last night."

I glanced over my shoulder at her. She was wringing her hands at her waist and biting her lip as if she wanted to flee but wasn't sure if she was allowed to.

With a slow nod, I took in her bare feet. They were cute and petite for someone with her height. The toenails were painted a pale pink.

"Well, that's good," she said.

I lifted my attention back to her face, and the effect her large green eyes had on me was like a punch in the gut. I turned my attention back to the pancakes and forced a big breath from my lungs. I was never so happy to hear footsteps coming down the hall.

"Good morning," a new voice greeted as Cora breezed into the kitchen.

Relieved to have her here and unknowingly playing interference between me and her roommate, I turned to greet her with a smile after I flipped a pancake. "Hey, you."

Her eyes warmed with pleasure. "Hey, yourself." Sweeping up to me, she wrapped her arms around my waist, stepped up onto her tiptoes, and kissed me long and slow. "Have I ever told you how much I love Saturday mornings?" She glanced around and frown-ed. "What? No strawberries today?"

I laughed and tweaked her nose. "You're up too early. I haven't gotten them out of the refrigerator yet."

I had to pass Zoey as I went to retrieve the strawberries. That smell of hers was particularly strong this morning. I held my breath until I'd passed by her again, hoping it didn't mess with my hormones today as it had the other night. "Are you sure you don't want any pancakes?" I asked her again. "We have strawberries too?"

She shook her head just as Cora said, "Of course she wants pancakes. Seriously, Zo. You can't turn down Quinn's pancakes. They're legendary."

I ducked my face. "They're not really. I use a mix."

"But he grills them to perfection." Cora opened a cabinet door and pulled down three plates. "You're eating."

So the three of us ate breakfast together.

Cora talked the entire time, meaning there were never any uncomfortable silences. "Quinn used to cook bacon to eat with his pancakes. But I can't stand the smell of bacon, so he stopped, just for me, and transferred over to strawberries." She grinned up at me and slid her hand up my forearm before returning her gaze to Zoey. "Isn't he just the best boyfriend ever?"

Zoey blushed but smiled obligingly. I wasn't sure what to do about her anymore. Before we'd met, I'd wanted us to be friends. I'd wanted her to like me. After learning how intensely some parts of me reacted to her, however, I wanted distance from her more.

I'd never do anything to betray my girl, but there was no need to create any undue awkwardness where I could avoid it. But what was I supposed to do when Cora wanted us both around her together?

The whole thing depressed me a little. I'd been so hopeful that I could befriend Zoey. If only there wasn't always this thrumming tension brewing inside me when I looked at her. Inappropriate urges kept bub-bling up. I wanted to move closer, inhale that lovely mysterious scent, touch her soft-looking skin, bury my fingers in her hair, then press her against a wall and lift her up until the base of her throat was level with my mouth, where I could bite—

Great. There I went again. Muscles coiled tight, I glanced up cautiously from the pancake I was devouring, hoping no one could guess where my mind had just gone. Cora was still carrying on about who was who in her crowd of friends, and Zoey hugged one arm over her chest and nodded as if she was trying to pay attention while her mind was wandering in a completely different direction.

I glanced away, smiling to myself because her reaction reminded me too much of what I did when Cora started gossiping about all her girlfriends. It really was too bad I had to stay away from Zoey. I think I would've liked her.

A hard knock on the front door interrupted Cora mid-speech a split second before the front slammed open.

"Hey, motherfuckers," a familiar voice called. "Don't tell me you little pigs ate all the pancakes yet, did you?"

Zoey sat up straight, her eyes wide. "Who is that?" she asked while Cora whirled to me, scowling.

"What the hell is *he* doing here?"

"I-I don't know." I started to stand, but Ten appeared in the kitchen entrance before I could waylay him. Grabbing onto the doorframe above his head, he leaned into the room and leered at us, wiggling his eyebrows. "Well, doesn't this just look like a cozy little threesome?"

Zoey gasped and set her hand over her heart.

Ten winked at her and glanced at me, knowingly.

I scowled. "What're you doing here?"

"And have you never heard of knocking?" Cora snapped.

Ten's eyes narrowed when he glanced at her. "I did knock, bitch. Weren't you listening? And if I'd waited for permission to enter, you wouldn't have let me."

"Got that right, *asshole*," Cora grumbled just be-fore I repeated, "Seriously. What're you doing here?"

"What?" He shrugged his shoulders as if he thought the question was incredulous. "Can't I pick my roommate up for football practice? You do remember we have practice this morning, right?" He glanced between Zoey and Cora again. "You didn't get other-wise...*occupied*, did you?"

I clenched my jaw, upset he was getting so close to some of the things I hadn't been able to stop my brain from thinking. "*Yes*, I remembered practice." I folded my arms over my chest and glared him down, silently commanding him to make another crack a-bout me being here with both girls. "And my truck is right outside. I can drive myself."

Ten dropped his arms from the doorframe. "Fine. Then I'm here for the pancakes, I guess." He sauntered into the kitchen and winked at Zoey. "Morning, Blondie. These two didn't keep you up all night, did they? You know, if they ever get too loud and rowdy, you're always welcome to come back to my place to get away from them."

"Ten," I growled. I was tempted to break his face.

Something must be seriously wrong with me. Friday night, I'd pushed Cane Belcher against a wall? Last night, I could've easily taken out K.C. for the way he'd talked about Zoey. And this morning, I wanted to break Ten's face. It was enough aggression in three days to freak me out. I never, ever wanted to take up any of my mother's abusive qualities. But here I was, feeling violent all over again.

"What?" Ten glanced at me with his eyebrows lifted. "It was a perfectly polite invitation." He smiled at Zoey again. "I honestly don't know how they are together, you see. *I* don't let her stay over at our place." He returned his attention to me. "Sit back down and relax already, pretty boy. Practice isn't for another forty-five minutes."

My jaw bunched. I was about to order him from the apartment when Zoey surged to her feet. "Let me get you a plate. The pancakes are amazing."

Wait? What? Zoey actually *wanted* him here? I couldn't even feel smug about her praise of my pancakes. She looked too happy that he was staying. Even her shoulders weren't as tense as they'd been since she'd entered the kitchen this morning. When she sent him a warm smile, I froze.

Oh, no. What if she *liked* him? What if... Nausea swirled up my throat. I have no idea why, but I didn't like the idea of her liking Ten. At all.

Ten seemed surprised by her generous offer. He lifted his eyebrows and shot a glance my way. I wanted to wipe that smug smirk off his face with my fist. And Cora was no help whatsoever. She just groaned and stuffed more pancake into her mouth.

"Well, hot damn. I like you, Blondie," Ten finally announced. He smiled charmingly as he seated himself.

I was still standing, glaring at him when I noticed Zoey was having trouble finding which cabinet the plates were in.

"They're in here," I told her, brushing past her to open a door to her left. When Zoey let out a quiet inhalation, I turned back wondering what was wrong.

I hadn't realized quite how close I'd moved to her until our gazes met and her green eyes, so pale they almost looked blue, were right there. A hitch in my breathing made me clench my teeth. Why did I keep noticing things about her, like how soft her cheeks looked, or how pretty her eyes were? I never noticed things about other girls. Cora was my *it*, everything I wanted and more. I didn't like how my blood went hot every time I simply looked at her roommate.

"Sorry," I mumbled, hastily grabbing a plate and shoving it at her before I backed off and returned to the safety of Cora's side, where my core temperature thankfully once again lowered to normal.

I accidentally met Ten's gaze as I slid into my seat. He lifted his eyebrows with a knowing smirk. I scowled back but quickly wiped it off my face when Zoey offered him the plate I'd handed her.

Ten winked at her as he took it. "Thanks, Blondie."

She blushed and played with a piece of her hair. "Oh, it's Zoey, actually."

"Yeah." Ten didn't seem concerned as he promptly filled his plate, piling on a good half a dozen pan-cakes. "But I probably won't remember that."

TEN

⚬ ZOEY ⚬

As soon as Cora kissed Quinn goodbye, telling him to have fun at football practice, she turned to me, suddenly serious. "So, my next dialysis treatment starts in forty-five minutes. It takes half an hour to get there. You want to come with me or not?"

The emotionless, matter-of-fact way she asked flabbergasted me at first. When I finally got my bearings straight, I nodded my head vigorously. "Y-yes, of *course*, I want to come."

"Then hurry up. We leave in ten." She strode past me and down the hall toward her room. "Don't worry about dressing up. It's not exactly glamorous there."

I was ready in five, yanking on the first shirt and jean shorts I came across. After tugging my hair into a ponytail, I hurried to the front room, worried Cora might leave without me. She just seemed so stoic and unresponsive about the entire thing.

Heart pounding because I had no idea how the procedure went, or what I was supposed to do while she was...doing whatever she did, I sat on the floor by the front door and slid on my shoes.

Cora exited her room just as I was getting back to my

83

feet. She had her hair up as well, with the shortened front strands smoothed back with a headband. And she wore no makeup, which made the sleep lines under her eyes stand out. "Ready?"

I nodded.

Not sure what I could ask without annoying her, but curious about everything, I silently followed her to her car.

The woman drove like a maniac. What took her half an hour to reach the treatment center, probably would've taken a normal person forty-five minutes. She talked on her phone to friend after friend the entire way, telling each one of them she was taking me shopping.

I bit my lip, wondering why she felt the need to lie. When she had to hang up to find a place to park at the center, I couldn't help but say, "It must get exhausting to always come up with things to tell people. Do you ever run out of reasons why you're gone so much?"

She glanced at me, and I couldn't tell what her eyes looked like through the large, dark shades she wore. But then a smirk creased her lips. "People will think I attend classes on Tuesday and Thursday, and on Saturdays..." She shrugged. "I keep active enough, no one questions it."

I nodded but still felt confused.

THE TECHNICIANS were startled to see me stroll in with Cora.

"Finally got yourself a support system going, huh?" one woman asked with an approving nod.

Cora blew her off as she slid off her shades and put them away in her purse before pulling out some lip gloss and freshening her mouth. "Can we get started already?"

I quickly learned that where my best friend was shy on details, everyone else at the center was over-flowing with them. I'd done some online research about all this, but what I learned in that first ten minutes left me reeling.

I learned that Cora had bypassed the home hemodialysis option, where she could've taken a ma-chine back to her apartment and learned how to treat herself multiple times daily. Instead, she'd opted for the in-center hemodialysis where a trained professional administered the treatment and she only had to go in three times a week on

Tuesdays, Thursdays, and Saturdays at midday.

Each treatment lasted three to five hours. I had no idea how she managed to hide four hours a day three days a week from all her friends—Quinn especially—but she seemed determined to make sure no one else found out about it.

"We're going to send your dietitian in to talk to you while they'll clean your access," Petey, the first guy to meet with her, announced before he left to check on another patient who was already hooked up and halfway through his treatment.

As I watched him check the monitors on the machine, I leaned in toward Cora where she was sitting up on a gurney. "Access to what?"

Cora glanced at me, her expression bland. She looked so calm and collected, while my heart wouldn't slow down. I was worried about everything they were going to do to her.

"Access to my fistula," she finally said.

"Oh." I nodded. Five seconds passed. And then I couldn't contain my curiosity a second longer. I leaned in again. "What's a fistula?"

She sighed and lifted her arm to expose the flat inside part she'd so carefully covered with concealer yesterday before the car wash. "It's this tube thing they implanted in here to access my blood and flush it through the dialysis machine to clean it."

With a gulp, I stared at her arm, not realizing there'd been anything surgically implanted under the skin. She'd had to go through a lot more than I was aware of for her dialysis treatments. But as soon as she had the transplant, she'd never have to worry about them again.

The sooner I handed over my kidney, the better. I didn't like knowing she had to spend so much time in this place. It smelled like antiseptic and sickness.

"Food police," a cheerful voice jerked me from my thoughts. When a small, spritely woman bounded toward us, she glanced at Cora before turning her attention to me.

"Melissa," she greeted, holding out a hand. "And you are?"

"Uh...Zoey." I shook hands with her. "I'm Cora's friend."

"Great." Melissa pulled up a rolling seat and propped herself next to Cora on the other side of the bed as me. "I'm the dietitian, and it's my job to make sure Cora here is getting a healthy diet and taking care of herself. And now you can help me keep an eye on her when she's away from here."

A sick smile lifted the corners of my lips as I glanced at Cora. I already knew there was no way I was going to be able to help her eat right. She sent me a passive smile that felt more threatening than reassuring, then she turned back to Melissa and lied through her teeth. The only thing she'd been honest about was the strawberries she'd had with her pancakes this morning. She even took credit for the egg whites I'd gagged down for her the day before.

I probably should've called her out and told Melissa what she'd really been digesting, but I didn't want to get Cora into trouble, especially when Melissa warned her that abusing alcohol could make her ineligible for a transplant.

I don't think I was able to breathe again until Melissa left and another technician returned, this one named Claire.

Claire was a lot more laid-back, and a lot less intimidating, so I was able to relax around her.

As she sprayed something on Cora's arm, right where Cora had showed me her fistula was, I leaned in to watch. "What's that?"

"It's an anesthetic to numb the skin," Claire answered easily, grinning at me. "Our Cora here doesn't like the needle pricks."

I smiled weakly, feeling even worse for my best friend. Cora hated needles, and yet she had to endure them three times a week. "Who would?" I said, studying Cora's face as she turned away as if bored. But I saw her flinch as the first needle was inserted.

I flinched with her.

Claire chuckled. "Oh, you'll get your turn to be stuck plenty if you're going to be her donor."

Great. Unease swirled through my stomach, but after four hours of sitting there watching Cora's kidneys get flushed out through her arm, I was more certain than ever that I wanted to be her donor. No one should have to go through this.

I was also more convinced she should tell people about her condition. Especially her boyfriend.

Quinn seemed like the caring type. He'd made sure I was okay in the warehouse at the car wash, but then he'd given me privacy. He'd even let Caroline talk out some of her problems to me at the pizza parlor without interfering. And that didn't even get into the things he did for Cora, like cooking her breakfast every Saturday and changing the menu in deference to her wishes, or carrying her up to her apartment after she'd drank too much, making sure she was comfortable in bed before leaving her, or knowing how to handle her hangovers. He'd definitely be the type to stand by her and pamper her through a difficult time. And I knew Cora loved to be pampered.

That's why I didn't understand her. But every time I broached the subject, she just hissed at me. So I shut up and focused on the reasons why I was here: to give up a kidney and start my own life. Nothing else really mattered.

TWO DAYS AFTER I got to watch Cora's dialysis, I started college.

ESU was bigger than I thought it would be. I wished I'd been able to attend some of the orientation classes, but hopefully Freshman Experience would help me adjust.

Using the trusty map I'd printed off, I hunted up my first class—Art Appreciation, a general requirement that was easy to get out of the way.

The room was huge and tall, with steps in the seating area that lifted up with each row of chairs so everyone could stare down at the professor while he taught. I felt like a complete mess. My bag was packed with all the supplies I hoped I needed as I entered the lecture hall, but I was so nervous I worried I might give myself indigestion.

I was early, because I hated being late, but surprisingly I wasn't the first person in the room; a couple more individuals sat scattered throughout. I ducked my head and started for a place at the end of a row, somewhere strategically in the middle section, when a voice called, "Zoey? Over here."

Surprised to hear my name, I automatically looked over, even though I was sure there had to be another Zoey around. But I was even more startled to find a familiar blonde waving at me. She grinned and patted the chair next to her.

Relieved to see a friendly face, I changed directions

and hurried to Caroline, who'd taken up a front row seat, directly in the center of the room. I'd feel overly exposed there, but it'd be worth it to sit next to her.

"Hi. What a coincidence. I had no idea we'd share a class."

She grinned. "I know. I'm so glad we do. I looked over Noel's schedule last night. But being a senior, he's already taken all his basic requirements. We didn't share *anything* together. I was so sure I wouldn't know anyone in any of my classes."

"Ditto," I admitted.

As soon as I settled myself beside her, she reached out and gripped my forearm. "Hey, thanks again for Friday night."

"I..." When my words stumbled over my tongue, I looked up from the notepad I was taking from my backpack to find the most sincere expression on her face. "Oh, but I didn't do any—"

"You were there for me when I needed someone to just...be there. Trust me, your presence helped. I was so worried I freaked you out, though, because of the way I acted at the—"

"No! Not at all." With a roll of my eyes, I admitted, "I would've freaked a little myself to learn what you'd just learned about your brother."

"I know, right." She leaned in to whisper. "I still can't believe it. I've been hiding in a hole all summer, worried he thought I was the most wicked person ever for—" She stopped abruptly, as if she'd just then realized I had no idea what had happened to her.

With a small clearing of her throat, she shoved some hair out of her eyes. "Anyway, come to find out, Noel hasn't been a perfect angel either." She grinned and patted my arm. "It was actually kind of a relief to learn. I mean, it's *weird*. Don't get me wrong. But...I don't know. I can't really condemn them for anything because I've seen them as a couple and they just click together, you know. How they hooked up just doesn't bother me." Biting her lip, she sent me a hesitant look. "Do you think that's wrong?"

I shrugged. "I don't know. I've always loved happily ever afters in romances. I love to see couples in love beat the odds. And those two really seemed to be—"

"They are." Caroline sent me a nod of approval. "They

really, really are."

She opened her mouth to say something else, but a call from across the room stalled her. "Caroline? Is that you?"

Caroline looked over, and her face instantly brightened. "Reese! What a happy surprise. I was so sure I wouldn't know anyone all day. But look, I have you two in my first class. This is Zoey. I met her this weekend at the football's fundraiser car wash. She's roommates with Cora, Quinn's girlfriend."

The brunette with a nose ring skipping toward us latched her attention on me. "Oh, I *love* Quinn." She gave a happy clap before carelessly flinging her bag onto the desk beside mine. "He's such a good guy, and a total sweetheart."

Caroline turned to me. "Reese is engaged to Ma·son, who also works at Forbidden with Quinn and Noel...and Oren." Her smile faltered when she said that last name.

I nodded. "Oh." Then I couldn't handle the curiosity anymore. "What *is* Forbidden, exactly?"

"It's a nightclub," Reese explained, plopping into her chair with a relieved smile before she kicked off her shoes and began to wiggle her purple-painted toes. Then she took a sip from the steaming cup she'd brought in with her. "All our guys are bartenders there."

"What...the hell are all you hens doing in *this* class?"

I turned to see a horrified Ten standing before us, a single thick textbook tucked under his arm. He spun and scowled at Caroline, his gaze accusing. "Where's your brother?"

She blinked and moved deeper into her seat away from him. "Um...I don't know. His own first class of the day, I would assume." Her eyes narrowed and lips pinched tight. "He didn't hold my hand and walk me to class."

"But *he* should be *here*." He pointed down to the exact spot where he was standing. "I saw his class schedule sitting out on the table in the kitchen at your place. He had this class, so I enrolled."

Caroline flushed. "Well, that must've been *my* schedule you saw because I know for a fact Noel isn't taking this class."

As Ten closed his eyes and lightly pounded a fist to his forehead, I darted my gaze between them. When Ten had told me he'd have to change his game plan around Caroline, I guess he hadn't been kidding. He definitely wasn't being as sweet or nice to her as he'd been before she'd tried to kiss him.

"Motherfucker," he groaned. "No Gamble, *and* I'm stuck in a class with not one, or even two, but *three* untouchables. This is going to suck...ass."

"I'm sorry, what?" Reese lifted a curious eyebrow. "Do I even want to ask what an untouchable is?"

"You know..." He twirled out his finger to encompass Reese, Caroline and me. "You're Lowe's woman. Can't flirt with you. You're Noel's little sis-ter." He scowled at Caroline. "Can't fucking go there. And you..." He flicked his attention to me, "...belong to Hamilton." Then he made a sweeping gesture over all three of us. "Ergo I can't touch any of you. Untouchables. And to make it worse, you all will probably be watching me with your judgey little eyes so I'll have to behave and can't hit on any other woman in this class either."

As Reese snorted, I gaped at him. I couldn't believe he was being so candid about his pursuits for other women...right in front of Caroline, when he *knew* she liked him. And what in God's name had he meant about me being—

"I don't care if you hit on anyone," Reese told him.

"Flirt away." Caroline gestured airily, as if she didn't care either.

"I belong to...*Hamilton*?" I repeated incredulously.

"Undisputedly." Ten sent me a short nod, ignoring the other two girls for the time being. "Apparently, if you move in with the woman he dates, he automatically assumes responsibility for you. I have henceforth been...warned off."

"You..." I shook my head. Wait. "*What*?"

"I know." He lifted his hands as if he totally agreed with my confusion. "I made one remark about your ass and he ordered me to back off and leave you alone."

"You did *what*?" If I wasn't sitting, I probably would've tried to cover my tush with my hands. I settled for crossing my arms over my chest to hide the girls from him, even though the button-up pink and white plaid blouse I was wearing didn't show a hint of cleavage.

"Fine." He rolled his eyes and blew out a dis-gusted breath. "I checked out your legs too. But God, I'm a guy, okay? I look at women. Why is that such a bad thing?"

"Probably because you're really lewd about it," Reese

offered helpfully. "I mean, do *I* make *you* feel like a piece of bacon for sale when I check you out? No. There *is* a tasteful way to look."

Turning all his attention to her, Ten hiked his foot onto the chair next to the desk where she was sitting and rested his elbows on his thigh while he wiggled his eyebrows at her. "So you check me out, huh, Buttercup?"

"Yes," she answered dryly and patted his cheek. "And I've found you completely lacking compared to my Mason. Sorry."

On the other side of me, Caroline cracked up laughing. Ten jerked his foot off the chair, scowling as he straightened. Then he sniffed at Reese. "Pfft. As if I want to be as pretty as Lowe, anyway."

"Well, good." Reese set a hand over her heart, looking relieved. "Because you don't even rank in his league."

Ten gaped at her. "Jesus, thank God I'm not a self-conscious pansy ass, otherwise that would've stung."

"Oh, don't worry," Reese assured him brightly. "I wouldn't have said anything if I didn't know what a huge, overinflated ego you have."

Ten opened his mouth but didn't seem to know what to say, not that Reese was paying him any more attention anyway. Her face brightened, and she leapt out of her chair. "Now *there's* a guy in my Mason's league. *Quinn*!"

Hearing that name made me stop breathing. I zipped my attention to where Reese was bounding past us, and sucked in a breath when I saw him in the opening of the lecture hall.

Oh, good Lord. I was going to share my first class with *Quinn Hamilton*?

€LEVEN

ZOEY

HE LOOKED GOOD in crisp dark jeans and a pale green shirt that clung to his heavenly chest. I couldn't look away because something about looking at him just seemed to bring me to life. I could suddenly smell better—the crisp graphite of a newly sharpened pencil pierced my nostrils—hear better—every crinkle of paper and shift of a book bag rattled through my eardrums—see better—the fluorescent lights sprayed down on his neatly combed dark hair—even taste better—the hint of mint toothpaste coated my teeth.

At first, Quinn didn't see Reese; he was too busy scanning the back of the room. When he did spot her, she was already right there—barefoot and all—plowing into him. He jerked a startled step away, but Reese tackled him into a hug anyway.

"I'm so glad you share a class with us, too." She grinned up at him adoringly as she pulled back to hook her arm through his and sweep him across the room to our group. "This will make having to put up with Ten much more bearable."

As I watched her drag him closer, I tried not to feel anything about the way she'd hugged him and clung to his arm. I told myself it was injustice on Cora's behalf, but sadly, I felt the same simmering heat and flushy cheeks as when I'd seen Cora touch him.

Clearly, he didn't know how to take Reese's attention. I could tell he wasn't comfortable with how familiarly she handled him, but he didn't want to be rude and pull away, either. It all lingered in his eyes as he sent her a tense smile.

Ten lifted his hand, scowling at Reese. "What the hell? Why didn't I get *that* kind of greeting?"

In answer, Reese clung to Quinn's arm tighter and even rested her cheek against his shoulder in a possessive move. "Because *you* never dove in front of a speeding bullet and *were shot* to save my cousin's life, that's why."

"Oh my God!" Ten cried, throwing up his hands in disbelief. "It was a flesh wound."

"Most beautiful, amazing, gallant flesh wound *ever.*" Reese found a puckered nick of flesh on Quinn's arm before she kissed it. "*This* is why my Eva's still alive."

My mouth fell open when I realized what she meant. "Wait. You were really shot?"

At my voice, he jerked his attention abruptly to me. His lips parted as surprise washed over his features. Cheeks flushing darker, he darted his gaze away until it set on Caroline next, which seemed to surprise him even more. "Oh," he rushed out the word, glancing between the two of us. "Hi." When his gaze settled on me, the heat that always consumed me in his presence flared even hotter.

Since he didn't seem eager to talk about his experience, Reese was more than willing to fill me in on what had happened. "Yes, he was shot. He was so brave and heroic about it too."

Ten snickered. "Aren't brave and heroic the same thing?"

"Shut up," Reese said pleasantly, without taking her gaze off me. "Eva, my cousin, told me all about it. This sick, sadistic, evil witch of a woman pulled a gun on her—"

"The same woman who—" Ten tried to cut in to add, but Reese punched him in the arm, silencing him.

Keeping eye contact with me the entire time, she continued her story, "...and pulled the trigger. She probably would've hit Eva right in the heart and killed her."

"Pfft," Ten muttered, rolling his eyes. "As if she could aim that good." This time, everyone ignored him.

"But Quinn was there, and instead of ducking for cover, he tackled Eva and took her to the ground right when the witch pulled the trigger."

She went back to patting Quinn's scar lovingly before Ten muttered, "Jesus, why don't you back up off the poor guy already? Are you not seeing the look on his face? I swear I'm about to get hives *for* him."

Reese looked up at Quinn's face and suddenly seemed to realize how uncomfortable she was making him. She jerked back. "Oh my God. I'm so sorry, Quinn. I keep forgetting how shy you are."

My heart thumped hard in my chest, but that word...shy. It resonated through me, making my ears buzz.

But Quinn Hamilton was *shy*?

I have no idea why I hadn't realize that before. All the signs had been right there in front of my face. I'd just been so focused on what I thought he'd be like from all the letters Cora had sent me. I'd never once imagined he'd be *shy*. I saw it as clear as day *now*, though, as I watched the way his face flushed and his gaze darted my way before he ducked his chin and mumbled, "It's okay."

That's when another enlightening fact hit me. I had a major crush on my best friend's boyfriend. For some reason—probably complete denial—I hadn't understood before why my body reacted every time he was around...or even whenever his name was mentioned. But learning he was just as introverted as I was...it was suddenly so clear why I'd felt such a connection with him.

How mortifying. Feeling my own face heat up, I lowered my attention to the books on my desk just as an arm swept them away.

"Wha...?" I looked up to realize Ten had grabbed everything that had been on my desktop as well as Caroline's and Reese's and was now holding them hostage under his arm.

"So now that we've established Hamilton's perfect, and gorgeous, and heroic, and all that awesome shit, can we please find our real seats?"

"This *is* my real seat," Caroline argued, scowling up at him. "Now give me by book back."

Ten snorted. "I don't think so, sweetheart. We are not sitting in loser lane." When the guy who'd been sitting next to Caroline lifted his face from the book he was reading, Ten tossed him a chin bob. "No offence."

"Yeah, I think he's still offended," Caroline reported dryly.

"Then maybe he shouldn't be such a loser sitting in loser lane," Ten tossed back before he took the stairs two at a time only to shoo off a pair of guys to get five desks in a row at the very back of the room.

When we all turned to watch him set our books back on the desks up there but didn't move to join him, he sent us a brief frown and waved us up. "Well, come on already."

"I think he wants us to sit with him," Reese whispered in a conspiratorial manner.

"I don't *want* to sit with him," Caroline huffed, scowling as she jerked to her feet. Hooking her thumb over her shoulder, she motioned to the guy still gaping at us after Ten had yanked his attention out of his book. "He called this poor loser a loser. That's just wrong."

She didn't seem to realize she'd just done the same thing as she angrily spun away and was the first to march up the aisle so she could sit at the desk next to Ten, where he was already slumped back in his chair with his feet kicked up onto the back of the empty seat in front of him.

The three of us still remaining on the ground floor shared an amused glance.

Then Quinn swept out a gallant arm. "Ladies first."

Reese grinned at him and patted his arm. "Such a gentleman." Then she found her shoes under the desk, slipped them on, and started up the steps to·ward Ten and Caroline.

Which left just Quinn and me.

Realizing we were alone, and he wasn't going to move until I did, I sprang to my feet. "Oh! Uh, thank you."

He fell into step just behind me. "I didn't realize you were talking this class." When he leaned in so I could hear him, I immediately smelled his spicy scent. "We'll have to share our schedule to see if we have anything else in common. I know Cora's taking Early American History with me next hour."

I glanced back as I reached the last row. "I have biology next hour."

He brightened. "I love biology. It's one of my favorite subjects."

I hated biology. And I think he read that answer

clearly from the expression on my face because he only grinned wider. "I took it last year from Professor Gilcrest. I still have all my notes if you want them to help you study."

I stopped in my tracks and spun around. "Oh my God, really? That's amazing. *I* have biology with Gil-crest." I began to bounce on my toes, which made him chuckle and in turn made me realize how dorkily giddy I was behaving. "I mean...thank you." I cleared my throat and smoothed back my hair. "I'd appreciate that." Beyond mortified, I spun away and hurried the last few feet to the seat next to Reese.

Quinn took the seat on the other side of me. "Not a problem. I can bring them when I pick up Cora to-night for our date."

The mention of my roommate cooled my temperament even more. My face heated with shame. I hadn't thought of Cora once during the past few seconds as I'd walked up the steps with her boyfriend.

I was such an awful, awful friend.

"Thank you," I repeated, not even daring to look his way, though it was impossible to miss him next to me. His mere presence took up so much room, his aura invaded my personal space.

"Selfie time," Reese announced, leaning in toward me so she could aim her camera phone at the both of us. "Quinn, get in here so I can send this to Mason and let him know who I'm sharing a class with."

Quinn obediently came in closer until his face was nearly brushing mine. Reese was squished in closer to me on the other side, but she still didn't feel nearly as close as he did. It only took her half a second to click off a picture. It felt like hours, though, that the warmth from his face radiated into the side of my ear.

Then Reese's phone flashed and she jerked away with a bubbly, "Thanks."

Quinn shifted away while Reese commanded Caroline and Ten to do the same pose with her as she'd made Quinn and me get into. Caroline paled but agreed, while Ten flipped her off before crossing his arms over his chest and tipping his head back as he closed his eyes.

"Where's Noel?" Quinn asked his roommate.

"Wrong Gamble." Ten cracked open one eye to spare Caroline an accusative glance. "Guess we didn't have to take this class after all."

"Aww. Were the three of you big, tough football players supposed to share mean, intimidating art class together?" Reese cooed. "That's so sweet."

Ten shot her a glare. "Zip it, shorty."

"Shorty?" Reese gasped and set her hand over her heart. "I'll have you know I'm two inches taller than Eva."

"Wow, I'm so impressed. I think I just pissed my-self from excitement."

"What an ass," Reese shot back as her phone dinged. She glanced at the screen before sniffing. "Hmph. Mason said he was sorry I have to share a class with you."

Sitting up, Ten leaned across Caroline's desk to point at Reese. "Well, you can tell Lowe to kiss my—"

"Excuse me." Caroline set her hand on his fore-head and shoved him back before framing her desktop with her arms. "This is my desk. My space. Get back."

He shot her an irritated scowl before falling back into his seat and rubbing his hand over his face. "This is going to be one long-ass semester."

I didn't mean to, but I glanced at Quinn. We shared a look where we both lifted our eyebrows as if to say this was actually going to be an entertaining semester.

"You guys sure are quiet over here," Reese said, making us jump and tear our gazes away from each other.

Quinn cleared his throat. "Sorry," he said just as the teacher arrived and started class.

Ten went back to closing his eyes and folding his arms over his chest as he rested his head back, while Quinn, Caroline, and I pulled out notebooks for note-taking. Reese, however, tugged a stack of wedding magazines from her bag and began to flip through them, the glint from her engagement ring reflecting light into my face every time she turned a page.

And so began my first college class.

TWELVE

QUINN

BLOOD PUMPED fanatically through my veins as I a dodged a linebacker and hurdled a fellow teammate who'd wiped out in front of me. Tucking the pigskin more snugly against my ribs, I sprinted up the field, free of the entire defensive line. Feet pounding behind me told me there were more on my heels, though. With fifteen yards left to go before making a touch·down, I bowed my head and plowed forward.

The cheering of my practice scrimmage team told me when I'd crossed into the end zone. A piercing whistle split the air.

"Good job, Hamilton," the coach's voice boomed, only to start yelling at the defense for letting me slip through.

Sweat clouded my vision as a hand pounded me on the back. "God damn, Ham. You're in rare form. What'd you eat for breakfast? Or should I say...who? I'm thinking it can't be the same nasty Cora you have every day."

I ripped my chinstrap open and pulled my helmet off to glare at Ten. "Not funny. That's my *girlfriend* you're disrespecting."

He lifted both hands as if to surrender, but his grin was still as cocky as ever. "I'm just saying, man... you have a lot more energy than usual."

"Whatever." Turning away, I jogged back toward Noel where he was having the team huddle up for another play.

Hot August sun poured down on us, making my heavy pads wet from my own sweat and sticky with every movement. I did feel more energized than usual, though it had nothing to do with what my irritating roommate was suggesting.

The idea still made me uncomfortable, though. I hated how he'd just put the image of Zoey into my head. Mere months ago, I didn't even know what it meant to eat out a girl, and now...I knew how it tasted. I didn't want to start wondering what another flavor would be like. I liked the flavor I had. I was faithful to my taste buds. Dr. Pepper was my drink. Strawberry was my ice cream. Pepperoni was my pizza. And Cora was my girl. What was Ten trying to accomplish by tempting me toward something else?

I didn't appreciate it.

"Change of plans," Coach called. "First stringers take four laps and hit the showers. Everyone else line up for a couple more plays."

Ready for a hard run to help jog off the sudden tension I was feeling, I took off toward the track circling the field. A lap later, I found myself running alongside Ten and Noel. Needing to exhaust more energy today than usual, I wondered if Noel would be able to stay a couple minutes longer with me after we ran. Coach had told me that if Noel kept working with me one-on-one to be a quarterback, I might even take over the spot of the second-string quarterback. That was the position I really wanted, so it'd be a double bonus if I asked Noel for a few tips before we finished for the day.

In my opinion, he was a better coach than Coach. He was more patient and could pick out a person's strengths and weaknesses. He knew exactly what kind of things I needed to work on the most to improve. The guy really was my mentor; I looked up to him more than about anyone I knew.

Case in point: when he'd realized his younger brothers and sister Caroline were being neglected by their mother, he'd driven hundreds of miles down to where they lived and gathered all three of them up, then brought them back to Ellamore to live with him. That was exactly the kind of family devotion to earn my respect. Made me wish I'd had a big brother when I was growing up.

But as the three of us jogged side by side, I noticed Noel was particularly quiet today. Usually, he and Ten carried on the conversation while we finished our end-of-practice laps. But Ten was the only one talking, describing this girl he was pursuing in his history class, and Noel wasn't responding at all. I usually only listened, so Ten wasn't too concerned about my lack of input, but he finally did scowl at Noel.

"What the fuck is wrong with you today?" He nudged his elbow into Noel's forearm.

"Hmm?" Noel ripped his gaze away from the baseball diamond not far from our practice field. "You know, if you guys won't tell me which baseball player had that picture of Aspen on his phone, I can find out other ways."

Ten groaned. "Jesus, man. Can't you just let that drop? I told you we took care of it."

Noel shot him a glare. "Would you be able to let something like that go? He was spreading around indecent pictures of my *woman*. Damn it." He stopped running and ran his hands through his hair as he continued to stare daggers across the football field to where the baseball players were also having an afternoon practice. "It was one of those fuckers... right...over...there."

Eyes hardening with intent, he began to stride that way when Ten caught his arm. "Whoa, man. We haven't finished our laps yet."

"Screw the laps. I need to kill that bastard. I need him dead. Right now."

"No, you need to screw your fucking head on right. It won't do your woman any good to expose yourself, which would, in effect, expose *her*. Now keep running."

Noel gritted his teeth, shook his head as if to fight off his rage and then started running again. Ten and I fell into step on either side of him.

"I wonder if the fucker got the picture from Marci Bennett." I knew Marci was the girl who'd taken the picture of Noel and Aspen together. She'd gotten Aspen fired...because she'd wanted Noel for herself. "What if she's spreading them around to everyone? What if—"

"She's not," Ten assured him.

Noel and I glanced at him together. "How do you

know?"

He snickered. "Because the picture on that phone was a fuzzy shot of what the Coach posted on the board in the locker room. And besides, I deleted all the pictures off Marci's phone...when she was putting her clothes back on."

My mouth fell open because that was the first I'd heard of this.

"You *fucked* her?" Noel exploded. "The bitch who ruined Aspen's career? What the hell, man?"

"Hey, I needed a reason to get access to her phone. And I've learned they're more willing to let you take naked pictures of them after you screw a dazed smile onto their face." He shrugged. "Actually, the me-photographing-her-nude thing was her idea, but hey...she was handing me her phone, so who was I to say no?"

When both Noel and I continued to stare at him as if he was insane, he lifted his hands. "What? I did it for you, man."

"You keep any of those naked pictures of her?" Noel finally asked.

Ten choked out an incredulous sound. "Really? You want to see her titties after what she did to your woman?"

"No, asswipe. I want to use them as leverage in case she had any more of me and Aspen that you didn't get off her phone."

"Oh. Well, I'm pretty sure I got them all. She was pissed as fuck when she realized what I did." Ten shrugged. "And anyways, I'm already one step ahead of you. I forwarded the least flattering ones of her to myself and I'm already using them to keep her quiet."

"Damn, man," Noel murmured as we finished up our mile run. "Thank you."

I was a little impressed that Ten had gone to so much work for Noel, too. He had his annoying moments, and a lot of them, but he could always be counted on in the friend department. Which made me feel kind of crappy.

I hadn't done anything on that level to help Noel. In fact, now that I thought about it, I wasn't sure if I'd done anything for him at all.

The whole idea still had me bummed when I went to pick Cora up later that evening. It was my one night this week I had off work to be with her, and of course there was a frat party she wanted to attend. So I planned on having a miserable evening, watching her drink and dance with her friends while I listened to all the jocks around me brag about how amazing they were. I wouldn't even have Ten there to keep me any company because he had to work, and Noel had stopped attending parties when he'd hooked up with Aspen and taken in his younger siblings. None of the other guys I worked with had ever done the frat-party thing. So yeah, I planned on being bored and abandoned most of the evening.

When I arrived at Cora's apartment, I was already antsy and uncomfortable about spending an evening surrounded by...people. But then Zoey opened the door for me, and my anxiety level went through the roof.

She had her hair up in another perky ponytail, and she was wearing glasses. She looked freaking adorable in glasses.

I swallowed, unable to say a single thing.

Then she smiled, and suddenly, I couldn't blink either.

"Hi." She sounded so happy to see me, my chest expanded with pressure. It felt as if someone was blowing up a balloon inside my ribcage. "Come on in. Cora's in her room...." She paused and cocked her ear as if she wanted me to finish the sentence.

A grin broke across my lips. "Changing?" I guessed.

"Exactly." Leaving the door open for me to make myself at home, Zoey turned away. As she did, her ponytail breezed past me, stirring up that mysterious smell. I started to step over the threshold when it hit me that the smell came from her hair.

"What kind of shampoo do you use?" I blurted out the question before my brain could tell me not to.

Zoey stopped walking and turned back slowly. "I'm sorry?"

Oh, crap. Her eyes narrowed suspiciously, letting me know good and well she realized I'd been smelling her.

I gulped, and motioned wildly with my hand to her ponytail. All the while, my face kept getting hotter and hotter. "I... you...when your hair whooshed past as you turned away...I didn't mean to—sorry."

She must've realized I wasn't trying to make a pass at her or anything because her shoulders relaxed and her lips loosened into a smile. "Oh, well, it's, um...wild cherry and jewel orchid, or something like that. I can't really remember. It's supposed to be for curlier hair..." Plucking at her ponytail to show me just how curly her hair wasn't, she shrugged with a rueful grin. "But it's my favorite scent, so I use it anyway."

"I don't blame you. I love that smell." I realized what I'd just said the moment the words left my lips. "I mean..." Mortified, I gaped at her with no idea how I was going to talk my way out of this faux pas, when a commotion on the television caught my attention.

"Are you watching *Pysch*?" I shut the door behind me and wandered into the living room, remembering the episode she currently had on.

"Yeah. You have me officially addicted. I started watching it last night when Cora was out and almost finished the entire first season in one sitting."

I began to smile until it struck me what else she'd said.

Cora had been *out* last night? She hadn't told me she was going anywhere. I knew she probably didn't sit at home alone on the nights I worked, but...

I shook my head. My girlfriend certainly didn't have to tell me every little move she made. Besides, I hadn't had much of a chance to talk to her since then. She'd probably tell me all about what she'd done as I drove us to the frat party tonight.

"It's helping me gag my way through my home-work," Zoey was saying as she settled onto a bare spot of couch that was covered in open textbooks. Sending me a brief accusing glance, she added, "You forgot to warn me how tough Gilcrest was. I mean..." She held up a stapled stack of papers and shook it at me. "This syllabus is insane."

"You're studying biology?"

Oh, man. Soaking in bio *and* watching *Psych*? I wondered if I could talk her into trading places with me for the evening.

"Yes. So I'm really hoping you were serious about those notes you were offering to share."

With a chuckle, I reached back and pulled out the sheets I'd rolled into a tube and shoved into my back pocket. Waving them at her, I stepped in to hand them over. "I was."

"Oh, thank God. You're amazing." She snagged them from my outstretched hand. "Thank you, thank you, thank you." She hugged the roll to her cheek and then kissed it.

My skin heated as I watched her press her lips to the paper I'd just had in my back pocket. She seemed to realize the intimacy of the moment a second later, because she froze, then glanced at me with a guilty cringe before she blushed and slowly moved my notes away from her mouth.

"Sorry. That was...really weird, wasn't it?"

Actually, it made me feel better for all the mortifying things I'd done and said since she'd opened the door. I sniffed and waved an unconcerned hand. "Not at all. I kiss my homework all the time."

When she laughed, I felt...I don't know, but it was one of those really good feelings, like you're floating off the ground because you're so happy.

Unable to stay back, I drifted closer. "What's Gilcrest making you learn first?"

"Oh! Here." Zoey shoved aside some books on the couch to make room for me. "I'm not exactly sure. It says on his syllabus, but..." She shook her head and sighed. "It's all Greek to me."

I held out my hand for the sheet, and she readily handed it over. When I scanned over her first assignment, I pointed. "Actually, this is Latin...not Greek."

The dry look she sent me told me just how much she wasn't impressed by my nerd knowledge. "Sorry." I cleared my throat. "Bad joke."

She rolled her eyes and fluttered a hand. "No. Go ahead and rub it in. I suck at biology and you rule. I got it."

I smiled out a silent laugh as I motioned to the syllabus again. "Looks like you'll be starting with human anatomy."

"Really?" She leaned in to read over my arm, which stirred up more of that wild cherry and orchid smell. "Why didn't he just *say* human anatomy, then?"

"Because Gilcrest only knows science jargon. But I think I wrote pretty common terms in my notes, so hopefully that'll help you."

Zoey pulled the notes into her lap. I found her biology book next to my hip, and we spent a few minutes going through the text, syllabus, and notes.

I know I got a little too involved in some of the things I explained. But it was so nice to know what I was talking about, I got a little carried away...and possibly a little off topic. Zoey didn't seem to mind though. She kept nodding and transferring her attention from my notes, to her book, to my face as I went on. Sometimes, she'd even write down something I said.

"And did you know ancient Greek doctors thought there was a vein in this finger," I tugged at the fourth digit on my left hand, "that led right to the heart? It's not true, of course. But they called it the *vena amoris*, which means—"

"Vein of love," she said.

My gaze shot to hers. "Oh, you know the story already."

She shrugged and smiled apologetically. "I knew that was why that was the wedding ring finger, but I didn't know it wasn't true." Disappointment filled her eyes. "So that finger doesn't really have a vein that leads directly to the heart? That's kind of depressing."

"I know. Sorry." I shook my head, feeling crappy for destroying a perfectly sweet theory. "I always liked that story of why couples wore their wedding rings on that particular finger, too. But, no, the vein structure in all the fingers is pretty similar."

"Yeah. That's too bad."

I opened my mouth to tell her I hated nothing more than being misled with lies like that, but then I also wanted to restore her faith in romance, except yeah, my mind was blank with something eternally romantic.

Cora saved me from having to come up with a response when she called from her room. "Hey, is Quinn here yet?"

"Yes," I answered for Zoey. "I've been polluting Zoey with more episodes of *Pysch*."

Cora grumbled something that sounded vaguely like "Be out in a minute," and slammed her bedroom door shut. Zoey and I shared a smile. But we both seemed to realize our time together was about up. Setting my notes aside, she smoothed her hands down her legs and let out a breath. "Well, thanks for taking the time to explain all that to me. It makes a lot more sense, now."

I straightened in surprise. "Really?"

Zoey blushed and ducked her face. "Yeah, I... yeah."

I was sure I'd only been confusing her more, but if she said it helped, then...cool. I bumped my shoulder into hers. "Actually I was glad for the distraction after practice today."

She glanced up, her green eyes wide with concern. "Did you get in trouble from your coach for that fight you were in?"

I frowned in confusion. "Fight?"

"You know..." She flailed out a hand. "With that guy you pushed against the wall at the party—"

"Oh! Right." I'd forgotten all about that. "No." I sighed and ran my fingers through my hair. "Nothing like that. I'm just worried about Noel. He's having a hard time, wondering who had that picture of his girlfriend. He's really ticked at Ten and me for refusing to tell him whose phone it was on. But if we told him—"

"He'd beat up Belcher," Zoey surmised with a knowing nod.

I glanced at her sharply, stunned. "You know whose phone it was on?"

"Oh! I..." She flushed and stammered a moment. "I hear things."

Of course she did. She was like me, a watcher and a listener. I nodded slowly. "Right."

"So...Noel would definitely go after Belcher if he knew?"

"Definitely." I blew out a breath. "He wanted to storm the entire baseball team today and start taking names. I don't know what to do for him. I don't blame him for being upset, but if he did anything to get himself kicked off the team, everything he's fought so hard to protect would be over."

Zoey cocked her head to the side. "What do you mean? What has he fought for?"

"I guess you realized at the pizza parlor that Aspen was his—"

"Teacher," she said with a nod. "Yeah. I caught that part."

I smiled. "Well, when this one girl who had a thing for Noel found out about their secret relation·ship, she took some...pictures of them and turned them in to Aspen's boss."

Zoey's eyes widened. "Wow. I'd heard most of that at the pizza parlor, but not the part about the girl who turned them in. Was it really just about revenge, because she wanted Noel and couldn't get him?"

I nodded, and sympathy filled her gaze.

"Poor Noel. Poor *Aspen*."

"I know. But what's worse, when Noel went to Aspen's boss and tried to talk him into getting her job back, he ended up making things worse and ticking the professor off until the professor threatened Noel. Now, if Noel does anything to put his football position at risk and lose us the championship this year, they're going to make Aspen's termination public and turn her and Noel into a national scandal."

Zoey shook her head. "That's so awful. Why would they do that to her?"

"I don't know. I've stopped trying to figure out why some people do cruel things years ago."

Hugging herself, she began to run her hands up and down her arms. "I can only imagine what Noel's going through right now, needing to protect his girl-friend by being calm and level-headed, but also wanting to defend her honor. He must be so torn up."

"He is." I studied her a moment, charmed by the level of compassion in her eyes as she worried about my friend's situation. I felt this urge to just reach out and squeeze her hand because I understood exactly what she was feeling.

"Ready, baby?" Cora asked, making me jump to my feet and spin toward her. Wearing her usual short skirt, skimpy top and high heels, she strolled into the living room with a dazzling smile, all jazzed up and ready to go.

The smile on her face always meant she was ready to have fun, and I usually ended those nights a very lucky guy.

Okay, so maybe I wasn't going to have a completely awful time at the frat party after all. Remembering some of the things she'd done with me at other parties, I stepped toward her and took her hand, just wanting to fast-forward to those parts.

"Yep," I answered her.

"Great." She tossed her hair over her shoulder and glanced behind me as I started us toward the door. "Have a good night, Zo. Unless...do you want to come?"

I froze mid-step, and it took me a moment to glance around to catch Zoey's response. I didn't realize I was holding my breath for her answer until she shook her head. "No, thanks. But thank you for the offer."

A hiss of oxygen rushed from my lungs. The bad part was, I wasn't sure if I'd been hopeful for her to say yes or to say no.

107

THIRTEEN

ZOEY

"THREE TO SIX *months*?" Cora squawked incredulously. "But you just told us she's a match. Her tis·sue type and blood group match mine perfectly. I thought you said that's all we needed for a trans·plant."

Sitting next to Cora at the doctor's office, I reached for her hand to give it a supportive squeeze, but she jerked her fingers away and kept glaring at her doctor.

He sent her a stern look over the tops of his bifocals before letting out a sigh. "No, I said blood and tissue had to match before we could even get started. Miss Blakeland will still need to go through a series of tests to ensure her physical and mental health."

Cora snorted as if that idea were absurd. "Like what?"

All the while I was gulping. But mental? What the heck did they mean by mental tests? Were they going to sic a psychologist on me? What if I ended up confessing about my childhood? Oh no, what if they didn't think I was of sound enough mind to help Cora?

I started to sweat. My heart pounded as the doc·tor began to explain. "We'll need her full medical his·tory and to perform an extensive medical examination. She'll probably have a few sessions with a psychologist."

108

Oh God.

"What the hell for?" Cora cut in.

"There are many psychological impacts that affect donors. He'll need to establish her motivation and—"

"Motivation?" Cora shook her head. "She's my best friend. She loves me. What else do you need to know?"

The doctor nodded with her as if he agreed that it was silly, but he said, "It's policy." Glancing at me, he softly added, "There should only be a few of those sessions."

I nodded, but inside I was ice-frozen scared. What if they uncovered how envious I sometimes felt of Cora? What if they decided I was a whack job and unfit to give her anything? She needed this kidney; I didn't want to do anything wrong to keep it from her.

Fingers cramping as they wrapped around the arm of my chair, I kept listening to the doctor list all the things they'd have to test me for. "There will be a number of blood tests to make sure you're not carrying any diseases: hepatitis, HIV, any infection that could be passed on. We'll need to see how well your blood clots. We'll have to monitor your blood pressure routinely. We'll have to check how well both your kidneys are functioning as well as your liver and some other organs. There will be numerous urine tests, and scans like ultrasounds and MRIs. Then you'll need to take an EKG, X-rays, Pap smear..."

Wow, they really were going to check me from top to bottom, inside and out. No wonder it took so long to get to the actual transplant part.

"After you pass all the tests, we can set you up with a consultation with the surgeon, who'll go over the operation with you, get you a date for operation and have you sign the consent form."

He smiled kindly, but Cora didn't smile back. "It really takes three to six *months* to get all that done?"

Lips pinching thin, the doctor answered, "Some-times longer if any abnormalities in her test delay things."

"Oh, mother," Cora muttered, glancing acerbically at me. "We're screwed."

I just stared at her, unable to believe she'd just basically called me abnormal.

BY FRIDAY, I felt more than abnormal. I felt stupid and deluded.

Six months ago, I'd been expecting to live my entire life under the strong thumb of my father. I'd pre-enrolled at the college he wanted me to attend and even set my degree as teaching, when the thought of getting up in front of a class scared the bejesus out of me. But Ernest Blakeland honestly scared me more. I'd always, always done what he'd wanted me to. I'd never broken one of his rules, snuck out of the house when he wasn't looking, or cheated on the amount of soap he wanted me to use when I washed the dishes. I'd followed each and every one of his rules like the good, obedient girl I had hoped to be.

It wasn't until Cora had called me with her dilemma that I'd even considered trying to break free from him. Because breaking free meant severing all ties completely. He never would've allowed me any kind of freedom. He liked total control. So if I was going to help my friend, I had to do it without his knowledge and without his permission.

The scariest decision of my life, and I'd made it so effortlessly without an ounce of regret. Yet now that I was here, risking the wrath of a man I knew would take pains to hurt me for retribution, I started to reevaluate the source of my reasons for coming.

Cora wasn't at all as I remembered her. I wasn't sure if I'd just built her up to be so amazing in my head because she'd been there in my life when I'd needed her the most or what. She'd been the one person who was nice to me when I'd felt alone. Maybe I'd blinded myself to her flaws.

Or maybe she'd just changed that much.

She'd been sitting on a bench outside the office the first day I attended public school as if waiting for me to come out with my class schedule and locker assignment.

"Hey, you're that new girl. Zoey, right?"

Startled to hear my name, I paused and sent her a nod. "Yeah."

With a smile, she scooted down and patted the open spot of bench beside her. "I'm Cora."

When I sat gingerly, she studied me for the longest time. No one had ever paid that kind of attention to me before, except my father when he was upset with something I'd done. It made me blush and duck my face.

Then she asked me a couple questions, to which I think I gave mumbled, one-word answers. After that, she told me about herself. She liked to talk about herself, and I liked having someone talk to me, so it seemed to work for both of us. We never shared any classes, so I didn't get to see her much during school, only those few minutes every day before the first bell rang on that very bench where we met.

After a couple months, she invited me over to her house for dinner. My father only agreed when he realized who her parents were. Mr. Wilder had apparently founded the country club with him where they were both members. In fact, before I'd been born, back when my mother had still been alive, Mr. Wilder and his wife had been close friends with my parents... which reminded my father of another reason he hated me. After I'd killed my mother in childbirth, my father had fallen out of touch with one of his closest friends.

But he'd reluctantly allowed me to occasionally visit Cora.

Her mother was so charming and nice. It boggled my mind when Cora would get irritated with her for asking too many questions about her day. I would've loved to have a mother who wanted to know what was happening in my life.

Mr. Wilder had acted shocked the first time he'd met me. I guess Cora never brought friends home with her, or something. I don't know. But he quickly got over it and when I told him who my parents were, he remembered them, telling me I looked like my mother. I loved hearing that because my father had gotten rid of most of her pictures.

I envied Cora for her parents, wishing they could've been mine, even though they'd been as strict with her as mine had been with me. Many times I'd called over to talk to her, her mom had told me Cora wasn't home. When Cora told me the next day that she'd really been home but she hadn't been allowed phone privileges, I'd wondered briefly if her father was just as abusive as mine.

I'd grabbed her hand and clutched it hard. "Do your parents hit you too?"

She'd wrenched back in surprise and blinked at me as if I was insane. "No. Why? Does *your* dad hit you?" She sounded so intrigued by the idea, I lowered my face in shame and buried my hands into my lap.

111

"No."

But she knew I was lying. She made me look her in the eye before she quietly asked, "Zoey. Does your dad hit you?"

"Sometimes," I whispered. "But only when I'm bad."

After that, she questioned every little bruise I had, and yes, most of them came from his brutal touch. The abuse became easier to take after Cora found out about it, though. I don't know why; maybe just sharing it with someone took off some of the stress.

She was loyal and never told anyone about it because I begged her not to. And she never made me feel bad about what happened to me.

I know those times I sat with her before school, and the fewer times I'd talked to her on the phone or visited her house, probably wouldn't seem like much of a friendship to someone else. But it was all I'd ever had, so it was everything to me. Enough to get me here.

But here I was, and now...now the friend I'd once known was gone.

Maybe the transplant would bring her back. I don't know. Or maybe I was still deluding myself.

I was probably being selfish for wanting her time and attention, but she hadn't stuck around the apartment a single night since I'd moved in. She was either out, visiting friends or with Quinn. I knew I didn't have to stay home alone—I was free now—but I didn't know what else to do. Homework and television kept me company most nights. Or sometimes I'd wander the apartment and try to acclimate myself to my new living space.

School kept me busy during the days, but the evenings still left me lonely.

By Friday of the second school week, I was debating whether I had the courage to take myself to a movie that evening when I entered art class. Cora would probably let me tag along with her if I asked, but I'd seen the kind of parties she preferred, and they were so not my thing.

"Morning, Zoey," Reese greeted as I found a seat next to her. She was sipping from a Starbucks cup and flipping through another bridal magazine.

I smiled as I dug into my bag for my notebook and pen. This hour every Monday, Wednesday, and Friday was the highlight of my week. I loved sitting with Reese, Caroline, Quinn, and Ten. They never failed to entertain me. And they made me feel included.

And not-at-all lonely.

"I thought you'd found a dress last week," I asked, noticing which advertisements she examined as she slowly flipped through pages.

"Oh, *I* have," she said, sliding me a wink. "But my cousin just got engaged *yesterday*, so I'm looking for her now."

"How exciting." She talked about Eva quite a bit, so I felt as if I already knew her cousin without having even met her. "Tell her congratulations for me."

"Sure. She's anxious to meet you, you know."

That caught me off guard. "What?"

Reese paused in her page flipping and looked up. "Eva. Yeah. I've told her all about you, and she can't wait to meet you for herself."

I totally wasn't expecting that. With a blink, I slowly shook my confused head. "Really?"

"Yep. You'll have to come with us when we hang out at the club some night."

By club, I knew she meant Forbidden. Just thinking about the place where Quinn worked got my blood pumping faster. He hadn't come by the apartment to pick up Cora for a date since the night he'd helped me acclimate myself to biology. But I still saw him in art class. Still sat by him in art class. Still had an unrelenting crush on him in and *out* of art class.

We didn't have assigned seats, but since day one, our group had continued to sit in the exact same spots every day with Reese in the middle, Caroline to her left, me to her right and Ten and Quinn taking up the ends.

"Since Eva's engaged to the owner, we can get in free," Reese nudged her elbow into mine and winked, "*and* underage without any hassle."

"Hey, guys," Caroline greeted as she trudged up the steps to our desks. Smiling warmly at me, she squealed happily when she saw Reese. "Noel told me about Eva and Pick! That's so exciting. Are you guys going to have a double wedding?"

"God, no." Reese rolled her eyes. "Mason and I are being slowpokes and waiting until we graduate. Pick and Eva need to hurry their nuptials along to help with the adoption process for Julian."

Eva and her boyfriend took care of two children: Eva's daughter Skylar, and Pick's stepson Julian. They'd been working toward permission to adopt Julian for a few months.

"Oh, can they finally adopt him? That's great." Caroline gasped happily as she started to sit. But when she glanced down at her chair before lowering herself, she frowned. "What's this?"

She picked up a sheet of paper that had been in her chair and flipped it over. As her mouth fell open, she looked up at us. Her face was wreathed in awe.

"Oh, wow, you guys. Check this out."

When she turned the sheet around to show us the drawing that had been sitting there, my mouth fell open. "Wow," was all I could think to say. It was a pencil sketch, like an exact replica of Caroline. And not just her face, but her entire body.

"Oh my God, that's you." Reese leaned forward to examine every perfect detail. She looked up at Caroline's face and then back at the picture. "I mean, that's really *you.*"

"I know. Isn't it amazing?" Caroline looked shocked speechless. Her gaze was dazed as she met my stare.

"Do...do you think I have a secret admirer or something?" She stepped closer to us and glanced suspiciously around the room, lowering her voice. "I don't know if that's creepy or flattering."

"Well, he put clothes on you, so...I'm going to go with flattering." Reese snagged the sheet out of Caroline's hand and made a giddy sound as she studied the picture some more. "You have a secret admirer! This is so wicked awesome. I want someone to draw me like this."

"Wait? How do we know the artist is a he?" I asked, frowning slightly.

Reese and Caroline looked at me as if I'd just spoken a foreign language. "What?" I asked, clueless and feeling really stupid.

Turning the page to show me the picture again, Reese lifted an eyebrow. "Someone drew her barefoot in a dress and curled up on the grass, sleeping under a tree."

"Yeah," I said slowly, totally not catching on.

"Seriously," Reese cried jabbing her finger into the page. "Don't you feel how sensual it is from the way the wind is blowing stray pieces of hair into her face, how the skirt of her dress is riding just the slightest bit high on her thigh. I mean, damn, I look at this and even *I* want her a little bit right now."

Caroline snorted out a laugh and covered her face. "I cannot believe you just said that."

"Well, really." Reese shrugged. "Can't you tell that whoever drew it likes her? Like, *likes* her." She sang out the last two words for emphasis.

"Oh." I said, finally getting it. It made perfect sense when Reese explained it that way. Then I tipped my face to the side. "Unless it was drawn by a lesbian."

Both Reese and Caroline burst out laughing. I started to grin, tickled that I'd managed to entertain them, but Caroline immediately sobered and ripped the sheet out of Reese's hand.

"Damn, I hope it's a guy and not a lesbian who likes me. I like beard scruff, six-pack abs, tight buns of steel, and that bulge in the pants way too much to go gay right now."

"Amen," Reese murmured with a dreamy sigh.

Suddenly, Caroline cleared her throat and turned away, tucking the sheet into her art book. I glanced over my shoulder to see what had caused her to hide the drawing so quickly. Quinn and Ten were absorbed in whatever they were discussing as they entered class. They paid us no attention, but we couldn't stop staring at them.

Both Reese and Caroline were right. Slight beard scruff, six-pack abs, tight buns of steel and that bulge really were powerful enhancements to the masculine race. They were definitely helping to keep me straight!

I wondered when Quinn would come by the house to pick Cora up for a date again. I kind of craved another biology lesson with him...which made me hope he never came by again, and Cora just kept going out to meet him as she claimed she'd been doing the last few nights, because I so very badly needed to nip this crush I had in the bud. The less contact with him, the better. Right?

He and Ten looked up at the same time to catch all three of us girls ogling them.

"What?" Ten demanded with an instantly suspicious frown.

"Nothing," Reese, Caroline and I answered in unison. When we abruptly became interested in our own things, Ten snorted.

"That was definitely something," he told Quinn. Falling into his seat next to Caroline, he sighed and stretched. "I bet it was about sex."

I flushed because that word...yeah, it wasn't something I'd discussed with anyone. Ever. Especially out in the open in a classroom where just anyone could hear.

Reese wasn't so scandalized, though. She snorted. "I know it's shocking, but unlike men, we women can actually think *and talk* about other topics."

"Hey, guys can too. Ham and I were just dis-cussing *football*, thank you very much. How I used my football image to score a chick last night."

I finally dared to glance over at Quinn for the first time since he'd sat beside me. He looked a little hurt that we hadn't told him what we'd been dis-cussing. I already felt bad enough that I had to keep Cora's secret from him, so while Reese and Ten bickered back and forth across Caroline's desk, I picked up my pen, opened my notebook and wrote, *"Caroline just found a drawing in her chair. Someone made a picture of her and left it there for her to find."*

I tipped it his way to get his attention. When he finally noticed, he paused, looking up at my face, then went back to reading. His eyebrows lifted as he opened his own notebook.

"And she doesn't want Ten to know?" he wrote.

I grinned. *"Exactly."*

"Don't blame her. Do you think it's a secret admirer?"

"That's the general consensus."

Quinn shook his head. *"Wow."*

"I know. I wonder who—" My cell phone dinged from my book bag, making me jump.

I didn't realize class had already started until everyone, including the professor, stopped to stare at me.

"Cell phones off, please." The teacher sent me an irritated glower before he went right back to lecturing.

Sinking lower in my chair, I cringed. "Sorry."

Fumbling to retrieve my phone and set it to silent, I checked the message first. It had to be from Cora. She was the only person who even knew I had a phone, much less what my number was.

Meet me in front of the library after this hour, was all she wrote.

I typed in a quick response, only to find Reese wiggling her fingers at me. "Ooh. I want your number," she whispered, snagging my phone from my hand.

I didn't get my phone back for the rest of art class. When Reese realized I only had one number in my address book, she and Caroline made it their mission to enter every number they thought I should have. They even confiscated Ten and Quinn's phones to make sure we all had everyone's numbers.

When I got it back at the end of the hour, I had a number for Reese, her boyfriend Mason, plus her cousin and cousin's new fiancé, not to mention Caroline, her brother Noel, his girlfriend Aspen, and Ten and Quinn. They also thought it fitting that I have the number for the bar where every guy in their group worked.

In the span of an hour, I went from having one contact to having eleven. I felt good—accepted and even liked—as I skipped toward the library after class, hoping Cora didn't make me late to biology with whatever she wanted to discuss.

FOURTEEN

ZOEY

CORA WAS ALREADY waiting for me, impatiently tapping her foot with her arms crossed over her chest. "What took you so long?"

I slowed my pace, my smile dropping. "Sorry. I just got out of class."

She let out a disgusted sigh and rubbed the center of her forehead, before thrusting a folder at me. "Whatever. Here, just take this."

I did, asking, "What is it?"

"It's a half-assed schedule and checklist of every-thing you'll need to do before the..." She paused and glanced around before leaning in closer and muttering, "the operation."

I nodded and started to open it, but she slapped it back closed. "For God's sake, don't open it *here*."

Holding in a sigh, I slipped it into my backpack. "Why didn't you just wait to give it to me at home, then?"

"Because I won't be home tonight. Or the rest of the weekend. Quinn and I are going away someplace *special* together." She smiled saucily and wiggled her eyebrows. "I got it yesterday at my...treatment and forgot to get it to you last night before I went out, but your first test starts

118

Monday, so...you need it now."

I nodded, ignoring the pang in my chest at thinking of her and Quinn someplace alone and romantic together...all weekend—

"Wait." I shook my head, confused. "What about your Saturday dialysis treatment?"

Cora gritted her teeth at me, probably upset that I'd said that word aloud in public, but I didn't care. I didn't want her to miss an appointment because she was going to be with someone who didn't know what was happening to her.

"Will you relax? I can get away for a couple hours for *shopping* and a *spa* or something."

Four or five hours was way longer than a few. I didn't see how she could hide something like that from him all weekend long. I wondered if she even planned on attending the treatment.

Missing them had to be dangerous. They cleaned out her kidneys. If her kidneys stopped working, she'd die.

I remembered the call I'd overheard her making with her dad last night before she left for the evening. When she'd assured him the nurse he'd hired to help her out was still doing a fine job, I'd turned from the supper I was making at the stove and watched her tell Mr. Wilder she loved him before hanging up.

"What nurse?" I asked, taking the grilled salmon off the skillet and sliding it onto a plate.

"The nurse I paid to tell my dad she was keeping an eye on me." She snagged the plate I'd just filled and moved to the table to start eating. "Seriously, you don't think my parents let me live here *alone* with failing kidneys without making sure *someone* was looking out for me, did you?"

"But..." I filled my own plate. "Why don't you just let the nurse do her job, then?"

"Because she annoyed the shit out of me." Cora hummed in pleasure deep in her throat as she took her first bite. "Fantastic," she told me with her mouth full.

I smiled vaguely and sat across from her. I had stopped telling her which foods were healthiest for her to eat in her condition. Instead, I just fixed them, without saying anything, and let her dig in. As long as something tasted good, she didn't care how good it was for her.

Staring at her now, I wondered who'd watch her diet

all weekend long. Maybe there was a way to tell Quinn what to make sure she ate without telling him why. More misery filled me as I realized he hadn't once mentioned his plans with her this weekend in class.

"Hey, guys." A male voice from behind us made me jump and spin around.

Noel Gamble gave us a friendly smile as he bounded down the steps of the library with his thumbs tucked into the straps of his book bag he had slung over his shoulders.

"How's it going?"

"Oh, it's *you*." Cora lifted her nose and turned slightly away from him. "Hello again." Ever since she'd learned he was dating his ex-teacher, she'd been very anti-Noel Gamble.

He nodded to her and turned to me. "Zoey. You should come by the house sometime and hang out with Caroline. She talks about you all the time."

Flattered by the invitation, I opened my mouth to thank him, but Cora sniffed, interrupting me. Both Noel and I glanced at her, then he returned his attention to me.

"So, anyway. I was wondering..." He glanced at Cora again, before sending me a big smile. "You don't happen to know the name of that baseball player who had the picture of my girlfriend on his phone, do you?"

My eyes widened, and my heartbeat echoed through my ears. Oh, man. But I never thought he'd try to pry that name out of *me*. I knew my eyes were big with fear and my face frozen with shock as I shook my head slowly, but I couldn't help it. I hated outright lying to people.

He narrowed his eyes slightly, and I knew he knew that I knew.

"You mean Cain Belcher?" Cora asked, turning back to us with interest.

Noel swung to her. "Cain Belcher?" he repeated.

I closed my eyes, wishing I could gag my room-mate right about then. Didn't she know Quinn did *not* want Noel getting that name?

When I opened my lashes, I found him studying me before he turned back to Cora. "Shorter, stocky, light-headed kid with the scar on his chin, right? *That* Cain Belcher?"

"Yeah," Cora agreed. "That guy."

"Right," Noel murmured, his grin transforming into a

fierce snarl. Then he stepped back and nodded to us. "Thank you, ladies." And he was off, marching across the campus.

Crap. This was bad. This was so bad. He was going to beat up Belcher.

"Cora!" I hissed, grabbing her arm. "How could you tell him that?"

"What?" She scowled and jerked her arm out of my grip.

"Quinn didn't want him to know that guy's name."

She shook her head and wrinkled her face. "Oh, whatever. Quinn never told *me* that. Why would he care anyway?"

"Because," I started, only to stop myself. It'd take too long to explain right now anyway. "Never mind." I hurried past her. "I gotta go."

"Don't forget your first session Monday," she called after me.

I waved over my shoulder, letting her know I'd heard her, and took off after Noel in hot pursuit. I dug my cell phone from my pocket and tried to punch out an explanation SOS text to Caroline, all the while trying to keep up with her brother enough to know which direction he was headed.

Caroline didn't respond. She probably had her phone turned off for her next class. Great.

Fingers shaking, I tried Quinn next. **Noel just found out about Belcher.**

After I pressed *send,* I looked up to keep track of my target, but he'd disappeared. "Oh, no." My heart sank into my stomach and I yelped out my surprise when my phone rang in my hands. It was Quinn.

Spinning in a circle in the hopes of spotting Noel, I answered. "Hello?"

"How do you know?" he asked without a greeting. "What happened? Where is he now?"

I gulped. Oh, great. I couldn't tell him Cora was the culprit. But then I spotted Noel. "Ooh. There. I'm following him across the main quad right now. He's walking between the history and math building. I think he's headed toward the ball diamond." Which was a good mile from here, but from the way Noel was stalking, I don't think he cared.

"Thank you. I'm in the history building right now. Be right there."

121

Quinn hung up. I wasn't sure what he wanted me to do, so I kept following Noel. I had to run for a while to get close enough, and then I still had to half jog to keep up with his determined stride. Afraid he might actually make it to Belcher before Quinn could intercept him, I called, "Noel?" as soon as we hit the beginning of a parking lot.

He jerked his attention to me and snorted out a hard laugh. "My sister got to you, didn't she? Told you I wasn't allowed to know. Like I didn't have the right to defend my own *girlfriend*."

I flinched and cowered back. He was mad, as mad as my father would get right before he'd take out his anger on me. Breathing heavily, I lifted my gaze even as I kept my chin lowered.

Instead of telling him that it had been Quinn, not Caroline, who'd informed me of anything, I said, "I...I was just trying to help protect you."

"Protect me? *Me*?" With a snort, he stepped menacingly toward me. "I think its *Belcher* you're trying to fucking protect."

I cowered down even more, but refused to shift my feet even the slightest inch away. I'd been hurt by a man before; I could handle it again, especially if it was for a worthy enough cause to save his, his girl-friend's, and maybe even Caroline's future.

"What would happen if you went after him?" I asked in a small voice.

"I'd fucking defend my woman, that's what would happen."

He stepped even closer to me, and I held my breath, trying not to hyperventilate. If he charged, maybe I could duck behind a car and escape. Maybe he'd get so preoccupied with trying to catch me and hurt *me* that he'd forget all about Cain Belcher.

"But I thought it would hurt her more if you went after him."

His face contorted with rage and hot, angry color. I closed my eyes and turned my head aside, bracing for a blow when someone shouted. "*Hey!*"

I barely heard the pounding of approaching feet before someone grabbed my arm and yanked me against a warm, solid mass. When I realized it was Quinn and he'd pulled me behind him to position his body between mine and

Noel's, I gratefully gripped the back of his shirt and buried my face into the warm cloth, right between his shoulder blades.

"Don't you ever intimidate her like that again." The serious tone of Quinn's voice was almost as lethal as Noel's, but instead of being afraid, I felt comforted. I knew with absolute certainty he would not let anyone hurt me.

I shuddered with the overwhelming realization, and he must've felt it because he reached an arm out behind him and caught my hip as if trying to reassure me.

"Man, what the fuck do you think you're doing?" Ten spun Noel to face him. I guess Quinn must've gotten a hold of him too. "How is killing douche-bag Belcher going to solve anything?"

"Because it'd make me feel better," Noel roared.

"Yeah, and then it'd get you kicked off the team, and then out of school completely, where your woman will be exposed to the world, and then ruin the futures of your brothers and sister."

"Damn it." Noel squeezed his eyes shut and bowed his head. Easing my grip on Quinn's shirt, I watched Caroline's brother lose his cool. "How can I just let that fucker get away with doing that to her?" When his voice cracked, I swallowed, feeling awful for him. His face twisted with despair right before he fisted his hands, roared out his frustrations and pounded his fist down onto the trunk of the nearest car.

I jumped and Quinn tightened his hold on me, shifting until I was more securely behind him.

"I want to kill him. I want to kill him so bad."

"I know. I know, buddy. And I'm sure you can. Someday. Just not today."

Noel clenched his teeth hard. "But I want to kill him today."

As Ten wrapped his arm around Noel's shoulder and kept talking to him as he walked them away, Quinn eased his grip on me.

"Are you okay?" He turned to catch my chin, and force me to look up at him.

"I think so." Staring into his bottomless blue eyes made me shudder from a different kind of fear, a fear that I'd never feel this way when I looked into anyone else's eyes again.

He nodded. "He wouldn't have hurt you. Noel can bluster, and he can go off the deep end when he's mad enough, but he'd never physically hurt a girl."

"Okay," I said, but I still felt as rattled as a toy in a baby's hand.

"You're shaking." He began to rub his hands up and down my arms as if I was cold. It didn't even occur to me to stop him.

"Zoey!" I heard a shout. When Quinn and I looked over, we found Caroline racing our way. "There you are. I just got your text. What happened? Where's Noel?"

Quinn dropped his hands from my arms. "Ten took him away. I think he's settled down for now. But who knows what he could do tomorrow or the next day, now that he has Belcher's name."

"Well, who the hell told him?"

I paled and opened my mouth, but I just couldn't put Cora's head on the chopping block. I was about to confess that I'd told Noel the name when Quinn murmured, "Cora. Cora told him."

He looked at me and I lifted my eyes to him. "I saw the text she sent you to meet her after class. And I forgot to tell her not to give Noel Belcher's name." He gripped the front of his hair and closed his eyes. "It's my own fault. I should've said something to her to keep her quiet."

Caroline patted his arm. "It's okay. It doesn't really matter, anyway. As determined as he was, Noel was going to find out one way or another."

Shaking his head as if he didn't want to be forgiven, he turned his attention to me. "Thank you. Thank you so much for calling, and for slowing him down. You just...you prevented a complete disaster."

"Oh, I didn't—"

He grabbed my hand and squeezed warmly. "Yeah. You did." He glanced at Caroline. "I'm going to go make sure Ten's keeping Noel calm."

"What?" Caroline shook her head in surprise. "I didn't know Oren was capable of anything but pissing people off."

ANOTHER WEEK passed. When Cora returned from her mystery weekend with Quinn, she gave me no de-tails about

124

it whatsoever, and he never mentioned it once in art class.

The next Saturday, his football team played their first home game. I didn't go; I went with Cora instead to her dialysis appointment.

Meanwhile, Noel Gamble didn't kill anyone, his girlfriend wasn't exposed, and Quinn didn't have a reason to touch me again, not the way he'd so protectively pulled me behind him in the parking lot when I'd had a showdown with Noel. He did show up on Wednesday evening to pick Cora up for a date, but I made sure I was safely stowed away in my bedroom until they were gone.

He surprised me the next morning when I left my bedroom to freshen up in the bathroom at the same time he was leaving Cora's room to head home. We both drew up short and stared at each other, until he said, "Morning," in a nervous, breathless kind of voice.

"Good morning." Ducking my face, I crossed my arms over my chest because I wasn't wearing a bra under my nightshirt.

"I, uh..." He closed his mouth and motioned with his finger for me to go first.

With a nod of thanks, I rushed into the bathroom and then pressed my back to the wall after I closed the door. I clenched my eyes shut until I'd heard him pass and leave the apartment.

I also started my testing for the kidney trans-plant that week. I had to skip at least one class every day, but my main purpose here wasn't to attend college; it was to save my friend's life. I could make classes up another semester if I had to.

The checkup with the gynecologist was the most embarrassing by far. I'd never had one of those exams before, and no one had even been where that doctor went before, so it was quite a mortifying experience. After the Pap smear was over, she prescribed me birth control, letting me know I could absolutely not be pregnant to take part in the kidney transplant. Blushing madly, I tried to tell her she didn't have to worry about that...ever. But she assured me the pills would at least work to regulate my periods.

Since I wasn't the argumentative type, I filled the prescription.

By Friday, I was ready to be done with doctors and tests forever, but I kept telling myself Cora had to go through a hundred times this torture. It'd only be for a few more months, and then everything would be okay.

Just a few more months.

I was still dragging as I entered art class. The doctor who'd given me a physical exam the day before had made me run for twenty minutes straight on a treadmill, testing my heart rate before and after.

Not used to running...or any kind of exercise, really, my sore legs screamed at me with every step I took up to my seat.

"I got another one," Caroline cheered, waving a piece of paper. When she finally stopped moving it enough to let me see the drawing, I smiled. It was basically the same picture as the first one, but a cute fuzzy kitten was now playing with Caroline's bare toes and her eyes were opened as if she'd just awakened.

"Isn't it amazing?"

I nodded. "The details are astounding."

Caroline touched the pencil strokes. "And now I want a kitten."

I laughed just as Reese bounced into the room, full of smiles. "Are you guys going to the club next Friday? Asher's playing his first gig then."

"Asher?" Caroline asked slowly, burrowing her eyebrows. "What're you talking about? Who's Asher?"

"Oh my God. Does your brother tell you *nothing* about his work? Asher...Asher Hart. He's the newest bartender at Forbidden, and Pick's let him set up this entire sound system at the bar so his band can sing there. And their first performance is next Friday. I'm so excited. I've heard them practice and, oh...my...God. Asher's voice...it'll melt your panties right off, ladies. I kid you not."

Ten snorted, appearing seemingly out of no·where. "Whatever. He's not that good."

"Oh...Yes. He is," Reese argued. "I have to molest Mason senseless every time I hear him sing. Seriously." She glanced between Caroline and me. "He has the best voice. Oh my God, did you get another drawing?" She snagged it out of Caroline's hand to inspect it. "Aww. I love the kitten. Now I want a kitten."

"Wait. What is that?" When Ten tried to peer around Reese's shoulder to see it, Reese slapped it to her chest so he couldn't.

"None of your business."

"I'll just make it my business then." He snagged it away from her, making her gasp in outrage.

"Hey," Caroline snapped as he stared at the drawing. "Stop manhandling my picture. You'll rip it." Scowling at him, she tore it from his hand about as roughly as he'd taken it from Reese.

"What the fuck is that?" he demanded. "Who's drawing your picture?"

She turned her back to him and busied herself by carefully tucking it into her book bag. "I don't know," she finally said.

"Caroline's got a secret admirer," Reese announced in a sing-songy voice. "Isn't that sweet?"

"Or creepy," Ten said, studying Caroline's face before he added, "The fucker got your chin all wrong."

"The hell if he did," Caroline muttered, crossing her arms over her chest and staring straight ahead. "It's absolutely perfect."

Smiling to myself as I listened to them squabble, I opened my biology book.

"Your first test in biology is today, right?" Quinn asked, almost in my ear.

I snapped upright, not realizing he'd made it to class yet. His dark hair was windblown, and his voice a little breathless as if he'd had to rush to get here. My skin buzzed with awareness as he slid into his chair, and his scent wafted past me.

"Uh...yeah," I said, watching him situate himself. "I guess there are some lab experiment questions, so it's this afternoon instead of next hour when I actually have class. I don't know if the few extra hours to wait are going to give me more time to study or more time to freak out."

Worry filled his gaze as he paused from getting prepared for class to look at me. "I have a free period at eleven if you need a last-minute cram session."

Oh, dear God. I didn't have a class then, either. But even as my brain told me to say I did, my mouth blurted, "I have a free period then too."

He straightened as if surprised by that, but then he smiled. "Cool. You want to meet up at the library or some place? I could quiz you."

No. No, I didn't want to meet at the library, because

actually, secretly, I really did want to meet up—anywhere—with him. But I knew I shouldn't.

My mouth worked faster than my brain, though. "Okay," I said. "That would be great."

FIFTEEN

QUINN

I HAVE NO IDEA why I asked Zoey to meet me in the library. Alone. I was an idiot, that's probably why. I was tempted to text Cora and see if she wanted to meet us there too, cut down on the alone-factor, but I didn't. I don't know why I didn't do that either. Or maybe I did know why.

Cora was not a library type of girl, and if I asked her to join us, and she said no—which she would—then I'd have to explain why I really needed her there, and then she'd know my hormones were unfaithful little turds who'd been responding to another woman aside from her.

I should've just not asked Zoey at all, but I had really liked helping her study the other week. It had been easy and relaxing and...I really liked her. It made me wonder if we could be friends after all. I knew a lot of girls who were pretty and I was never worried about my attraction to *them*. So why had I been so leery about my fascination with her? I could totally do this.

Yeah, I was that sure of myself...until I walked into the library and saw her sitting at a table with an opened textbook in front of her. A wall full of windows was letting the sun in, and the way the light hit her almost made her glow. As if sensing my presence, she looked up, and yeah, I knew exactly why I shouldn't be her friend.

This was no mere attraction. What I suffered from was total, debilitating awareness. Every freaking inch of me tuned in to her. Her green eyes had my stomach churning. Her smile made my mouth go dry. The way her perfect fingers lifted to push a long piece of hair out of her face had my jeans suddenly tighter.

Up until four months ago, I'd never even seen a woman naked. But now I had. I'd touched and licked and experienced things that blew my mind. My body couldn't stop itself from wanting to touch and lick and experience those things again...with Zoey.

My step faltered. I shouldn't do this. I so should not spend any more time with her. But her smile wavered, and I saw the hint of hurt pierce her eyes. No way could I let her down.

Besides, no matter how forceful a couple of my urges were, I would never ever betray Cora.

I could handle this.

"Hey," I said, setting my book bag on the table next to hers. "How much time do we have?"

And great, my mind went straight to the gutter with that question. How much time could I strip her bare and thrust into her—

But Zoey didn't seem affected, thank goodness. She checked her wrist. "Forty minutes."

I nodded and sat across the table from her, tense but also a little charmed that she actually wore a watch. I don't think I knew any girl anymore who wore one. My grandmother had always worn a thin silver watch. I still had the sentimental piece of jewelry stored in a little box in my closet.

Zoey pulled some papers from her bag and started explaining what she needed to know. Her test was over cell biology, so I glanced over the study guide she'd scribbled on and started to quietly quiz her about proteins and ribosomes and amino acids. She did great for the most part but a couple acronyms like RNA, RER, and ER tripped her up, so we went over those again.

Half an hour later, I lowered the study guide and raised my eyebrows. "I think you have this."

"Really?" A hopeful grin lit up her face. I loved putting it there.

With a nod, I said. "You'll get an A, no problem."

"Gosh, I hope so." She tucked a piece of hair behind her ear before slipping her study sheet into her biology book. "I know how much you like it, but biology is one class I do not want to have to retake."

I smiled, not offended. As she pulled her bag closer to cram the book inside, I noticed an opened three-ring binder sitting on the table that had been hiding under her biology book. "Oh. Here. Don't forget this." I reached out and snagged it for her only to notice her handwriting taking up every line. A couple words caught my attention.

A thin ray of light slashed across her arm as if scolding her for disobeying her father and stepping outside—

"Sorry," Zoey rushed out, breathlessly, snatching the pages from my hand before I could read any more.

She blushed and ducked her head as she shoved the book out of sight inside her bag.

I knew she didn't want me to say anything, but my curiosity got the best of me. "What was that?"

"Nothing," she started. But when she glanced at me, something in my face must've changed her mind, because her shoulders slumped. "It's stupid," she added, looking exposed and alone. "Just...I'm taking a creative writing class."

"Really?" When she hurried to her feet to leave, I stood up as well. "I didn't know you were a writer."

"Oh, I'm not." She looked at me quickly, and then just as quickly looked away. "I mean...I just dabble here and there. It's silly, really."

As she started for the exit, I fell into step beside her. "How is that silly? I think it's amazing. I have no creativity whatsoever when it comes to storytelling. So I'm in awe of your ability."

"But I'm not...and you...you're..."

I couldn't help it. I smiled. Usually, I was the one fumbling for words. "I'm a biology nerd?" I guessed as I opened the door for her to precede me outside.

She snorted, but quickly covered her mouth and blushed over her response. After delicately clearing her throat, she lowered her hand. "Uh, no. Nerd is the last word I'd use to describe you."

I had been a nerd in high school, though, so it was nice

131

to learn my image was somewhat improving. "The jock thing kind of screwed it up, huh?"

With a laugh, she kept pace with me across the campus. "Maybe that's it. You're a unique hybrid mix."

Hybrid. Hybrid was so much better than freak. I liked the word *hybrid*. Almost as much as I liked her laugh.

"Is biology your major?" She moved closer to me to allow a bigger group to pass by, and her scent wafted up to my nostrils. My body instantly tensed. I'd managed not to get close enough to smell her throughout our entire study session, and now...now I just wanted to bury my face in the crook of her neck and inhale as deeply as my lungs would let me.

I shook my head and let out a breath when the group passed because she moved back out of my space.

"Uh..." Crap, what had we been talking about? She looked up at me, her green eyes so big and innocent and questioning.

Major! Somehow, my brain ignited the memory.

"Pre-med," I blurted, then rolled my shoulders to relax myself. "I'm a pre-med major."

"No way. Really?" She seemed pleasantly surprised. "You're going to be a doctor?"

I nodded. "I'd like to be a heart surgeon."

Her eyebrows crinkled. "Okay, that sounds really specific. What made you go with *heart* surgeon?"

"My grandma." It was those eyes, I swear. So curious, and interested, and green. I started spilling everything. "She, uh, she d-died when I was nineteen. Car accident."

Zoey's lips parted and her face filled with sympathy. She wasn't even aware how much my grandmother had meant to me, but she knew...some-how sensed how hard I'd taken her death.

"I'm so sorry." She sat her hand on my arm before letting it fall away. I instantly missed it the moment her touch was gone, wanting her fingers to return, to comfort me some more. "You don't usually see... I mean, grandparents are supposed to go from natural causes, not—"

"I know," I said, shaking my head. "Gran was so full of life too. She had plenty of years left in her. A strong heart. Yeah... That's why they took it. She was an organ donor, and they used her heart to put into someone else who needed it."

Zoey's green eyes widened. "Wow."

I nodded in agreement and glanced across the campus at all the people milling by, and the trees sprouting flowers and leaves...at *life* abounding. "I love knowing her heart is still out there, beating. Giving someone else a second chance."

Zoey bobbed her head too, and then quickly dashed a tear off her cheek. "It is pretty amazing."

"That's when I knew I wanted to be a part of that process. I wanted to put hearts into people who needed them."

It took me a second to realize she was no longer next to me. But when I glanced over for her reaction, she was gone. "Zo—?" I turned back to realize she'd stopped in her shoes and was staring at me as if I'd lost my mind. "What's wrong?" I immediately back-tracked to her and took her elbow. "Are you okay?"

She moved her head up and down in a robotic kind of way but continued to stare at me with slightly parted lips and wide eyes. Finally, she said, "You want to transplant organs."

"Yeah." I furrowed my brow, wondering what was wrong with that.

Then her entire face bloomed into a sudden smile, telling me there was absolutely nothing wrong with it. "I think that's amazing." She began walking again before she bumped her elbow into mine. "And you say you're in awe of my dream to be a writer. You want to save lives, Quinn. *That's* impressive."

She hadn't said becoming a writer was her dream earlier. She'd said it was just a hobby she dabbled in, but I'm glad she let it slip now. I liked learning more about her.

I let her words settle in my head a bit before I said, "I may want to save lives, but art, like the stories you want to write...that's the kind of stuff that makes life worth living."

When Zoey looked at me this time, something powerful fisted into a knot at the base of my stomach. "What?" I asked softly, needing to know what she was thinking more than I needed my next breath.

She shook her head as if she wasn't going to tell me, and then she murmured, "I was always scared to tell people about my writing. Everyone would say it's silly and stupid and tell me to get a real dream, but...when you say things like that, it makes it feel..." She shrugged and glanced away with a far-off look. "Almost important."

"But you are." I wanted to touch her, shift the hair out of her face, slide my fingers up her cheek, and press my forehead to hers. My guts actually ached because I held myself back. But I was even too afraid to hold her hand, so I shoved my fists into my pockets. "We all have paranoid moments where we think everything we do is silly and stupid, or completely inconsequential. But stories are a way to connect with others and realize we're not alone in our crazy, mixed-up thoughts. I think what you do *is* important. It keeps introverted people like me from going insane."

Tears glistened in her eyes as she smiled up at me. But I didn't hug her. No, I did not. And I didn't kiss her. I didn't grab her hand, yank her around the corner of the nearest building, or take her against the first wall we came across. No matter how insistent some of my urges were, I managed to hold back.

"Thank you," she whispered.

Even though I didn't do any of the things I craved, I still felt completely satisfied in that moment. Because I'd made Zoey smile.

SIXTEEN

ZOEY

THE APARTMENT was quiet when I let myself inside after class. I thought I was home alone until I heard a strange sound down the hall. Immediately apprehensive, I froze.

It took a couple seconds for my vocal chords to work up the courage and function before I could hesitantly call out. "Hello? Cora?"

"Back here," I thought I heard her answer.

Unease prickled the back of my neck, so I dropped my book bag to the floor and hurried down the hall and into her room. I heard the vomiting from her bathroom as soon as I entered.

"Oh, no." Dashing past her bed, I flew toward the opened doorway and skidded to a halt in the entrance of the bathroom.

Cora sat on her knees in front of the toilet, her back arched up with the force of her heaves as she emptied her stomach.

"Cora!" My knees weakened and I almost landed beside her on the cool tile. But I managed to sit on the edge of the bathtub so I could gather her hair out of her face. "What's happening? Are you okay?"

For a couple minutes, she was too busy to answer. I had to look away so I didn't get sick myself, but the sound and the smell still turned my stomach, and I gagged more than

135

once.

Tears were matted to Cora's face as she came up for air. "I'm fine," she finally said, wiping her cheeks clean. "It's just nausea."

Just nausea my butt. But I nodded and left her for a moment to fetch her a glass of water. When I re-turned, I watched her gulp the entire cup full.

"Could..." She had to pause to regain her voice before she asked, "Could you get my Nauzene in the bottom drawer next to my bed?"

She so rarely let me help her. Eager to do some-thing, I stood up so fast I made the blood rush to my head. The dizziness blurred my vision for a moment before I could kneel beside her bottom drawer and pull it open.

I swear, the entire thing was filled with medicine, some prescriptions, some over the counter, and some vitamins. "My God," I murmured, wondering how much of this she had to take every day.

Two minutes later, I still hadn't found what she needed. She finally had to call, "The bottle's in a white box, blue words."

I spotted it seconds later and pulled it free. After shutting the drawer, I returned to the bathroom. I wanted to question and lecture her so bad.

She rarely followed any of her dietitian's suggest-ions. And as often as I tried to feed her the right food, I really didn't see her most of the day, so she could be eating anything when I wasn't around. And I had no idea how much alcohol she drank.

"Go ahead," she mumbled after she chewed and swallowed her pill.

I blew out a breath. "You're not going to die, Cora," I said, and then I shook my head because that was probably one of the worst things I could've said. But, really... "I'm here to help. This is going to pass. And the dialysis will be over soon. Just a couple more months and you'll have a new kidney, and you won't have to worry about any of this again. I know you said you wanted to live your life how you wanted because no one knew how long they had left, but not watching your diet is just going to make you miserable and maybe even delay things until you can get through this."

Cora closed her eyes and bowed her head before pressing a palm to her temple. "I know," she reluctantly admitted.

"You're right. I just...It's easier to pre·tend nothing is wrong when I eat...whatever. And drink...whatever."

"I know." I cringed, wishing I could trade places with her, even just for a day so she could get a little escape. Just a small respite. "But—"

Down the hall, someone knocked on the front door. A second later, a familiar voice called, "Hello? Cora?"

Cora and I exchanged a glance, mine begging her to finally just confess everything, hers pleading with me to keep silent.

I blew out a surrendering breath as footsteps drew near. Another knock fell outside her bedroom. "Cora?"

"In here," I said. Cora sliced me with a lethal glare half a second before Quinn appeared in the bath·room's opened doorway.

He took one look at his girlfriend still planted on the floor in front of the toilet and bolted inside.

"Oh my God. What happened? Are you okay?"

Cora shook her head and lifted a hand. "I'm fine. It's nothing. Just...the flu, I think."

Quinn landed on his knees beside her and instantly pressed his palm to her forehead. "You don't have a fever. Does your stomach hurt?"

"It feels a lot better now." Resting her cheek on his shoulder, she asked, "Could you carry me back to bed?"

"Of course." Quinn scooped her up without a smidgeon of protest. When he turned her my way, I hurried out of the doorway to let them through.

Quinn met my gaze as he passed. I knew there was something in my expression that made him blink in confusion. Maybe it was the sympathy he didn't see because I was too busy silently screaming at her to just tell him everything already. Maybe it how solemn I was, and he'd just figured out something was seriously wrong. Or maybe he just wanted me to leave.

That one I could do.

Because I couldn't stand there and watch her lie to him. She obviously liked him taking care of her; she cuddled into him like a content kitten and closed her eyes with a small sigh as he tenderly tucked her into the sheets. So, why didn't she just *tell* him?

"I'm going to set your nausea tablets here on top of the nightstand," I said.

"Thanks," Cora murmured weakly, and Quinn once again glanced at me, his gaze penetrating something so deep inside me I felt stripped bare.

QUINN

A STRANGE FEAR clutched me as a pale, stone-faced Zoey walked stiffly from Cora's room. She looked...I don't know. She looked shell-shocked. And Cora looked like death warmed over with bags under her eyes and her face flushed as if she did have a fever.

Something wasn't right. And it was not the flu.

I sat next to Cora on her mattress and let her curl up with her head in my lap. Stroking her hair, I watched her close her eyes and breathe deeply, trying to fall asleep.

"Are you pregnant?" I finally asked.

Her eyes fluttered open and she scowled at me. "Why do guys always automatically assume a girl's pregnant as soon as she upchucks?"

Okay, so she wasn't pregnant. "Bulimia?" I asked next.

She sighed as if already exhausted by my interrogation. Then she closed her eyes without answering me.

I continued to sift my fingers through her hair. "I know this isn't just the flu, Cora. You've continuously lost weight for as long as I've known you. Every day, you seem to get more fatigued. This is something so much more than a common cold."

Keeping her eyes closed, she refused to answer me.

"You're beautiful to me," I tried again, "exactly how you are. Please don't think you have to lose weight... for any reason." I ran my finger down the center of her spine, feeling each dip and bump in her vertebrae.

Her lashes flickered open before she looked up at me. "I'm not bulimic," was all she said.

I ground my teeth. "Then what are you?"

Again, she refused to answer, just stared at me as if I was an idiot for even bothering to ask. I didn't understand what was going on, and I hated this. Couldn't she see I only wanted to help her?

"Zoey knows," I finally said. Why would she tell Zoey, and not me?

She sniffed and glanced away, pushing my hand off her

head. "So you're going to go hound Zoey until she gives up all my secrets?"

"No. I shouldn't have to learn anything about *my girlfriend* from her roommate. I want *you* to tell me." When she remained mute, I gnashed my teeth. "Why don't you trust me?" I whispered, aching from the pit of my being.

"Trust?" She rolled her eyes. "Baby, this isn't about trust. It's about *privacy*. Why do you feel you have to know everything about me?"

Sucker punched right in the stomach, I pulled back and shook my head. "I don't..." My tongue felt twisted in my mouth. I was going to start stuttering any second, so I glanced away and concentrated on breathing through my nose.

"Can't you just be here for me and let me have my privacy?"

Silently, I nodded.

So, I sat there, just being with her, and I gave her privacy, even though it gutted a part of me. I stroked her hair, and stayed quiet so I wouldn't irritate her with questions.

As soon as she fell asleep, I eased her head off my thigh and settled it gently on a pillow. She looked exhausted, though I knew she'd been getting enough sleep. Frustration, anger, and hurt raged through me, dueling for supremacy.

Strangely, the hurt won.

After I walked down the hall and saw Zoey sitting on the couch, watching an episode of *Psych*, I fell down on the cushion beside her. I didn't say anything; I just stewed in my misery as I stared through the television screen, seeing nothing but Cora sitting on the floor of her bathroom in front of the toilet.

Visions of my time with my mother swirled through my head. The beatings, the boyfriends laughing at me for being a freak as they threw beer bottles at me whenever I'd race through the living room to get to the kitchen. Then high school. Never fitting in, always being on the outside.

When I'd first started seeing Cora, I thought I'd finally found a place to belong, someone to share all my thoughts and secrets with. But there was so much she refused to open up about. Sometimes, I still felt like I was on the outside, a freak who didn't belong in her life.

Unable to control my bubbling emotions a second longer,

I spun to face Zoey. Refusing to face me, she continued to stare at the television as the show played on with the volume low.

"Why won't she just talk to me?" I blurted out, the anger in my voice hopefully blotting out the pain.

She sniffed and pulled her knees up to her chest so she could hug them. "I don't know." She kept staring at the television, and I hated that she wouldn't look at me, either. "But I wish she would."

So did I. Not only was Cora putting a strain on my relationship with her, but I think she was putting one on her relationship with Zoey too. Zoey looked strung tight enough to snap with the slightest nudge.

"Don't worry," I told her. "I'm not going to ask you."

A tear slipped silently down her cheek. "Thank you." She kept watching the show, though I'm pretty sure she also had no idea what was going on in it.

An urge rose inside me. I didn't understand why it was suddenly so important to me, but I just needed to connect with someone...in any way possible. I needed to...I don't even know. I needed to know someone understood me. Hell, I'd settled for just understanding someone else. I had to somehow feel tethered to the planet and not like some foreign being invading everyone else's space.

So I asked, "Can I read one your stories?"

Zoey whirled to me, her green eyes wide. I expected her to tell me no, but she blushed. "You actually *want* to?"

Did I? I don't know. I hadn't even thought about it until just now. But the more I thought about it, the more I did want to. "Yes," I said.

"I..." She flushed and ducked her face. "I don't know. They're not really—"

"Please."

Her eyes went even wider until she almost seemed frightened. But I think the sincerity in my gaze finally won her over because she swallowed. "Okay."

She stood up and glanced down to where I was still sitting. "They're, uh...they're in my room." When she nervously tucked her hair behind her ear, I knew she wanted me to follow her. To her room.

I stood up. "Okay."

I hadn't been in her room since she'd moved in. It had the same pale blue walls and white bedding that had been in here before she'd come, but she'd man-aged to make the space her own. She had books and clothes and two stuffed teddy bears in the wicker chair in the corner. A row of shoes lined the foot of her bed, and the yellow scarf she'd worn to school last week was wrapped about her bedpost.

And it smelled like her.

I drew in a deep breath of wild cherry and orchid but stayed near the entrance as she moved forward to pull a spiral ring notebook from the white shelf over her bed.

But my curiosity got the best of me, and I moved closer. "Are *all* those full of stories?"

She nodded. "I don't know why, but I have to write them by hand."

"So you only have one copy? Don't you worry about something...happening to them?"

She shrugged. "I plan to type them into the computer someday. But for now, I like them like this."

She hadn't handed the notebook over yet and was actually cradling it protectively to her chest. So I reached out my hand. Her eyes lifted to mine. After a moment of hesitation, she finally gave it to me.

"Thank you," I said, realizing how much she'd just put her trust in me. I felt honored. Now if only Cora had—

My girlfriend appeared in the doorway, her mussed hair sticking up around her head and a blanket wrapped around her shoulders like a cape.

I nearly jumped out of my skin.

"Cora!"

SEVENTEEN

⤜ QUINN ⤛

CORA GLANCED passively between Zoey and me, her bruised eyes sharp with censure. "Well, this is a sight no girl likes to see. Her boyfriend alone in her roommate's bedroom."

"I was showing him my stories," Zoey blurted out at the very same moment I said, "She was showing me her stories."

We glanced at each other and then broke out grinning together.

Cora growled. "Seriously, baby. What're you doing in here?"

I'd never seen her jealous or so possessive of me before. It made my stomach churn with guilt as I wondered if she knew just how attracted I was to Zoey. "Seriously," I answered. "I was borrowing one of her stories to read." I cocked my head to the side. "What're you doing awake again? Can't you sleep? Do you need something?"

"No, I cannot sleep, *okay?* But, Quinn, just don't." She entered Zoey's room and shuffled toward me. "I know you're only trying to be your nice, gentlemanly self and act interested, but trust me, her cute little children's stories aren't your thing." She plucked the notebook I was holding and haphazardly flung it on top of Zoey's neatly made bed. Then she smoothed her hand intimately up my chest, the heat from her palm soaking through my shirt. "I think my pills are kicking in. The nausea's all gone, so let's rent a movie and snuggle on the couch. Huh?"

As she turned and strolled from the room, I frowned after her, upset that she'd just done that to Zoey. When I turned back, Zoey's face was a deep humiliated red. With a huff, I retrieved the notebook Cora had tossed aside. Zoey opened her mouth and lifted her hand to stop me, but I spoke over her.

"Thanks," I said and waved the notebook to show her that I *did* want to read her story. A sick worry worked into her features, so I added, "Children's stories actually happen to be my favorite. I think I've read *Holes* about a dozen times." I left her there to find Cora in the living room.

"Make us some popcorn, will you, babe?" Cora didn't glance over at me as she flipped through the options on the screen.

"You don't think it'll bother your upset stomach?" I asked.

With a muffled curse, she tossed her remote to the floor and cupped her head with both hands. "Damn it," she screeched. "Why can't people just leave me alone and let me eat whatever the hell I want to eat?"

Startled when tears fill her eyes, I rushed to her. "I...I'm sorry. Cora? Are you okay?"

"I just want some popcorn," she sobbed against my chest when I pulled her into my arms. "Why couldn't you have just *made* it? Why did you have to nitpick and harp and question *everything*? If I didn't think I could handle it, I wouldn't have requested it."

"Okay, okay," I soothed, stroking her hair, and wondering what the heck was happening. I was pretty sure she wasn't flipping out about popcorn, but I had no idea what was really going on.

Maybe if I knew what was wrong, I could help. But...she wanted her privacy.

She would let me make her popcorn, though, so after she settled down again, I made some popcorn.

I was still in the kitchen waiting for it to finish when I tugged the rolled-up notebook from my back pocket, but before I could get started, Cora called my name. "Quinn?"

"I'm in the kitchen. Everything okay?"

"What're you doing in there?" She sounded accusing.

I crinkled my eyebrows. "Uh...I'm popping the popcorn...like you wanted." Worried something was affecting her memory, I left the popcorn still popping and started down the hall as she called, "Where's Zoey?"

I stepped into the living room. "In her room still, I guess. I don't know. Why? What's wrong? Do you want me to get her for you?"

She sat on the couch with her blanket pulled snug around her shoulders and her knees up to her chest. She definitely wasn't behaving like Cora tonight.

When she looked up at me, I almost panicked. What the hell was going on with my girlfriend? Was she on drugs? Had some guy messed with her? My mind went crazy. But all she said was, "I want you to sit by me."

So I sat by her.

Zoey must've realized that I couldn't leave Cora's side, because she carried in a bowl full of popcorn just as Cora decided on a movie and started it.

"Here. You guys left this in the microwave."

"Thanks." I reached up and took it from her, and Cora cuddled in closer to me.

"Want to watch with us?" I asked Zoey, tightening my arm around my girlfriend to let her know I wouldn't leave her side. "We're just getting started."

Zoey glanced at the screen and look undecided.

"Yes, do," Cora coaxed. "Watch a movie with us. You and I haven't spent nearly enough time together since you moved here."

That seemed to be the clincher for Zoey. She joined us on the couch, sitting next to Cora.

It took me about five seconds to realize Cora had picked a horror movie. She knew I hated them. But I didn't say a thing about her choice. Maybe she just wanted a reason to cuddle into me and clutch my arms, because she spent the next two hours smashed against me doing just that.

When the final credits rolled, she groaned and flopped her cheek onto my shoulder. "I don't want to walk all the way back to my bed."

I offered to carry her, which she gladly accepted. As I glanced at a pale, shaken-looking Zoey and told her good night, Cora wrapped her arms around my neck and cuddled her nose into my throat.

"Will you stay the night?" she whispered in my ear.

"Of course." I knew she didn't want to do anything and I wouldn't have tried after seeing her so sick, but her sudden, strange clinginess scared me. I wasn't too sure what to think about what was going on with her.

But she continued to cling to me when I crawled under the sheets with her and spooned up behind her. "I like it best when you're here." Her hand settled possessively on my forearm before she sighed into her pillow and went to sleep.

I stayed up long after she was out, trying to figure out what most of this evening had meant. Cora had wanted me to take her to a party tonight, but she hadn't even mentioned how much she'd missed not going after I'd found her sick. She usually hated missing a party for any reason; she liked to bemoan the fact that she'd missed it until she found her way to another event.

Tonight, she just hadn't acted like herself at all. I kissed her hair and hoped to God she was okay.

When I finally fell asleep, nightmares plagued me. Reason number one why I never watched horror movies. They never failed to make me dream about my mom.

I jerked awake sometime late in the night in a cold sweat. Cora was sleeping peacefully. I touched her forehead for a temperature, but she felt cool, so I shoved the blankets off me and patted barefoot out of her room, down the hall, and into the kitchen. A night-light above the sink guided my path as I went to the refrigerator and found a bottle of chilled water. When I noticed the notebook I'd started to open while I'd been popping popcorn still sitting on the kitchen table in the corner, I opened the water and went that way.

A lighthearted children's story sounded like the perfect cure to get me over a scary-movie-induced nightmare.

ZOEY

I GASPED MYSELF awake, my haunting dreams chasing me into consciousness. The movie Cora had picked out had been about a girl who'd tried to leave her abusive spouse, but ended up being chased down by him.

So, of course I had to dream that my father had chased me down and caught me here. Arms prickling with goose bumps, I sat up in bed, breathing hard. It was the dead of night and I felt like I needed to check the front door, just to make sure it was still locked. After finding my glasses on my nightstand, I crawled off the mattress and tiptoed down the hall.

But I still felt jittery after finding everything bolted properly in place, so I stopped by the kitchen and got a water from the refrigerator. I was unscrewing the cap when a voice from the table said, "Hi."

I yelped and whirled around, dropping the bottle and spilling water all over the floor.

"Sorry." Quinn popped up from the table and dashed to the paper towels sitting on the counter. "I thought I'd scare you more if I didn't say anything before you saw me."

I retrieved the bottle, grateful not much had spilled. As Quinn wiped the floor clean, I cradled the water to my chest because I realized I once again wasn't wearing a bra under my nightshirt...in Quinn's presence.

"Can't sleep either?" I asked, not sure what to say, or if I should say anything. Maybe I could just slip back to my room and leave him here alone.

He shook his head and sent me a look after he tossed the used paper towels into the trash. "I hate those stupid scary movies."

A smile burst across my face. "I do too. I have no idea why Cora loves them so much."

"And that she doesn't like quality shows like *Psych*," Quinn added, smiling back.

"Clearly, she has issues." Unable to stay away, I wandered to the table to see what he'd been reading. When I realized it was the notebook I'd given him, I sat, wondering which one it was. I'd been too nervous earlier; I'd just picked out the first one my fingers had touched and shoved it his way without seeing the title I was handing away.

Tucking my feet up on the seat with me, I rested my chin on my knees and read a few words. Ahh. This one was about the dragon slayer who ended up making friends with the dragon. Very *How to Train Your Dragon* like. I know, I was *so* original. Except they weren't Vikings in my story, the main character was a girl, and the main dragon was not named Toothless.

Glancing up at Quinn, I sighed. "I kept dreaming about someone breaking into the apartment, so I had to make sure it was locked. But now that I'm up, I know I won't be getting back to sleep any time soon."

He sat back in the chair he'd been in when I'd come into the kitchen, and he lifted his water in a silent kind of cheers. "Same here."

I clinked my bottle gently against his. He smiled, and we drank together in silence.

"How'd you do on your biology test?" he finally asked. "I totally forgot to ask earlier, what with that guy breaking into his ex-wife's window and trying to cut her apart with the saw and all."

I grinned and rolled my eyes. "I think I did okay. I feel really good about it, anyway."

"That's great." He tilted his water bottle toward me again. After another bump, we drank some more.

"Caroline got tickets for me to go with her to your home game tomorrow," I said, thinking I should make small talk, and actually *wanting* to make small talk with him. "I even bought an ESU shirt to wear to it. I'm kind of excited."

"Really?" His eyes lit up. "You're going? That's cool. I didn't know if you even liked football."

I shrugged. "My father's a fan, so...I learned about the game from watching him watch it."

Quinn watched me curiously before he shrugged. "I didn't know much about it myself until I joined the team. I was homeschooled until high school."

"Really?" My jaw about hit the floor. "No way. So was I." That was so strange.

He nodded and glanced away. "Yeah, I know. Cora mentioned it before."

I gulped. Oh. "She did?" What else had Cora told him about me?

Not meeting my gaze, he nodded again. "I never planned on trying out for the team, but the coach saw me walking down the hall one day and said with my size, it was a shame I wasn't trying out. So I decided to go for it, and ended up being the starting quarter-back by the end of high school. Of course, I was twenty at the time, so I'd matured a lot more than the other guys."

I tipped my head to the side, curious. "Why were you twenty when you finished high school?" He obviously had no learning disability to hold him back. His biology help had told me that.

When his mouth opened, but no words came and a strange expression entered his face, I held up a hand. "Sorry. Ignore me." That information was none of my business. "Still...that's so cool that the football coach came to you. You must've been a natural." I smiled, glad to hear he'd turned out a success after his beginning had been so similar to mine.

Quinn shrugged bashfully. "I was big enough to handle a hit here and there, but I still had decent aim with my throwing arm." He glanced at me only to suck in a sudden breath. "Ouch. That must've hurt."

Before I knew what he was doing, he reached out and slid his fingers over the top of my shoulder where my shirt had slipped down revealing bare skin. The graze of his flesh against mine made me shiver. When my nipples instantly went hard, I jerked back with a gasp.

His eyes widened as if he'd just then realized what he'd done. Snapping his hand back to himself, he immediately apologized. "Sorry, I just...they surprised me. I'm so sorry."

When I realized he was talking about the scars and that's what he'd touched, I immediately covered the area with my hand.

"The way they're in a straight line like that..." He shook his head and his eyes filled with compassion. "That's crazy. Someone must've possessed some insanely controlled temper to do something like that."

I shook my head, instantly denying it, but Quinn merely whispered, "Zoey." He lifted a hand to stop me from protesting. "I know what cigarette burns look like." Then he reached for the hem of his own shirt and lifted it. I got an eyeful of perfectly formed abs before he twisted to show me his back.

My mouth fell open. Not only was he marred everywhere with belt-inflicted scars, but little white and red dots were scattered sporadically, showing me how many times someone had taken the butt of a cigarette to him and burned him.

Tears filled my eyes.

He dropped his shirt back into place. "My abuser just wasn't as neat as yours."

I opened my mouth and met this gaze, but no words

came.

"Cora told me about you before you ever moved here," he admitted. Then he glanced away. "I've wanted to say something to you for a while, let you know I understood and that I'd been there, too."

I wiped at my wet cheeks and finally managed to asked, "Who...?"

"My mom," he answered with a blank nod. "But only until I was twelve. That's when she overdosed and died. I went to live with my grandma after that. I'd never had any kind of schooling at that point. Gran knew I would've been horribly out of place if I started public school then, so she homeschooled me until I was ready for ninth grade. I don't think a lot of people knew I was seventeen my freshman year of high school."

"Wow," I whispered. My hand trembled as I reached for him, but I kept reaching until my fingers were covering his.

He slipped his around until our palms pressed together. Then he sent me a sad smile. "I was worried about you when you first showed up. I'd had years to get over what I went through before I moved out on my own. But you were just escaping. I didn't know how easily you'd adjust. I wanted to let you know I was here to talk...you know, if you ever needed to, but I wasn't sure...I'm sorry. I didn't know how to broach the subject."

I smiled and nodded, sniffing with a new batch of tears wetting my eyes. "You're doing a very good job of it now."

He half smiled, half laughed. "Yeah. Better late than never, huh? I guess we should've watched a scary movie together weeks ago."

When I blurted out a laugh only to mop up more tears, he stood and tightened his grip on my hand to urge me out of my chair as well. "Come here."

My stomach fluttered with unease and excitement as I followed his instruction without question. I stood, and he pulled me into a hug.

I'm not sure if I'd ever really been hugged before. It was...amazing. I rested my cheek on his shoulder, inhaled his heavenly scent and hugged him back as hard as I could.

Warm lips pressed against my forehead. "It'll get better. I promise you."

More tears fell and I squeezed my eyes closed, wishing this moment would never end. But footsteps in the hallway approached and Cora's voice lightly called, "Quinn?"

"Right here." His arms loosened around me, but he didn't lurch away with any kind of guilt.

He was still lowering his arm from around me when my best friend appeared in the doorway, rubbing her eyes and yawning. She jerked to a stop when she saw us. Dropping her hand to her side, she gazed back and forth between us with confusion. "What the hell?"

"You caught us," Quinn said with a grin as he held out his arm to draw her into his side. "We're both complete chickens who couldn't sleep after you made us watch that awful movie."

Cora went to him willingly but frowned at me in concern when she saw the tears in my eyes.

They fell a little harder because it'd been so easy for him to turn to her after sharing such an intimate moment with me. I felt completely altered after being held in his arms, but obviously he hadn't feel the same, which only made the guilt inside me fester and grow.

I was developing feelings for my best friend's boyfriend. This was worse than awful. It was deva-stating.

"No, really," Cora said, looking up at Quinn. "What's going on here?"

He kissed her temple and pulled her tighter against him. "We ended up sharing a couple horror stories of our own."

Cora's shoulders fell. "Oh, so you finally told her, huh?"

He nodded. And I realized Cora already knew all about his past, probably ten times more than what he'd just told me. *They* were the ones with all the intimacies between them. Not him and me.

Feeling like a stupid, young fool, I murmured, "I think I can finally go back to sleep now. Excuse me." My gaze met Quinn's. I wanted to thank him for opening up to me, for making me feel better, but I didn't know how, so I said nothing.

I slipped past them and hurried to my room, shutting myself inside and crawling under the covers until I had the blankets over my head, so I couldn't hear anything that might be happening outside my room.

EIGHTEEN

QUINN

GUILT GNAWED at me as a white-faced Zoey fled the kitchen, and it wasn't because my girlfriend had walked in on me hugging another woman. I felt guilty because Cora had interrupted my moment with Zoey, as if I'd just cheated on *Zoey*—not Cora.

That was so messed up, it left me reeling. But I'd just shared something with Zoey that I'd never shared with Cora. We had connected on an entirely different level. I'd opened up to her and for some reason, I knew she'd been able to see me. The real me, not someone I had to strive to be. Just me.

"Let's go back to sleep, my big man." When Cora reached for my arm, I just couldn't follow her. My head was everywhere; I felt that anything I did right then would be wrong. But staying the rest of the night with her while I was this way had to be worse.

I pulled my arm away before she could touch me. She shot me a surprised glance. I winced and rubbed the back of my neck. "How's your stomach feeling?"

She nodded. "Better. In fact..." A grin spread across her face. "I'm willing to show you just how much better."

Her fingers reached for my chest this time. My body reacted to the ideas she put into my head, but I was still too affected by what I'd just experienced with Zoey. So I caught Cora's wrist, brought her hand to my lips and kissed her knuckles before smiling softly at her.

"Actually, if you're feeling okay, I was going to head home. We gotta get up early in the morning to get ready for the game tomorrow." I paused to send her a hopeful glance. "Are you going to make it to this one?"

She sighed and let her shoulders slump, telling me how much I'd just dissatisfied her. "I can't. Zoey wants me to spend the day with her."

From the attitude in the way she answered me, I didn't believe her. In fact, I think she only said no as a way to punish me for not giving her her way. The urge to apologize rose in my throat, but I swallowed it down even though I wasn't sorry; I just hated dis-pleasing anyone.

Then another thought occurred to me. "*Zoey* wanted you to spend the day with her?" I asked, cocking my head to the side. "But she just told me she was going to the game with Caroline tomorrow."

Cora's brow puckered with confusion, and then she slowly shook her head. "No. I didn't say Zoey. I said Rachel."

"Uh...no. You said—"

"I said *Rachel*," she bit out aggressively and stepped closer to me, her mouth tight with displeasure. "Maybe you have so much Zoey on the brain that's what you thought you heard."

I flushed and glanced away. I'd been certain she'd said Zoey, but crap, *had* she said Rachel? *Was* I thinking about Zoey too much?

Mumbling, I nodded. "Okay. Sorry." Great, I'd ended up apologizing anyway. "Call me after the game whenever you get home then. I don't have to work. We can do something if you want."

Cora's frown immediately ironed into a smile. "Sure thing, baby." She smoothed her hand over my chest and reached up on her tiptoes to give me a kiss. I'm not sure why I shifted my face at the last moment so that she merely glanced the side of my lip instead of giving me full mouth-to-mouth contact. Kissing her right then just didn't feel right.

I stroked my fingers down her hair, though, and gave

her a smile before bidding her farewell. Then I escaped the kitchen. I controlled the next impulse I had; I didn't glance back at Zoey's closed bedroom door as I walked down the hall.

THE NEXT DAY, we won our second home football game of the season. Cora never called. I tried contacting her but was sent straight to voice mail, so I just chilled at home before heading to bed.

Late that night, I once again woke in the early hours, all because of a disturbing dream. But this one wasn't a nightmare. Not by a long shot. Yet it rattled me just the same. Testosterone flowed so thickly through my veins that my erection literally throbbed for release. I was tempted to reach down and take care of myself, just to alleviate some of the pressure in my groin, except I felt too guilty.

It had started as a normal enough wet dream. I was rolling around naked on a bed with Cora until she pinned me down on my back and crawled on top of me, straddling my lap. Just when I swear I could almost feel her sit on me and take me inside her, Zoey appeared out of nowhere. Her heady shampoo scent filled my nostrils. She was wearing the same sleep shirt she'd been in the night before, with her bare cigarette-butt-burned shoulder on display. But this time around, her nipples were hard and poking through the thin cloth.

Her green eyes were full of heat and longing when she met my hungry gaze. "Eat me," she begged as she gathered up the hem of her nightshirt, exposing her legs and climbing on top of me to frame my head with her thighs. I wanted my mouth on her and my tongue inside her so bad; my jaw began to ache and my mouth watered.

I closed my eyes, eager for her to sit on my face, just as Cora did sit on my dick, taking me deep and tight.

My eyes shot open as I realized I was awake and alone in my own bed, gripping myself and pumping my fist up and down the heavy column. I hadn't meant to take care of myself at all. But I ached so much I actually hurt. And my hand kept moving, sliding up and down, no matter how loudly my brain was shrieking at me to stop; I didn't stop until I was coming all over my stomach. And I just kept coming. It was one of the strongest orgasms I'd ever had. I ground the heels of my feet into my mattress and gritted my teeth as I humped my hips into my fist. It would've been so much better if I'd been inside a woman. I tried to picture Cora's face as the last strong burst left me, but it ended up being green eyes I saw watching me, not blue.

Feeling awful because I hadn't been able to help myself, I covered my head with my hands and physically tried to push the stray leftover images of Zoey and Cora together out of my head.

I couldn't get back to sleep, so I ended up taking a shower—a freezing one—at the crack of dawn.

Becoming sexually active must've ruined me. Now that I knew what certain things felt like, I wanted them. A lot. It had been over a week since Cora and I had been together, which was actually the biggest dry spell for us.

I was a mess; there was no other way to explain it. It seemed like no matter what I did, it was going to be the wrong decision. Sleeping with Cora last night would've been bad because I knew I would've had thoughts of Zoey. But not sleeping with her had felt wrong too, because I'd *already* been having thoughts of Zoey.

I just needed to stop having thoughts about Zoey. Except the more I tried, the more thoughts of her that came.

Physical exercise seemed to be the only thing to clear my head when something was bothering me, so I found myself at the university's twenty-four-hour activities center. The weight room was dead at this time of day, which left me with free reign of the place.

I spent a couple hours there.

The burn in my muscles when I finished felt good. I kind of didn't want to stop, so I jogged another mile around the indoor track and finally hit the showers before heading home. Ten was still asleep when I arrived, so I made him some breakfast.

The smell of frying bacon and eggs finally roused him. When he stumbled bleary-eyed into the kitchen, he mumbled something that I took for a greeting and went straight to the refrigerator to grab his usual morning dose of Sunny Delight.

We were both silent as we sat to eat. He was probably sporting a hangover from the after-game party he'd no doubt attended. And I was too jumbled with nerves to even look him in the eye. But every time I glanced over, he was quietly munching and just studying me, making me feel like he could see into my head and know every dirty dream I'd ever had.

"Didn't see you at the celebration last night," he finally said, after draining the last of his juice.

I shrugged and glanced away. Cora hadn't even gone to my football game, so I don't know where she'd been for the after party, and she was the only reason I attended any of them, so I hadn't seen the need to go.

"Your woman not in the party mood?" Ten pressed.

I gritted the back of my teeth. "She didn't go to the game." I tried not to let it show how much that bothered me. Most of the time, our games took place on Saturday afternoons; she wouldn't have classes or work—since she didn't even have a job. But she always had a reason for not attending them.

After listening to her belittle my position on the team, I knew football didn't mean much to her, so I didn't want to hold anything against her. But I had kind of hoped she'd want to attend at least one game, if for no other reason than to see *me* play.

"How the fuck could she not go to the game?" Ten frowned at me. "She's dating a starting player. A starting *sophomore* player. Doesn't that kind of make her a shitty girlfriend for not—"

"Stop," I warned, sending him a death glare. "She couldn't make it. Leave her alone."

"Her *roommate* made it." Ten lifted a challenging eyebrow. "I saw Blondie sitting with the Gamble family before the game started."

I narrowed my eyes, desperately wishing he hadn't brought *her* up. "Well, obviously *she* didn't have any·where else to be."

"Even Gamble's woman was there, and she has more reason not to step foot on campus than—"

I shoved abruptly to my feet, cutting into his tirade. I already knew he wasn't a Cora fan; I didn't want to listen to him bashing her a second longer. "You're taking care of the dishes this morning, right?" I asked. "Good." I walked out of the kitchen, leaving my stunned roommate gaping after me.

I was already a confused bundle of nerves; I didn't need

him irritating the situation. It didn't seem possible that someone could be upset with his girl-friend as well as worried about whatever secret she was keeping from him, all the while feeling guilty for having dreams about another girl. But there I was, experiencing something I was certain no one had ever experienced before.

When Cora called later in the day, I couldn't even talk to her because I didn't want her to hear all the guilt, upset, and worry in my voice. But then I grew even guiltier for avoiding her, so I called her back two minutes later.

She sounded tired, which made my guilt explode. I asked if she wanted me to come over and take care of her until I had to go into work that evening, but she said she and Zoey were going to spend the evening together. Girl stuff, she claimed. So I stayed away.

Monday progressed painfully. I spent extra time in the weight room that morning so I had to hurry through my shower. My hair was still wet when I rushed into art class. That was one miserable hour... and not because of my hair. When the scent of Zoey's shampoo wafted my way as soon as I sat down, I hardened my jaw and tried to breathe through my clenched teeth and not my nose. Then she went and smiled at me and told me hello, and congratulated me on the team's win. The entire time, I kept picturing that dream. The way her lips had pursed before she'd told me to lick her between the legs, the way her eyes had softened with need. I couldn't get that freaking dream *out* of my head.

What was worse, I had it again Monday night. Twice. Her and Cora both crawling all over me, kissing and licking things they shouldn't, taking me to new heights of pleasure. I won't even go into how sinfully, wickedly, deliciously awful both Tuesday and Wednesday nights were.

By Thursday, even my co-workers noticed some-thing was bothering me. Ten had actually been giving me my distance. But it only took Pick one glance when he'd been strolling out from the office before we opened to glance my way at the bar and slow to a stop.

"You doing okay, Hamilton?"

I nodded and mumbled something about being fine as I kept my attention on taking chairs off tables. Pick glanced toward Ten, who shook his head no, and I clenched my teeth, wishing my roommate would mind his own stupid business. Because of his headshake, Pick didn't let the issue drop.

Moving closer, he talked in a lower, more confidential tone. "What's going on? You got bags under your eyes. You been getting enough sleep?"

I shrugged, still not looking at him. "I've had a couple disturbing dreams," I admitted reluctantly, for-going to mention that I would then wake up and touch myself, each and every time, only feeling worse after each episode.

"Nightmares?" Pick asked, his brow knitted with concern.

He'd only been my boss for a few months. Before that, we were co-workers. But for as long as we'd worked together at Forbidden, he'd been the protector of the group, the paternal figure, though he couldn't even be five years older than the rest of us.

"Not quite nightmares," I admitted. "Just...things I shouldn't be dreaming about."

Pick understood immediately. His eyes sharpened as he lifted an eyebrow. "Or *people* you shouldn't be dreaming about?"

My face heated, and I wanted to fist my hand and hit something: a wall, the table, myself. I hated not being able to keep a straight face. Blushing had to be the freaking bane of my existence.

With a chuckle, Pick slapped me companionably on the back. Then he called across the bar to where Asher was sweeping up something from underneath a table in the corner. "Hey, Hart. You ever dream about a woman you shouldn't?"

Asher glanced up, looking surprised to be singled out. But then he grinned and shrugged. "I dreamt about *your* woman last week. She went down on me while I was singing on stage, and man...she had a sweet mouth."

My jaw fell open. I couldn't believe he'd so readily admitted such a thing...and to Pick's face. But Pick just chuckled and grinned approvingly. "Hell, yes she does."

I glanced between him and Asher, wondering why he wasn't more upset.

"I can do one better than that," Ten spoke up. "I had a dream once of Pick's woman going down on Lowe's woman."

Mason popped up from behind the bar to scowl at him, but Ten just lifted his eyebrows in challenge. "What? They may be cousins, but as close as those two are, you *know* they've at least kissed before."

Mason and Pick exchanged a knowing glance, to which Ten went crazy. "Holy shit, they *have*, haven't they? Fucking awesome. Did you guys *watch?*"

"We're not saying anything," Pick said, only to let out a huge grin.

"Well, hell," Noel spoke up from behind the bar. "Now I'm going to dream about those two ganging up on Aspen and going down on her."

As the guys laughed and started mixing and matching up which one of their women would star in their next wet dream, I shook my head. "So *all* of you have dreamed about...threesomes?"

Everyone stopped talking to stare at me as if I was insane. "We're guys," Mason finally answered. "So... yeah. Pretty much. Why wouldn't we?"

I blushed, not knowing how to answer that. I'd never had one of those dreams until this week. I had no idea they were supposed to be *normal?*

"Damn, it must've sucked growing up home-schooled by your widowed grandma," Noel murmured, sympathy ruling his gaze as he studied me.

I shook my head, because no, it hadn't. I'd loved my grandmother desperately. Finally being able to live with her after my mother had died had been a saving grace. I didn't even mind much that it left me socially clueless so much of the time. Gran had done the best she could for me, and I'd be eternally gratefully for that.

"I'm surprised you haven't picked up more shit from listening in on all that raunchy locker room gossip you must hear," Pick mused.

"I don't spend much time in the locker room." I hated changing in front of people because someone always asked about my scars, so I typically rushed to get in and out.

"Well, anyhow," Pick went on. "I wouldn't sweat a-bout any dream you have. I've had some crazy-ass dreams that don't mean shit. Okay, bud?"

I nodded, and strangely enough, I felt better. Listening to the guys openly admit to having thoughts about other women while over half of them were in committed, faithful, monogamous relationships let me know I wasn't as awful or alone as I thought. I was just a typical, flawed human.

NINETEEN

∞ ZOEY ∞

ONCE AGAIN, I couldn't sleep. Awake at two in the morning, I sat up in bed, turned on a night-light and began to write. I was quickly coming to realize the stories I wrote in the middle of the night were some of the craziest yet most colorful and eventful ideas I'd ever come up with.

So, I made me some hot chocolate and went to town. But as hot chocolate was wont to do, it went straight through me, so I had to pee before I could finish the last page of my short story.

My mind was elsewhere as I flushed, already planning out the final paragraphs. I didn't even realize the water was overflowing until I was washing my hands and cold wet toilet water crept in over my toes.

Yelping out a startled scream, I jumped back and gaped in horror as it kept flowing over the toilet seat.

"Oh my God. *No!*" I leapt forward, not sure what to do, but the water didn't stop flowing. Thinking there had to be a shut-off valve somewhere nearby, I peered behind the tank and tried to ignore the ick factor of more water covering my feet.

I was no plumber. I had no idea what did what, but I

knew I had to do something, so I turned hard on the first lever-looking thing I found.

And the stupid thing came off in my hand.

Water spurted out the hole I'd just created and sprayed me right in the face. I gasped and lifted my hands to protect myself.

No way was I going to touch anything else after that. Soaking wet, I sprinted out of the bathroom and pounded on Cora's door before shoving it open. "Cora! Cora?"

The light from the hallway splayed over an empty, neatly made bed.

Oh God. She couldn't be gone *now*.

Trying to calm myself, I blew out a breath, but I could hear the water still drenching the bathroom. Water dripped off my face and coated my clothes as I raced barefoot from the apartment and down the hall to the elevator. I would've run the entire eight flights down, because I was in a running mood, but the elevator was faster...even though it felt like it took forever since I had to just stand there and wait for it to take me to the ground floor.

Henry, the faithful doorman, was not in his usual spot. I stared wide-eyed and gripped my head, not sure what to do now. I was sure there had to be a super somewhere in the building who could help me, but Cora had never told me who or where to go for emergencies like these.

So I had to ride the elevator back up to our apartment and find my cell phone in my room to call her. But her phone immediately went to voice mail.

She'd told me she was going to spend the evening with Quinn before she'd left earlier, so I didn't even think. I called him next.

Surprisingly, he sounded awake when he answered on the second ring. "Hello?"

His voice sent a jolt through me, but I shook it off as quickly as possible. "Hi," I rushed out. "I'm so sorry for waking you. It's Zoey. I'm looking for Cora, but her phone's turned off. Please tell me she's still there."

"Still...here?" he sounded vaguely confused. "She's not with me if that's what you're asking. I thought she said she was doing something with you tonight. Everything okay?"

My roommate had lied. Again. What a surprise. But I had no time to dwell on that right now.

"Um...sure." I cringed. "No, not really. I broke...

something in the bathroom. Water is spraying everywhere, and I don't know how to turn it off or where the number for our building's superintendent is. Then Henry wasn't at the front door. And Cora's..." Who knew where Cora was.

"I'll be right there."

Even as my insides leapt with relief and joy, they shuddered with worry. Him, me, alone. Not such a good idea. "No, Quinn. You don't have to—"

But he'd already hung up.

Well...

I scowled at the dead phone, but the sound of rushing water from the bathroom called my attention back to things at hand. So I hustled down the hall and peered in at the disaster. Everything inside was splattered and drenched.

Hoping to catch as much of it as possible, I dashed to the kitchen and threw open cupboards, looking for as many bowls and pots and pans as I could find.

Ten minutes later, I'd devised a system where I held a bowl right over the direct spray and could aim it to pour into a pan on the floor. When that one got full, I aimed it to the next pot in line beside it and tried to wrangle the full bowl into the bathtub with one hand to drain it. My arms were screaming in agony; I wasn't sure how much longer I could keep this up. So it was a relief to hear someone knock on the front door.

Letting go of my hold on the main bowl, which let the water spray out again, I hurried to answer the door, hoping the building super had miraculously sensed a problem and was here to rescue me.

But it was Quinn.

"Is the water still on?" he asked, his gaze running over my soaked clothes and hair.

"Yes." Miserable and almost in tears, I clutched my wet head. "I have no clue how to turn it off."

He stepped into the apartment. "Let's have a look." I followed him back, nearly having to skip into a run to keep up with his long-legged stride. He wore a ball cap, tight black T-shirt and jeans that looked...really nice on him, especially when he bent over to reach for something behind the toilet.

Half a second later, the water stopped spraying him in the chest. He let out a sigh before he sat back on his haunches to glance over at me.

I scowled and crossed my arms over my wet chest. "Oh, that's not even *right* how fast you fixed that."

He grinned. "Sorry." Then his gaze skipped around the bathroom before he murmured, "Wow."

"You're telling me," I grumbled as I waded inside toward him. "Now show me what you did, so I'll know what to do the next time this happens."

"You just turn that lever there to turn the water off," he explained, stepping aside and pointing so I could squeeze in closer to see.

"Oh. Well, cool. That's actually what I would've chosen next. But I kind of lost my experimental nerve after the first doohickey thing I twisted came off in my hand."

Quinn chuckled and glanced at my row of pots and pans. "Yeah, I probably would've lost my experimental urge too."

I straightened and smiled at him as I wiped stray drops off my arms. "Thank you so much for coming. I don't know what I would've done without you. And you got here so fast."

"I wasn't too far away. I was driving home from work."

"Oh," I said lamely as my gaze spanned down to his outfit. He must get good tips if that was what he wore to work.

All wet like that, he looked really—

"Oh my God," I yelped, realizing *just* how wet he was. "I'm so sorry you got soaked."

"Looks like I wasn't the only one." When his gaze met mine, he grinned, and before I knew it, I was grinning back. Within seconds, we were laughing at the mess around us.

"Why don't you change into something dry," he finally suggested, "and I'll get started cleaning up in here?"

The very idea made me recoil in horror. I already felt awful about him having to come over and rescue me. No way was I leaving him here to clean what I had messed up. "But you're wet too," I argued.

He glanced briefly at my chest. "Not as wet as you are."

That's when I remembered I wasn't wearing a bra, and with my white nightshirt soaked through, he could see...everything. Flushing hard, I crossed my arms over my chest and retreated to my room to change.

Quinn had a good portion of the bathroom mopped dry with a heap of towels when I returned. And he'd dumped out all the pots and pans and put them back in the kitchen.

"Seriously, you didn't have to do all this," I said, shaking my head as I watched him toss that last wet towel into the hamper.

He merely shrugged as he took in the outfit I'd changed into: baggy flannel pants with frogs on them and an equally large, but dark T-shirt.

"It was no problem. You'd already had quite a night. I was happy to help."

I wasn't sure what to say to that. So I cleared my throat and glanced away. "Well...thank you...again. I have no idea how to repay you."

"No, you don't—" he started, waving his hand, only to pause and glance down the hall toward Cora's room. "Actually, do you mind if I stick around until Cora gets home? Just to make sure she's okay?"

My eyes grew big. Whoops. I'd kind of forgotten about Cora. "No, not at all. Here let me try her cell phone again. Maybe she was just out of service for a bit."

But Quinn shook his head. "I already tried. She still has it turned off."

"Oh. Well..." I kicked at a spot on the carpet. "*Psych* time?"

"Sure.' He nodded, looking glum, but started to follow when the wet squish under his shoes made me pause.

"You have to be miserable in those wet things. Do you have any extra clothes in Cora's room? I could throw the ones you're wearing in the dryer."

He scratched his ear, not looking very hopeful, but checked Cora's room anyway. He exited a minute later, wearing nothing but the sleep pants he wore on Saturday mornings when he made pancakes. My gaze dropped briefly to the wet shirt and jeans he gripped in his hand, but strayed right back to his bare, rippled chest.

But holy...moley.

Yeah, he looked good shirtless.

"This was the only thing I could find," he said softly, tugging bashfully at his pants.

I bobbed my head stupidly. "That's fine." And, wow, was it fine. *He* was fine. "At least you found something."

Actually, it was too bad he'd found anything, because Quinn Hamilton in nothing but his boxers had to look— yikes. I probably shouldn't let my mind stray there.

I bumbled forward jerkily and held out my hands for his wet clothes. He handed them over, looking a bit reluctant but letting me take them regardless.

I tore my attention from his chest and hurried his clothes to the utility room where I shoved them into the dryer and cranked it on.

When I found him in the living room, still gloriously shirtless, he'd settled on the couch and started up our show.

"Looks like you're already on season five," he said, appearing shocked by my progress.

"Yeah, I..." I tucked a piece of hair behind my ear. "I'm definitely a fan now."

He grinned at me. "That's so cool."

I knew I should've taken the side chair, but I could see the television from a better angle on the couch, with him, so I sat beside him, leaving a whole cushion of space between us.

He sent me another glance and then started the show.

When neither of us laughed at the first one-liner, I knew something was wrong. Quinn picked up his phone and glanced at the screen, and it struck me how worried he was.

I'd learned not to worry so much about Cora. She seemed like one of the most self-sufficient people I knew. When she needed help, she knew how to get it. I was almost glad he didn't know about her kidneys; he'd probably be through the roof right now.

I scooted closer to him and patted his knee. "She's okay." I was going to make sure she stayed okay. Just a few more months of testing, and she'd be as good as new again.

He glanced at me, his eyes swirling with misery. Then he blew out a breath and tugged me closer to him so he could wrap his arm around my shoulder.

Tipping his face to the side until our heads touched, he murmured, "Yeah," but he didn't sound so sure of his claim. "I bet she's fine."

We fell asleep that way, watching *Psych,* pressed up against each other with his arm around my shoulder and my cheek resting against his shoulder.

Cora woke us when she unlocked the front door. Yawning and stretching, we stirred to find the show was long over. We were getting to our feet when she stumbled inside.

She faltered to a stop, glancing between us. "What's going on?" She focused on Quinn. "Where's your shirt?"

"It's in the dryer. Where have *you* been?"

She pulled back, blinking as if she couldn't believe he'd dare to answer her question with another question. "I was out working on a group project for my World Geography class. I told you that. Why are you here, alone, with my *roommate*?"

He glanced at me, answering, "She called, looking for you. She thought you were with me. I thought you were with *her*."

I thought I detected a bit of accusation in his voice, so I quickly said, "The water line to the toilet broke and I didn't know how to turn it off or how to get a hold of the super. You weren't answering your phone."

She looked down and pulled her phone from her purse. "Oh, I must've turned it off. Hmm. Wonder when I did that." She turned it on and checked over the half a dozen or so messages from both Quinn and me. Then she looked up and smiled at us brightly. "So...everything's fixed now?"

"No," Quinn said. "The line's still broken. You'll need to get a hold of your super." Then he leaned in and sniffed her. "You smell like alcohol."

She scowled. "Well, yeah. We finished the project a couple hours ago and then went out for a few drinks. Is that okay with you, *dad*?"

He nodded even as he answered, "I just...I could swear you said you were staying in and doing something with Zoey tonight."

"Are you sure?" When he kept bobbing his head up and down, she sighed and pressed her hand to her temple. "I don't know, maybe I did say that. But I meant I was going to work on the group project with Sydney and Kallie and all of them in my World Geo class." When Quinn didn't respond, she looked at him. "You believe me, *right*?"

Again he stayed silent, but he swished his head up and down, letting her know he did believe her.

"Good." She let out an exhausted sigh. "Well, I'm beat, so I'm going to bed."

When she started down the hall, Quinn followed her. He went into her bedroom with her, and then he shut the door.

I slumped against the wall and hugged myself. I felt sick because I knew what he was going to be doing with her. And I felt even sicker because I could've sworn Cora told me she was going to be with Quinn tonight. But why would she lie to both of us?

TWENTY

⚜ ZOEY ⚜

"WANT TO RIDE to class together?"

Cora's question made me stumble to a halt just as I reached the front door of our apartment Friday morning. After the night I'd had dealing with the plumbing, my limbs were sore and my head ached from how exhausted I was, but strangely enough, I felt kind of exhilarated.

My roommate's question warmed me from the inside. This might've been the first time since the car wash that she'd asked me to do anything with her that didn't involve her health. But she just had to pick the worst day ever to ask, didn't she? For once, I actually had plans.

"Sorry." I winced in genuine apology. "But I'm going over to Caroline's straight after class."

Caroline wanted me to go to the show with her tonight and watch the newest bartender at Forbidden sing with his band for the first time. It'd also be a first for me. It'd be the first time I'd step inside a bar. We were supposed to go to her place this afternoon after classes and get ready together.

"Where's Quinn?" I asked, thinking Cora could ride to class with him since he'd stayed the night.

But that question made her eyes narrow. "He had to leave early for his morning weight training session."

I winced. He'd gotten off work at two thirty last night, and then stayed up later to help me. And then he had to go in early for weight lifting? I suddenly had no reason whatsoever to complain about being tired. Poor guy.

Stepping between me and the door, Cora crossed her arms over her chest. "Well, I was going to have this discussion in the car, but since you obviously already have *plans...*" She sneered the word as if she couldn't believe I'd make my own plans. It made me feel guilty because I was here in this town for her, to make sure she stayed healthy. What was I doing, going out with Caroline to football games and con·certs?

"Are you okay?" I asked, immediately concerned. "Did one of your tests—"

"I'm fine." She rolled her eyes and sighed. "This is about Quinn."

I blinked, totally confused. "Quinn?"

"*Yes!* Your crush on my boyfriend is getting a little ridiculous."

Not at all expecting her to say that, I stumbled back a step and pressed my hand to my heart. "Wha—no... *Excuse me?*"

I couldn't even believe...

Yeah, I was too flabbergasted to think.

"I mean, it was cute at first," Cora went on in the most conversational tone as my jaw dropped farther and farther. "This is probably the first time you've actually liked someone from the opposite gender. Right? I mean, for a while there, in high school, I thought you were a lesbian and into me, but... no...from the way you watch my boyfriend, like *all* the time, it's obvious you're definitely into guys. I just hope you know you could never have him."

"I...I..." Heat infused my face...and my chest...and my stomach. I didn't even know what to say to that. So I fumbled out a few more unintelligible words before sputtering, "Oh my God, Cora. I have never...not even once thought your boyfriend would—"

"Good," Cora said perkily, clasping her hands together. "Because even if you tried, he'd never go for someone like *you.* He's into much more knowledge·able, sophisticated women. Naive, gullible little innocents just aren't to his taste."

My heart flopped heavily into my stomach, not only because it hurt to hear how I could never get a guy like Quinn because I was too...*me*, but just knowing she felt the need to warn me away from him, as if she thought I'd even *try* to steal him from her, was just...yeah. Insane.

"I don't know why you even feel the need to say this to me." I shook my head. "You know *me*! I'd never...*ever*..."

"You're right." Cora smiled as if pleased. She patted my arm and stepped aside to let me go. "I do know better. I guess I was just getting a little possessive of the man I love."

Hearing her say the L-word rattled me more than I cared to admit, and I had to look at anything but her while I nodded, agreeing with her assessment.

"Thank goodness that's all settled then. Have fun at school."

I shook my head, feeling more unsettled than ever before. I stared at her a moment, then I had to say, "I think you should tell him, though. He deserves to know. Quinn is a really good—"

Cora lifted her fingers to stop me mid-word. Then she narrowed her gaze. "Yes, he is a really good guy. But he's *my* guy. Not yours. It's completely my decision what I do with him and what I tell him." She stepped threateningly closer. "And if you ever even *think* about interfering with that, or telling him what I don't wish for him to know, you'll regret it for the rest of your life. Understand?"

I couldn't even respond to that. I simply brushed past her and hurried from the apartment. But I felt cold, deep inside, all the way to school.

What was worse, Quinn was already in art class, sitting in the chair next to mine when I arrived. And then he had to go and smile at me as if he were happy to see me.

"Hey, did you get the super called this morning?"

"Yeah." I nodded vaguely, unable to look him in the eye as I sank into the chair next to him. "Cora showed me where the number was kept." *And then she threatened me to stay away from you and keep secrets from you.*

When I dared to meet his gaze, he was watching me strangely, as if he knew something was wrong. I offered him a tight smile, but my chest was constricted with fear and worry. "He said he could get to it tomorrow."

Quinn nodded and then opened his mouth to say something, but thank goodness Caroline and Reese interrupted, calling out to me and asking for my opinion on shades of fingernail polish. They were both excited about the concert that evening, so for the rest of the hour, I whisper-gossiped with them and made a point to ignore Quinn completely, even though it hurt to turn my back to him.

He tried to talk to me as soon as class let out, but I sent the group a big, fake smile and waved goodbye before hightailing it out of there.

My nerves were jittery and strung out; I was al-ready on edge when I entered my writing class later on. And that's when I learned we were having open critique.

∾ QUINN ∾

SOMETHING WAS up with Zoey.

Despite the lack of sleep, I'd actually felt rejuvenated when I'd woken this morning.

Last night had gone so well. If ever a guy were to fall prey to temptation, it would've been when he was stuck alone in close quarters and half-dressed with the girl who made his thoughts stray. But I hadn't done one inappropriate thing with Zoey. It felt as if I'd passed some kind of test.

Knowing I could one hundred percent behave myself around Cora's roommate, I felt good and refreshed, and ready to befriend her without any reservations.

I'd sought her out in the library a couple times before, but every time I'd actually seen her sitting at a table studying, I'd been too much of a coward to approach, worried about anything and everything happening. But now that I knew nothing *would* happen, I wanted to see her. Something had definitely been bothering her in art class, and I had to make sure she was okay.

As luck would have it, I caught sight of her entering the library when I was still a few buildings away. Her back was to me as she skipped up the steps. She looked like she was in a hurry, so I picked up my pace to catch her. But when I entered, she was nowhere in sight.

I checked out a couple of the tables I'd seen her sitting at in the past, but they were all occupied by others. She had to be somewhere in the building, but the library was a big place with lots of private nooks and crannies for secluded studying.

I had an entire hour to kill, so I just kept looking. When I came to an area that was rarely inhabited, I turned down a row of bookshelves and saw her sitting on the floor at the end, against the wall with her knees drawn up to her chest and her head bowed, her hair covering her face.

There was something "wounded animal"-like about the way she was sitting. Charging forward with concern seemed like a bad idea. So...as I crept closer, I whispered. "Zoey?"

Her head flew up, and she stared at me from wide, tearstained eyes.

My heart cracked. I'd never seen her cry before, and she looked so lost and alone. I wanted to yank her into my arms and cradle her close just as much as I wanted to hunt down whoever had hurt her and pulverize them.

"What's wrong?" I eased to my knees next to her.

"Nothing." She eyed me warily but didn't skitter away.

I arched an eyebrow, letting her know it was definitely not nothing.

She blew out a breath and stared forward, wiping frantically at her cheeks. "It's really...nothing," she repeated. "It's stupid."

Situating myself so I was sitting beside her on the floor with my knees bent up and the shadows covering us in our little nook, I waited until she stopped trying to pat her face back into order before I said, "It's not stupid to *you*."

She glanced at me. "But it's probably stupid to *you*."

"I still want to hear about it."

After shaking her head, she hugged her knees tighter and went back to staring straight ahead as if I wasn't beside her.

Knowing she wasn't going to instigate our talk, I cleared my throat. "When I was little, I hated it when my mom drank. She was nicer when she was sober, hit me less, treated me as an actual human being. It was when she had alcohol in her that everything went bad. So I went to the library and did all kinds of re-search about how to stop drinking. I came up with a, I don't know, a kind of step-by-step program to help her quit. I drew up a bunch of posters and graphs and spent nearly a month to create this little presentation to help her, because everything I read said alcoholism was a disease. I thought she'd *thank* me if she saw how much work I'd gone through to help save her."

"What'd she do?" Zoey whispered, her eyes wide with worry as she glanced at me.

"She got mad." I watched a new tear glisten on Zoey's cheek, and I wanted to wipe it away. "She threw a beer bottle at me and yelled at me for being such a freak. Then she chased me until she caught me in my bedroom. She hit me until I passed out, and...I don't remember anything else after that."

Zoey shuddered and hugged herself. "I kind of *prefer* passing out during a beating. I don't like remembering...or feeling it."

I reached over slowly and unpeeled her fingers off her forearm from where she was hugging herself, then I squeezed her hand gently. "Will you please tell me why you're so upset? I know what it feels like to think something's important, only to find out someone else thinks it's stupid. I promise I won't think any less of you. I just want to help."

She lowered her face and sniffed. "We had open critique in my writing class today."

I pulled her hand against my chest and squeezed it a little bit harder. She didn't have to tell me she'd gotten some bad comments about her story. She wouldn't be sitting here, sobbing, if it'd gone okay.

I didn't say anything, just stroked the knuckles on her hand and waited for her to talk. A minute later, she sniffed again, blew out a shuddery breath, and wiped at her cheek with the back of her free hand. "Not one person liked it. It was stupid, silly, immature. The teacher went into a big long tirade about the differences between true literature and... and...whatever drivel I'd written. Talking animals are bad. Stories with no connection to the human condition are worthless—"

"Now wait a second," I butted in, frowning. "*The Silver Belt* had all kinds of connections to deeper things. And the frog in that was the funniest character in the entire story."

Zoey jerked her face up, her eyes wide as she blinked them. "Y-you actually read *The Silver Belt* already? All of it?"

"Well...yeah. And it connected with me, like, really well. I kept thinking about it long after I finished. How Truman always felt like he was on the outside of everything, left out as if he was missing the biggest step of how to be a true fisherman. I feel that way practically every day. Not about fishing, but other things. And I'm serious about that frog. You're not allowed to take him out of that story."

She gave a watery laugh, and I swear, watching her smile made my entire day. "You really liked him?" she asked, her voice uncertain.

"I've read it three times," I said. "So I don't think the problem is your writing. It was just...your audience. I don't think they wanted to teach you to be a better writer, they wanted to teach you to write a certain way. I just hope you know not everyone wants to read their kind of stories. Some of us prefer the talking animals. And there's nothing wrong with that."

She nodded and brushed the last of her tears off her face. "Okay. Thank you." Her eyes lifted to mine. The trust and gratitude I saw made my chest fill with this awesome pressure. "I just wish I would've known that before I turned in my first story."

I pulled her closer and gave her a one-armed hug. "So do I." Because I seriously hated to see her cry.

"Thank you again, Quinn. I don't know what I would've done if you hadn't come along and—"

"Hey, no problem." I bumped my shoulder into her to get her to look at me. Then I grinned, flashing my dimple in pleading. "Just promise you'll let me read more of your talking animals, and we'll call it even."

She rolled hers eyes but grinned back. "You don't seriously want to read more."

"Heck, yes, I do." I stood up, dusted off my pants and then held down a hand to her. "Until then, what do you say? Want to work on some biology?"

Groaning as she stood, she gifted me with a dry glance. "No. But...I probably should. You're a better teacher than the professor."

I grinned. "Thank you. Now let's find a table around here and get our geek on."

When I tightened my grip on her hand, she tightened hers right back. I felt good that hour, helping her with her homework and making silly jokes about people against talking animals. She finally loosened up enough to joke back with me. I was never so happy that I'd been able to get past my physical reaction to her so we could finally be friends.

Because I *really* liked being Zoey's friend.

Twenty-One

⚜ Zoey ⚜

My FIRST TRIP to the Forbidden Nightclub to watch the band Non·Castrato play their first gig started with me full of nerves.

Not surprising, huh?

Since Caroline was adamant that I go with her, I drove to her place as soon as classes let out. She claimed she had "the dress" she wanted me to wear.

I wasn't really a dress person, but she kind of sucked me into her enthusiasm, so I agreed and even started to get excited about it, too.

I met her two younger brothers—the older one, Brandt at fourteen, even flirted with me, making me blush, which in turn made Caroline chase him away. Then I met her brother's girlfriend, Aspen...officially. Caroline had also talked Aspen into going. But I could tell as soon as I arrived that the poor ex·teacher was a quivering ball of nerves.

Caroline forced us both into dresses, short ones that fell way above our knees, and tops that con·formed sexily to our figures. Then she went and put pants on herself. When I asked what *that* was about, she waved a hand, saying, "Pfft. I don't have anyone to impress," which really confused me because I didn't have anyone to impress either. But when I said that, she merely sent me an unreadable Mona Lisa·

type smile and said, "You look great. You're wearing it."

I'm not sure if I really looked that great, but it was soft and it made me feel pretty, so I gave in. And I think Aspen felt the same way. But even as she longingly eyed her reflection in the mirror, she made it seem like she didn't want to leave the boys home alone.

"Are you sure you're okay with heating up leftovers for supper?" she asked Brandt.

He snorted. "That's how we ate every night before moving here."

Aspen paled and opened her mouth, probably to say she wasn't going to leave them alone, but Brandt waved her on "We'll be fine. Just go. Have fun. Make Noel sweat by showing up, looking like that."

Biting her lip, Aspen nodded and was helplessly swept along as Caroline hooked her arms through Aspen's and then mine.

"I don't know about you two, but I'm totally looking forward to tonight. I'm feeling good vibes."

I was mostly just feeling nervous vibes, but I hoped she had more reliable vibes than I did.

We arrived before the club opened. Caroline tapped on the front glass doors until her brother appeared on the other side. He grinned when he saw us, and let us in. His eyes were only for Aspen.

"I couldn't believe it when Caroline texted and told me she'd talked you into coming. I swear you haven't been here since..." His eyebrows lifted and Aspen blushed while they shared an inside secret.

After he pointed at Caroline and said, "Behave," he grabbed Aspen's hand and swept her away toward the bar, leaving Caroline and me behind. We glanced at each other as we huddled together just inside the entrance. One bartender was in the back behind the bar, setting up a row of glasses while a handful of waitresses pulled chairs off the tables and four guys milled around the staging area. No one seemed to pay any attention to the pair of us.

"Have you ever been here before?" I asked.

She shook her head but hooked her arm through mine. "I guess we'll learn our way around together."

We didn't have to worry long about where to go, though; someone started tapping on the glass doors behind us. Caroline glanced around only to grin. Hurrying to the entrance, she pulled the door open for a waving Reese.

"Thank goodness you're here. Zoey and I have no clue where to go."

"Hey, chickie." Reese pulled her into a half hug. "Let me show you guys around then." She swept out an arm. "This...is Forbidden. There's the bar, the stage, and that hall there leads back to a kitchen, office, bathroom, storage and a new private reception room. And that's about all there is. Except for this..." She'd led us to the bar where she rested her elbows on the countertop and half leaned over it so she could ogle the guy behind the counter with his back to us as he finished stacking a row of glass cups.

"Oh, sexy bartender," she sang out. "I think you dropped something there. You really ought to...*bend over* and pick it up."

Instead of bending, the bartender whirled around and sent her a devastating grin. "What're you doing here so early?"

Batting her lashes, Reese sent him her own smoky smile. "I couldn't stay away from you."

Striding to her, he grabbed the front of her shirt and pulled her even further over the bar until she was more than halfway hanging over his side. Then he kissed her hard and long.

Feeling hot around the collar after witnessing such a scorcher, I glanced Caroline's way to find her looking back at me with raised eyebrows.

"*Wow*," she mouthed the word as she fanned herself. We started laughing in unison.

Reese unlocked her lips from the bartender and grinned back at us. "Oh, sorry! Caroline, you've al·ready met him, so...Zoey, this is my boyfriend, Ma·son." Then she rolled her eyes and slapped her hand to her forehead. "I mean, my *fiancé*, Mason."

Caroline snickered and bumped her elbow into mine. "Yeah, I think she kind of figured that out al·ready."

Mason chuckled. "Hi again, Caroline." Then he glanced at me, "And Zoey. Reese described you perfectly."

Reese let out a dreamy·sounding sigh. "Isn't it awesome? He actually *listens* when I ramble." When she leaned in for another kiss, Mason seemed eager to supply her with one.

They were still locking lips when a new guy exited the back hall. Face full of piercings and arms laden with tattoos, he scowled when he caught sight of the necking couple. "Hey! No baby-making on my counter, please." He smacked Reese lightly on the butt, making her yelp and jump away from Mason. Then he winked up at her. "Not unless you have a little loving for me, too."

"Hey, cousin." Reese dutifully smacked a kiss to his cheek and wrapped her arm around his neck as he wrapped one around her waist to pull her off the bar top and back onto the floor.

Folding his arms over his chest, Mason just scowled at them. Reese was too busy asking the newcomer to notice, though.

"Where's my girl?" she asked.

"She's back in the office, still looking for her panties."

"Pick!" Gasping, Reese smacked his arm. "That was way more than I wanted to know."

He just chuckled and brought attention to his pocket as he stuffed a peek of cloth deeper out of sight. "So I really shouldn't tell you she's not going to find them, huh?"

Reese rolled her eyes and seemed to notice Caroline and me lurking nearby. "Oh, you need to meet Zoey. Zoey, Pick. Pick, Zoey."

Curious brown eyes veered to us. "So, this is the beauty I've heard so much about lately? It's a pleasure."

Caroline and I exchanged confused glances before Pick came forward and took each of our hands in a warm greeting. "Long time no see, lovely Caroline." After he smiled at her, he turned to me, "And Zoey. Welcome to Forbidden."

"Hey, I want in on the introductions."

One of the guys from the band strolled over. When I turned, he had his gaze set on Caroline. "It's about time I got to meet you two. The way the guys talk, I feel like we're old pals already."

Realizing he was Asher, the new bartender Reese had gushed about, I studied him a bit more intently. He was slimmer than the other bartenders but had a very arresting face with lips that were probably too pretty for a boy but looked good on him. His eyes were a sparkling green and his dark hair was longish and styled to the side.

Caroline and I shared a look, and I knew she was thinking exactly what I was thinking. Yowza.

Simultaneously, we turned back to him.

"I didn't realize we were famous," she said. "What exactly does everyone say about us?"

His grin grew mischievous. "Oh, you know. Caroline and Zoey did this today. Caroline and Zoey did that. The way I hear it, you guys are quite a pair."

Caroline shook her head, looking as dazed as I felt when we shared another glance, this one confused. "We really don't do all that much, actually. But, wow, I didn't realize my brother took so much interest in everything we did."

Asher's eyes sparkled as he leaned in to her, lowering his voice. "I didn't say it was your brother who was always talking about you."

Her lips parted as a look of awe spread across her face. We both knew if it wasn't Noel feeding everyone the gossip, then that left only two people who could possible know so much about us...two other Forbidden bartenders who shared an art class with us.

"Then, who..." She shook her head, but her eyes lit with hope.

Asher merely winked. "You'll never get me to tell." Patting her shoulder and mine both, he glanced be-tween us before adding, "Thanks for coming to watch me sing tonight. I hope you like the show."

And then he was strolling off, making us gape after him. Caroline leaned in closer to me. "Oh, yeah. I like him."

I nodded dumbly. He definitely had a certain appeal.

"Patrick Jason Ryan!" a blonde screeched, march-ing out from the back hall, where she stopped and set her fists sternly on her hips.

Pick lifted his face from the cash drawer he was slotting into the register. "Yes, my love?"

"Oh, don't you give me that innocent little smile. You know what you took from me." She held out her hand, palm up. "Give them back."

He just grinned. "Now, you know better than that. That's not how to go about getting anything from me, Tink."

Tink's eyes lit with pleasure and she murmured, "You're right. I know a much better way to get what I want from you."

But when she went to stroll toward him, Reese lifted her hands and squeezed her eyes shut. "For the love of God, just give her undies back already. I swear, the two of you are even making my unborn babies blush."

"Ree Ree," Tink cheered, when she saw Reese. "I didn't know you were here already."

They came together and hugged. While Tink had blonde hair and Reese had dark, I could still tell they were related from the shape and color of their eyes.

"And look." Reese steered Tink around to face us. "Caroline and Zoey are here, too."

"Zoey?" Eva pulled back and glanced around blindly until her gaze settled on me. "You mean, *the* Zoey?"

She sounded as if she couldn't believe it, but when Reese nodded, she studied me up and down, before a knowing smile lit her face. "You were exactly right about her, Ree Ree."

Reese just laughed. "Of course I was."

I glanced between them, but neither seemed willing to let me in on the joke, so I had no idea what Reese had been right about. It must not have been anything bad, though, because Eva came to me and immediately pulled me into an enormous hug. After greeting Caroline, she returned to me and looped an arm around my shoulder to ask me all kinds of get-ting-to-know you questions, like my year in college and what my major was. After I politely answered everything, she shook her head and glanced toward Reese again. "I can't believe it," she murmured, sounding almost in awe. "She's freaking perfect for him."

"Wait, what?" I blushed at the unexpected comment. "Who're we talking about?"

But Eva just tsked at me and patted my cheek. "Oh, honey, you'll figure it out soon enough. Just know, Reese and I will be cheering you on the entire time."

"Um..." I shook my head, completely confused. "O-kay."

Eva glanced at Caroline. "And we're cheering for you and..." She glanced around before turning back to us, "*your* other half, too."

Caroline glanced at me and lifted her eyebrows. I shrugged, so she shrugged, too. "Thank you?" she finally told Eva as if it was more of a question than an answer.

I felt strangely elated after that. I still had no idea what was going on with all the other-half talk, but Eva seemed to accept me, so a giddy little smile stole over my face.

I liked the Forbidden Nightclub.

Caroline must've felt the same because she leaned in to whisper, "I think we've been accepted into the inner circle."

She sounded ecstatic about that idea.

I glanced at her, hoping she was right, when Pick clapped his hands together.

"Time to open. You guys ready for this?" he asked the band. Asher sent him a thumbs-up. Pick glanced toward the waitresses and then the bar, where his brows lowered into a scowl. "Wait. We only have one bartender. Where the hell is Gamble?"

"Right here," Noel called as he exited the back hall, one hand laced possessively with a blushing Aspen's.

Pick sniffed. "Oh, how the tables have turned. Wasn't it *you* who used to rag on me about always being late to work?"

Noel scowled back at him as he led Aspen forward. "I'm not late. I've been here the entire time."

"And seeing to the extreme comfort of our customers too, it seems." Setting his gaze on Aspen, he sent her a grin and extended a hand to her. "Hey again, beautiful. Nice to see you tonight."

Aspen took his hand and he aptly stole her away from Noel, leading her to the bar. "You should watch the show from here. Best seat in the house." He helped her up until she was sitting on the counter instead of on a barstool. Then he glanced around. "Tinker Bell?"

"Right here, lover." Eva ran her hand up his back until he turned to her and grinned.

He kissed her on the mouth, lingering before he asked, "Can I help you up?"

She nuzzled her nose against his. "Please do."

Reese popped up beside Eva and patted the open space beside her. "Caroline. Zoey. Sit with us."

Caroline hurried over and I trailed behind. It felt like we were getting VIP treatment to sit on top of the bar. After Caroline seated herself beside Reese, I hesitated. It didn't feel as if I belonged with these people. They were so nice and full of outgoing vivacity. I felt like a great big blah of an outsider.

Pick glanced at me and held out a hand. "Need some help up?"

"Oh!" I gulped, touched by his invitation. No matter how I felt, though, it seemed they were accepting me with a warm welcome. Unable to turn him down, I took his hand and stepped onto the bottom rung before hoisting myself up next to Caroline. "Thank you."

"Now there's a sight for sore eyes," Pick said, glancing appreciatively down the counter at the five of us women. "You ladies sure know how to decorate my nightclub." He paused in front of Eva to give her another kiss before he wandered toward Asher, who was lingering around the base of the stage and fiddling with a few wires.

One of the waitresses had unlocked the doors. A doorman had appeared somewhere and was letting a line of people in through the entrance. And the place was beginning to fill.

"Any of you ladies thirsty?" Noel asked. "I know the only one here not underage is Aspen, so...can I get you some sodas?"

Caroline groaned and rolled her eyes, while Reese said, "Mason can get my drink."

"Mine too," Eva was quick to add.

When Caroline opened her mouth, her brother pointed at her warningly. "No way. You're just getting soda."

As she scowled and narrowed her eyes, I spoke up. "I'll take a Sprite."

Noel grinned approvingly at me before glancing pointedly at his sister. Her shoulder slumped as she mumbled, "One for me too, I guess."

We'd just gotten our drinks and were slurping from the straws when Caroline tensed beside me. "Oh God. Oren's here," she said under her breath as she leaned in close.

I turned to watch the bouncer let him into the club. A pair of guys immediately jumped on him from behind and greeted him with tackles and laughs.

"I can't believe he came tonight since he doesn't have to work." Poor Caroline. She seemed so tense and on edge as she fiddled with her straw and watch-ed every move he made.

"Maybe he wanted to see the band perform too."

She didn't answer, probably hadn't even heard me.

So I watched him too as he made his way through the crowd. I was a little jealous how personable he was. He seemed to know everyone, girls and guys a-like. When one girl he greeted lifted up onto her tip-toes to whisper something into his ear and make him grin, I reached out and grasped Caroline's hand. She clutched my fingers for dear life.

He finally noticed us when he turned toward the bar, or maybe it was the row of five women sitting on the countertop that caught his attention. But his gaze lingered on Caroline before he ordered a bottled beer from Noel.

Finally, he approached us, swaggering closer. I thought Caroline was going to squeeze my fingers clean off.

"Well, if isn't a whole *row* of untouchables," he mused, glancing down at the five of us as he took a sip. He looked almost sad as his gaze slid over Caro-line and kept going.

But Eva cheerfully called, "Ten-Ten, what're you talking about *untouchables*? You can come over here and touch me any time you want. If you get too inappropriate, my man'll just knock your head off."

"Invitation accepted." He moved to her. "Hey, Milk Tits. You still breastfeeding those kids of yours?"

She rolled her eyes but perked out her chest. "What do you think?"

"Oh, yeah." He laughed and rested his arm on her leg as he drank his beer and gazed out into the gathering crowd. He didn't seem to be in any hurry to leave, which didn't help ease Caroline's grip on my hand at all.

Yikes. I wondered how long it'd take for permanent damage to set in since there was obviously no blood circulating to my fingertips.

"*Zoey*? Is that you?"

I glanced around at the call and blinked when I saw Cora.

"Hey!" She climbed up onto the bar beside me and engulfed me in a huge hug, which I stiffly returned. The last time I'd seen her, she'd been threatening me to stay away from her boyfriend. And now...now apparently we were back to being friends.

Bipolar much?

"I didn't know you were coming tonight," she called over the growing noise of the club.

"Yeah, I...Caroline invited me," I said, then I couldn't help but glance over her shoulder, looking for *him*.

And there he was.

Twenty-Two

⋙ Zoey ⋘

WHEN I SPOTTED Quinn ordering drinks from Ma·son further down the bar, my heart skipped a beat. Then I remembered how Cora had chastised me for always looking at him just this morning. I forced my attention to her.

My roommate sent me a knowing little smirk but kept talking as if we were still on good terms. "Isn't it crazy; we've both been so busy this semester, we've barely had time to talk. And yet here we end up together at the same club." When she spotted who was sit·ting beside me, her gaze cooled. "Oh, hi, Caroline."

Before Caroline could answer, Ten called, "Wow, they're just letting *anyone* in tonight, aren't they?"

Cora scowled right back. "I wasn't talking to you, dick breath."

"Hey, hey, hey," Eva cut in, petting Ten soothingly on top of his head. "No one calls our Ten·Ten a dick breath but me."

"So, *ha*." Ten sneered at her. "Take that, whore."

Cora opened her mouth to spit something back, but Quinn showed up with two glasses, diffusing the tension in the air. He carried something pink with fruit floating in it and another cup that looked exactly like what I was

183

drinking.

"Hi, Quinn," Caroline greeted, making me blush because I probably should've said hello too instead of just ogling him like a moron.

He glanced at her in surprise. "Oh! Hi." Then his gaze moved on to Reese and Eva before swerving back to Caroline's other side where I sat. When he found me, his scanning stopped. "Hi," he called again. "I didn't know you were going to be here."

I shrugged. "Caroline," was all I had to say in explanation as I tipped my head her way.

He smiled as if he understood. "I had to coax Cora into coming too, so I could watch Asher's first performance."

As he handed Cora the pink drink, Eva opened her arms to him. "Quinn! My hero. Come give me some sweetness, you handsome thing."

Quinn ducked his face slightly but obliged, step-ping onto the first rung of the stool in front of her so he could reach her. She enveloped his large frame and then smacked a kiss to his cheek.

Sneering, Cora leaned into me. "He only puts up with that bitch because she's doing his boss."

I wasn't so sure about that. It seemed like Quinn was genuinely fond of Eva. I remembered the gunshot wound he had on his arm from saving her life. He had to like her, even if it was just a little. When he pulled away, he smiled one last time and nodded before finding his way back to Cora's side.

"So which one is this Asher guy?" Cora asked, possessively curling her arms around his shoulders from behind.

"He's the lead singer." Quinn pointed as the band took stage.

Wrapping her legs around his chest next, Cora rested her chin on top of his head and checked out Asher. "He's cute,' she finally decided right before her fingers trailed down the front of Quinn's chest. "But not as cute as you."

I thought I was going to be sick so I quickly took a drink of my Sprite, only to realize Caroline's fingers were wiggling in mine.

Oops. I guess I'd been the one squeezing too hard this time.

Beginning the evening's events, Asher stepped to the

microphone and introduced Non-Castrato. Caro-line tapped her hand on my leg, showing me just how excited she was. Pick appeared in front of us to boot Ten aside so he could rest *his* arm on Eva's leg. So Ten moved down the line and ended up closer to Caroline, Cora, Quinn and me.

"For our first song, we're going to do something a little different. We've already gotten our first request from a very persistent fellow. So we're going to cover this song for his woman."

"Aww, that's so sweet," Caroline said with a smile.

"Pick, please don't tell me you made them play our song?" Eva demanded as the drumbeat counted off.

"No," Pick muttered, "but now I'm pissed at who-ever did, because that was a damn good idea."

As the music began, I realized they were playing Adele's "Rolling in the Deep," but they'd layered a little heavier of a rock beat to it.

"Oh, this is Aspen's favorite song," Caroline said, just before we heard a gasp from the end of the line, as Noel snagged his girlfriend around the waist before pulling her back off the bar until she was on the ground with him.

They hugged each other and kissed, and Asher began to sing. His voice was perfect, not like Adele's but something just as amazing and raspy that fit the heavier beat.

Aspen and Noel began to dance with each other, and Caroline's eyes watered as she covered her mouth. "That is so freaking sweet. I had no idea my brother was such a romantic."

"Disgusting, isn't it?" Ten asked.

Caroline sniffed and sent him a glare, bumping his shoulder with her knee.

My glaze slid unwillingly to Quinn. His lips had tipped up in a smile as he watched Noel and Aspen. Then, as if he felt my stare, he looked up. Instead of frowning at me for staring, his smile only widened. Then he returned his attention to the main couple.

But my chest still pounded from that half of a second we'd shared.

I shook my head. I was so pathetic. I couldn't believe I had such a raging crush on my roommate's boy-friend. Bad enough that Cora even knew about it, now I was longing for stolen little glances that probably meant nothing to him.

No wonder Cora had been so nasty and unfriendly to me

lately. She probably thought I was actually going to try to steal him.

I forced my attention back to Noel and Aspen just as the song drew to a close. Noel let go of Aspen to kneel down in front of her and pull a ring from his pocket.

Caroline gasped. "Oh my God. *Oh my God!*"

Aspen took a step back, and her mouth fell open as tears filled her eyes.

I couldn't hear the actual proposal from where I sat, but I could tell what her response was when she leapt at him, hugging him and kissing him.

"Dude," Ten spoke up. "I can't believe you're freaking proposing to a break-up song."

"Shut up," Caroline hissed, slapping his shoulder. "Before I punch you in the nuts."

"What?" He glanced at her in shock before he motioned to Noel and Aspen, who were still kissing. "I'm just saying...that can't be good luck."

"It's her favorite song. Who cares what the lyrics say?"

Ten snorted. "Obviously no one." He turned away, taking a huge gulp of his beer, and focused his attention on Asher singing.

I watched the tense set of his shoulders and the tormented expression on Caroline's face before glancing away to focus back on Noel and Aspen. But, yeah, they were still connected at the mouth.

"Wow." I turned away from the bar completely to face outward. "They're really going at it."

Next to me, Cora laughed. "Oh, Zoey. You poor innocent little virgin. Look at your blush."

To my mortification, she said it loud enough that all the Forbidden people could no doubt hear her. Just wanting to sink into a hole and die, I continued to blush as she went on. "We totally need to get you some experience. Quinn, baby, let's set Zoey up with one of your single friends. We could do a double date."

Quinn froze and sent her a look that told her going on a double date with me was the last thing he wanted to do. It was the last thing I wanted to do, too. I didn't want to see him and Cora hanging all over each other any more than necessary, much less purposely trap myself into a front row seat of watching it all night long. But knowing Quinn didn't want to spend an evening with me either, hurt.

Why didn't he want to hang out with me?

I opened my mouth to tell Cora there was no way I'd go on a double date with her and Quinn—blind dates equaled hell in my book—when Ten suddenly turned to us.

"I'll do it."

Everyone stopped drinking whatever they were drinking and gaped at him. Caroline even choked on hers.

He shrugged, taking in all the expressions focused on him. "What?"

"Since when do *you* double date?" Quinn asked.

"Since now, I guess." Glancing at me, he grinned and wiggled his eyebrows. "What do you say, Blondie? It could be fun."

I glanced toward Caroline. Her expression was surprisingly blank. She was watching the band as if she wasn't listening in on every word we said.

"Uh..."

I couldn't say yes. I didn't *want* to say yes. But what if Cora kept pressuring me until she found someone else, someone I didn't know. Ten was the antithesis of any guy I would consider dating, but for some reason I trusted him, and I somehow knew he didn't want to go out with me because he was interested in me. He had some kind of agenda. And what·ever it was, I'd rather take a chance on him and his ulterior motive than someone else.

"I don't know," I mumbled. "I guess."

QUINN

I GUESS.

She'd said *I guess.*

Why in the world had she said *I guess*?

Did she *like* Ten? I could tell Caroline was into him, but I'd never caught that vibe from Zoey. So why would she ever agree to go out with him? And what's more, why had *he* asked her to? Ten didn't do the dating thing. He was more of a one·night stand kind of guy.

Zoey was part of our group too. Why would he risk strife within the group to go out with her? Strife with *me*?

I was irritable as I dressed for the bar that evening, not to work but to go out...on a double freaking date.

"'Bout ready yet, princess?" Ten appeared in my opened

door and caught my eye in the mirror before he stepped inside and dropped onto my bed, rumpling the bedspread.

"Almost." Tugging at the cuffs of my shirt, I found my shoes in the doorway to my closet and pushed my feet into them with probably a bit too much force.

I turned to face my roommate, who looked as if he could just close his eyes and sleep on my mattress for the rest of the night. Wanting to shove him off, I muttered, "Let's get this over with."

Ten stopped swinging his foot and blinked up at me. "Damn, Hammy. You sound about as enthusiastic about tonight as I feel."

Unable to keep my thoughts bottled a second longer, I said, "If you didn't want to go, then why did you *volunteer*?"

"Finally!" Ten cheered, spreading his arms wide as he bounded off the bed. "The lecture. I've been waiting for this little talk since the moment your woman orchestrated this whole fucking night."

"My woman didn't—" I clenched my teeth and scowled at him, following him from the room as he left. "What little talk?" I growled.

"The one where you warn me away from Blondie and tell me to keep my hands to myself or you'll break them off at the wrists."

Dang it. How did he know I was dying to give him that very lecture? I shook my head though, refusing to admit it. "Why would I tell you that?"

Ten paused, glanced back at me, and then stepped closer. "Because you can't handle the idea of *anyone* putting his hands on her, that's why."

I rolled my eyes, but inside, my stomach burned. Listening to him say that made me want to curl my hands into fists and punch something. Punch him. Because what he said was true.

This was bad. This was so bad.

My roommate gave a sudden grin before he patted my shoulder in reassurance. "Don't worry, bud. I feel the same way."

With that, he turned around and strolled off. I blinked. He felt the same way? He wanted to murder anyone who even thought about touching Zoey? He...wait. Did this mean he *liked* her?

What about Caroline? I thought he had a thing for

Caroline. Why couldn't he just keep his sights set on Caroline?

"What?" I asked, hurrying after him.

He laughed and opened the front door of the apartment, stepping aside to let me exit first. I didn't. I just stared at him.

So he threw his head back and gave an exhausted sigh. "Believe it or not, I like Blondie exactly how she is. All sweet, and innocent, and untouched. But Cora wasn't going to let up until she found someone to take your girl out. And you and I both know someone else would probably try to get into her panties. So...*I* volunteered."

I shook my head. This just wasn't anything Ten would do. I couldn't compute or make any sense of it. "What?" I finally said. "Does this mean you're not going to try to, you know...?"

As I waved a hand, he lifted an eyebrow. "Get into her panties?"

I curled my lip into a snarl as I growled, "Yes."

"Nope. I am not." When I continued to stare at him, letting him know I didn't trust him, his face went serious. He patted my chest. "I'm doing this for you, Ham."

I shook my head. "I don't understand."

With another long, drawn-out sigh, he closed his eyes. "One of these days, hopefully one of these days *soon*, you're going to realize you don't have to stay with a girl just because she was the first person you fucked. Putting your dick into Cora didn't commit you to her for the rest of your life, man. And when you catch on and figure out you're allowed move on and be with a girl you actually *like*, I want her to be nice and preserved for you."

I blinked, stunned senseless by what he'd just said. There was so much in there I wanted to dispute, I wasn't even sure where to start.

I held up a finger. "First of all, Cora and I are not breaking up. And I'm not with her because she was my...I'm with her because I *love* her and I *want* to be with her. Okay? I'm not planning on straying...espec-ally with her roommate. Are we perfectly clear?"

"No." Ten made a face. "We are perfectly *not* clear. How could you claim to love *Cora*? You admitted to me just last week that she's hiding something from you. She doesn't go to your football games. Plus you're dreaming about—"

"Just stop." I held up a hand, getting upset. "No one is perfect. I certainly wouldn't be your roommate if I couldn't handle a few flaws. Cora isn't required to like football, and she's allowed to have her privacy. She accepts me as I am, and that is something I thought I'd never find."

Ten lifted an eyebrow. "*Accepts* you?" he repeated slowly. "What the hell? You're not some freak show just wandering around, waiting for some benevolent soul to finally take you in."

"You know what I mean." I glanced away, feeling stupid. "I'm not normal. I'm not like...you."

Unable to hide his shock, Ten pulled back and shook his head. "Why the fuck would you *want* to be like me? Hell, *I* don't even want to be like me half the time. And I am most definitely not normal."

"But you're...you..." Feeling my stutter approach, I gritted my teeth, hating all my ineptitudes. "You can talk to people," I finally pushed out.

My roommate snorted and rolled his eyes. "Yeah, what a talent. I can piss off pretty much everyone I talk to, too."

But I just stared at him, because to me...being able to socialize *was* a talent.

With a sigh, he slumped his shoulders. "Okay, fine. You're quiet. You're introverted. You're too nice to be rude to anyone. You open yourself up and are willing to trust more than just about anyone I know. Being as sensitive as you are means you have a bigger heart. And if I ever see you try to change and harden that heart of yours, I'm going to throat punch you. Don't be ashamed of being a big, soft teddy bear, Ham. The world needs more people like you, otherwise it'd just go to shit. Now..." He stepped back and spread his hands. "Can we go pick up our dates, or do you want to hold hands, sing a couple rounds of "Kumbaya," and dig into our feelings some more?"

I frowned and shook my head. "You're the one who started this conversation."

"Yeah, well...I must be on crack. Let's go already."

He headed for the door and I reluctantly followed.

We didn't talk on the ride over. I was afraid to say much of anything else. I think Ten was in the mood to set me over the edge for some reason, because he started up again as soon as we parked in Chateau Rivera's parking garage.

"So...if Blondie looks really good, you're not going to kill me if I go for a goodnight kiss, are you? I won't even use tongue. Okay, maybe a little tongue."

I sent him a dry look and parked the truck. He snickered and stepped out, leaving me to follow. "Didn't think so."

I wanted to smart back something like, "*I thought you wanted to keep her preserved for me*," but that would make it sound like I actually wanted him to, when...okay, the thought of Zoey dating someone—anyone—didn't sit well with me. Just thinking about someone else pressing his mouth to hers—

Crap, I forgot where I was going with this line of thinking. Ten had scattered my brain with that con-fusing heart-to-heart he'd pushed on me before coming here. He was making me think about Zoey again.

I kind of hated him right now.

"Think she'll be wearing a dress or pants?" Ten asked when we stepped into the elevator.

I glanced over at him. "Cora?"

He sniffed and glowered back. "*My* date, asshole. Why would I care what *yours* is wearing?" Then he grinned to himself and looked up at the number as we rose to the eighth floor. "I bet Cora bullied her into a skirt. Hopefully a short skirt. Blondie does have some nice legs."

I rolled my jaw and cracked my knuckles, commanding myself not to respond.

As soon as the elevator stopped and the doors opened, I shot out into the hall...mostly to keep myself from maiming my roommate. What was worse, I heard the jerk laughing softly behind me.

More than ready to get this night over with, I stormed to 8E and knocked once before letting myself inside. I needed a big dose of Cora's bubbling smile right now. I strode down the hall toward her room, leaving Ten to let himself inside.

Cora was in her room, but she wasn't alone.

Ten had been right. Cora had gotten Zoey into one of her dresses. And it had a short skirt. It wasn't tight like Cora's, but fluttered around her thighs in a loose skirt that would flare out into a bell if she twirled. Stalled just outside the doorway, I looked in at the two girls whose backs were toward me as Cora attached a necklace around Zoey's neck. It was long and disappeared down into her cleavage.

She looked good. They both looked good. I started to speak, make my presence known, but then Cora said something that had the words evaporating in my throat.

"You're so lucky to be getting Ten tonight."

I froze, not sure what to do. What to think.

Zoey jerked at the comment and twisted to look into Cora's face. "What do you mean?"

"I don't know." Cora shrugged. "He's just...social, you know. Quinn can be cute with his country-bump-kin ways, but Ten's just a little more world-savvy, and he can...I mean, I bet he can dirty talk in bed like you wouldn't believe."

I turned away blindly, unable to believe she was comparing me to Ten...and finding me lacking. I'd always thought she liked me the way I was, that she *accepted* my...my country bumpkin ways. I didn't need her to love everything about me, but...I don't know.

I was still too hurt and reeling to think properly.

I started to stride back down the hall but I realized Ten was standing at the end, watching me. His jaw was hard, and his eyes narrowed. He'd heard every-thing I'd just heard...because I really needed my humiliation to be complete right now.

"Hey!" he called loudly, his voice arrogant. I thought he was talking to me for a second, until he added, "We're here. You hens ready to go or what?"

Zoey was the first to career through the doorway, moving a little too fast. She skidded to a halt when she saw me, her eyes wide and guilty.

I don't know why *she* felt guilty. She hadn't been the one talking smack about her own boyfriend, finding him lacking, and telling her roommate she was lucky because she didn't have to be *my* date for the evening.

Cora breezed out of the bedroom behind her. When she saw me, her face lit up...just as it always did. I stared at her, wondering how she could smile at me as if I mattered, as if she didn't wish I was more out-going and experienced. It made me wonder if every smile she'd ever given me had been so false.

"Ooh, you look so handsome," she said, coming up to me and looping her arm through mine before kissing my cheek.

I remained stiff, unable to relax or fake my own smile. But I let her press her mouth to my cheek and I didn't brush her away. I quietly asked, "Are you ready?"

My gaze moved to Zoey, who immediately bobbed her

head, her eyes wide and worried. And for once in her life, Cora didn't have to "change" her clothes. I made no comment about that, when on any other night, I would've feigned a heart attack because she was actually ready on time. I simply took her hand and led her from her apartment.

TWENTY-THREE

⤜ ZOEY ⤛

As QUINN SWEPT Cora away, I shuddered out a breath and glanced at Ten. He stared after them as they passed and then turned to me, only to wiggle his eyebrows. "Thank God I got the sweet, *pretty* one for the night, huh?"

His words let me know he'd heard everything Cora had just said, comparing him to Quinn.

Setting my hand against my roiling stomach, I glanced past him toward Quinn and Cora. When they were far enough away that they couldn't hear me, I asked, "He heard, didn't he?"

Ten's eyes went hard as his teeth flashed. "Oh yeah."

I sucked in a breath. *Oh God.* "Is he okay?"

"What do you think?" Ten lifted an eyebrow, his gaze dry and yet ticked off.

"I think I'm going to be sick," I admitted.

"You and me both, Blondie." He took my elbow and led me from the apartment. "Let's just do this al-ready."

I hated knowing Quinn was hurting as much as I hated not being able to do anything about it, unless I wanted to publicly call Cora out on it, which totally wasn't my style. Besides, as vindictive as she'd been lately, she'd probably announce to the world—or more specifically, to Quinn—about my embarrassing crush on him. Since I didn't want that getting out, I felt trapped and forced to watch him suffer.

Tonight was going to be awful. I just knew it. It was already starting all wrong. Quinn was upset, Cora was clearly in denial, and Ten wasn't his usual cheerful yet annoying self. I just wished he'd say something crude and totally inappropriate to put me—or more specifically *Quinn*—at ease.

We ended up taking Cora's car. Quinn drove, Cora took the front passenger seat, and Ten didn't even make a crack about sitting in the back alone with me.

In fact, he slumped down on his side of the car, closed his eyes and pretended to sleep.

Cora chattered and talked as if nothing whatsoever was wrong. I watched Quinn, but other than saying nothing—which wasn't out of character for him in the least—he didn't act as if anything was bothering him.

"I think tonight's going to be so much fun." Cora twisted in her seat to grin at me. "Wouldn't it be cool if two roommates started dating two roommates? We could be an awesome foursome."

Not bothering to open his eyes, Ten muttered a very dry, "Yeah. That'd be *so* awesome." Then he leaned toward me and quietly murmured, "No offense, but that never in hell is going to happen. I don't do virgins, because technically, no one does virgins, hence the whole virgin status thing."

I leaned his way as well, whispering back, "No offense, but I don't really do man whores either."

He opened his eyes and grinned. "Then I guess we're good." He offered me a fist bump. When I clanged my knuckles against his, he whispered, "This would probably be the beginning of a beautiful friendship, except I don't make friends with chicks, so...I'll probably never talk to you again after tonight."

"That's okay. I don't like your crude jokes anyway."

He laughed outright, which caused Cora to turn around curiously and Quinn to lift his gaze to the rearview mirror.

Ten slapped the back of Quinn's seat. "Looks like I got the more *entertaining* date, thank God."

I was tempted to reach out and pinch him for stirring that pot. But it did cause Cora to narrow her eyes, which didn't break my heart any. I couldn't believe she was being so delusional as to think Quinn hadn't heard her comparison of him and Ten.

"As if anyone would *want* to entertain you? It'd take a freak to match your awful sense of humor."

Quinn glanced at her sharply. "Did you just call Zoey a freak?"

He'd been so stony and silent after she'd insulted him, but now that my head was on the chopping block, he was ready to jump to my defense. My heart ached, and soared, and then ached some more.

Cora fumbled over her words. "What. *No!* Of course not." She glanced back at me. "You know I didn't mean it that way, right?"

I wished I could say something witty and scathing to help side with Quinn and let her know I was still upset with her for what she'd said about *him*, but I had nothing. I hated confrontations, and I'd never be able to have one around more than two people. "Don't worry about it," I mumbled and lowered my gaze.

"I don't think you're freakish," Ten spoke up. "In fact, I think you look amazing tonight, like *someone's* wet dream come true."

Quinn stomped on the break when he almost drove through a red light. Then he whipped his gaze around to glare at his roommate. When Ten merely grinned back, I cleared my throat.

"Um...thanks?" Though I wasn't sure if I was that grateful for such a compliment.

The light turned green.

Quinn hit the gas.

And no one else spoke until we reached the bar.

The night seemed to be getting worse by the second. Quinn and Cora didn't bother to hold hands as the four of us walked to the front doors, where the bouncer recognized Quinn and Ten and let the four of us in without carding or charging us.

Since Asher had been hired at Forbidden, he'd set up all kinds of musical entertainment. Tonight was supposedly their first night to have karaoke. So as soon as we stepped through the doorway, some guy on stage began an awful rendition of Alicia Keys' "Fallen."

"Oh my God. Kill me now." Ten groaned and el-bowed Quinn. "Remind me to *never* work on karaoke night."

"Ooh, there's Rachel," Cora announced, bouncing on her

toes. "Let's go sit with them."

But Ten braked. "Over my dead fucking body. That chick annoys the hell out of me."

Cora scowled at him. Then she glanced at Quinn as if silently asking him to step in and side with her.

"Why don't you go over and say hi?" he suggested. "We'll find a table."

Her mouth fell open. I think this must've been the first time he hadn't given her what she wanted.

I was tempted to cheer for him and root him on, even though I knew I shouldn't. I should be Switzer-land.

I totally wasn't Switzerland.

"There's an open table," Ten announced, nodding toward a small round tall table that actually had two guys sitting at it.

"But—" I started, only to stop when he approached the men and told them we needed their seats.

My jaw dropped as they actually obeyed and left. They even apologized to me for sitting there first. I gazed after them before looking up at Ten.

"They're freshmen football players," he explained.

I shook my head but sat in the chair across from Quinn so I'd be by Cora and Ten. But Ten caught my arm and shook his head. "Hell no, honey. I don't sit by other dudes if I don't have to."

He tugged me out of my chair, stole it for himself, and forced me to sit between him and Quinn. As Ten lifted his hand to flag down a waitress, I glanced at Quinn. He was waving a hello to Noel and Asher at the bar, who both waved back, and then he turned to catch me watching him.

His eyes saddened, but he forced a smile. Then he glanced toward Cora where she was sitting with her friends and chattering away. His sad, forced smile died completely.

I glanced at my hands in my lap and picked at the blue fingernail polish Cora had put on me, suddenly wishing Caroline were here. Or Reese and her cousin Eva. Anyone to spruce up the dismal start of this agonizing double date.

"Bottoms up," Ten announced, startling me as he took a handful of drinks from the waitress who'd arrived with them.

Quinn scowled at the glass his roommate slid in front of him and lifted his face to transfer his frown to Ten. "This is alcohol."

"I know." Ten rolled his eyes. "You're drinking tonight. I've even decided to play DD so both of you," he included me in his glance as he nudged a glass toward me, "can relax and just...enjoy the evening."

Quinn snorted and glanced away, letting him know that wasn't going to happen no matter how much he drank.

I tucked my hair behind my ear and eyed my own drink before admitting, "I've never drank before."

"Neither have I," Quinn added, "and I'm not starting tonight."

"Yes, you are," Ten ground out. "I swear, your asshole's probably puckered so tight right now you've gone and made yourself constipated. That cannot be good for you. Drink. Relax. Have fun."

I leaned in toward Ten and quietly murmured, "But his mom was an abusive alcoholic."

He blinked at me, and I could tell from the surprise on his face, this was news to him. But then he recovered and announced, "Well, my dad's a hell of a nice guy, and my mom hasn't sworn a day in her life." Then he shrugged. "We don't always take after our parents."

Quinn looked at him as if considering his words.

"Are you sure you'll stay sober enough to drive?" I asked, feeling the urge to be a little reckless because I wanted Quinn to be able to relax and maybe forget what Cora had done to him...even if it was just for a few hours.

"Smell." Ten offered me his cup, so I'd know it was soda pop. But I took my investigation a step farther and took a drink from his cup to taste a sip. Pure Dr. Pepper. Handing it back to him, I smiled my approval.

"So, what did you give me?" I asked. "Some kind of girly frou-frou drink?" Caroline had insisted those tasted the best.

"Fuck no." Ten snorted. "It's a Long Island Iced Tea. It's what both of you have."

I nodded, then licked my lips and drew in a breath as I bolstered myself. Then I reached out and took a small sip.

Quinn sat up as he watched me. He looked as if he was ready to perform CPR if I started choking, but I merely nodded my head as the new flavors slid down my throat. There was a bit of a tang to the flavor that made me want to shudder, but over all, it tasted...fine. Mostly like cola.

"That's actually not too bad."

Ten rolled his eyes. "I *am* a bartender, you know. I can tell which drinks will agree with which people."

"Well, thank you." I smiled at him and took an-other sip. Then I turned to Quinn. "I just realized you're a bartender who's never drank before. That's so cool. In my writing class, they would consider you a rounded character instead of flat and clichéd because of that kind of contradiction."

I could tell by the change in his blue eyes that my compliment pleased Quinn. Proud of myself, I took another sip. Maybe tonight wouldn't suck quite so much after all.

"What kind of character would I be?" Ten asked, leaning forward with interest.

I lifted my chin and announced, "I believe they would call you *quite* a character."

Ten snorted out a small laugh and murmured, "Keep drinking, Blondie."

For a couple minutes, both guys just watched me nurse my Long Island Iced Tea. Quinn still had yet to touch his, but at least Ten had stopped trying to egg him on.

"So, I don't think I know what your major is?" I turned to Ten expectantly, since he was supposed to be my date for the evening and all. A girl was supposed to talk to her date, wasn't she?

"Architecture," he answered and spun his soda glass in a puddle of its own sweat stain.

Just as I frowned, Quinn lifted his face. "You told me your major was construction."

Ten just shrugged. "Pretty much the same thing; they both create buildings, right?"

"Actually, no." I shook my head. "They're not the same at all."

"So, which one is really your major?" Quinn pressed.

"Architecture," Ten repeated.

Quinn and I glanced at each other and frowned. He immediately turned back to his roommate. "Then why did you lie to me?"

After another shrug, Ten took a long drink. "I don't know. Architecture seems like a pansy-assed, artsy-fartsy major. Construction's more...you know, manly. I didn't want you thinking I was a pussy when we met."

Quinn pulled back, his eyes wide with shock. "*You* were worried what *I* would think of you?"

"Fuck, yes. You were a big-ass dude who really rocked it

on your first day of practice your freshman year." Then he waved both of his hands as if fake apologizing. "Excuse me for wanting to impress you."

"Weird," Quinn murmured, staring as if he'd just met Ten for the first time. Then he shook his head and glanced at me. "He wanted to impress *me*."

"So I heard." Wanting to hug Ten for making Quinn feel better, I turned to him. "Aren't you a senior?"

"Yeah. Why?" He glanced at me and narrowed his eyes as if commanding me not to follow my own path of logic. But I did anyway.

"Then shouldn't you have taken a *lot* of art classes by now?"

Quinn finally caught on. "Wait. Why *are* you in a beginning art class with us?"

Ten drew in a deep breath. I could tell he was getting uncomfortable when he glanced away. "Be-cause I knew you still needed to take one, so I badgered my advisor into letting me take it again, to keep you and Gamble company." His negligent shrug was a little too careless though. He was putting on an act. "Wasn't my fault I saw the wrong class schedule sitting on Gam's table and thought it was his instead of his sister's. The three of us would've owned that class."

Quinn shook his head. "No," he murmured softly, studying Ten intently. "I don't think you mistook that schedule at all. I think you knew it was hers all along. I think you just wanted a reason to be close to her and get to know her more."

Ten sent him a frown and snorted. "Whatever, man. You're on crack."

"And you wanted *me* there, not Noel, to act as a buffer, because you knew you couldn't cross the line if I was around, but you still wanted to get as close as you could because you were curious what she was like."

"That's it," Ten muttered, reaching for Quinn's glass. "If you're not drinking, then I am. This fucking karaoke is killing me."

But Quinn snatched the cup away from him and quickly tipped it up, starting to gulp.

My mouth fell open as I watched.

Ten's did too. Then he shook his head. "Bastard," he muttered.

Quinn grinned as he set the cup down. "Sorry, but I guess you're going to have to DD after all." Then he arched an eyebrow and lifted a threatening finger. "And don't ever lie to me again."

The two men had a mini stare down that seemed to end in some kind of draw because they both loosened their stances in the same moment and turned to me in unison. I sank lower in my chair, not sure what to expect from them.

Ten snickered. "Aren't you going to ask Hamilton what *his* major is?"

I shook my head. Quinn wasn't my date for the evening. I shouldn't be talking to him at all. But what I said was, "I already know his major."

"Really?" Ten lifted his eyebrows and glanced to Quinn before turning back to me. "And how's that?"

"Uh...he *told* me." I shook my head, wondering why that was such a big deal.

But Ten only seemed more intrigued. "That's funny. You guys seem to talk a lot for people who generally...don't talk."

"Stop," Quinn warned him icily, letting me know there was some inside thing between the two of them going on that I knew nothing about.

Instead of backing down, though, Ten seemed more challenged. He turned to me abruptly.

I shied away.

He opened his mouth, but must've rethought what-ever he was going to say because he immediately turned back to Quinn to ask, "Where'd your date go, anyway?"

Quinn glanced around the bar before spotting Cora at a new table, drinking a pink drink, and chatting with a new group. "She'll be over soon, I'm sure."

Ten sighed and ordered us all a new round of Long Island Iced Teas.

Feeling miserable for Quinn, I opened my mouth and blurted out the first thing to come to my head. "If you could be powerful or honest, which would you choose?"

"Why can't you be both?" Ten asked.

Quinn, however, mulled the question over before admitting, "Honest. It seems like you have to be meaner when you're powerful. I don't want to be mean."

I nodded. "So, then...if you had to choose between *nice* or honest...?"

"I'd choose nice."

A smile bloomed across my face. "You believe in lying in order to keep from hurting someone, then?"

He shrugged, but didn't seem to question why I was asking him this stuff. Heck, I wasn't even sure why I was. I just wanted to talk. To him.

"I don't know," he admitted. "I just can't handle hurting anyone."

"Yeah," I murmured thoughtfully. "Me neither."

ʒWENTY-ʒOUR

ఞ TEN ఞ

AND THAT'S about the point where I totally lost track of the conversation. The two Long-Island-Iced-Tea drunkards at the table with me started talking about all kinds of shit I didn't follow, and yet they knew exactly what they were raving about.

"Did you know the corneas are the only cells in the human body that don't receive blood from the heart?" Hamilton told Blondie.

She puckered her lips thoughtfully. "Does that mean the heart can't see?"

I groaned and realized their happy juice had definitely kicked in, especially when Blondie giggled and then swayed as she clutched her forehead. "Whoa. I'm getting woozy."

Hamilton grabbed her arm to steady her. "I know," he slurred and glanced my way. "This shit is potent. I feel..." He nodded slowly. "Yeah."

I lifted my eyebrows, wondering if he was drunk or high.

Blondie giggled again and pointed at him. "I've never heard you cuss before."

"I don't," Hamilton said blankly before Blondie charged, "But you just said shit."

He laughed and pointed back at her. "So did you."

As they giggled together, I rolled my eyes to the ceiling. Oh, dear God. Someone shoot me now.

"I don't know why I was always so scared to drink," Quinn announced. "My mom used to get so mad when she drank. That's when she'd beat me the hardest. So I always thought I'd lose my temper too if I ever drank. But I don't feel mad at all. I'm just...happy."

My gut twisted as I listened to him so nonchalantly announce something like that. I'd seen his back before, so I knew he had to have been beaten once upon a time. I just figured school bullies though, or someone else he hadn't been related to. To learn it had been his own mother, the one woman who was supposed to protect him from all kinds of bad shit, made me want to look that bitch up and beat *her*. It also made me want to call my own mom and tell her how fucking awesome she was.

But it'd been too long since I'd voluntarily called her, so...yeah, didn't want to give the old broad a heart attack or anything.

I was just starting to feel shitty about how I treated my parents while they might possibly be the best parents in the world when Blondie had to go and say, "My dad didn't need alcohol to hit me. So, I don't know why I was always so scared to drink. I guess I'm just an overall coward."

My eyes grew wide with that little piece of information.

Well, shit. *Both* of them had been abused? No wonder they'd turned out so much alike.

Fuck, I really was an ungrateful asshole to my mom and dad.

"You're not a coward," Quinn insisted, taking Blondie's hand. "You're...you're...resilient."

I squinted, wondering how the fuck "resilient" was such a complimentary word to use on a chick, but hey...to each their own, I guess, because the freaking word seemed to work on Blondie.

She murmured, "Thank you," and stared at him with a pair of longing green eyes that made me want to reach across the table and thump Hamilton on the back of the head. Hard.

Prime opportunity to kiss her, I wanted to tell him.

Kiss her already.

Why wasn't he kissing her?

God, what a pansy.

Instead of kissing, they just kept staring until Ham blinked and then grinned. "Staring contest?" he offered.

Dear fuck. *Really?*

I groaned and covered my face. I was going to have to work on my boy, big time. Who the hell offered a staring contest instead of *kissing* a girl? I might actually have to defriend him after tonight.

Blondie laughed and glanced away, blinking rapidly. "God, no." She rubbed her eyes. "I've never been able to play very long in a staring game before."

"It makes your eyes water too much?" Hamilton guessed.

She shook her head. "No. It's just...too intimate, I guess."

I lifted an eyebrow. Wow. If staring was too intimidating for her, I'd hate to see what she'd do if I made her watch some porn.

Thank God, Hamilton seemed similarly bewildered. He barked out a surprised laugh. "*Staring?* Intimate?"

"Hey, don't make fun of me." She pushed lightly on his arm. "Staring is like step two in the Twelves Stages of Intimacy."

"Wait." I held up a hand and leaned in, feeling the need to interrupt. "The twelve stages of *what?*"

Blondie glanced at me, before turning back to Quinn. "Intimacy," she repeated before gazing be-tween the two of us. "Haven't you guys ever heard of Desmond Morris's twelve steps of intimacy before?"

Ham and I both shook our heads. "Who? What? No, never heard of him."

She laughed. "Desmond Morris. He's this famous behavioral scientist, or something. I don't know. He wrote a bunch of books about studying the mating patterns of human couples."

Ham's eyebrows arched with interest. "And you've actually *read* one of his books?"

"No." She blushed. "But I read a small five hundred-word article about his famous twelve steps."

I let out a surprised snort of laughter. "What a nerd." She was totally meant for my biology-loving roommate.

"Hey," she muttered, insulted. But Quinn waved her quiet.

"No, I want to know about this. Are there really *steps* for intimacy?"

"Well, obviously." She rolled her eyes and sighed. "You

don't see people just jumping into bed with each other without any buildup, now do you?"

"Actually—" I started, but Blondie held up a finger in my direction, shushing me.

"Trust me. When it matters, you don't. You lead up to it. Familiarize yourself...one step at a time.

"So what're the steps?" Hamilton asked, genuinely interested.

I rolled my eyes, already bored out of my mind, but Blondie decided to humor him.

"You're in luck. I think I'm actually drunk enough to remember. Step one, you make eye-to-body con-tact." To demonstrate, she dropped her gaze down to his chest. Wiggling her eyebrows, she murmured, "Oh, yeah. Looking good."

Yep, she was drunk.

Ham cracked up, and okay, so did I. But then Blondie slid her gaze from his body up to his eyes, and suddenly it wasn't so funny anymore. Hamilton's laugh died as he stared back. The tension between them made me pull back in my seat, feeling like a freaking voyeur all of the sudden.

"If you find the figure pleasing," Blondie said into Hamilton's eyes, "you move your attention up to make eye-to-eye contact."

"Someone actually wrote a book about this?" I asked, snorting.

Blondie shrugged but kept her gaze on my boy, who seemed trapped in her hold. "Someone has writ-ten a book about everything."

"But—"

Ignoring me, she kept talking to Ham. "So Morris says a man and woman make eyes at each other, throw out a couple sparks and if things feel good from there, the 'hi, how ya doing?' comes into play." She held out her hand to shake with Ham. "Which brings us to step four."

"Wait. What was step three?" I asked as my entranced roommate reached out and took her hand.

Okay, fuck. Fine. I was starting to get interested in all this twelve-step bullshit, because damn, Hammy seemed to fall for it, hard.

"Voice to voice." She sent me a quick, irritated frown. "Keep up."

I gulped as I watched them intertwine fingers. Then I

glanced around to make sure no one else was looking.

Yeah, yeah, I know I wanted to shove these two together and make them kiss, like two seconds ago. But honestly, Hamilton needed to dump his current woman before moving on to the one he was actually meant for, otherwise he'd never forgive himself. And...well, shit. I didn't care if they were only holding hands, that fucking article Blondie had read must've known what the hell it was talking about. I couldn't recall ever being as intimate with any chick as those two seemed to be now.

"What's next?" Hamilton murmured, unable to take his eyes off *my* date.

"After ste—uh, step four, which is hand to hand, things move away from visual and auditory and to·ward the...the physical."

"Like what?" he asked softly, repeating step two and fucking the shit out of her with his stare.

I resituated myself in my seat. If anyone else watching this didn't get as sucked in as I was, then they had to be fucking dead from the neck down.

"Uh...the, uh..." Poor Blondie. Steam was rolling off her, she was sizzling so hard for him. "Step five would, be...arm or hand to shoulder."

"We've already done that," Hamilton said, making me lift my eyebrows and wonder just when he'd put his arm around her. But then he went and explained it. "The night the pipes broke in your bathroom. On the couch. Remember?"

Blondie nodded. "Yeah."

Touching on a couch, huh? I was impressed.

Ham's gaze dropped to Blondie's mouth. "What's step six?"

We all knew what he *wanted* step six to be. Horny bastard. I couldn't believe he was this far gone after only two and a half Long Island Iced Teas. But I loved it. I was so getting his ass drunk every time I possibly could from here on out.

"S·step six. Hand to waist," Blondie said, her face flushed and chest heaving.

My roommate was the fucking man. He was get·ting a girl all hot and bothered by just asking her questions. Fuck, the two of them were making me horny just from *listening* to his questions.

"And then?" Hamilton leaned in as if he was going to slip his arm around her waist.

Blondie closed her eyes. "Mouth to mouth," she said.

Shit. I had to stop them. Now.

"Hey, is that Cora headed this way?"

Hamilton lifted glassy eyes and looked around, but he didn't spot his girlfriend anywhere. "I don't see her. Oh, wait. There she is; dancing with that guy."

"Hmm," I said. "Could've sworn that was her coming this way and waving, trying to get your attention. Sorry."

Blondie opened her eyes and met my gaze. With a blush, she straightened in her seat and made a production of smoothing down her shirt and trying not to look guilty.

I tapped my fingers on top of the table and kind of regretted interrupting their moment, even though I know they'd both thank me for it...if either of them knew what I'd just saved them from.

"Seriously," I muttered when the next singer started on "My Girl." I motioned toward my roommate. "Ham, you sound better than that in the shower every morning. Get up there and sing so all those other losers who can't hold a tune don't get a turn."

Blondie turned curiously toward him, her lips twitching with a smile. "Do you really sing in the shower?"

"No!" His face turned red before he rolled his eyes and mumbled, "A little."

"A little every fucking morning," I taunted.

"Aww," Blondie cooed, touching his arm. "That's so cute."

Ham glanced at her, then quickly ripped his gaze away. "I used to stutter when I was younger. My grandma took me to singing classes to help with it."

What? "I had no idea you used to stutter," I said just as an equally surprised Blondie said, "I've never heard you stutter."

"Yeah, well." He rolled his eyes. "The singing actually helped. A lot."

Blondie squeezed his bicep. "So, you'll sing now. Pretty please."

He laughed, and a blush tinted his cheeks. "Heck, no."

"I'll sing with you," she offered, batting her eye-lashes and making Ham fall into another one of those staring trances she was so good at putting him under.

I lifted my eyebrows. "*You'll* sing?" I asked. "Do you sing in the shower too, Blondie?"

She shrugged. "No, but I'm just drunk enough to try anything right now."

Oh, that was it. "Do it, Ham," I urged.

I had no clue what was emboldening him, but he grabbed her hand and surged to his feet. "Okay, we're doing it, then. As long as you'll really sing with me."

She nodded. "I said I would."

As she followed him toward the stage, I folded my arms over my chest and sat back in my chair, ready to enjoy this show. I even pulled out my phone to take a video for future blackmail against Hamilton.

Once the man before them wrapped up his song—thank fucking God—Ham and Blondie stepped onto the stage. I wolf-whistled, making Blondie glance my way and blush. Then she grabbed Hamilton's hand and they stepped in front of the mic together.

As the beginning chords started, she leaned in and called, "Cora! This one's for you."

I frowned. That bitch shouldn't have had any part of their song. But from across the room, Cora turned and gaped up at the stage where her boyfriend and roommate were standing together and swaying lightly to the beginning chords. Then Hamilton leaned in and started singing. And shit, he was good. Really good.

Cora stood up and covered her mouth with her hands as she listened to him. Even Hart came out from behind the bar where he was working to listen. He paused by my table and asked, "What the hell? I didn't know Quinn could sing."

"Join the club."

Then Blondie joined in at the chorus. I whistled a-gain because she wasn't half bad. She and Ham turned to watch each other as they sang, and I couldn't contain my grin.

They wanted each other so bad.

I watched Cora for her reaction to their sizzling chemistry, but I don't think the clueless bitch even noticed. It was more than obvious to me that they were singing to each other...not to her.

As soon as the song ended, their faces lit up with accomplishment. I think Ham would've gone in for a hug, but his girlfriend jumped onto the stage and tackled him, kissing him all over the face before shoving her tongue down his throat.

Blondie's face absolutely crumpled.

Ah, hell.

I waited until she'd made her way robotically off the stage before I startled the shit out of her by wrapping an arm around her shoulder. "And that, my new chick friend," I said into her ear, "is what we call majorly fucked up. Her mouth should not be on him right now."

She looked up at me, her heart in her eyes. Pity ricocheted through my guts.

"I thought you didn't have girls for friends," she uttered as if in a daze.

"Well, I'm making an exception for you." I led her straight up to the bar, where we'd be closer to the alcohol, and I got her rip-roaring drunk.

She tried to find Quinn in the crowd with her gaze, but his slut girlfriend was still dry-humping him, so I turned Blondie's attention back to me before she could spot him.

Half an hour later, I had her back in the employee bathroom, bent over the toilet as I held her hair back and she emptied her stomach.

"Okay, that one was gross," I admitted.

"S-sorry," she sobbed, just before her stomach re-belled again.

"Don't apologize. Just get it all up."

So, she did. She spent the next five minutes spewing everything out of her system.

And this was actually one of the better dates I'd ever been on.

Reason number one why I didn't bother to date. Dating sucked ass.

Fuck 'em and move on, I always said...and was probably going to keep saying, especially since the one girl I might've made an exception for was utterly for-bidden to me.

"Thank you," Blondie said, glancing at me from wet, bloodshot eyes. "You...you're really not that bad of a guy after all."

I groaned and shifted my eyes toward the ceiling. "Yeah, just...promise to never tell anyone that. I have a reputation as a douchebag to uphold."

"I promise," she told me seriously.

I grinned and shook my head. "You about ready to get off the floor yet?"

She nodded but didn't move.

"Up and at 'em, Blondie." I stood and reached down for her arm.

And that's when Gamble appeared in the doorway.

"What's going on?" he asked suspiciously.

I glanced at Blondie and then the toilet. "What's it *look* like is going on?"

Gam just kept watching as I helped Blondie stand and then held her arm as we made our way into the lounge where I assisted her to the couch, where she slumped down ungracefully.

"I saw you two head back this way almost half an hour ago." Gam sent me a stern glance.

I rolled my eyes. "Well, sorry, but you're not going to catch us doing anything indecent. I tend to wait until *after* the drunk chick empties her stomach be-fore I start taking advantage of her. Jesus, man. Really?"

"I'm just saying...she's Caroline's friend. I don't want to see anything bad happen to her."

I knew damn good and well whose *friend* she was. "Well, as you can see, she's fine. All her clothes are on, lipstick isn't smeared, virginity intact. Okay, *dad*?"

Gam just scowled at me. "You don't have to be a prick about it."

Sighing, I rubbed my face. "Where's Ham? We rode here with him tonight. Is he about ready to go or what?"

With a snort, Gamble shook his head. "I think he's too busy practically screwing his woman on the dance floor to realize what time it is."

Hearing that, Blondie curled into a ball on the couch and proceeded to sob.

I seared my buddy with a glare. "Way to go, ass-hole."

"What?" He gaped at Blondie as if she was some kind of alien. "What did *I* say?"

"Just..." I waved him away. "Go tell Ham we're ready to leave *now*, will you?"

TWENTY-FIVE

ᨀ QUINN ᨁ

I WOKE WITH the headache from hell splitting through the center of my cranium. A whimper later, I squeezed my eyes shut and clutched my temples, wishing to be put out of my misery.

"Morning, lover," a voice cooed in my ear and a hand slid up my bare thigh. Cora rubbed against me, her naked breasts crushing my bicep. "I've been waiting for you to wake up."

I tried to unstick my dried tongue from the roof of my mouth. "What...what time is it?"

"Too late for you to make pancakes, but that's okay." Five very greedy fingers curled around my morning wood. "I'd rather have sausage anyway."

My eyes nearly crossed as the pain in my head mixed with the pleasure spreading from my groin.

"You were so amazing last night," Cora murmured in my ear just before she nipped the lobe with her teeth. "Do you remember how awesome it was?"

No.

I blinked up at the ceiling, trying to remember last night at all. But I came up with a big blank nothing. Why couldn't I remember what had happened?

"Best night of my entire life." My girlfriend moaned as she pumped me a little faster.

I reached out and caught her around the waist, dis-covering she was as naked as I was. She mewed when I slid my hand over her bottom. Then I urged her to slide on top of me, and she was more than willing to climb onto my lap.

Cora found a condom and was sliding it into place before I could even go searching for one myself. And then she was lowering herself onto me.

Twenty minutes later, we were both still panting, she was sprawled against my chest, too bonelessly weary to move, and I still couldn't remember a single detail from the night before.

"Okay," I finally admitted. "I don't remember last night at all."

I began to rub her back, hoping she didn't get up-set because whatever had happened last night had set her off this morning until she'd been chanting how much she loved me just five minutes ago when she'd come...for the second time.

But instead of getting mad, she laughed and rub-bed her nose against my throat. "Yeah, you did have a bit much to drink."

My eyes opened wide. "I *drank*?" A sudden vision hit me of downing a big gulp and then laughing at something I said to a girl...except the girl I'd been laughing with hadn't been Cora. At least, I don't think it'd been Cora. I swear, it'd been Zoey. But I'd been leaning into her until we were almost touching as I'd laughed, which couldn't be right.

"Why was I drinking?"

"Ten talked you into it, or something. I don't know."

"*Ten*?" Oh. Right. The double date. I winced, hoping Zoey had fared okay with Ten, since I obviously hadn't been in the right frame of mind to keep him in line.

"You and Zoey both got plastered."

My eyebrows crinkled. "We did?" Now that just sounded weird.

Cora started kissing her way down my chest. "Yep. And then you sang to me on the karaoke."

My eyes widened. "*What*?"

"Then you danced with me until we came home and made love for the rest of the night. I've never seen you so insatiable before. It was like you just couldn't get enough of me."

I flushed, wishing I could remember *that*.

But then another flashing memory popped into my head. I'd been squeezing my eyes closed as I gasped for breath and pounded hard and without finesse into a woman. I'd been thinking about Zoey, though.

My gaze sprang guiltily to Cora. I'd been thinking about her roommate while I'd been inside her. That had to be the absolute worst thing I'd ever done. I wanted to apologize and beg her forgiveness, but no way did I want to actually confess to her what I'd done...or why I hadn't been able to "get enough of her" last night.

Oh God. I think I needed to throw up.

"You were, like, the man I always knew you could be." Cora rolled off me to curl against my side. Gazing lovingly at me, she kept running her hand up and down my chest.

I knew it was wrong, but I couldn't tell her. There was no point. It'd only hurt her, and I couldn't take it back now. Wishing I could do something—anything—to make it up to Cora, I rolled toward her and nuzzled my nose into her neck, breathing in her scent and silently apologizing for picturing someone else while I should've been concentrating on nothing but her. She purred at my apologetic cuddling and clutched handfuls of my hair.

"So I've been thinking," she murmured.

I rolled her onto her back and moved above her to trail the tip of my nose down the slope of her breast. This morning, I swore, I would have nothing but Cora on my mind, nothing but Cora in my heart. Whatever she wanted, I'd make sure she got it. "What've you been thinking?"

"You know the way Noel proposed to Aspen... It was kind of in public, and yet is was behind that bar and hidden behind all the girls sitting up there so no one else but our group could really see what was happening?"

"Yeah?" I said between batting my tongue against her nipple.

She arched under me and began to breathe hard as she petted my hair, encouraging me to continue.

"Okay, well, I was thinking, I'd want something even more public than that. I'd want *everyone* to see and know how much you loved and adored me."

I deserted her nipple and lifted my face to stare into her eyes.

But had she just said...?

She grinned up at me and cupped my face. "As much as I want you again, baby, I don't have time for another round this morning. I have to be out of here within the hour."

I frowned. After what she'd just said to me, I was kind of hoping she'd want to spend the entire day together. I didn't have class, practice, a game, *or* work...which was rare for me. I was ready to give her everything, *especially* after she'd just suggested that she wanted to marry me.

"Where do you have to go?" I asked, bewildered.

"Rachel demanded we go shopping." She popped out of bed, but I just sat there, stumped, as I watched her slip on her underwear.

Then I sat up, running my hand through my hair, wondering how shopping with Rachel could be more important than me...after she'd just had the best night of her life with me and was mentioning proposals.

But she'd given me plenty to think about as she scooted me out the door ten minutes later. Marriage and proposals skipped through my brain.

Even as I thought about all that, I glanced around the apartment before leaving, hoping I'd catch a glimpse of Zoey. I wanted to ask how her night had gone and if her head was killing her as much as mine was killing me. But she was nowhere in sight. So I left without getting to talk to her.

ZOEY

I HID OUT IN MY bedroom for the rest of the week-end. After listening to Cora moaning Quinn's name Saturday morning when I woke, I curled into a ball and cried.

My head was pounding, my mouth was beyond dry, and I needed to pee. But I refused to venture from my room until I'd heard both Quinn and Cora leave.

Once I was alone, I tried watching a little *Psych* on Netflix. But it reminded me too much of Quinn. When Shawn and Jules finally had their first kiss on the show, I started bawling all over again.

So, I did some homework to distract myself, but bi-ology was what I needed to work on the most. Remembering when he'd helped me study, I, yep...cried even more.

I couldn't believe I'd almost kissed him. I couldn't believe he'd turned around and spent the entire rest of night and into the next morning with *Cora*. I couldn't believe...well, there was a lot I couldn't believe, and it was giving me a headache.

When Monday rolled around, I considered skipping art class. What if I burst into tears the moment he walked in?

I knew I couldn't hide from this forever, though, so I attended. I even arrived early so I could already be in my chair and prepared before I saw him. Except Caroline was chewing on her bottom lip and anxiously waiting for me outside the building.

She leapt forward and grabbed my arm, making me jump. "So how was Saturday night?"

I groaned and closed my eyes, covering my face with both my hands. "I almost kissed him," I admit-ted, needing to confess it to someone.

"What?" Caroline gasped. "You...oh my God. I can't..." She sounded like she was going to start crying, so I dropped my hands and opened my eyes.

Blinking rapidly, she asked, "Did he push *you* away too?"

I shook my head, confused. "Huh?"

"Oren," she pressed.

"Oren?"

"Oh my God, Zoey." She snapped her fingers in front of my face. "Keep up. You just said you almost kissed him."

What? "No, I didn't. Why would I kiss *him*?"

"Because you just said you did...Saturday night... on the date you went on with him."

I groaned and buried my face back into my hands. "Oh my God, I totally forgot about the date part. I am the worst person ever. Not only did I almost betray my oldest friend, but I almost kissed one guy while I was on a date with another one."

"Wait. What?" Caroline gripped my arm. Hard. "If you didn't kiss Oren, then who...." Her eyes shot open wide. "You did not," she whispered and glanced a-round before hissing, "You almost kissed *Quinn*?!" Then she gave a happy squeal and literally jumped up and down. "Ohmigod, *cool!*"

"Shh." I yanked on her arm to hush her. "It was...we were...drunk. And talking...and we leaned in toward each other, but no...you know what? I don't think we almost kissed at all. We just moved in closer to each other to hear each other better over all the noise. Yeah. I would never kiss another woman's boy-friend. It just...no..."

Caroline arched an eyebrow. "I know you like him, Zoey," she said softly. "You don't have to lie to me."

Tears filled my eyes, but I quickly swallowed them back down. I hadn't meant to lie to her. I'd just been in denial.

"Damn, what a pair we make," she said, taking my hand and squeezing my fingers, "liking guys we can't have. Or won't have us." She started to lead me into the art room but stopped when she saw someone loitering in the back, where our chairs were located.

Jerking me to a halt at her side, she pointed and whispered, "Look."

Someone wearing a sweatshirt with the hood up was placing something in Caroline's chair.

I elbowed her. "Oh my God. It's your secret admirer! Can you see his face?" No one had turned the lights on in the room yet and he was sheathed in shadow.

When he glanced our way, we both quickly ducked out of the doorway, then we just as quickly peeked back inside as he began to jog down the steps. I was beginning to think the way he moved looked familiar when he stepped into a pocket of sunlight coming in through the windows.

My mouth dropped open and Caroline clamped her hand hard around mine when Ten hit the last step and turned in the opposite direction as us, escaping out the other side of the lecture hall.

Like a streak, Caroline took off and raced into the room and up the steps.

"It's... Zoey... Look."

Too wide-eyed and breathless to explain, she spun the page around to show me what Ten had left for her.

I set my hand over my chest, my mouth dropping open. It was the same picture her admirer had been leaving her all semester, but this time the Caroline in the picture and the kitten were rolling around in the grass, laughing.

"*Ten's* your secret admirer?" I lifted my dazed gaze to her, and she stared back, looking just as shocked as I felt before the biggest smile bloomed across her face.

"He is." She covered her mouth as tears glistened in her eyes. And then she started to laugh. "Oh my God. He really is."

She sat down blindly in her chair and kept staring at the picture he'd put so much time and detail into drawing. "I can't believe he's such a good artist. None of the crap he turns in for class assignments ever looks this good."

I sat beside her, taking Reese's spot. "I found out on Saturday he's actually an architecture major."

She blinked at me. Then she shook her head. "But why would he be taking a beginning art course if he was a senior with a major in architecture?"

I probably shouldn't tell her, but I drew in a breath and did anyway. I was tired of lying to so many people about so many things. "I think he knew that wasn't your brother's class schedule he saw on the table at your house. I think he just...he wanted a reason to be close to you."

Caroline huffed out a breath. She gazed wildly around the room for a minute before focusing on me again. "But...he pushed me away. I tried to kiss him, and he—"

"You're his best friend's little sister. He knows he should stay away."

Her mouth fell open. "Well, fuck that. If Oren...if he really, truly, honestly *likes* me, Noel is *not* getting in my way."

With a laugh, I blurted out, "I wish I could be more like you."

She snorted. But I think she was too thrilled about the idea of Ten actually liking her to bother arguing with me. Instead, she started to fluff her hair and pinch her cheeks. "Shit. I knew I should've dressed up today. How do I look? Be honest."

I grinned. "You look lovely."

Reese arrived then, carrying a Styrofoam cup. "Starbucks is freaking bound and determined that I not get my white chocolate mocha today. They were out of lids and I almost spilled this on me twice already." She nearly tripped over her feet and spilled it again when she saw me sitting in her chair. "Oh! Hi."

"Sorry." I started to stand and give her her chair back. "We were just talking."

But she waved me back down. "No, it's okay. Stay. I can sit by Quinn. He always smells good, anyway. I can drink my latte and sniff him all hour."

Yes, that's what I usually did all hour too, sans the latte. He entered the room then, talking to Ten who entered with him, now wearing a T-shirt.

Everything inside me perked to attention.

Next to me, Caroline sucked in a breath.

Quinn looked amazing; his hair was styled as if he'd hand combed it and his shirt was one of those plaid, form-fitting button-up things that conformed to his large frame snugly enough to make my mouth water.

"...and then she scratched the shit out of my back when she came," Ten was saying. He lifted the back of his shirt that I could now read: "*Hey! The chick who usually sucks my dick has a shirt just like yours.*" Then he twisted his torso to show off long red scratch marks on his back to Quinn...except *all* of us saw them.

My mouth fell open as I glanced at Caroline.

Her face went sheet white as she surged to her feet. "Oh. My. God." Gritting her teeth, she glared at Ten as if she would gladly murder him in that second. She literally quivered as she fisted her hands at her sides.

He paused when he noticed the force of her attention. Dropping his shirt casually back into place, he frowned. "What's wrong with you?"

"You know what," she snarled. "*You* are. You make me absolutely sick. The way you whore around is appalling. You'd have to dip your dick in acid to clean off all the girls you've ever had."

Pulling back in surprise from the venom of her statement, he started to shake his head, only to snort and ask, "Why would I *want* to clean that shit off? Took me years to build up that much pussy."

"Oh...you..." Her rage was so toxic I think it bub-bled over into me, because I suddenly felt the urge to—

Snatching Reese's cup off her desk, Caroline upended the entire drink on Ten's head.

"My mocha!"

"*Shit*, woman! That's hot."

My mouth fell open as chaos erupted: Caroline fuming, Ten trying to shake off the wet steam oozing down his face and appalling T-shirt, and Reese be-moaning her lost drink. Then Caroline shoulder-checked Ten hard before she stalked off down the steps and out of the room.

Quinn glanced at me questioningly, then he did a double take when he seemed to realize Reese was going to sit by him today instead of me. I swear a smidgeon of hurt entered his eyes, but Ten stole our attention when he started cussing.

"What the *fuck* was that about?"

I didn't feel like telling him Caroline had figured out he was her secret admirer, but Reese had no problem clearing her throat and saying, "Maybe next time don't talk about your sex life in front of her, *o·kay*, moron? Maybe then I can actually *drink* my morning dose of sugar and caffeine instead of watching it wasted all over your stupid, idiot head."

Ten spread his arms and gaped at her. "I'm covered in second·degree burns over here and you're worried about your fucking drink?"

"Well...*yeah.*" Reese rolled her eyes. "And you're fine. They're probably not even first·degree burns, you big baby."

Ten sniffed and turned around to march off. "Un·believable."

Reese sniffed too. "I'm not going to be worth any·thing without my fix." She stood up and wished Quinn and me a good day before she too took off.

Leaving me alone with Quinn Hamilton.

My breath hitched in my chest as I glanced un·easily up at him.

But he just smiled his usual, warm smile as if he hadn't been inches from kissing me two nights ago, as if he hadn't broken my heart when he'd turned to Cora after singing to me, as if I was just a friend who meant nothing more than biology study sessions and the occasional conversation. Then he took Reese's abandoned chair and sat next to me.

"I haven't seen you since Saturday to ask if you had any fun on the date," he said, pulling out his note·book and flipping it open.

My lips parted as I stared at him.

When I didn't answer him soon enough, he looked up. "Cora says we both got pretty drunk." He leaned in closer and lowered his voice. "Are you like me? I can't remember...*anything.*"

My mouth worked, but when no words came, I closed it. He didn't remember? *Any* of it?

I wasn't sure if I should feel relieved or crushed.

I began to shake my head, slowly at first and then with a little more speed. "No," I croaked. "No, I don't remember anything, either."

He blew out a relieved-sounding breath. "Cora says I sang a song to her on the karaoke." Rolling his eyes, he gave a rueful laugh. "That must've been awful."

No, it really hadn't been. He'd had a good voice, a voice I could've listened to forever.

Then a thought struck me. Had Cora not told him I'd sung that song *with* him?

My bottom lip quivered, but I bit the inside of my cheek and refused to cry.

The professor started class, but apparently Quinn was in a chatty mood. He began to write on his note-pad before he bumped his leg into mine to get my attention.

"*I have a favor to ask.*"

I looked up at him, and he smiled at me big, his dimple melting my resistance. No way could I deny him anything. "*What's that?*" I wrote back.

"*Would you be willing to skip classes tomorrow and go with me to help pick out a ring...for Cora?*"

I stared at his words. Then I reread them.

A buzzing filled my ears and lead weighed down my stomach. But no matter how many times I read his words, they said exactly the same thing every time.

I must've stared too long, because Quinn nudged my knee again.

I veered my gaze up to his face. The question in his eyes snapped me back to the present. I blinked, then blinked a little more before I mouthed the word, "*Wow.*"

It wasn't necessarily a *good* wow, but he smiled anyway as if pleased by my reaction. His eyes lit up, his mouth swooped into that sexy curve I loved, and his entire face just...glowed.

He was happy, so freaking happy while I was afraid I might vomit. I closed my mouth and forced each breath through my nose. Then I nodded because I was totally unable to write the word yes.

TWENTY-SIX

ZOEY

"So THIS WAS unexpected," I finally found the courage to admit the next day.

I sat in the passenger seat of Quinn's truck as he drove us to the jewelry store. So he could buy Cora an engagement ring.

He glanced at me. "Hmm?"

"Your, you know..." I flailed out a hand. "The ring. Your engagement. I didn't... I mean, I didn't realize you were that serious about her...that you guys were that serious."

His cheeks reddened as he grinned out the front windshield. "Well...yeah. It was pretty unexpected. I mean, I hadn't been planning it or anything."

"But yesterday you just, what...woke up with a wild hair to propose *marriage* to someone?"

Okay, I might've sounded a tad bit bitter there, be-cause he glanced at me in surprise.

"I mean..." I rushed to add, except he was already shaking his head.

"Cora isn't just someone. She's my girlfriend. I've been dating her for months. We're in love." He cocked me a searching glance. "You don't think I should ask her? You think it's too soon?"

Face flooding with heat, I waved my hand. "I wasn't saying you shouldn't ask."

He nodded. "Then you think I should?"

Grr. Why was he making me answer this? I just wanted to lean forward and bang my head against the dashboard. I was the last person on earth who should answer that question.

All the *no* reasons floated through my head first.

Because I want you for myself.

Because she lies.

You're too young. You haven't dated her long enough. She doesn't even like football. She lies. And I want you for myself.

Ugh. I couldn't tell him any of that.

So I thought up the yes reasons.

She's sick and she needs support, the kind some·one warmhearted like you could give. Any woman would be lucky and honored to receive a question like that from you.

You love her.

And with that reason in my head, I lost my taste for all the *yes* motives. I stared out the side window of his truck. He loved her, and there was no way to argue my way around that.

"I think you should do what you feel in your heart is the right thing to do."

Quinn was quiet for a minute. "She woke up so happy on Sunday morning. I mean, she even said Saturday night was the best night of her life."

No, it had been the best night of *my* life. And then Cora had stolen it from me by hopping onto that stage and kissing him after he'd sung that song to *me*.

"And I can't remember what happened, but some·thing did. Something big. I think it was something amazing."

I swallowed, sinking lower in my seat, wondering if it had been something amazing with me...or some·thing amazing with Cora. I was tempted to tell him... about us, how we'd talked, flirted, almost kissed, how he'd gazed into my eyes when we'd sung that song together. But what if I was wrong? What if the amazing thing he thought he remembered had really been something afterward that had happened with Cora?

What if I was trying to steal my roommate's boyfriend while he wanted to buy her an engagement ring? That would make me the lowest of low, especially when she was so sick and...

I drew in a shaky breath. Since moving here, Cora hadn't been acting as I remembered her from home. But maybe the lies and the secrets would stop after the transplant. She had to be scared; I knew I would be. Maybe fear was just making her lash out. And maybe she'd been so distasteful to me lately because she didn't like the way I always looked at her boy-friend. I certainly wouldn't blame her for that. So what if she and Quinn really did belong together and I was hampering it by making him question his reasons?

"She dropped a hint too." Quinn glanced at me swiftly before returning his attention to the road. "A pretty big one. On Sunday morning, she pretty much told me *how* she wanted me to propose."

I nodded and swallowed. "Well, then. It sounds like you know what she'll say when you ask."

He shifted in his seat, looking uncomfortable. "You still don't think I should ask her, though, do you?"

Sucking it up, I smiled at him. "Actually, I'm happy Cora found someone who's so sure about her, and who treats her as well as you do." I set my hand on his arm and ignored the thrill that touching him sent through me. "I think you're going to make her an amazing husband."

He nodded humbly, his grateful smile killing a little part of me. "Thank you. That means a lot, Zoey."

"You really didn't have to buy me lunch."

Across the outdoor table from me, Quinn looked up from his sandwich. "I wanted to. Plus, I'm starving." He sank his teeth into the bread and moaned.

"Nothing like finding the best ring ever to rouse your appetite?" I guessed.

He grinned, rather proudly. "It was a pretty amazing ring, wasn't it?"

I nodded. "It was definitely *my* favorite."

With a laugh, he dunked a handful of fries into his ketchup. "I could tell. Once you saw that one, you didn't really look at any of the others."

"What can I say? I have awesome taste."

"Yes, you do." He paused to reach across the table and cover my hand with his. His fingers were large and warm. I wanted to flip my palm up and press the two together. But I refrained as he sent me a serious look. "You were amazing today, Zoey. Thanks for going in there with me. I don't know how I could've done this without you. You're the best."

I shrugged, even though the crack in my heart widened a couple more inches. "It was no big deal. I'm honored you thought to ask me." Honored and yet heartbroken.

Quinn grew somber. "No, seriously. You really are the best, you know. It's..." He glanced away before turning back to smile at me, killing me with his dimple. "It's not easy for me to make friends. Cora and the guys at Forbidden are really the closest I've ever gotten to anyone. But you...you're one of the best friends I've ever had. I'm glad Cora talked you into coming here this semester. I think you really helped settle her down some. I'd been getting worried that she was partying too much and just...she was starting to get so wild. But you calmed her back down to more like how she was when I first met her." He squeezed my fingers warmly and then let go. "Thank you."

Brushing my bangs out of my eyes, I changed the subject before I could start bawling all over him. "So how're you going to propose?"

"Well." He sat back and took a breath. "Her favorite place to eat is Jenny's Crab Shack, so I was going to go in before taking her there and see if the waiter can bring the ring in with the meal, hanging from a pincher or something like that. I'm not looking for-ward to doing it out in such a public place." He sent me a sick kind of smile. "But that's what she wants."

I nodded. "Yeah. I can see Cora getting a kick out of that kind of proposal."

Quinn nodded. "But I still don't know what I'm going to say."

"What?" I set my hand over my chest. "The future heart surgeon doesn't know how to phrase a wedding proposal?"

When he flushed, I rolled my eyes. "Just keep it simple. Get on one knee, take her hand, and stare lovingly into her eyes. Then say something like, 'With every beat of my heart, I belong to you. I love you, Cora Lorraine Wilder. Will you marry me?'"

Quinn gazed at me. When he didn't respond, I flushed and ducked my head. "Okay, so that was probably too corny, but I thought the heart reference would be cute, since, you know..."

"No. No." He shook his head. "It wasn't corny at all. It was...it was perfect actually. Thanks, Zoey."

My heart beat hard in my chest as I realized in that moment, I didn't just have a crush on Quinn Hamilton. I loved him.

Oh, God. I loved him.

"Hey," he murmured softly, knocking on the table in front of me to get my attention.

When I lifted my face, he pointed at a couple passing by us on the sidewalk. "You can tell he likes her."

They weren't holding hands or even touching, and they were facing their attention down instead of a-head of them where they were going, but I totally agreed with Quinn's assessment.

Still, I had to ask. "How can you tell?"

He smiled softly. "Watch. He picks a leaf off every tree they pass. It's like he has to keep his hands busy to keep from reaching for her." And on cue, the guy reached up and tugged at a new leaf from the tree he passed.

I grinned at Quinn. He grinned back and returned his attention to the couple as if he was waiting for the guy to bypass the next leaf and reach for the girl in-stead.

"Shawn and Jules kissed," I blurted out.

He turned back to me slowly. Then his eyes widened. "On *Psych*?"

I nodded. "I saw it this weekend."

"How far along are you? I'm going to have to catch up."

I began to play with my food, realizing I hadn't touched a bite. "Do you think they'll end up together?"

"I don't know," he answered. "I hope so. They bet-ter."

"Yeah. I hope so too." Because if they didn't, I'd probably lose my hope in love altogether.

Twenty-Seven

❧ Quinn ☙

I HAD A HOME game on Thursday and was off work on Friday, so I planned to take Cora to Jenny's Crab Shack then.

We won our game, of course. We always won. With Noel at the helm, we were practically unstoppable. We'd actually won so hard I got to play quarterback for the last five minutes.

Jazzed about that and nervous about my proposal to Cora, I couldn't stop drumming my fingers on my thigh as I sat at the table and waited for our main course to arrive.

Any minute now, they'd come out with our food...with her ring. I kept trying to remember the words Zoey had said, the words that I'd thought would make the perfect proposal, but my head was fuzzy and I couldn't concentrate long enough to remember anything.

I picked up the glass of water and took, like, the hundredth sip for the evening. I was worried about my mouth drying out when the time came, but then I was equally worried about drinking too much and having to go the bathroom at exactly the time they brought out the ring.

The staff had been tickled to participate in my plans when I'd brought the ring in earlier. I guess they were all

227

romantics at heart too. I kept seeing waitresses and waiters stealing secretive grins my way every time they passed, which made my stomach knot with even more nerves.

I don't think I'd ever done anything so big and public before in my life. But for Cora, I would. Except...what if she said no? What if I'd totally been reading her wrong last Sunday morning?

Heck, what if she said *yes*? Was I really ready to get married?

Across from me, Cora's phone dinged with an incoming text. About the twentieth text she'd received since we'd gotten here. I glanced at her as she picked up her phone and read the screen. Whoever she was talking to had quite a bit to say, because she studied the screen for a while before grinning and typing back an answer.

When my own phone chimed, I glowed, thinking she'd just written to me.

But when I checked my screen, it was from Zoey. **Relax already. You look like you're going to toss your cookies any second.**

I lifted my face and glanced around until I spotted her sitting all the way across the restaurant on a stool at the bar.

When she realized I'd found her, she smiled and waved, giving me a big thumbs-up as she swung her legs cheerfully.

I don't know why, but knowing she was here immediately eased my nerves. I let out a breath and all my muscles stopped clenching.

Then I shook my head and texted her back, since Cora was still on her phone. **What're you doing here, crazy girl?**

I couldn't stay away. I'm dying to see Cora's expression when she says yes. That's okay, right?

I rolled my eyes. **Sure. Just make sure she doesn't see you before then. Or she might get suspicious.**

You got it, boss.

When I read that and glanced at her, she sent me a salute. Then she wiggled in her barstool as if she was doing some kind of sit-dance. I had to cover my mouth with my hand to keep from laughing aloud.

Across from me, Cora actually did laugh.

My gaze shot to her.

Still smirking at whatever she was reading, she began to answer her text. Curious what was pulling her attention

228

away from our date, I asked, "What's so funny?"

Her head zipped up, her eyes wide. "What?"

I tipped my attention to her phone. "Who're you texting?"

"Oh. Uh...Zoey."

I glanced toward Zoey. She was most definitely *not* texting Cora. I looked back at my girlfriend. And it hit me.

Oh...hell.

"You're lying." The words seemed to echo from my mouth and reverberate inside my head. Why would she lie about who she was texting?

Cora looked up again, and I saw the flash of panic in her gaze. "Excuse me?"

"Who...are you texting?" I said with a little bit more force.

Cora scowled. "I just told you. *Zoey.*"

"No." I shook my head slowly. "You're not texting Zoey."

I glanced toward Zoey again just as a new text chimed from Cora's phone. Zoey's phone was still sit-ting on the bar behind her. She frowned at me, looking concerned, and motioned with her hands as if to ask what was wrong.

I turned back to Cora. Busy trying to open the new message, she didn't notice me stand up and lean across the table until I'd snagged the phone from her hand.

"Hey," she yelped, glaring at me and trying to retrieve it. But I'd already read enough.

She wasn't just texting some other guy, she was texting lewd, sexual things to some other guy, telling him she'd try to sneak out to him tonight because her mouth was watering for his dick.

My pussy is so wet for you right now. As soon as I'm done with this stupid dinner, your cock better be hard, because I'm climbing on it as soon as you open your door and I'm riding you until dawn.

I kept reading, and everything in my chest just kept sinking lower and lower. Cora ran around the table and once again tried to take her phone back. I held out my hand, keeping her away. She hit my shoulder and started to curse me. But I didn't feel her fists or hear her words. I was still reading, unable to look away.

"Damn it, Quinn." She started to cry. "It's not what you think. Just give me my phone back...now."

"Not what I think?" I murmured, looking up at her.

"So...you're not having sex with this guy who..." I glanced down and starting reading her text aloud, "made me come so hard the last time you were in me I almost orgasm just thinking about it?"

"I..." She had no words to talk herself out of the truth.

An uncontrollable, hard laugh left my lungs. "Oh my God. *Oh* my God, Cora." My ears began to ring. "I cannot believe you."

This was impossible to process. My girlfriend had cheated on me.

"Quinn," Cora started, but I held up my hand.

"No. Don't even...just, *no.*"

"No. Please...just listen to me..."

I shook my head and threw her revolting phone on the table. "I think I've had enough of reading what you have to say, I don't want to listen to any of it."

"Damn it." She stomped her foot in a pout. "How the hell did you know it wasn't Zoey?"

My mouth fell open in shock. She was upset be-cause she'd gotten caught, not because she was break-ing my heart all over Jenny's Crab Shack? I couldn't freaking believe her.

"Because she's sitting right there!" I helpfully pointed Zoey's way.

Cora spun around and gaped at Zoey. Zoey jumped off her barstool, clearly startled. She hurried toward us, but I couldn't handle her right now either. She knew; she *had* to know. How could she live with Cora and not know? How could she go with me to pick out a ring and not tell me?

Oh God, why had she let me do that and let me make a complete fool of myself?

I felt doubly betrayed.

Just then, the server, wearing a huge smile, approached our table. "I hope you guys have a big appetite tonight."

The blood drained from my face. Life could not possibly get any more humiliating than it was in this second. Actually it could, because I was half a second away from puking my misery all over the floor.

But Zoey plowed into the server, sending the bucket full of crabs flying everywhere. I watched in a daze as she apologized to the waiter as if she totally hadn't meant to tackle him.

"I should've watched where I was going," she said as she

crawled through butter sauce and crabs and shrimp until she curled her fingers around something she picked up and cradled to her chest. When she looked up, her eyes met mine.

I saw pity, and I couldn't handle it. I whirled away and stalked from the restaurant.

"Quinn, *wait.*" Cora raced after me. She grabbed my arm and whirled me around.

"What was that? Was that a ring she picked up? Are you going to *propose* to me?"

Her eyes lit with a smile, but I snorted. "No." *Hell, no!* "Because I never want to see you again. It's over, Cora."

This time, she didn't go after me when I stormed away, and I wouldn't have let her stop me if she'd tried.

ZOEY

CORA WAS A sobbing mess. It was hard to under-stand anything she was saying. I still wasn't sure what had just happened between her and Quinn, but he'd been so upset, more upset than I'd ever seen him before.

Through all Cora's tears, I finally understood that he'd seen something on her phone he was never sup-posed to see. So I grabbed her phone, and then *I* saw something I never *wanted* to see.

"Oh my God, Cora. You...you're cheating on Quinn? *Quinn?*" I stared at her, wondering when she'd lost her freaking mind. "How...how...how *could* you?"

"I love him, Zoey. I swear I do. Quinn is the best boyfriend I've ever had. I don't want to lose him. What do I do?"

"How about not having sex with other men?" That'd be a good start.

She huffed out a sound of irritation. "Those were just flings. Quinn's the real deal. No one's ever been as good to me as he is. I really do want to marry him. But I like sex. What's so wrong with that?"

"Oh my God, Cora. You can't have your cake and eat it too. Marriage means monogamy. And you...you just lost the best thing that's ever happened to you."

I turned away and left her in Jenny's Crab Shack too,

with Quinn's engagement ring a little buttery but tucked safely in my pocket.

I cried a little bit, wandered around town a lot, re-fused to return to my apartment where Cora was. About an hour after everything fell apart, Caroline called, frantic.

"Oren just showed up here with a black eye and really upset, mumbling something to Noel about how Quinn will never forgive him for what he did. What the heck *happened?*"

"I don't...I don't know. I'm not sure. Cora cheated on Quinn, and they broke up."

"What? Cora cheated—Wait. Oren wouldn't possibly be stupid enough to...not with *Cora*? Would he?"

"I don't think so." I shook my head. "No, the texts I read weren't from him. She definitely cheated with someone else." Or maybe a couple someone elses from the sounds of it.

"That lying fucking whore. I mean...I'm sorry. I know she's your—"

"She is not my friend," I snapped. "Not right now. She lied to me too. I had no idea." I'd helped Quinn buy her a ring. I'd...Quinn probably thought I knew about this. He probably thought I'd purposely led him on a merry goose chase. "I'm sorry, I have to go."

I hung up on Caroline and raced toward Quinn's apartment.

QUINN

WHEN I STORMED through the front door of my apartment, Ten was slouched on the sofa, eating from a bag of potato chips and drinking a beer as he watched television.

I slammed the door behind me and began to pace the front room.

"I'm sensing turmoil," he said mildly.

I picked up one of his textbooks off the coffee table and heaved it as hard as I could against the wall.

"And I'm sensing it has something to do with...classwork?"

I sent him a glare. "Cora cheated on me."

Ten dropped his beer. "Shit, man." He popped to his feet. "So, it's true then?"

I stopped pacing. "What? Wait, you *knew* about this?"

"What? No! Fuck, no. I've just heard—I mean, come on, man. She was a total slut before you hooked up with her, but—"

"She was *what?*" I marched toward him. He backed up a step.

"Dude, we called her Cora the Whora. How did you never know that? Before you two hooked up, she'd had just about every guy on the team."

He must've realized that was the very worst thing he could've possibly said because his eyes widened a split second before I grabbed his shirt and hauled him close until we were nearly nose-to-nose. "Really? Did she have *you?*"

Ten didn't answer, but his face paled.

I let go of him and stepped back. "Oh God. She did."

"Ham. Man." He inched toward me, reaching out, but I slapped his hand away. "It was only one time, before you ever met her, before you even knew she existed." When I just stared at him, he closed his eyes and winced. "Okay. And then one time after."

"After..." I repeated slowly. "After what? After I *met* her, you mean?" I'd slept with her the very first night I'd met her.

Ten held up his hands in surrender, his eyes pleading. "I didn't know you were going to start dating her. I swear to God. You'd just lost your virginity to the girl. I thought you'd call it good and move on to other pastures. She's a one-time kind of slut, not someone you *date*. And *she* came on to me a couple nights after you guys first hooked up, so I thought, why the hell not? We were both unattached—or so I thought—and I was horny. When I heard the next day that you'd asked her out again, I cornered her and demanded to know why the fuck she'd done that to me. But she said she didn't know you were going to call her again."

I growled. "I didn't call her again. I asked her out on an official date the morning after the very first night we *met*. And she said yes."

Ten winced. "Then she lied to me. I promise you, Quinn, I would never betray you like that. I had *no* idea you were still interested in her after your first time."

I couldn't listen to any more. So I punched him.

In the face.

He wasn't expecting it and shouted out his surprise

before catching his jaw in his hands and cursing up a storm.

As he danced around the room to alleviate the pain, I pointed toward the door. "Get out of my apartment."

Breathing hard, Ten straightened. He opened his mouth, but I shook my head, finished listening to him. "Just go."

He drew in a deep breath, nodded, and left me alone. After he was gone, I took the beer he'd left on the coffee table and I got drunk. I was still drunk when a knock came on the front door.

I didn't feel like talking to anyone or being civil, but I stood up and checked to see who it was anyway.

It was Zoey.

Twenty-Eight

⤳ ZOEY ⤳

I KNEW HE was drunk as soon as he opened the door. I covered my mouth as I stared up at him. "Oh, Quinn."

While my eyes wanted to fill with tears, his eyes remained dry. And hard and accusing. "Did you know?"

"What?" Pain sluiced through me. I shook my head fiercely. "No! How can you even ask that? You know... you know I had no idea. You know I...I never would've helped you with the ring, or...or...oh God. She betrayed me too. I'm supposed to be her friend, her closest confidante, and she kept something like this from *me*. I'm...I had no idea."

With a relenting nod, he stepped back and let the door fall open. "Well, this seems to be the party for the betrayed. Come on in."

I stepped over the threshold, smelling the alcohol immediately. When I spotted the half-empty bottle sit-ting open on the coffee table, I started for it. "We need to cut you off."

But Quinn caught my arm and whirled me to face him. I gasped when my chest bumped into his. "How 'bout we don't," he said softly.

I gulped and lifted my gaze. He stepped in toward me, and I backed up a pace. As if my retreat irritated him, he

235

turned me and pressed my back to the wall.

"Quinn?" I said, my voice small. My skin buzzed with apprehension. His expression looked so severe. I had no idea what he was thinking, and that scared me. I wasn't afraid of him exactly, but I was definitely afraid of the moment. Anything could happen, but what I feared most was what I'd *let* happen.

A relieved breath rushed from me when he released my arm. But the small moment of freedom didn't last. He slid the back of his finger up my bicep toward my shoulder, making me suck in a shaky inhale.

"It's funny what you remember when you're drunk, you know." His gaze seemed fixated on the place he touched me. "Like I was just sitting here, remembering the last time I drank. Do you remember that night, Zoey? Do you remember what we almost did?"

He cupped my cheek with one palm while he pressed his other hand against the wall beside my face, so close that his wrist brushed my hair. I gulped and tried to soak deeper into the sheetrock. But he was still right there, invading all my senses.

"Do you?" he pressed.

I closed my eyes. "Yes," I whispered, because in that moment I didn't know how to lie to him.

He let out a harsh breath. "Why didn't I remember that until now? I almost had my mouth on you but I stopped because I wanted to be *faithful* to my girl-friend. What a joke. *Faithful?* She doesn't even know the meaning of the word."

"Quinn," I started, but he took his other hand off my cheek to set it on the wall too, neatly trapping me into place.

"Do you think I'm a joke, Zoey?"

"What?" Flabbergasted by the question, I shook my head. "No. Never."

His gaze met mine. "Does she? Does *Cora*? She's probably laughing at me, right now. Isn't she?"

Again, I swished my head back and forth. "N-no. The last time I saw her, she was crying."

Mouth curling into a hard smile, he let go of me and stepped back. "Good." But as soon as the word left his lips, he shuddered and his eyes filled with pain and remorse. "What is wrong with me?" Cupping his head, he backed away some more until the backs of his legs hit the couch, and then he slumped down, sit-ting on the cushions and still cradling his head in his hands. "I'm *glad* she's crying? How wrong is that? Hours ago—just hours ago—I thought she was the love of my life, and bam." He snapped his fingers. "Just like that, I hate her? That doesn't even seem possible. But it is. I mean, seriously, I want nothing to do with her. I don't want to see her, I don't want to talk to her, I don't even want to think about her. She's dead to me. How can I be that coldhearted after I was *this* close to asking her to...?"

He shuddered again and bowed his face, looking more tormented than I could handle. Unable to stay a-way, I peeled myself from the wall where I'd still been hovering and went to him.

"You're not coldhearted." I set my hand on his shoulder. "You're just...brokenhearted."

When he leaned into me, I shifted my fingers from his shoulder to his hair, and he wrapped his arms a-round my waist. So I wrapped mine around his head. His large frame quivered again.

"Oh, Quinn." I wanted to help him, anything to end his pain. So when he tugged me down onto his lap, I went willingly; I even kissed his hair.

His arms banded even tighter around me as he said, "Thank you," in such a broken voice that I had to bite my lip to keep any more tears from spilling. "Thank you for coming."

He pressed his lips to the side of my head, just above my ear, and I rested my cheek on his shoulder. We sat there for I don't know how long, but it was long enough for me to grow warm and realize how hard yet completely comfortable he felt under me.

And speaking of hard—and under me—something had grown noticeably stiffer against my bottom. Realizing how inappropriately I was sitting on his lap, I started to move off him, but his hand snaked out and caught me high on the thigh.

"Don't go."

I fell still. Unable to help myself, I kissed his temple. "How can I help you? Tell me what to do."

He drew in a breath, smelling my neck and brushing his nose lightly along my pulse. Then his hand moved slowly up my thigh until he was gripping my hip. I grew moist and tensed, hoping he didn't find out.

"Make it go away," he whispered against my throat. "Make me forget."

With a shiver, I shook my head, not under-standing, or maybe I was too hopeful to really think I understood. "How?"

I'm pretty sure it wasn't his nose that touched me next, right under my ear. It felt too wet and soft, like tongue, followed by the crisp nip of teeth. I gasped, and my head fell back as my fingers bit into his shoulders, unable to control the crackling surge of heat between my legs.

As his thumb stroked my hip, burning through my clothes, scorching my skin, and shifting dangerously too close to where I was throbbing and wet, he pulled back to look me in the eye. "I almost had my mouth on you that night," he slurred. His gaze fell to my lips. "Except I wasn't free. And now that I am...I still want to kiss you. I've wanted to kiss you so many times. So many nights. I'd dream about you and wake up aching. Then I'd touch myself, wishing it was your hand, not my own. I'd walk through the library almost every day, just to see if you were there."

I drew in a sharp breath, unable to believe what I was hearing. After weeks of crushing on him, wishing I was his, and knowing I could never be, weeks of knowing he loved someone else, after helping him pick out a ring for *her*, it didn't seem real that I was hearing what I was hearing.

He leaned in as if to kiss me, but he stopped only inches away. "I want you, Zoey. I tried to stop it. I even bought Cora a fucking ring in an attempt to convince myself I didn't want you. But in the end, she turned out to be a cheating whore...and I still want *you*."

I whimpered. "Oh God." Was arousal always this intense? It was the first time I'd ever been so turned on, and I was nearly crippled by the lust. My skin sizzled with warmth. My breasts went tight and achy, and the heavy clenching deep in my womb made me press my thighs together. Quinn's erection under my bottom grew hotter.

I was more aware of him then I'd been of another human being on earth. Quinn's presence was so large, so *there*, it just took control. The heat from his body scorched me as his breath tickled my cheek when he leaned in another inch. I gulped, unable to control my erratic panting, and tried to focus on his neck.

Why I chose his neck, I have no idea. But right then, even the freckle on his pulse looked too damn sexy to calm me. I wanted to sink my teeth in it and taste him. I think I even swayed toward it.

"Did you know," he murmured, causing my nerves to wrench in eager, delicious contact with the sound of his voice and the wash of his warm, moist breath on me, "that when you're sexually aroused your heart starts pumping fast to circulate the blood to all organs that're preparing to fuck? So you start breathing harder to support the oxygen rushing through your lungs."

I squeezed my eyes shut and bowed my head, trying desperately to slow my breathing, but instead I ended up jerking in a loud, shuddering gasp that made it overly obvious just how out of control my lungs were.

He cupped the side of my neck just under my ear-lobe, his fingers skimming around to the sensitive part of my nape while his thumb just barely grazed my lower jaw. The tip of his nose brushed the rim of my ear.

"Are you listening to me, Zoey? Do you hear me breathing just as hard as you are?"

A relieved sob tore from my throat and my eyes flashed open when I realized he *was* breathing as hard as I was. I lifted my face and met his gaze. His eyes were glassy and bloodshot, but the expression was just as uncertain and hopeful as I knew mine was.

He took my hands and laced our fingers together. More pressure tightened around my chest. I couldn't believe this was happening. Quinn was touching me, and I was letting him. We both wanted what was coming next, and we both knew it. It was so crazy, yet amazing, a complete dream come true. I didn't even care how wrong it was.

He watched me as he pressed our foreheads together. My breasts swelled and pulsed with pleasure.

I whimpered, needing something, I have no idea what, but I knew Quinn could supply it. And he did. He dipped his face until his lips glanced the very corner of my mouth. I turned my face his way, seeking more, but he shifted back, teasing me out of my mind.

His gaze flitted from my lips to my eyes. Ever so vigilant, he read my expression, testing my response. "Is this okay?"

That's when I couldn't stand it a second longer. I dove at

him and kissed him for real, fitting my mouth completely against his. I had no idea what to expect, but the rush of endorphins to my head, the weightlessness in my stomach and the curling of my toes surprised me.

Quinn groaned and abandoned my hip to catch my face in his large, warm palms. His mouth moved over mine, and the tips of his fingers felt abrasive and hard and delicious as they skimmed through my hair.

I arched up, needing to get closer. My heart beat wonkily in my chest as he tugged me in until I was straddling him and pressing my throbbing core to his straining erection. I felt everything, the hard plane of his chest, the strength of muscle in his powerful thighs, the steel bulge of his arousal pressing into me. His mouth attacked mine as he kissed me hard and ruthlessly.

And I wasn't freaked out. That might've been the craziest part of it all. I trusted Quinn implicitly. He could do anything, absolutely anything, because I knew I'd want it and I'd like it. I was already that far gone. So when he began to rub little circles over the hinges of my jaw with his thumbs, I followed his lead and let my lips part for him.

His tongue swooped in, and he claimed me in a whole new way. Mine slid against his, eager but hesitant. He made a sound of approval that hummed from his throat. Then he wrapped his tongue around mine and showed me how to make them dance. Even with the hint of alcohol, I loved the way he tasted, all fresh and crisp and completely Quinn. Hungry for more, I clamped my thighs around his hips and ground against him.

He groaned and pressed right back against me.

Yes! That was it. Right there.

I broke free of the brutally hot kiss and gasped for breath. Quinn tucked his face into my throat and panted as he continued to ride his hips hard against me. It seemed like the most natural thing in the world to wrap my legs around him and imagine him deep inside me.

"What's the next step after kissing?" he rasped breathlessly.

"Wha...what?" I shook my head, my brows puckering in confusion.

"Steps of intimacy," he repeated. "You know...arm to shoulder, mouth to mouth. What's next?"

How he could remember something like that at a time

like this, I'll never know. I couldn't even remember my own name.

I shook my head, only wanting his mouth back on mine. "No idea."

"That's okay." He stood, picking me up by the butt, my legs still anchored around his waist, and he started to carry me down the hall. "We'll just figure it out as we go."

I couldn't believe this was happening, not even as he paused at a doorway where the door was three-quarters shut and he nudged me inside a dark room. I buried my face in his neck and hugged the solid expanse of his shoulders, seeking comfort from his familiar smell. My excited, overeager senses buzzed with anticipation, even as they jerked with worry.

What the heck was I doing? This was my best friend's boyfriend. Or at least he had been up until two *hours* ago. That marked him as strictly forbidden. I shouldn't be touching him the way I was touching him, wanting him the way I craved every inch of him, or licking my way up his neck the way my tongue was licking without my permission.

But he tightened his arms around me and groaned out another one of his approving hums, telling me he wanted this just as much as I did.

He was drunk though, which probably meant I was taking advantage. It was up to me to stop this.

Oh God. How was I going to find the will to stop this?

Quinn set me on the mattress once he found the bed. There was a moment in the dark that we were separated, when I knew I had to act, had to say no. But then he flicked on the bedside lamp, and I looked up at him. I opened my mouth to say...something, but the hungry need in his eyes fried my resistance. No way could I tell him no, not after he was finally looking at me the way I'd been dreaming he would for weeks.

His crystalline blue eyes glittered with a predatory awareness as he set a knee on the bed and began to crawl toward me. I had no idea why I went on retreat, maybe because he looked as if he wanted to devour me whole. I wasn't graceful with my crablike crawl away from him while he was more than supple in his stealthy prowl forward. By the time he climbed on top of me, I had stumbled back into a supine sprawl with the back of my head flattening into one of his pillows.

Triumph flooded his smile as he gazed at me. My lips trembled when I tried to smile back. I didn't know what was about to happen, I didn't know how it'd feel, or how it'd affect us afterward, I just knew I wanted it anyway. Desperately.

Quinn must've sensed my nerves. He studied me with his glassy, inebriated gaze before catching a piece of my hair and whispering, "Are you scared?"

I shook my head, though I'm sure I probably looked like a liar from how wide my eyes were and how badly my lips trembled.

But scared? Of him? Never.

Nervous? Yes. Definitely.

He gently smoothed his rough fingers over my face before tucking my hair behind my ears. "Have you ever done this before?"

I almost blurted out a laugh. But done *this*? I'd never even kissed anyone before he'd brushed his mouth against mine only minutes ago in the front room. So, no, I'd never lain on a bed underneath a guy, and I'd certainly never done what he was really asking.

I settled for shaking my head a second time.

Tenderness entered his face. I think he liked my answer. He kissed the tip of my nose. "Can I show you how?"

I nodded, and he flashed me his dimples.

"We have to communicate a lot," he whispered, "let each other know what we do and don't like."

I smiled, because, "I like everything so far," I whispered back.

When I circled his face with the tips of my fingers, hoping he liked that, his gaze met mine. "So, do I."

Then this expression entered his face, like awe, as if he couldn't believe it was me under him and not someone else. It reminded me of the exact way I felt. I was here with Quinn, like *this*. I just could not believe this was happening.

"What else should I know?" I asked, eager to learn.

"Kissing," he said right before he lowered his mouth to mine. "Kissing it important."

Our lips absorbed each other, exploring and moving until our tongues joined in, and it was just as powerful as our first kiss. Maybe more so.

"I like kissing," I gasped out, cradling his face and burying my fingers in his rich, thick hair as he nib·bled his

242

way down my neck.

"It gets better."

Oh, God. I swallowed and then sucked in a hard breath when his teeth nipped at a sensitive spot on my pulse.

Body on fire and throbbing in more places than I could count, I arched up against him. "How? Show me."

"Touching," he said. "Touching and kissing both."

Thus began the pleasure assault of his fingers. Up my neck, into my hair, clutching my scalp as he kissed me deeper, then down again, over my shoulders, along my arms, catching my hip, curving around the swell of my bottom and digging his nails in as he canted my hips up and ground his erection into my core.

I couldn't take much more of this. I had to... I had to...

"Can I touch you too?" My voice was high and desperate.

"Yes." He took my wrist and pressed my palm flush against the center of his chest, right over his heart. "Touch wherever you like. Learn me, Zoey."

Dazed that I was actually doing this, I watched my hand, entranced as I moved it down, over his shirt. Mesmerized by the power and strength I felt rippling under the cotton, I moved back up, still unable to believe I was touching him *however* I pleased.

He pulled back and sat up on his haunches long enough to grasp the back of his shirt and tear it off over his head. And oh, my... My greedy hands returned to him, a little more certain, and a lot more curious.

"You're so warm and hard, yet soft."

"Not as soft as you." He leaned down and kissed me again, petting his hand down my side until he reached the hem of my shirt. I was too busy delighting my way over his bulky, warm arms and thick shoulders, then pausing at the stubble on his jaw, before having a field day in his hair, to care what he did with my shirt. It didn't even alarm me when his fingers swooped under the cloth and skimmed over the flesh at my waist. Heck, I arched my back to give him more access. He took it, moving his palm up and his mouth down until they met at my breasts. As he cupped the bottom half and kissed the top through layers of cloth, I reacted wildly, not expecting how strongly an electrical current would shoot right out the ends of my nipples, and definitely not ready to feel it deep in my core.

I clutched him, my hands curling instinctively around

his back to anchor him against me. When my fingers encountered scar tissue, I faltered. Crap, I'd forgotten about his wounds. Quinn jerked and made a sound in the base of his throat as if he wasn't quite sure how to react to my discovery.

I wanted to inspect each laceration and love them, kissing every single one of them. But now didn't seem like the time, so I ventured south until I came to the waistband of his jeans. Needing him to know he hadn't repulsed me in any way, I kept going, inside his jeans, under the band of his boxers and down until I cupped cool, smooth buttocks. Then I squeezed.

He groaned and bit down a little more enthusiastically onto my breast before he was whipping my shirt over my head.

For a brief moment, I panicked. What if he saw how skinny and puny I was and turned disgusted? What if—

"It's okay," he murmured, stroking one side of my hair as he buried his nose into the other. "You're so beautiful. I just want to see you." He pulled back. "Just want to worship every inch of you."

I blew out a shuddered breath and nodded. His smile warmed. Then his gaze lowered. I held perfectly still. When he reached for the strap of my bra and slid it off my shoulder, I closed my eyes and concentrated on breathing. But he stilled.

"Zoey?"

My lashes fluttered open.

He shook his head, almost as if he was confused. "Don't be scared. I'd never hurt you."

Tears filled my eyes. I nodded and sent him a huge, watery smile. Then I removed my bra myself. He watched, seemingly spellbound. After I unbuttoned my pants, shimmied them down my legs, and kicked them off, I hooked my fingers into the tops of my panties, but he caught my hand. "Not yet. I just... I-I don't know if I could trust my own control if I saw all of you right now because...wow."

He blew out a breath.

Feeling good, feeling bold and uninhibited, I reached for the top button of his jeans. "Can I see all of *you*?"

Another strained breath escaped him, but he nodded and removed both his jeans and his boxer shorts.

I thought I was ready for my first glimpse of his cock,

but I wasn't at all. My head went dizzy as the long column bobbed proud and free from his body. I knew the mechanics, what was supposed to happened, what went where, and I began to wonder how the heck that huge, long thing could fit anywhere inside me. He'd rip me in half.

Oh, crap. How bad was this going to hurt?

"Trust me," he said, reading my mind as he smoothed his fingers over my hair. "It'll work. As long as you're wet, it'll work perfectly."

Well, we didn't need to worry about that then. I was already wet. Embarrassingly wet. My panties were so damp they'd soaked through.

I blushed hard, but he merely smiled. "After the touching and kissing comes the licking," he instructed. He lowered his head and licked one of my nipples into his mouth.

My back came off the bed as I shrieked, startled by the intensity of sensation that surged through me. But Quinn didn't just lick. He commenced to suck as well, lavishing one breast, then the other until I was a panting, aroused mess.

"Quinn," I begged, needing him to help alleviate all this throbbing pressure he'd created.

His lips were red and swollen when he lifted his face to grin at me, his blue eyes still glazed with alcohol but also, I think, arousal.

"Ready for another biology lesson?"

"What?" I gasped in disbelief, my chest heaving. How could he even think about—

My eyes crossed when he slid his hand down and touched me through my drenched panties.

"I want to teach you about flowers. Flower anatomy."

What had he just said? Nothing was computing. So I just bobbed my head and slurred, "'Kay."

"Like humans, flowers can have female reproductive organs, male reproductive organs, or they can have both." His fingers curled around the band of my underwear, and he began to lower them over my abdomen, then my pubic hair.

I sucked in my stomach, unable to catch a steady breath.

After he peeled the cloth down my legs and tossed them over his shoulder, his gaze focused on me, right where I was wet and aching. I didn't mean to, but I squirmed until I'd arched my hips an inch off the bed in a silent plea for attention.

His lips spread with a masculine kind of pride. "First, you see the petals that cover the reproductive organs." His gaze lifted to mine as one of his fingers stroked *my* petals. "That's the prettiest part, I think. So pink and delicate, hiding the best things inside it."

I bit my bottom lip as my thighs quivered with need.

His attention fell to where he was gently thrumming his finger up and down my labia. "Some flowers react to sunlight and open their petals during the day, exposing all their carpels to the world." He swiped his finger between my lower lips, making me cry out and jerk from the mattress. "Am I your sunlight, Zoey? Is that why you opened your petals?"

I didn't respond past a needy whimper, but I don't think I needed to. He already knew the answer. He wasn't just my sunlight; he was my everything.

"This receptive tip here would be the stigma. It catches all the pollen for germination." He slipped his finger over my clit and rolled it delicately under the pad of his finger. "It's definitely caught me."

He massaged the nub relentlessly, focusing on nothing but the circular movement of his touch. My body seemed to compress into that one spot, coiling all feeling there as if waiting for the right moment to release it and zap the sensation back out the ends of my arms and legs.

"Nectar is what attracts the bees who carry off the pollen to other flowers where they get more, but me...if I were a bee, I don't think I'd be a good pollinator. I think I'd taste one brand of flower and like it so much I'd become addicted. I'd never want to go off to another one ever again."

After dipping his face, he licked me, right up through the center of my petals, swiping up a mouthful of my nectar. I shrieked and clutched the blankets under me, my thighs quivering and chest heaving while the hard tips of my nipples burned for the same attention.

Lifting his face to look up at me, he groaned. "God, yes. That's the flavor, right there. That's what would keep me coming back for more, every time."

Which is exactly what he did. His tongue went back for more, working faster, making his strokes longer, and applying pressure harder until I was squirming under him, grabbing handfuls of his hair, and whimpering completely incoherent words. It was so much more than I ever thought this could possibly be, and yet something seemed to be missing, like I needed—

As his tongue continued to lavish ceaselessly, his finger went lower, circled the damp rim of my sex and then pushed inside.

I cried out. The muscles inside me greedily contracted around his fingers before the tightening in my womb went crazy. I didn't know how to control it; there *was* no way to control what happened next. I choked out the most embarrassing sound, and yet I didn't care. I was freaking flying. My body went hay-wire in the best way possible and Quinn, the source of it, just kept feeding the explosion with his mouth and fingers.

By the time I settled down, I was limp and exhausted, yet exhilarated and at peace, satisfied in a way that boggled my mind.

Quinn took his mouth off me and slid his finger free. I whimpered from the loss, but I still felt too good to really care. When he sat up and our gazes met, he looked a little feverish, his eyes desperate and his skin slick with sweat.

Feeling as if I'd taken on all his alcohol, I offered him a drunken smile. "Whoa," was all I could think to say.

He laughed, and his flushed face crinkled with genuine pleasure. "I wish I could take a picture of your smile right now." He reached out to unstick a sweat-clogged piece of hair from my cheek. "I want to memorize it and carry it around with me always."

Too blank to think up an appropriate response to his sweet words, I nodded. I wanted to thank him, pile my own heap of sweetness right back onto him, and praise him for being...him. But I'm pretty sure he'd just scrambled all rational thought right out of my head.

So what I ended up saying was, "There's more, right?"

His blue eyes sparkled as he nodded. My gaze fell down to his cock where he was still kneeling between my spread legs. Hard, and long, and completely intimidating, it dripped with anticipation, stirring up a new arousal in me I had thought for sure he'd licked away.

Before, I'd been worried about the fit, but after his finger had been in me and I'd loved the way it had filled me—and had wanted even more filling me—I was actually eager to feel the real deal. Spreading my legs wider, I lifted my hips to him, displaying everything I had to let him know I wanted it. I had no clue where my inhibitions had gone, but with Quinn Hamilton hard and dripping before me, those things had high jacked themselves out my body and taken a vacation.

"Show me," I said.

Again, he nodded without speaking. After spotting his crumpled jeans hanging off the side of the bed, he dug into the back pocket, pulled out his wallet and flipped it open. As he pulled out a condom, a moment of reality struck. Hard. I experienced another slap of guilt.

He'd probably bought that condom, thinking he'd use it on my roommate.

Oh, God. What was I doing? I shouldn't be doing this. He was Cora's. She'd had him first, and probably opened herself in this very position to him many times. I should never be allowed—

But then he tore open the package and began to sheathe himself. It was beautiful to watch. He rolled the small layer of latex down with such care, holding on to the tip as he went. Then he wrapped his fist around the base as if to insure everything was in pro·per place.

When he started to let go, I choked out a sound of resistance. "No. Don't."

He looked up, startled. "What's wrong?"

I blushed, embarrassed by what I wanted and averted my gaze. "Nothing."

"No, tell me. Zoey, please."

He touched my hip and looked so worried, as if he thought I might stop everything, I had to tell him. Ducking my face, I admitted, "I...I liked watching you...touch it."

His mouth fell open. He looked down at himself and then back up to me. Then his lips twitched. "What? Like this?"

He touched himself again, rewrapping his palm around his thick girth. Then he went and pumped his fist slowly up and down the entire length.

"Oh, God." I drew in an awestruck breath. "Yeah. Like that. Is that...is that how you masturbate?"

He nodded and closed this eyes, his throat working as he kept on with the movement of his hand. "This is what I did when I thought about you."

"It's breathtaking," I didn't mean to admit aloud.

His pupils seemed to dilate and his shallow pants went even more erratic. "You could do it too." When his gaze slid between my legs, a spark of arousal shot through my pussy, startling me. "You could touch yourself where I just touched you."

My mouth worked before I could form the words. "W-would that...I mean, would you like that?"

Face going from red to deep purple, he nodded, his eyes intent. "Only as much as you seem to like watching me do it."

Oh. Wow. That much, huh?

I slowly, hesitantly reached down. But my fingers had barely begun to fondle, eliciting an excited tremble in my womb, when Quinn lost it.

"Fuck," he rasped, his teeth locked tight as he stared dumbfounded at my hand between my legs. "I can't...I'm sorry, I can't wait. I have to..." He let go of himself to grasp my thighs. As he pulled me down toward him, into his lap, he thrust his hips forward. Like two matching pieces of a puzzle, we came together.

Quinn pushed inside me without pause or hesitation. I cried out from the shock and nip of pain as he filled me completely. His overly long eyelashes fluttered as he tipped his head back, making the muscles in his throat strain.

He said something, then said it again. I wasn't sure if it was *Jesus* or *Jeez* or a strange version of both, but the word seemed to be ripped out of him. When he finally looked down at me, he appeared dazed and drugged. But he only had to glance into my eyes before his own widened with realization.

"Oh shit, Zoey. I'm inside you."

"I know." If there was only one thing in the world I knew in that moment, it was that he was full and hard and deep inside me.

"Are you okay? Does it hurt?" He didn't wait for me to answer before demanding, "How bad does it hurt? I'll pull out."

He started to retract his hips, but I stopped him, clamping my thighs around him. "No. Don't. It's not bad. Just a little sting. It's already...it's not so...just give me a second."

Quinn nodded, watching my face. Panic etched into his expression, his gaze drifting to my white cheeks and my wide eyes. "It's not fair. Why does it have to hurt for you and feel so good to me?"

249

I smiled and buried my fingers in his forearms. "Does it feel good to you?"

His laugh was surprised, as if he couldn't believe I even had to ask. "Yeah," he admitted. His hips started to move, but he gritted his teeth and held them still again.

Beginning to grow accustomed to the stretch my inner muscles made to accommodate his girth, I shifted and started thinking that moving might not be such a bad idea after all. But I knew he wasn't going to budge until I okayed it. I liked knowing that. I liked having some power and control here, even though he was the experienced one who was teaching me everything.

Wiping beads of sweat off his brow, I said, "Maybe if you kissed me, you could share some of that good feeling."

"Okay," he said as if willing to try anything.

It'd been too many minutes since his mouth had last pressed against mine. He felt fresh and new, as if I'd never kissed him before. A light tang on his tongue made me realize exactly what I was tasting. I knew I should be embarrassed, but just then, I didn't care.

Quinn moaned and rolled his hips. I don't think he realized what he'd done. But I did. Oh, how I noticed the way it felt for him to retreat and then penetrate again, rubbing his heavy length against a bundle of nerves. My toes curled and my fingernails dug into his scalp. When I arched my hips up to meet his next thrust, he spiked his tongue deeper into my mouth and pounded a little harder, a little faster.

"Yes," I sobbed. "*Yes.*"

He slid his hands under my bottom and lifted it off the mattress so he could control the angle and depth of his plunges. My body quickened and that sensation I'd experienced only minutes before crested once more.

"Quinn!"

"Zoey," he groaned, gripping my hips and pouring into me.

We came together, and it was the best biology les-son of my life.

Twenty-Nine

✥ Quinn ✥

I CAME AWAKE slowly, murmuring her name and reaching for her. An unexplainable energy flowed through me. I honestly couldn't remember ever feeling this happy. Last night...wow. Last night had honestly been the best night of my life, and it was all because of the woman lying beside me. I smiled, giddy beyond words and already trying to think up a way to keep her here in bed for the rest of the day. To keep her forever.

I rolled onto my side and into the pillow she'd used, rustling up the wild cherry and jewel orchid smell of her shampoo. But my fingers met with cooled sheets.

My eyes flashed open. I sat upright in bed, only to find myself alone.

"Zoey?" I croaked, my voice hoarse and raspy.

No one answered except my own, lonely echo.

Panic clutched my throat as reality struck me over the head like a club, reminding me how much alcohol I'd guzzled last night.

The first night I'd gotten wasted, I had remembered nothing from the night before...nothing until last night. This morning, I remembered every·thing. Every single detail, every time I woke in the night to take Zoey again, every time she accepted me and let me back into her body. I lost count of how many times we'd come together; after a while, the rounds blurred together until I stopped pulling out and just stayed inside her until I was hard again.

I'd taken her from behind, underneath, against the headboard, in her mouth. I'd wanted her every way possible, and she'd been willing—so freaking willing and eager—to let me do whatever I wanted.

"Oh my God." I clutched my head, my hangover coming on strong as memory after memory flooded me. I hadn't just taken Zoey's virginity, I'd completely demolished it.

Only *hours* after breaking up with her roommate.

Ripping the sheets off me, I flew out of bed and found my clothes from last night scattered around the floor. It wasn't until I was yanking my jeans up that I spotted a feminine-looking piece of pink cloth peeking out from under the bed. I bent to pick it up and un-wadded it to find panties in my palm. Zoey's panties. She'd been in such a rush to escape, she'd left her underwear behind.

That couldn't be good. But what really made the dread rise in my gut was seeing my engagement ring for Cora sitting on my nightstand.

"No, no, no," I chanted as I shoved my feet into the first two shoes I found. They totally didn't match, but I had a left shoe on my left foot and a right shoe on my right foot, so that was good enough for me. I tucked her panties in my pocket and raced for the door.

Okay, fine, I smelled them before slipping them out of sight. And they smelled exactly how I remembered her. My mouth watered, detecting the taste of her divine nectar. When my cock hardened, I muttered, "Stupid pecker."

If my drunken hormones had just lost me my friendship with Zoey, I would never forgive myself.

I drove to her apartment. I didn't even think. I just had to see her. Had to make sure she was okay.

Noel texted me on my way over. Twice. I ignored his messages until I parked in the parking garage of Zoey's building. When I opened his message, I was reminded I was late for practice.

You're coming to practice, right?

I didn't answer. I didn't want to think about foot-ball right now. And I didn't particularly want to see Ten, who would be there.

Man, you HAVE to come to practice, Noel wrote in his next text. **Coach won't let you start the next game if you don't.**

A minute later, he tried again. **Ten just covered for you. He fed coach a big lie about how sick you are.**

Good. Ten *better* have covered for me. He owed me that much at least. I had thought Noel would leave me alone then, but he didn't.

You're going to forgive him, right? It's TEN! You HAVE to forgive him. The guy's driving me nuts with how worried he is.

"Yeah, and you're driving *me* nuts," I muttered aloud, finally punching in my response. It felt strange to type a curse word, but I didn't regret it in the least. **Did you fuck Cora too?**

Noel's response was immediate. **WHAT? NO! GOD no.**

That was all I needed to see. I shut my phone off and slid it into my pocket, the same pocket with Zoey's panties. The soft cotton brushed against my knuckles and I shuddered, remembering when I'd slid them down her legs and had my first look at her completely naked.

I looked up just in time to see Terrance opening the door to her building. When Zoey stepped outside, I sucked in a breath and climbed from my truck. She was so beautiful. I still couldn't believe I'd been inside her just hours ago. I'd seen her naked and touched her. Licked her. Loved every freaking inch of her. My hormones buzzed with awareness, even as I shook my head, unable to believe we'd actually done everything we'd done.

She wore her hair down this morning, which worried me since she was always big on ponytails. Plus she had on her glasses, which she never wore when she left her apartment. The wind blew her hair in her face and she pushed it out of her eyes in her usual Zoey way. My chest filled with pressure, with possessiveness. She was mine. Only *I* had ever done to her the things we'd done last night. As wrong as I knew I was for sleeping with her only hours after breaking up with her best friend, I couldn't stop the perverse satisfaction that bubbled up my throat. No matter what happened, a part of her would always belong to me. I'd been her first.

As if feeling my eyes on her—I loved how she seemed to know I was watching her—she looked over and saw me. She slowed to a stop, so I stepped away from my truck to go to her. Her lips parted and her eyes widened. I couldn't tell if she was happy or horrified to see me. But I was about to find out. I had to talk to her.

It was impossible to take my eyes off her; that was probably why I completely missed who exited the door behind her.

"Quinn?" Cora's voice stopped me cold in my tracks.

I met my ex-girlfriend's gaze and panicked. Crap, why hadn't I even thought about her when I'd raced over here?

Hope sparked across her face. I gritted my teeth and shook my head. Slinking a step back, I scowled at Cora.

She began to rush toward me, but I couldn't talk to *her*. Not yet. Maybe not ever. I spun around and hurried off, slamming my door in my hurry to escape.

Cora reached my truck about the time I cranked the engine. She tried to open the door, but I'd already locked it. Scowling at me, she pounded on the window.

"Quinn. Damn it, talk to me."

My head was still swimming with all the filthy words I'd read on her phone, every intimate detail she'd written to other men, so I did something I'd never done before. I flipped her off and gunned the gas, backing out of my spot.

Mad because she'd tried to talk to me, because she'd prevented me from checking on Zoey, because she was still breathing, I drove blindly for a couple minutes, until I realized I needed a destination. I needed a plan. But I didn't know where to go or what to do.

Attending practice started to sound good. What better place to unleash some of the anger and anxiety gushing through me? I could tackle and hurt, and get hurt. I craved that.

But I wasn't ready to face Ten again. Not just yet.

So I found myself at Forbidden.

Asher was on the stage, rearranging microphones and preparing for the second night of karaoke. It seemed strange that my double date with Zoey and Ten had only been a week ago. I'd taken my first swallow of alcohol, I'd nearly kissed Zoey, I'd spent the rest of the night with Cora, and then I had bought her a ring and tried to propose to her. All of that within seven days, and I'd still found enough time to squeeze in completely shattering Zoey Blakeland's innocence.

Feeling sick to my stomach and still rocking a hefty hangover, I glanced around the quiet club. "Is Pick around?"

Asher straightened and turned my way, not having realized I'd come in. He tipped his head toward the hall. "He's in the back. Hey, help me move this speaker, will you? It's a heavy bastard."

I nodded and moved forward to assist him. We grunted and strained for a couple minutes to rearrange the stage until he had everything where he wanted it. He didn't ask questions or try to strike up a conversation, which I appreciated. I'd learned that when he was in a certain mode, he became too focused for social niceties. Which worked perfectly for me. A little labor without having to come up with words was exactly what I needed.

But as soon as we had everything where he wanted it, he grinned at me as he dusted his hands off on his jeans. "Thanks, man." I could see a conversation approaching, so I mumbled something and hurried down the hall to knock on Pick's office door.

The last time I'd been in the owner's office of this club, it'd been located in another room, and another man had been behind the desk. I'd gotten shot that day and seen two people die. Strangely enough, I felt more rattled today than I had then.

"Come on in," Pick called from inside.

After taking a big gulp of air, I entered. I wasn't sure what I was going to say; I just knew I needed help. Advice. Something.

Anything.

And I trusted Pick more than anyone to be confidential and helpful.

When he glanced up and saw me, he let out a relieved sigh. "Thank God, it's you. I'm working on this bitch of a schedule. Do you think you can work to-morrow, Monday, and Tuesday night? Lowe has chic-ken pox. *Chicken pox!* Can you believe that fucker? What twenty-two-year-old gets chicken pox?"

"I don't know," I mumbled as I began to pace. "But, yeah, sure. I can work them. No problem."

"Thanks, man." Pick started to pencil me in when he must've finally noticed how badly I was wigging out. His pencil stopped moving a good minute before he lifted his eyes. "Everything okay?" he finally asked.

"No." I captured my head with both hands and walked a little faster, needing to vent out some of the adrenaline churning through me.

Pick sat his pen down and straightened, finally lifting the rest of his face to give me his full attention. "What's going on?"

I knew he was good for discretion, but I still didn't mean to blurt out quite everything that vomited from my mouth. "Last night...I broke up with Cora. She was cheating on me. And then I got drunk and had sex with Zoey, like, all night long."

Groaning, I squeezed my head harder and closed my eyes to block out the buzzing between my ears.

When I risked a glance at Pick to gauge his re-action, he was just staring at me with the blankest expression. Finally, he said, "And then you woke up, right? Because this was another one of your crazy-ass dreams. *Right?*"

Collapsing on his couch, I buried my face in my hands and groaned. "I wish, but no. This one wasn't a dream."

"Holy shit," Pick exploded. "I mean, *shit.* Holy shit, man. You..." He shook his head. "I mean, we're really talking about *you* doing this, right? Not Ten. *You?*"

I seared him with a glare and he immediately apologized. "Sorry, I just..." He held up a hand and blew out a long breath. "It's just a shock, that's all. Sorry about that." He smoothed his fingers down the center of his chest as if straightening a tie he wasn't wearing. "I'm calmer now."

"Yeah, well, *I'm* not. Twenty-four hours ago, I was with one girl, settled down, completely committed in our relationship and thinking I was going to spend the rest of my life with no one but *her*, and then bam, a few hours later, I'm inside her roommate, and...God, I can't even...I'm not...I don't even know. I have no idea what to do about this."

"Yeah," Pick said, looking a little shell-shocked himself, which didn't ease my nerves at all. Then he cleared his throat and shook his head. "So, um...are you sure it's over between you and Cora?"

I sent him a sharp look, a little incredulous he even had to ask. "*Yes.*" There was no doubt in my voice at all. "I hate her. She killed anything *and* everything I ever felt for her the moment I read the texts she sent to another guy...to *multiple* other guys."

"Are you sure?" Pick cocked a leery eyebrow. "I mean, about your feelings? All this *just* went down. You may think you hate her now, and then realize... shit. I mean, you weren't just upset and hurt and struck out at her by sleeping with her friend... Did you?"

"*What?*" I surged to my feet, my face molting hot with anger. "*No!* God, no. I would never...not to Zoey. Not with any *girl*, but definitely not her."

Pick nodded, looking relieved. "Hey, man. I was just making sure."

I ran my hand through my hair and began to pace in a circle. "I still...I mean, she was a virgin. I was drunk. I shouldn't have...I know I need to talk to her, but I have no idea what to say. She was gone when I woke up, and I drove to her place without thinking, except Cora was there, so I took off without talking to her, and...I just... It was her first time," I repeated stupidly. "I know I have to apologize, but—"

"No, no, no." Pick stood up and waved his hands, instantly nixing that idea. He came around to me. "Whatever you do, you do *not* apologize to a woman *ever* for having sex with her. Unless you freaking *forced* her. Shit, you didn't force her, did you?"

I scowled. "No."

"Okay, good. That's good. It's a start. We can work with that." He paused beside me, eyeing me with a worried gaze.

Shaking my head, not comprehending, I asked, "Why can't I apologize to her?"

"Because you just completed one of the most personal, bonding acts a woman can go through. You don't ever want to tell her that was a mistake and you regret making that kind of connection with her."

"But I do regret the *way* it happened," I argued. "No girl's first time should come from a drunk guy mauling her after he just found out he'd been cheated on. She's not...she's not some rebound lay."

"Perfect." Pick snapped his fingers and pointed at me. "Tell her that."

I blinked at him and waited for him to say more, but he just shrugged. "What?"

"Well, what do I say *after* that?"

He shrugged and then patted my shoulder sympathetically. "No idea, man. Sorry. Every situation is different. You're going to have to wait and see how she reacts to the first part before you proceed with the rest of your conversation."

I swallowed, feeling sick again. "Great."

I'd be going into this blind, and I had a bad feeling that when I came out of our talk, Zoey would no longer be in my life.

Fear clutched my throat.

I began to remember every moment we'd talked be‑fore last night, how we'd been able to open up to each other and share some really personal things with complete trust. Zoey might just know more about me than any other living person on the planet. She was a confidante and a friend. The fact that I still wanted to have sex with her in every speed and position ever made was completely inconsequential. I didn't want to lose her friendship.

PICK LET ME HANG around his office for a couple more minutes. He talked me through a few scenarios until I felt a little better, but I was still bone‑deep scared. I still wanted to see Zoey as soon as possible. And I still needed to know we could repair what I had obliterated between us. But Pick thought I should give her a day to adjust and deal with what had happened.

He reminded me that she probably felt as if she'd betrayed Cora and might not want to see me just yet, because my presence would only heighten her guilt. Knowing she was going through that made me feel worse, but I decided to follow his advice. Ergo, I had to wait at least twenty‑four hours before tracking her down.

I left his office with a grateful thanks. When I exited the hall and entered the main part of the club, I slowed to a stop, catching sight of Ten as he pushed through the front door.

Checking the time, I realized practice must already be over. Damn. I wasn't ready to deal with him. Stick‑ing to the shadows of the hallway, I narrowed my eyes and watched him stalk toward the bar.

"I need alcohol. Bad."

"Well, you came to the right place." Asher flipped up a cup and served him a shot of tequila.

Ten didn't even say thank you; he snagged the cup from the bar and downed it with a hard swallow, then he gritted his teeth and focused on Asher. "What the fuck did you do to your hair?"

Asher chuckled as he flicked his head to the side, letting me see the blond ends he'd dyed into his dark hair, which I hadn't noticed earlier when I'd come in. "Caroline thought I'd look cool with highlights. So...I went and got some. Who gave you the black eye?"

"Caroline?" Ten repeated incredulously, narrowing his eyes, and completely ignoring Asher's return question. "You mean, *my* Caroline?"

Asher arched an amused eyebrow. "*Your* Caro-line?"

Ten flashed his teeth in a silent snarl. "*Noel's* Caroline. Caroline Gamble. You know who the fuck I mean, damn it."

"Oh, well then..." Asher grinned. "Yeah, *that* Caro-line."

Face growing dark, Ten leaned across the counter toward Asher. "Since when are you and Caroline such great buddies?"

Asher gave a shrug as he refilled Ten's shot glass. "Since we met at my first gig last week, I guess. We exchanged numbers and started texting—"

"You *what*?" Ten snagged the next drink and swallowed it whole before slamming the empty glass back down. "Does Noel know you two are suddenly so tight?"

Asher made a face as if he wanted to contradict Ten's terminology, but then he said, "Yeah. I mean, I think he knows. Why? We just *talk*. What's your deal, man?"

"My *deal* is that I don't want some fucking prick talking to her and thinking he can get into her panties because over my dead body is that happening. Ever. Got it?"

Asher grinned suddenly, as if he finally had Ten exactly where he wanted him. "Why not?" he taunted. "She's cute. She's fun. She's sweet. I think it could be good between us."

"And I think my fist would feel good slamming right into your throat, motherfucker."

A full laugh exploded from Asher. "Man, you are so obvious. If you want me to stay away from her, just tell me you like her, and I will."

"I like her," Ten nearly roared. "Stay the fuck away from her."

"Fine." Asher shrugged as if it were no problem whatsoever to step aside and let Ten have a go. Then he poured Ten a third shot.

"Fuck," Ten muttered. "I can't believe you got me to admit that."

"What can I say?" Asher looked pretty proud of himself. "I'm just that good."

"Fucker," Ten muttered, before glancing around. "Where's Pick?"

"He's in the back, talking to Hamilton."

Ten straightened; his face paled. "Ham's here? Shit." His gaze veered toward the hallway and instantly found me, watching them. Then his shoulders heaved as he drew in a deep breath. "Hey." His voice was cautious, respectful, regretful.

I didn't answer, but I did step out of the shadows before stopping again, my arms folded over my chest. He grew uncomfortable under my direct stare. He cleared his throat, glanced away and tapped his empty shot glass against the countertop, motioning for Asher to pour him another.

Asher glanced between us and then poured. He watched Ten down that shot before Ten grabbed the bottle from his hand to pour himself another. As Ten tossed that back as well, Asher pointed back and forth between us. "So, if you two are breaking up, does that mean I have to pick sides? Because I'd rather just stay neutral if it's all the same to you."

"Fuck you," Ten said, shaking the bottle to find it empty. "Get a different alcohol, will you?"

When Asher did, Ten swiped it out his hand, muttering, "Stop looking at me like that, fucker."

"Wow." Asher let out a low whistle. "You know, I'm not sensing any appreciation. And here I'd just agreed to step aside so you could have Caroline, too."

"You did not agree to step aside so I could have her, ass wipe. I'm never having her, either. You *a greed* to step aside, because you know your stupid rock-star ass is worse for her than my dumb man-whore ass. Jesus." Ten sucked down the next shot and then shook his head and bowed his face as if the alcohol was starting to get to him.

Pick strolled out of the hallway and slowed to a stop when he spotted the newest arrival. Setting his forearm against my shoulder to lean against me, he studied Ten passively. "Well, if it isn't Can't-Keep-It-In-His-Pants Tenning."

Ten slowly looked up and scowled at Pick. "Not a good time for that shit, man."

Pick just smirked back. "Didn't we warn you to never tell him about you and Cora?"

"Say what?" Asher asked as I tensed and glanced at Pick.

How did he know Ten and Cora had—

Pick slid his arm off my shoulder to pat it reassuringly.

Ten's eyes narrowed as he glanced between us. "Fuck," he said. "I should've known Ham would tell you."

With a chuckle, Pick shook his head. "Actually, he didn't. But I figured it out from the tension between you two and that black eye you're sporting."

"Wait. What loop am I being left out of?" Asher snagged Ten's shot cup and cleaned it before Ten could demand more. "You're not saying *Quinn* gave him the shiner, are you? And, Ten, you really didn't fuck Cora...did you?"

"Oh, yes he did," Pick announced so openly that I flinched from hearing it said aloud and in such a mild, blasé tone.

"Holy shit." Asher's eyes bugged before he turned an accusing gaze on Ten. "Man, what the hell?"

"Relax," Ten growled. "It was before they started dating..." Guilt crept over his face before he more quietly added, "...or so I thought."

Asher lifted both eyebrows. "But I thought you hated Hamilton's woman."

"She's *not* my woman," I bit out, only for Pick to pat my shoulder again. Unwillingly, the twitchy muscles under his touch calmed.

Asher didn't seem to know how to respond to my outburst. He slid his surprised gaze from me to Ten.

"Why do you think I hate her?" Ten admitted, glancing apologetically my way. "The bitch lied to me and said you two had only been a one-time deal."

I studied him for a moment before something suddenly became clear to me. "Is that why you never let her stay overnight at our place?" Ten looked away, the apology on his face morphing back into guilt. I snorted. "You were afraid she'd crawl out of my bed and right into yours."

Wow, that was a sobering thought. All this time, my own roommate had known she couldn't be trusted to keep her legs together around other men, and I'd been a clueless idiot. "Well, thanks for letting me know what she was really like. Appreciate it."

"Hey." Ten turned back and lifted his hands in defense. "She was so into you after you guys started going hot and heavy, I kind of thought she might've changed for you. I *hoped* she had."

"But just not enough to trust her overnight at our place, huh?"

Ten sighed and ran his hand through his hair. "I don't know what you want me to say. I told you I was sorry. And I am. If I could take it back, I would. The last thing on earth I'd ever want to do is betray one of my friends. I feel like shit, okay."

I didn't want to give in, but I knew he was speaking the truth. He didn't betray his friends, otherwise he would've satisfied his craving for Caroline a long time ago. But he stayed away, in honor of Noel.

"So, what do you say, Quinn?" Pick squeezed my shoulder again. "Are you going to forgive the dumbass for accidently sleeping with someone he probably shouldn't have?" When his gaze met mine, I realized he wasn't referring to just Ten and Cora; he was reminding me of Zoey.

I glanced away, the shame catching me in the throat. What I'd done with her was fifty times worse than anything Ten had done with a girl he thought was completely available and willing.

After blowing out a breath, I nodded. "Yeah," I said, my voice rusty as if I hadn't talked in a week. "I guess. Whatever."

"What? *Really?*" Ten straightened, looking bewildered. "Just like that? You forgive me?"

He stared at me in disbelief as if he wanted more from me. "What?" I said, scowling back. "Don't expect a hug or anything."

Pick and Asher burst out laughing. Looking a little sick to his stomach, Ten spun on his stool to face the bar, and then reached over to snag the bottle out of Asher's hand so he could tip it up and just let the alcohol guzzle down his throat.

Scowling, Pick pointed at him. "Hey, you're paying for that entire bottle now, fucker."

The front doors came open. The four of us turned as

Mason strolled into the club. His face was dotted with red splotches but he was whistling under his breath. He stopped when he saw us staring, though. Glancing around, he sent us a perturbed scowl. "Well, thanks for inviting *me* to the party."

"Hart and I are just keeping Hamilton here from killing Ten," Pick explained. "What're you doing out and about? I thought you had chicken pox."

"I do, but..." Mason pointed toward the stage, only to frown and scratch his arm. "I promised Asher I'd help him reset the stage for karaoke night. Except..."

"Quinn already helped me." Asher nodded to me with a grateful smile.

"Yeah," Mason said slowly, sliding his gaze his way. "What is *Quinn* doing here, though?" Then he glanced at my roommate. "And Ten too, for that mat-ter. I thought Gamble was filling in for me tonight."

"Ham broke up with Cora," Pick announced.

Again, the calm, level way he said it made my jaws clench. Coming from his mouth like that, it sounded like some average, everyday thing had happened, whereas I was barely keeping myself together from all the trauma. I wanted to rage and break things, and curl into a ball and die, and then shrivel up from mortification, all while the things I'd done with Zoey kept whirling through my brain, keeping me perpetually guilty and horny at the same time.

To say I was an utter mess was probably the understatement of the century.

"Oh, shit," Mason uttered, turning to Pick. "You finally told him how she hit on you, huh?"

I spun toward Pick and gaped at him open-mouthed. He backed away slowly and lifted his hands, his eyes wide with culpability.

Oh my God. She *had* hit on him.

"*What the fuck!*" I gripped my hair, wanting to pull out every lock by the roots, just...anything to relieve the anger and humiliation inside me.

Mason turned wide-eyed to Ten. "Did Hamilton just say fuck? Or is my fever messing with my ears?"

Ten smacked him in the arm. "Way to go, asshole. You turned him to cursing."

"Does anyone else here know something about my life that I don't?" I demanded, glaring down every man in the room. "I thought you guys were my *friends*."

They'd always made me feel included and welcome, like one of the crew. To realize they still kept things from me did not sit well. Did they think I was too stupid to keep up, too naive, too—

"You *are* our friend, Quinn." Pick's calming voice didn't really calm me this time. And when he set his hand back on my shoulder, I shrugged it off and glared. He lifted his palms and took a step back.

"So, what? You think I'm too *fragile* to handle the truth, then?"

"No." Pick scowled and shook his head. "Not at all. We think you've had to deal with a lot of new experiences in the past few months that you've never dealt with before. We know how sheltered you were; you didn't get a normal teenager's life. So when it comes to women, sex, and love, you didn't get to wade in like the rest of us. You've had to jump straight off into the deep end. It's because you *are* our friend and we're completely loyal to you that we didn't interfere or bother you with things we didn't know for sure. We just wanted you to have fun with your first girl. And Cora didn't exactly *hit* on me, as Lowe phrased it. She just put off this vibe like she wanted to, so I shut her down before she could. So she didn't. I could've totally been reading it wrong, and I didn't want to cause you any undue paranoia, so I never said anything."

"And I swear, if I'd known she'd already agreed to go out with you again when we fucked, I would've told you, straight up," Ten added. "I've been watching her like a hawk, waiting for the first moment I could catch her with someone else, but the bitch is slick, I'll give her that. She hides her secrets well. I never caught her with anyone else while you two were together, so I couldn't rat her out to you."

"The love of my life is alive today because of you," Pick added. "I would bleed for you, man. If there was ever anything we didn't tell you, it's because we care about you."

I nodded, but I still felt like a fool. I'd been blind to so many things. I didn't want anyone to think they had to hide anything from me for my own good, to lie to spare my feelings.

From here on out, I wanted to be tough. And a-ware. Screw nice; I wanted honesty.

THIRTY

∽ ZOEY ∾

IT'S CRAZY HOW fast a day can spiral out of control. Aside from the fact it felt as if my contacts had dried and glued themselves to my eyeballs, I woke to the most amazing sensation in the world: Quinn's warm hard flesh pressed against mine.

For the longest moment ever, I just stayed there, piled on top of him with his heartbeat doubling as my pillow and our legs entwined while I breathed in his incredible smell. Hypnotized by the rise and fall of his chest under my ear, I listened to his breathing, simply astounded to be with him. My fingers that had been resting on his shoulder slipped down his arm, thrilled by how warm and soft his flesh was as it covered steel-hard muscle.

Under me, he let out a breath, a half moan, half sigh. I grinned, keeping my lashes fused together, al-most afraid to open them in fear I might find some-thing other than what I knew I was feeling under me. Then his leg shifted and I could feel his shaft against my hip as it hardened.

The insides of my thighs crackled with lightning pleasure and if I'd been wearing panties, they would've gotten soaked. My body recalled every moment of last night as I tried to count in my head just how many times Quinn had been inside me. Four? Five?

He'd been so relentless. Passionate. Starving...for me. I

think he'd craved me just as much as I'd craved him.

Joy burst inside me. I honestly couldn't remember ever feeling this happy. I slid my hand down, wanting to wrap my fingers around his growing excitement as I kissed his heartbeat right through his chest.

Just before I reached his morning wood, he curved his hand around my butt in a warm caress and sleepily murmured, "Love you."

I froze, my fingers halting just below his navel. Opening my eyes, I took in green sheets and the shoulder of the naked man under me. Elation zipped through my veins, buzzed in my ears, and caused an electric jolt to spasm through my chest.

But Quinn *loved* me?

Should I say it back? I wanted to say it back. I wanted to laugh, and squeal, and scream. The moment was so utterly, breathtakingly perfect, I couldn't even breathe properly. Unable to believe he'd told me that, I lifted my gaze just enough to take in the side of his jaw. He needed to shave. I looked higher to find his eyes closed. He was still asleep.

Oh my God, he even loved me in his *subconscious*? That was just...wait.

I knew I was a shy, sheltered, naive person, but I was also fully aware guys didn't just go falling in love with a girl after one night, even if it had been the best night of my life. I mean, only yesterday, he'd been planning to ask Cora to—

Oh...no.

Cora.

Guilt and fear and pain swirled through me as his declaration of love continued to sting. Twenty-four hours ago, he'd been Cora's boyfriend, and he'd woken up in Cora's bed. He was used to being with *her*. What if he'd been talking to *her* in his half sleep? I'd heard him tell her he loved her before. It might just be habit to say it to her first thing in the morning. Made sense that he'd been talking to her, not me.

What didn't make sense was me, waking up with him this morning, or me thinking this had been one of the best moments of my life. What didn't make sense was me thinking he loved me.

Holding my breath, I lifted my face higher, but his eyes were still closed and his lips were parted as he breathed easily. Then his palm slid limply off my bottom as he drifted back into a deeper slumber.

And just like that, the best feeling in the world was replaced by the worst. I didn't belong here. I'd just stolen something from both Cora *and* Quinn that I could never give back. I was a vile, terrible, awful betrayer.

A tear slipped down my cheek. I chased it with my fingers, wiping it away before it could drip off me and onto Quinn. I shuddered out a sniff and gently, slowly tried to ease off him.

We'd been up most of the night, only catching cat-naps here and there until one or the other of us woke ravenous for more. I forgot how many times I stirred to the feel of him with his mouth on my breasts, or his tongue between my legs, his cock entering me from behind while his fingers slid around my hips to play with my clit. There was still a tender spot on the back of my shoulder when he'd bitten me from coming so hard in that position.

His hands had possessed me, stroking so much of me that he now owned every inch. His scalding touch had branded me as his.

And yet a part of him still belonged to *her*. His lips wouldn't have formed those words if he didn't. Right?

He slept on as I carefully climbed off him. After last night, he had to be exhausted. I knew I was. Exhausted and sore, especially between the legs and around my breasts.

I cupped both sensitive places to cover myself as I hobbled across his floor and hunted up my clothes.

It didn't even seem possible that I was about to do the walk of shame. Yesterday at this time, I'd been a virgin and was sure I'd stay one for a very long time.

More tears flooded my cheeks. I kind of wanted him to wake up and catch me, to pull me back onto the bed and into his arms and reassure me that last night had meant as much to him as it had to me. That he'd really been talking to me when he'd spoken those words. But I feared the moment he woke too, because I knew that was the total opposite of what he'd actually do.

I couldn't handle seeing the regret in his eyes, the guilt, the apology, the disgust and distress. I yanked on my jeans, not even bothering to search for my underwear I couldn't immediately spot. When some-thing stabbed into my hip through the cloth of my pocket, I nearly lost it all over again. With shaking fingers, I pulled out Quinn's ring for

Cora. It was still buttery from the shrimp scampi it had landed in.

Trying not to vomit from self-disgust, I set the ring gently on Quinn's nightstand. I spent a moment watching the two together, him and his ring for an-other woman. And then I fled.

As soon as I hit the hallway, I skidded to a halt, remembering Ten lived here too and might be lingering about. If Ten caught sight of me like this, my horror would be complete. But no man stirred. No Quinn. No Ten. Just one lost, scared, guilty Zoey.

I didn't let myself cry as I drove back to Chateau Rivera. I held it in and concentrated on driving. I didn't want to face Cora right now, but I didn't know where else to go. I hoped she was sleeping in as she usually did on Saturday mornings. Except crap, it wasn't exactly morning any longer, was it? But it *was* late enough that she would've left for her dialysis appointment already.

And oh man, the thought of her dialysis only made bile rise in my throat. I really was the worst person on earth. I had not only betrayed my best friend, but I'd done it when she was at her weakest and most vulnerable, sick and frail.

It did relieve me to know I could slip inside my room to be alone without her around, though. Except when I made it to the apartment and opened the door, I let out a shocked yelp when I saw someone standing in the front foyer.

"Oh my God," I gasped, setting my hand over my rapidly thumping heart as I focused on Cora's face.

She looked awful. Bags under her eyes, hair a ratty mess, clothes rumbled and hanging loosely from her thin frame.

"What're you still doing here?" I panted, out of breath from receiving the shock of my life.

She shoved the back of her hand across her nose and sniffed. "I'm waiting on you, idiot. What do you *think* I'm still doing here? I've tried calling your phone all morning."

I hugged myself, unable to look her in the eyes. "I turned it off."

"So I guessed. Look, I know you're still pissed at me because I didn't tell you about *the other guys*," she said. She was so nonchalant about saying the other guys, I winced, freshly hurt on Quinn's behalf. Just how many other guys had there been? "But are you really so upset you're just going to leave me hanging on the whole kidney transplant?"

I blinked, clueless. "What?"

"We're supposed to go in together this morning. You have more tests while I'm getting my treatment."

"Oh." Oh, crap. I'd forgotten all about that. I'd been too busy getting freaky with her ex all night long to think about doctor's appointments. The color drained from my face and guilt layered itself on top of the guilt I was already feeling. "I guess I don't have time for a shower, huh?"

I gulped, unable to think about anything but all the things I'd be washing off if I did have time.

"Fuck, no. You don't have time." She grabbed my arm, startling me. Quinn had touched me there last night. But then, he'd touched me everywhere. "Let's go."

I pulled away. "I really need to change." And my contacts were killing my eyes. Plus I couldn't handle feeling her hand on me.

She gave me five minutes, and then she bustled me out the door.

Still in a shocked daze over everything that had happened, I couldn't wrangle my thoughts into any order. My mind was all over the place. It felt so strange to stand mildly by Cora's side in the elevator when only hours ago I'd had her boyfriend's cock in my mouth. Ex-boyfriend, I reminded myself. Ex-boyfriend's cock. Quinn's gorgeous, long cock that had—

I gasped out a sound, garnering a strange look from Cora. But I darted my attention away.

As soon as we reached the ground floor, I shot out of the slowly opening doors and dashed for the exit, barely thanking Terrance when he let me out of the building. I didn't know how to do this, how to pretend I hadn't spent the entire night in Quinn's bed.

And then, as if thinking about him had conjured him, there he was, across the parking garage, standing by his truck. I jerked to a stop, not sure what to do. The wind whipped through his hair and flattened his T-shirt against his front, showing off every rippling muscle he had and reminding me what they'd felt like under my fingers.

Suddenly, I could feel him again inside me, could taste his kiss on my tongue, smell his perfect scent. My body reacted; I wanted him so bad, wanted him pressing me into his mattress and covering me with his hard warmth.

When he stepped forward, a hopeful yet uncertain expression, a shudder of longing tore through me. He'd followed me.

But then Cora said his name, and I nearly jumped out my skin. She raced past me, rushing to him, and horror filled his face. He turned away, yanking open his truck door, and slamming himself inside. When he started the engine, she banged on his window, but he sped away without slowing down.

I didn't know what to think, what to do. I just knew he'd come here for me, not her.

He'd wanted *me*.

Maybe he *had* been talking to me when he'd spoken in his sleep. Or maybe I was making a mountain out of a molehill. He'd probably just come to apologize and tell me he regretted everything.

"Well, come on already," Cora yelled at me, her hands on her hips.

So...we went. I still had her life to save.

I was so silent in the passenger seat I think it made Cora nervous. She finally huffed out a sigh, and grumbled, "I suppose you want to talk about last night, huh?"

I jumped. Last night? My brain immediately brought forth a dozen images in my head of last night: of Quinn on top of me, under me, behind me, pinning me to the wall. I paled and shook my head. "Not really."

Cora lifted her eyebrows. "*Seriously?* And here, I was so sure I'd get the self-righteous, indignant speech about fucking around and being unfaithful. I was actually expecting a bunch of questions like why. *Why, Cora, why?*" She finished the last three words on a whine as if trying to imitate me.

I shrugged and turned to stare out the window, ignoring the insult. She had a lot more to insult me about than she could ever guess. "I guess I've stopped wondering why you do things that make no sense to me."

She didn't have an answer for that. She made a huffy sound, and then said, "Well, I certainly didn't *know* he was going to propose."

I shot her a dry glare because she was still lying to me. "Oh, so you would've been faithful if you'd just known he was so serious about you?"

She shrugged, letting me know she wouldn't have been

faithful, no matter what. She didn't apologize for it, I noticed. She acted haughty and justified, as if she'd done absolutely nothing wrong, as if she hadn't just broken the heart of a man who'd been seconds—*seconds*—away from asking her to be his wife.

Just then, I hated her. And I didn't feel sorry for sleeping with her ex-boyfriend. And worst of all, I didn't feel bad about having such awful, terrible thoughts like I usually did when a stray awful, terrible thought entered my head. I just felt disgust for the woman sitting across the car from me.

But then the second passed, and the guilt and shame crashed down. I cowered in my seat, needing a distraction. "What kind of checkup am I getting today?" I asked quietly.

I'd already been through the physical exam. A doctor had looked me over from top to bottom, thoroughly, even going as far as to scrutinize every mole on my body to make sure they didn't look cancerous.

"Psychological, I think."

"Psycho...?" A cold sweat misted my skin. I turned to look at her, feeling like I might vomit. "What? No. I...I can't. Not today. Can't I do something different this time?" *Anything* different.

I could already picture the shrink drilling me for the truth.

Just how jealous of Cora are you? How much do you resent her perfect parents, her perfect social graces, her perfect boyfriend? Just how sore are you between the legs from stealing him from her and having sex with him all night long?

Today was the absolute worst day ever for someone to go picking around inside my brain.

Cora just sent me a dry glare, no pity whatsoever in her hateful gaze. "I didn't set the appointments. You're going."

"SO, ZOEY. WHY DO you want to give Cora your kidney?"

It was the easiest, most obvious question ever. And yet it rendered me completely blank, because in that moment, I couldn't remember why I was still so deter-mined to do this. The only thing I could think to say was that it was because

I'd told her I would. I would not go back on my word.

But after licking my extremely dry lips, I pushed out my shaking voice, "Be·because she's my best friend."

Lie. That was such a lie. A year ago, it would've been the truth. Hell, even a couple months ago, it had been the truth. But today, I didn't even know if I'd consider her a passing friend.

Across the overly hot room, the psychologist nodded and made a note on his pad. For some reason, I wondered if he was really making a notation about me or if he was just playing tic·tac·toe with himself.

Then he lifted his face and sent me a smile that creeped me out more than it settled my nerves. "From Cora's notes here, it says she was a year older than you and took you under her wing. Is that right?"

I blinked as he shuffled through a few pages as if to find the line he was quoting. But...what? Cora had already talked to him? Cora had...? What exactly had she told him about me? What did he already know?

My breathing began to escalate. "I..." I nodded because nothing he said was a lie. "Yes, I guess."

"And she's the, uh, the spearhead of your friend·ship? You're the follower?"

I didn't mean to frown, but something about the way he phrased that rubbed me all kinds of wrong—though, okay, that was how it had been back in high school. I had followed along with whatever idea Cora had, done whatever Cora had wanted to do, followed like a good, faithful little sheep.

But here in Ellamore? Yeah, that wasn't the way of our friendship at all.

I didn't tell him that, though. I didn't tell him she felt like more a stranger to me these days. So I shrugged and agreed with his assessment. "Sure."

He nodded as if self·congratulating himself for his brilliant deduction. "It sounds as if Cora is a pretty important person in your life. She said you didn't have a great home life, so she kind of acted as your family. Like a big sister. I guess I'm saying I'm worried about attachment issues. I don't want you to think of her as your crutch."

Whoa! *What?*

The last thing I thought of Cora as was a crutch.

Okay, maybe two years ago when she'd "taken me under her wing," I'd latched on to her friendship be·cause it was the only thing I'd had. But then I'd had a year severed from her to learn how to deal with things on my own, and the only reason I'd come here to Ellamore was to help *her*, not so she'd take care of *me* again. Lately, I'd actually been dreaming up ways to peacefully cut ties with her after the transplant was over.

"Sharing your kidneys between the two of you isn't going to make you one person or tighten any emotional connection between the two of you. You're still going to be your own person, and she's going to be hers. You do realize that, right, Zoey?"

What the hell?

I nodded, because I didn't know how to answer without telling him he was insane. I didn't want to be *one* with Cora. I didn't even want to be *like* Cora.

But I really wanted to know what kind of story she'd fed him. Remembering how she'd told me she'd thought I was a lesbian with a crush on her, I sank lower into the couch, hoping to God she hadn't told him *that*. But he was making it sound like I *was* obsessively in love with her, so...she probably had.

"I...I know that," I said, not sure what else to say without outright telling him his idea was completely whack.

"And then there's the possibility that her body might reject the new kidney. What would you do if the transplant wasn't successful and she didn't make it?"

"I don't know," I whispered, and honestly, I didn't know. I hadn't thought of what would happen after. I'd been too focused on just getting it done.

"I...I guess I'd finish school," I said dumbly.

He lifted an interested eyebrow. "Here? At ESU?"

I nodded. "Yeah. I mean, sure. I've already enrolled and am halfway through a semester."

Plus, Quinn was here. Which was a totally inappropriate, awful thought to have right now, but I couldn't stop myself from thinking about him being in my future.

"So, you think you could handle being here by yourself, without any family or friends around?"

I kind of wanted to laugh in his face. I had more friends here than I'd ever had at home. Caroline, Reese, Quinn. Even Ten. The idea of leaving actually made me recoil with dread. This place was my home now. And the friends I'd made since coming here were the closest family I'd ever had.

Clearing my throat, I met Dr. What's-His-Face's gaze. "I think I'd make it just fine on my own if I had to."

He nodded, scribbled another notation, or maybe he'd just beaten himself at tic-tac-toe. I don't know. I didn't care. He was so far off base with all his questions, it wasn't even funny. But, whew...I guess I needn't have worried that he'd pull out all my deepest darkest secrets and make me admit how guilty I felt when it came to Quinn and Cora.

BOTH CORA AND I were quiet on the ride home. I expected her to ask how my session with the quack had gone, but she didn't. And I didn't ask how her dialysis went. She looked better than when we'd left the apartment, so I guess it had helped.

She chewed on her lip and stared stonily out the front window, so I turned my attention out the passenger side window.

We were about five minutes from the apartment when she finally spoke. "I think I'm going to get Quinn back."

Dread zapped its way through my body as I turned slowly. "What?"

She nodded without glancing at me. "Yeah," she said as if she'd just come to that conclusion. "It's nicer to have a boyfriend than not have one. And he pampered me the most, always let me have my way, didn't crowd my space. And the sex. Wow. Once he learned what to do with it, that boy knew how to work a cock."

My stomach roiled, but oh God, I already knew how well he knew how to work one. And that was so, so wrong.

With a harsh laugh, Cora shook her head. "Strangely, he was actually the dream boyfriend."

I shook my head, not getting it. "What do you mean, strangely? Why is that realization *strange*?"

I'd thought his dedication, loyalty, and adoration had been amazing. Awe-worthy. Refreshing. It'd never been *strange* to me. Watching the way he'd treated Cora when they were together had given me faith in love and shown me it truly did exist in a healthy, amazing way. It had been beautiful, not strange.

But Cora shrugged. "Oh, you know. At first, he was just

kind of a trophy. The cute, clueless, brainless, muscle-necked football player no other groupie had gotten a hold of yet."

Groupie? She'd been a groupie?

"But then, he'd been so eager to please me. So desperate for attention." Another negligent shrug left her shoulders. "What can I say? I'm a girl. I like to be adored. So I let him worship me for a while. But then he got really good in the bedroom, and he kept pampering me and showering me with everything I want-ed. I mean, *everything*. And well...he's hot. Plus his dick is, like, enormous. So...I just kept him around."

"Are..." I swallowed because this was incredibly hard to listen to. "Are you saying you never loved him?"

Cora just sent me a look. I think that meant that answer was an obvious no. It broke my heart for Quinn, because he *had* loved her. He'd been willing to marry her. How could she just...?

"He was the most devoted man I ever dated. I don't think I'm finished with him yet."

I snorted. Maybe she should've considered that be-fore she slept with those *other guys*.

She glanced at me, her scowl cross. "What? Don't you think I can accomplish it?" A secretive smile crossed her lips. "Oh, I know how to accomplish it. I know exactly what he likes best."

She meant during sex, and that made me feel more vile than ever, because what if she *did* know how to entice him into forgiving her? What if she could draw him back into her clutches, into her bed? What if—? No, I couldn't even consider it. He couldn't go back to her after what he'd done with me. He just couldn't. Even if he never touched me again and refused to even talk to me, he couldn't be with her again, either.

"But you *cheated* on him," I argued, without meaning to. The words just blurted from my mouth because I didn't even want her to try to get back together with him. "He broke *up* with you."

"Meh." She didn't seem concerned about that fact. "I guess maybe it's time to drop the big bomb and tell him about my kidney failure. You *know* that'll bring a bleeding heart like Quinn back where I want him."

My mouth fell open incredulously. "You...you're going to

play the sympathy card and use that *against* him?"

The acid in her glance scorched into me. "What're *you* so bent out of shape about? Aren't you the one who's been badgering me for months to tell him about it? You're finally getting your way."

I'd only wanted her to tell him about it way back before I'd spent the night with him, given him my virginity and fallen irreversibly in love with him.

I paled as a thought struck. If Cora told him, he'd know that I'd known about her all along. He'd never forgive me for keeping it from him, because if I'd have just told him, he never would've left Cora, no matter how many other guys she'd slept with. She was right; he was a devoted bleeding heart who would stand by his dying—albeit cheating—girlfriend's side.

Oh God. What if he thought I hadn't told him because I'd wanted him all to myself? What if... Wait.

What if—subconsciously—I *hadn't* told because I *did* want him all to myself?

What if I was a worse person than Cora?

I couldn't urge her not to tell him now. I just couldn't.

"Do whatever you want." I turned to stare out the side window again. But inside my chest, my heart crumbled to pieces.

Quinn was going to hate me.

THIRTY-ONE

QUINN

CORA SHOWED UP at my door Saturday night while I was eating supper with Ten. He'd cooked for me by ordering pizza. Even though I wasn't hungry, I'd just bitten into my first slice of supreme when her knock came. Thinking—hoping and praying—it might be Zoey, I started to rise, but Ten waved me back down.

"I got this."

I could tell who had come to call when he immediately started ranting. "Oh, you fucking, worth-less, lying, cheating whore. How dare you show your face here? Why don't you turn around and go back to sucking on whoever's dick you just came from?"

I stood and moved behind him to see Cora glaring at him from the hallway. When she caught sight of me over his shoulder, her eyes lit up.

She rose onto her toes and waved. "Quinn? Hi. We need to talk."

I shook my head and snorted, turning my face to the side. "I don't want to talk to you."

"Hear that? He doesn't want to talk to you. Bye-bye now." Ten began to shut the door in her face, but she slapped her palm against it and scowled at my roommate before she boldly stepped into our apartment.

"We're *going* to talk," she said.

Ten huffed out his irritation but leaned against the opened door and arched an eyebrow my way, as if waiting for me to give him permission to throw her out. But I knew how persistent Cora could be. She'd probably keep pestering me until I finally gave in and talked anyway...even though I'd already said every-thing I'd wanted to say to her.

It was over; how many more ways did she want me to phrase it? But it seemed easiest to just get this over with now, and let her say what she'd come to say so I wouldn't have to deal with her any more after this.

Folding my arms over my chest, I drew out a big sigh. "Fine. Talk."

"Stupid, noble idiot." Ten shook his head in disappointment. "Man, I can't believe you."

"Well, no one asked you," Cora snapped at him.

Stepping away from the door, he towered over her and narrowed his eyes. "The only reason you're here is to beg him to take you back. But you're only wasting your breath. There's no way in hell he's going to let your lying, faithless, whore ass anywhere near his dick ever again."

"Ten," I muttered with another long sigh. "Just let her talk so she'll go away."

For the first time, Cora looked hurt. She glanced toward me as if uncertain, which made me think Ten had been right. She'd come here to win me back.

A headache formed between my temples. I sighed and rubbed at it, wanting to be anywhere but here.

"Fine." Ten swiped his wallet off the coffee table. "I'm out of here. Call me when the bitch is gone." He slammed the door on his way out.

"He's not very happy that you lied to him either," I explained when Cora just stared at the closed door as if bewildered.

She turned to me slowly. I braced for the apology, for the tears, and maybe some pleading. I totally didn't expect her to clear her throat and paste on a cheerful smile. "So, I've given you a day to adjust to the shock and get over what happened."

My mouth fell open. *Say what?*

Folding my arms over my chest, I arched an eyebrow. "Oh, you did, did you?"

"Mmm hmm." She nodded and blasted me with another grin. "I know it didn't sit well with you, so I'll agree to be strictly monogamous from here on out."

I blinked.

Was she freaking delusional?

After waiting for another beat to make sure she wasn't somehow pulling my leg, I slowly shook my head. "When did you ever think what we had was some kind of open arrangement where you could just sleep with *whomever* you liked?"

"Well..." I don't think she was expecting such a direct question like that, because she faltered. "I...we never had that talk. I thought you *knew*—"

"*No*, dammit." I stepped closer to her. Her eyes widened as she lurched a step back. "I didn't know. Who would know that? And we didn't have the talk because we didn't *need* to have that talk. No normal couple has that kind of talk." I was a social idiot here, and even *I* knew that. "Starting a relationship with someone implies monogamy."

She opened her mouth to speak, but I held up a finger.

"And you *knew* that otherwise you wouldn't have bothered to hide it from me and lie about it."

"I only kept it quiet to spare your feelings."

I laughed in her face. "No, you did it because you're a lying, faithless whore...just like Ten said."

Cora's jaw fell open. "I cannot believe you just called me that."

Yeah, well, I couldn't believe that's what she'd ended up being. Setting my hands on my hips, I glanced away. "If Ten was right, if the only reason you came here was to get me back, you should just go now. We're *not* getting back together. Ever."

"Are you sure about that?" She stepped closer and lifted her hand to run her index finger down the center of my chest.

She was lucky I didn't break her finger for touching me. But I managed to restrain myself. I settled for catching her wrist in a viselike grip and sending her a glare.

"What?" She giggled and sent me a flirty smile, stepping closer. "You can't tell me it wasn't amazing between us, especially in the bedroom."

I glanced away dryly. "I've had better."

I didn't realize what I revealed until she gasped.

A split second later, her free hand came around to crack me across the cheek with a stinging, loud slap.

Totally not expecting that to happen, I couldn't stop it from cranking my face around.

Jaw on fire from her palm, I slowly turned to stare at her.

"You *fucked* someone else?" Fury oozed from her pores. "When did you fuck someone else?"

I closed my eyes, calling myself ten kinds of idiot. She knew she'd been my first. She'd always known she was my first. When I opened my lashes, I found her quivering as she glared at me.

"Don't worry," I assured her with a cold, hard voice. "Unlike you, I didn't cheat."

"But..." She shook her head, her eyes showing me how furiously her mind worked to calculate the time in her head. "We've only been apart a *day*. How could you find someone else in a fucking *day?*"

I shrugged. It seemed like something Ten would do at a time like this, and I could certainly do with a little bit of Ten's attitude right about now.

"Oh my fucking God," she roared. "I cannot believe this. You stuck your dick in another woman. You fucking *bastard.*"

When she curled her fingers, claws extended, and went for my face, I caught her wrists again, stopping her. Then I propelled her away from me. She must've realized I wasn't going to let her hurt me, because her next strategy was to grasp her waist and double over as if in extreme pain before she burst into hiccupping sobs.

The weeping was so extreme, I arched an eyebrow because it was so obviously fake.

In the past, tears had always melted me. I absolutely could not stand watching a woman cry. But Cora's put·on tears enraged me. And the crude way she'd described what Zoey and I had done sent me right over the edge.

I leaned forward. "Imagine how I felt *yesterday*, finding out you'd let other men stick *their* dicks in *you*."

When she looked at me as if I'd betrayed her, I shook my head. "Are you forgetting which one of us was *faithful?*" I jabbed a finger at her. "*You* cheated on *me*, Cora. *You* betrayed *me* and slept with I don't know how many other men while we were together. So I moved on. How dare you stroll in here, without a single apology, and just expect me to...I don't know, *thank* you because you're willing to give us another try? Well, no. It...is...over. It was over the minute I read that text. And whatever I've done with anyone else since that moment is none of your damn business."

"But...you're mine." She stomped her foot, the pinch in her eyebrows a pathetic glare. "I *created* you. I—"

"You what? You *created* me?" My mouth fell open, wondering what the heck that was all about.

"Yes." She hissed at me. "You were nothing. A pathetic little naive, gullible nobody. So malleable and easy to control. Just like Zoey."

"Zoey?" I croaked. I didn't like hearing her name come from this woman's mouth, this woman I thought loved me and loved being with me, this woman who'd lied to me and broken my trust. "What does *Zoey* have to do with this?"

"Nothing." Cora shrugged. "You just reminded me of her. That's why I chose you."

I shook my head, more confused than ever. "Excuse me? Did you say you *chose* me?" She made it sound like she'd taken a trip to the pet shop to pick out her next lapdog.

A sick nausea churned in me when I realized that's exactly how she'd always treated me. Like a lapdog, someone to fetch her slippers, rub her feet, make her breakfast, lick her pussy.

She sent me a proud, triumphant grin. "The night of the auction, I did choose you. Like a shy, lost little puppy. It reminded me of how Zoey had always been. So I knew I could do to you what I'd always done to her."

I clenched my teeth as my stomach tightened with dread. "And what exactly did you always do to her?"

Her grin turned sly and mischievous. "Whatever I wanted. You see, timid, lonely people like you two are *starved* for a little attention. All I needed to do was feed you both a couple compliments, and you were devoted to me for life. Zoey will do anything for me, because I'm like, I don't know, her god, I guess. She worships the ground I walk on."

I tipped my head to the side, more curious than anything. I probably should've been mad to learn she thought so little of us. I should've felt hurt and incredulous. Well, okay, I was incredulous. And mad and hurt. I couldn't believe she'd always been this way. I guess I'd just been too stupid and naive and gullible to see it. And okay, maybe I was angrier than I thought, because knowing she'd done the same exact thing to Zoey flamed the fire.

"So, Zoey and I are just puppets to you? And I was like your...arm candy?"

"Arm candy?" She brightened and then laughed. "Yeah, I like that term."

"Well, I don't. You can go now. I think I've heard enough."

Grabbing her arm, I dragged her a little more roughly than I should've toward the door. As I pulled it open, she began to resist.

"Hey, I'm not—"

"I don't care. Your gullible, naive creation just grew a mind of his own. Get. Out." As soon as she stumbled into the hall, I slammed the door. She star-ted to pound, but a minute later, I heard Ten's muffled voice. Seconds after that, she was gone. And my roommate returned.

"So." He glanced around the room as if looking for broken furniture. "What'd she have to say?"

I slumped onto the sofa and picked up my pizza, but I couldn't eat it. "Quite a bit."

"Lots of begging and forgiving, huh?" Ten snorted and shook his head. "Figures."

"No, actually. She never said sorry. She never begged. She just snapped her fingers and then told me to come to heel and return to being her gullible, naive lapdog."

Ten paused, scrunched his eyebrows together. "Come again?"

I gave him the basic rundown of everything she'd said, to which he hissed, "That fucking bitch." When he turned toward the door as if to leave, I caught his arm. "What're you doing?"

"I'm going to go find her and punch her in the fucking lady parts. That's what I'm going to do. How dare she? How—?"

I sniffed and shook my head. "Wasn't like she lied, though. I *was* her—"

"Oh, don't you even," Ten warned, pointing a finger at me. "Don't let her lies get to you. You're a *good* per-son, Hamilton. You have a gentle, caring heart, and ugly, vile people like her will always try to take ad-vantage of that. But I said it once before, and I'm going to say it again. The world needs more people like you. So don't even think about turning hard because of this, or I'll never forgive you."

"So what do you expect me to do? Just keep being a weak, stupid—"

"You're not weak. And you're sure as hell not stupid. It takes more guts than I'll ever have to open up to people the way you're willing to."

I tossed my piece of pizza back into the box and buried my face into my hands, aching to hurt some-thing as violence brewed inside me. "I was such a fool," I admitted, my voice muffled in my hands.

"Well, now you're wiser. Never trust cruel, heartless bitches. Life lessons learned. Let it teach you, but don't let it tear down who you are at the core."

I started to nod, before I shook my head and frowned at him. "Wait. That doesn't sound like anything you'd ever say."

"I know," he grumbled and rolled his eyes. "There's nothing but fucking talk shows on when I'm home between classes and football practice. And all they talk about are *feelings*. Man, we're seriously going to have to get cable before my balls turn into ovaries."

I laughed, and it felt good to smile and think about something other than feelings. But Ten just scowled. "I'm not kidding. I'm learning way more than I want to about all that touchy-feely shit. It's not cool."

Picking up my pizza again, I took a bite and relaxed for the first time all day. I was still ticked at myself for letting Cora treat me the way she had, but as Ten had said: lesson learned. No woman was going to get that far under my defenses again.

Until the very next one did. Until Zoey did.

THIRTY-TWO

QUINN

REESE DIDN'T MAKE it to art class on Monday. She texted Caroline, telling her Mason's chicken pox was taking a toll on him. But two seats—not just one—remained open between Caroline and me that hour.

Every time the door opened, admitting a late student, my chest wrenched, thinking Zoey would enter.

She never did.

Ten slept the entire hour, which left only Caroline and me. She kept shooting me worried glances. I wondered if she knew. She and Zoey had grown close; but would Zoey confide something like this in her? I'd had to talk to Pick about it. Maybe Zoey had needed to talk to someone too, like Caroline.

Maybe Caroline would know what I should say to Zoey when I finally saw her.

Class let out early, thank God, and the two of us gravitated toward each other. I opened my mouth to ask when she'd last talked to Zoey, but she patted my arm and sent me a sympathetic smile, waylaying my question.

"I heard about you and Cora."

I jolted, not expecting or wanting to hear sympathy about *Cora*. I hadn't even thought about Cora today. I'd been too busy wound up about my upcoming talk with Zoey.

Gritting my teeth, I nodded and sent Caroline a stiff smile, even as my gaze strayed to Zoey's empty seat. God, I hated knowing I'd scared her away from art class.

"And don't worry. If you think Zoey knew anything about it, I can assure you, she was just as surprised and upset by Cora's faithlessness as you were."

I glanced at her, and suddenly I knew; Zoey hadn't told her about us. A sigh escaped my lungs, but I nodded. "I know she didn't."

Caroline opened her mouth again, but something a girl from across the room said caught our attention and stopped her from speaking.

"...Kavanagh didn't even look like the kind of teacher a student would want to fuck."

"*Excuse me?*" Caroline spun toward the group of girls talking together as they gathered their things.

As she marched toward them, a yawning, stretching Ten appeared at my side. "Where's she going, looking all pissed like that? I didn't talk in my sleep, did I?"

I shook my head. "She just heard someone bad-mouthing Aspen."

"Fuck." He swiveled her way. "Should we stop her?"

I glanced at him, shaking my head in confusion. "Stop her from doing *what?*"

He lifted his hands. "I don't know. She's a Gamble. A *pissed-off* Gamble. They lose their shit when they're pissed."

"Oh, crap." He was right.

But Caroline had already reached her target. She paused in front of the four girls and slapped her hands to her hips as she focused on one short redhead. "What did you just say about Dr. Kavanagh?"

"Umm..." The girl who'd been talking blinked at her as if she couldn't believe she'd been interrupted. "That's really none of your business. This is a private conversation."

"Private?" Caroline lifted an eyebrow. "Yeah, it was so private I could hear it in this public classroom from twenty feet away while you *bashed* a respected professor from this university."

The gossipmonger snorted and rolled her eyes. "She's not a professor here anymore. I heard she got fired for sleeping with a student."

"Oh really? You *heard?*" Caroline glanced back at us and

I could see she was about to blow.

Tensing, I wondered if she lost her temper the same way her brother did. I turned to Ten. He shared a worried look with me.

Caroline snickered at the girl. "Well, I heard you fucked that guy right there last night." She motioned blindly toward Ten. "And you liked it up the ass best."

The girl's eyes widened with horror as she glanced at Ten.

Next to me, he slipped into character without pause. Grinning, he blew the girl a kiss. "Hey, baby." He notched his voice seductively low. "Hope your tushy isn't too sore this morning. You liked it rougher than I was used to giving it, so I got a little carried away."

"Oh my God," the girl cried, backing away from him and trying to crowd into her friends, but her friends suddenly didn't want anything to do with her. She shook her head frantically. "No. I...I don't even *know* that guy." Gaping at Caroline, she shook her head. "You're *lying*."

Caroline widened her eyes as if she'd just realized she'd made a mistake. Then she covered her mouth with her hand. "Oh, but that's what I *heard*. And since I heard it, it has to be true, right?"

"What the hell are you talking about?"

"I'm talking about Dr. Kavanagh, bitch." Caroline moved right up into the girl's face. "Spreading lies about a person is called defamation, and it's illegal. But what's more important is that it really sucks when it's someone else spreading it around about *you*, doesn't it? So maybe from here on out, you should watch your fucking mouth whenever you start spewing trash about someone *else* you don't even know, like my *sister*, Dr. Kavanagh. Because that trash might not be the truth."

Notching her chin high, she turned her back on the girl and stormed proudly from the room.

"That..." Ten pointed after Caroline with his jaw fallen open. "Holy shit, Ham. That was so fucking awesome." He turned to look at me, his eyes glassy with shock and admiration. "She's totally fucking awesome." When he started to trail after her as if in a daze, I caught his arm.

"Whoa. Where do you think you're going?"

"To kiss the fucking shit out of her. I *have* to."

"What about Noel?" I reminded him with an arch of my

eyebrows.

He immediately blinked his gaze clear. Then, rip·ping his arm from my hold, he scowled at me. "Fuck you, man. Couldn't you have let me daydream for half a fucking second before going and saying *his* name?" With a sniff, he stormed away, but at least he took off toward the opposite door Caroline had used.

I blew out a breath and glanced at Zoey's empty seat. I wished she'd been here to see Caroline. She would've been so proud and amused. And she probably could've cooled Ten down better than I had.

Unable to help myself, I pulled up my phone and found her number. I knew I should wait until we were face to face, but I couldn't handle this a second longer. I needed some kind of contact with her.

So I typed in a simple, **Are you okay?**

Almost immediately, she answered. **Are YOU?**

Relieved she'd responded, that she wasn't avoiding me completely, my shoulders loosened. I left class and made my way outside into the cooling late September day. I wished she had answered my question instead of posing another, but right now, I'd take what I could get. She was at least talking to me.

No, I typed. **I'm absolutely freaking out. Too much is happening all at once and I can't keep up. Most of all, I want to talk to you. In person.**

I gnawed on my lip after sending that off, but in·stead of responding to it, she asked, **Did I miss any·thing in art class?**

Gritting my teeth, I lifted my face from the phone's screen to calm myself, but when I did, I caught sight of Zoey up ahead, entering the library. Hurrying after her, I typed as I went. **Yeah. Caroline overheard some girl gossiping about Aspen. She completely put her in her place. But now Ten's more in love with her than ever.**

I darted into the library and caught sight of her a·head, pausing to read my text. A smile lit up her face. **I was actually asking if we had a new assignment, but WOW. I wish I could've seen that.**

I wish you could've too. It was epic. Caroline was so cool and controlled through the whole thing. Are you in the library? I'm coming to talk to you face to face.

In front of me, she faltered as she read that. Then she

zipped her head up and glanced around frantically before darting around a corner to evade me.

My heart tore open, knowing she didn't want to see me. I blew out a breath, but kept on with my path. She could take any route she wanted; I knew where she'd end up. So I beat her there, to the same spot where she'd cried over her badly graded writing assignment.

Crossing my arms over my chest, I propped my back against the wall and waited. Two minutes later, she careened around the corner, not watching where she was going because she was too busy glancing be-hind her, making sure I wasn't dogging her heels.

When she finally faced forward and caught sight of me, her eyes went round as she skidded to a stop.

"I guess this means you're pretty mad at me, huh?" I said, gritting my teeth when my voice broke. "Leaving before I wake up, skipping classes we share, eluding me when I follow you into the library. I messed up big time. Didn't I?"

Her face fell. "No," she whispered as she pressed her hand to her chest and shook her head vigorously. "No, you didn't. Not at all. I...I just didn't know what to say to you. I don't know how to apologize enough to—"

"*Apologize?*" I stepped away from the wall, because now that I was seeing her, I had to be closer. I don't think I could ever get close enough to satisfy the urges raging inside me. "What do *you* have to apologize about?"

She lifted her gaze. Her eyes were so green and scared; my fingers rose to touch her cheek but she flinched, so I dropped them back to my side, ashamed that I'd scared her.

"I took advantage of you," she whispered as if con-fessing a horrible sin. "You were drunk."

An incredulous laugh left my lungs. Then it was my turn to shake my head. "If anything, I took advantage of *you.* I was the aggressor. I was the one with the experience. I *knew* where everything was heading."

"But I...I wanted...I wanted it."

When she bowed her head in shame, I moved in closer and lightly slid my hand down her arm. "I wanted it too."

She looked up, her eyes hopeful. I probably would've kissed her then—my body was churning with arousal, being this close to her—but she took a step back and drew in a sharp breath. "Cora would kill me if she knew."

Cora's opinion wasn't high on my priority list, but after her reaction to learning that I'd been with someone else, yeah, she probably would lose it if she found out that the someone else I'd been with was Zoey. She would not make things pleasant for Zoey. So, I nodded. "Yeah. She came to see me last night."

Horror dawned in her eyes. She sank even further away from me. "So...she told you?"

I snorted and rolled my eyes. "Oh, she told me plenty."

"Are you getting back together with her?"

The anxiety on her face, telling me she not only thought that was a possibility but a very likely one, shocked me. Why in the world would she believe I'd ever have anything to do with Cora again?

"No!" I think the force behind my answer startled her. She pulled back and blinked before shaking her head as if confused.

"I don't..." She really was confused...which con·founded me. Finally, she frowned. "What exactly did she tell you?"

I squinted as I watched her, wondering what she thought I'd been told. But then I shook my head. "Oh, just that you and I were more like sheep to her than people. Easily manipulated and controlled." I shrugged. "Stuff like that."

"Wait. *What*? But I thought...She told me she was going over there to get you back."

"Yeah." I nodded. "She tried."

Her mouth fell open. "By comparing you to *sheep*?"

"You too. That's why she said she chose me as a boyfriend. Because I reminded her of you. She said we were both gullible and naive and would do whatever she wanted."

Zoey's eyes widened in disbelief. "She *said* that? In order to try to win you *back*?"

I nodded and lifted my eyebrows. "Basically, yeah."

"Oh my good Lord." Zoey ran her hands through hair and turned away before coming back to me. "I thought she was going to tell you—" She cut herself off abruptly and looked up into my eyes. "She wasn't like this when I knew her a year ago. She wasn't even like this through all our emails. She was—"

"Oh, trust me. I believe you. She wasn't like this when I started dating her, either. The girl's a freaking sociopath. As long as you give her what she wants, she's going to be all nice and caring. But the minute you cross her..." I shook my head and laughed softly. "She didn't bring you here because she likes you, Zoey. I don't think she's *capable* of liking anyone." I moved in even closer to her. "She brought you here for a reason, because she wants something from you."

Zoey's eyes were big and lost as she whispered, "I know."

I took her hands, worried for her. "Don't give it to her. Don't give in and let her have her way."

She opened her mouth as if she was going to disagree with me. But then she closed her eyes and shook her head. "It's not that simple."

I don't know what had her so conflicted but I hated seeing her this way. I let go of one of her hands to skim the backs of my fingers down her cheek. I wanted to keep arguing with her, begging her to get away from Cora while she still could, but there were other bigger things to discuss. "You never answered my question."

She leaned her cheek into my fingers and her lashes fluttered before she pulled away. "What question?"

"*Are* you okay?"

Her chin trembled, and I swear she was a micro-second from crying, but then she pulled her shoulders up tight and blurted out a small laugh. "I don't..." Her gaze strayed away from me. "I'm about like you, I guess. Sorta freaking out about everything."

"Feeling guilty?" I asked.

She closed her eyes and nodded.

"Sore?"

Cheeks flushing, she glanced up at me. I couldn't help it, I smiled.

She groaned. "Quinn." Then she buried her face in her hands.

The need to pull her close and kiss her hair and hug her against me rose so strong in me, I actually fisted my hands to keep from reaching for her. "I don't know what to do here, Zoey," I finally admitted, ducking my face to talk closer into her ear. "I know the timing was all wrong. Two hours after breaking up with one girl is not—"

When she made a sound of desperation, I shut up about that part.

"But never...pretending it didn't happen and going our separate ways now that it *did* happen seems wrong too. You are not a one-time kind of girl and I most definitely don't want to be the guy to make you one. You don't deserve that, and I...I..."

Her eyes were red when she uncovered her hands from her face. "What're you saying?"

"I'm saying this is your decision. Do you want me to leave you alone? Or do you want to...I don't know..." I glanced away, feeling like an idiot. "See where this is going?" I turned back to her. "It's completely up to you. I'll respect whatever you want to do?"

Her lips parted and her lashes fluttered as she blinked. I held my breath, not sure which decision I was hoping for until she said, "I think...I think we should never do...what we did...again. Cora's my roommate and...and getting mixed up between you two isn't—"

Disappointment crashed through me, but I nodded emphatically as if I totally understood and agreed. "It's okay," I told her. "I understand. And the last thing I'd ever want to do is get you tangled up between us. It makes sense to just...not go there." But sense or not, I still wanted to go there...a lot.

Zoey nodded but looked about as crushed as I felt.

I turned my attention to the bookshelf and tried to keep it together. "If you ever need anything, though, just call, okay? I'm still your friend. Nothing can change that."

Her head bobbed again. "Okay," she whispered. "Thank you."

"Thank *you*," I said back to her and leaned in to kiss her temple, inhaling that last little bit of her shampoo scent that I could breathe in. "Thank you for being there for me when I needed someone the most. And I'm sorry for..." I shook my head, not sure what I was sorry for. But I felt like hell for the way all this was affecting her. "I'm sorry for..."

She spun away and ran off.

I cursed under my breath and then leaned toward the nearest bookshelf and tapped my head against it a few times, hoping to knock some sense back into myself. I hoped to God I'd just made the right decision by letting her go, but I felt so bad, I couldn't see how it had been the right thing to do at all.

THIRTY-THREE

❧ ZOEY ❧

IN THE SPACE OF a just a few days, my life went from the lowest point ever, to the highest, and right back to the lowest...and then it just kept rolling on as if nothing had ever happened. I had to skip more classes on Tuesday to get more tests done on my kidneys. When Wednesday came, I approached art class with dread.

I know I'd told Quinn it would be better if we put some space between us, but I missed him, and I regretted every word I'd said to keep him away. He'd insisted we were still friends, but I knew we weren't. We'd never be as close as we'd been before Friday night.

It was for the best, though...wasn't it?

I honestly didn't know. I was still too much of a mess to think logically. When I entered class, Ten, Caroline and Quinn had already arrived, and only one space sat open between Caroline and Quinn, making me wonder if they'd booted me out of the group. I certainly wouldn't blame them.

I slowed to a stop, not sure if I should approach, but then Caroline caught sight of me and waved me up with a relieved smile. Quinn glanced up, and his blue eyes immediately heated with all kinds of emotions I couldn't read.

I wasn't sure if he wanted me there, but I went to Caroline anyway.

"Reese is still home with a sick Mason, so it's just the four of us today."

"You ever had chicken pox before, Blondie?" Ten asked as Quinn shifted his knee aside enough to let me know he was making room for me to squeeze in between him and Caroline.

I glanced at him and met his intent blue-eyed gaze. He smiled as if happy to see me, but his eyes still seemed sad and regretful. Gulping, I forced my attention to his roommate. "Chicken pox?" I repeated distractedly, wondering why he was asking about that. "No. Why?"

"Neither has Ham," he said pointing out Quinn. "That's insane. I thought everyone got chicken pox before they reached middle school."

"Oh, well...I didn't go to middle school."

"Neither did I," Quinn added.

We glanced at each other again, and so much passed between us in that one stare: longing, guilt, excitement, dread, joy, suffering.

"Well, Lowe did, so why the hell hadn't *he* ever contracted it before? Working all these extra hours for him sucks ass, because I wanted to take Ham out and get him some pussy."

Quinn wrenched in his seat. "You *what?*"

Ten shook his head sadly and made a tsking sound. "Damn, is lack of sex making you lose your hearing, too?"

Mouth opening slightly as if he wanted to talk, Quinn darted a quick glance to me before he closed his lips and refused to respond.

"I said..." Ten leaned across Caroline's desk to talk more loudly toward his roommate. "First night we're both off...we're going out...and you're getting laid."

"He can't," Caroline spoke up suddenly. "Quinn's helping me with my...homework that night."

Zipping his attention to her, Ten scowled. "Since when do you and *Ham* do homework together?"

Caroline narrowed her eyes and scowled right back. "Since...since..." It was so obvious she was lying, Ten rolled his eyes. But she growled and finished with, "Since *now*."

"Pft." Ten waved her off. "Homework can wait. His poor, neglected dick cannot."

Quinn cleared his throat and shifted lower in his seat. He ducked his face, clearly not a willing participant in the conversation. "I really don't want to go out any time soon."

"That's because some cheating whore"—pausing to hold up a hand in my direction, he added, "tons of offense to your *friend*," and then he returned his gaze to Quinn—"ripped your self-confidence off by the balls. But don't you worry, buddy ol' pal. We're going to get them back. I don't care if we have to strap on a fuzzy, leopard-printed pair. I can't handle watching you go around without your nuts. Ergo, we're going to find you the easiest, nastiest, hottest whore, and you're going to get right back on that horse and fuck the shit out of her."

"Like, oh my God," Caroline squealed in the perfect Valley-girl imitation. "An easy, nasty whore? Can you find me one too?"

Ten leered her way. "Only if I watch while you make out with her."

Caroline fluttered her lashes before lowering her voice. "Oh, you wouldn't be invited."

He scowled. "That's not even right."

Sharing a triumphant smile with me, Caroline beamed as if she'd accomplished her main goal of the day: getting under Ten's skin.

"Anyway," Ten went on, shaking his head as if he had to clear it. He slapped the top of Caroline's desk to get Quinn's attention. "Pack your pockets with rubbers, 'cause it's going to happen."

A painful sizzling heat spread through my abdomen just thinking about Quinn with anyone else, letting her watch him roll a thin layer of latex over his glorious length. The recipient of that view didn't even exist yet, and I already wanted to scratch her eyes out. I wanted to pull the hair of every girl to ever look at him.

So I was more than relieved when he growled, "No. It's not."

"You know what'd be really awesome," Ten went on, completely ignoring Quinn's refusal. "If you found one of Whora's really close friends to fuck. That would be the *ultimate* revenge. Stick it to the ex while you're sticking it to her bestie. Oh, yeah. What about that redhead? What's her name... Tamsen or something?"

I darted my gaze away so I couldn't see Quinn's expression. I didn't think my heart, which was plunging into my stomach, could take the devastation if I saw any kind of guilt in his eyes...for already *sticking it* to one of Cora's friends. I sat stiff and frozen in my chair, not daring to move a single muscle. Then I wondered what Ten would say if he knew Quinn had already followed his suggestion.

Oh God. I might be sick.

Next to me, Caroline huffed out a breath. "Will you stop already? You are so disgusting."

"What?" Ten lifted his hands into the air. "Excuse me for trying to help out a buddy who just had his pride stomped on."

"I would think he might be a little more concerned about the blow to his *heart* right now."

Ten snorted and waved out a hand. "What the fuck ever. That woman did not have his—"

"You know what." Quinn sat up in his chair and slashed out his arm to motion for Ten to shut up. "I don't want to listen to this conversation anymore. I'm not going with you to find any woman. And I don't want to talk about what happened. End of discussion."

"Damn it, man." Ten's shoulder's fell. "This is not healthy. I'm trying to save your ass here. Guys *need* to sow wild oats and test the waters or they're going to end up having a midlife crisis before they're thirty, blow all their money on some cherry red convertible and turn into a cheating asshole. And knowing you, now that you're over with her, you'll try to rebound right back into some meaningful, *monogamous* relationship. Which is worse than worse because if the whore hadn't fucked around on you, you probably would've ended up asking her to marry you."

Cheeks flushing, Quinn briefly darted his gaze my way. I sucked in a breath, surprised he'd never told Ten about the ring he'd bought Cora.

"And no stupid-ass motherfucker should marry the first girl he fucks. That's all there is to it. She was your first, she absolutely cannot be your last."

Oh my...Cora had been the first girl Quinn had ever slept with? That meant she and I were the *only* two people he'd ever slept with. My cheeks burned with that knowledge as Quinn's gaze bore hard into Ten.

Next to me, Caroline lurched unsteadily to her feet. I glanced up to find her face pale and eyes deva-stated. "Excuse me," she mumbled, rushing away.

The three of us still sitting gaped dumbly after her as

she fled the classroom, bumping into and dodging around students still entering.

"What the fuck?" Ten finally said, sounding dumb-founded.

He glanced at me, then Quinn. Quinn shook his head and looked my way.

"I...maybe I should go check on her," I offered, reaching out to gather Caroline's books she'd left on her desk.

Ten stood. "No. It was *my* big mouth. *I'll* go." Scowling, he swiped his hand over the top of his hair in an angry, distressed gesture. He looked as if he'd rather have his testicles removed than seek out Caroline, but he slapped her textbook closed, tucked it under his arm and jogged down the steps toward the front of the lecture hall.

Quinn and I exchanged a glance. His mouth opened again. I knew he wanted to say something about everything Ten had just blurted out. I could tell by looking at him, it had left him humiliated and yet worried about me.

Wanting to put off this particular conversation because I was still a little too bowled over by what I'd just learned, I quickly said, "Should we follow them? I mean..." I flailed out a hand. "Ten and Caroline."

"Uh..." He glanced after Ten, then rolled his eyes and ground his teeth. "Yeah, probably."

Together, we gathered our things and without saying a word, we left the classroom.

"Which way do you think they went?" I asked just as I heard Ten saying, "*Hey.*"

Quinn nodded his head that way, and we moved together to peek around a corner and into a quiet hall, where Ten was catching Caroline's hand and whirling her around.

Obviously not expecting the move, Caroline yelped and nearly tripped into him before she pulled away. "What the hell?" she exploded. "Why did you follow me?"

Ten opened his mouth. Then he shrugged and scratched his head. "Fuck, I don't know." He motioned vaguely at her and shoved her textbook at her. "Why did you leave?"

When she didn't answer, just stared at him, he shifted from one foot to the other and asked, "So what stupid shit thing did I say this time to set you off?"

"*This* time," she muttered, and sent him a snarl. "You know what? Never mind. Just...forget about it."

When she began to walk away again, he snagged her

wrist one more time. "Oh, hell no. I made the effort to follow you and find out what was wrong. You're *talking*."

"Uh, *no*. I'm not. Not when you're being an ass-hole."

Ten snorted. "I'm always an asshole, and it's never stopped you from speaking to me before. What difference does that make, anyway? You can talk to an asshole just as well as you can a nice guy. Now, spill it."

"Fine." Caroline crossed her arms over her chest and glared up at him. "You know that crack you made to Quinn about no guy ever marrying the first girl he screws?"

"Yeah." Confusion reigned on his face. "What about it?"

She let out a long sigh and glanced away, pulling her arms more snuggly around her. "Sander said *I* was his first."

When she said nothing else, Ten squinted and leaned in closer to her. "Who the fuck is Sander?"

Caroline lifted her face to send him a searing glare. His eyes widened before he said, "*Oh*." Then he wrinkled his face into a grimace. "Sander? His name's *Sander?* What a stupid, fucked-up name."

A grin lit Caroline's face before she contorted it into a scowl. "Says the guy who goes by *Ten*."

Ten shifted closer to her. "*You* don't call me Ten."

She lifted her chin and stepped in toward him as well. "And I'm never going to."

"They're going to kiss," I leaned up on my tiptoes to whisper into Quinn's ear. "It looks like they're going to kiss. Doesn't it?"

He nodded and glanced at me, and whoa, suddenly it felt like *I* was going to kiss...Quinn. His lips were right there and his eyes were hooded and sleepy sexy as if kissing me—and maybe a little more—was the only thing on his mind.

Oh my God, I wanted to kiss him so bad.

I lowered my gaze. "Do you think we should let them?" I asked...when really I was asking if we should let *us*. There was all kinds of wrong about kissing Quinn Hamilton again. But I could only concentrate on how right it would feel to press myself against him again, to wind my arms around his neck and—

"I don't know." He glanced toward Ten and Caro-line. "Noel would lose it if they got together. But you can tell how much they like each other."

When his gaze veered back to me, I was sure he wasn't

just talking about Ten and Caroline liking each other.

"Yeah, they do. But the things keeping them apart are kind of a big deal."

He winced and twenty feet away, Ten seemed to come to his senses as well.

"Let me tell you something about *Sander* and his claim about you being his first. The douchebag was lying."

"What?" Caroline shrieked. I think she was a second away from slapping him or scratching his face off.

"Just...hear me out. The rich prick went out and found the poorest, most beautiful, loneliest girl from the crappiest trailer park across town, fed you a bunch of pretty words to get into your panties, and as soon as he knocked you up, he went running and crying to mommy and daddy to take care of it. Yeah...I'd say the fucker's been around."

My mouth fell open. When Quinn and I turned to look at each other, I knew he was as shocked to hear about Caroline's past as I was.

"Wow," Caroline said, her voice cracking. "When you say it *that* way, it really does make me look like a pathetic, naive idiot."

"No. Shit, don't cry." His eyes filled with the saddest, achiest expression. But as soon as he reached out her way, he fisted his hand and brought it back to his mouth. "Damn it, I didn't tell you that to make you cry." Then he threw his arms in the air as if defeated. "Jesus, fine. I'm going to say three more things, and then we're never going to talk about this again, okay?"

She nodded.

"Okay, good." He nodded too as if he had no idea what three things he wanted to tell her. But then he held up a finger. "Number one. I'm an idiot. A hundred percent of the shit that comes out of my mouth should not be taken seriously. I have no filter and I don't think anything through. Nothing I say should ever have the power to make you cry. *Two—*"

"Wait." Caroline lifted a hand to stop him. "If number one is that I shouldn't listen to you, then why are you even bothering to go through numbers two and three?"

Ten growled out a sound of impatience. "Fine. *Ninety* percent of the shit that comes out of my mouth should be ignored. Numbers two and three should not. In fact, two and three might just be the most important things I'll ever say to you. So, *two...*"

He paused a moment as if waiting for her to intervene. When she didn't, he continued. "Sander fucking lied to you. He is a liar, and an asshole, and that's how he works to get a girl's attention."

Caroline straightened her back, looking freshly ticked off. "And you know this from experience, I assume."

"No. There are a million freaking ways to get a girl to spread her legs for you, and lying isn't one I use, but I know that trick when I see it. And he used it on you. You were used, and you should not spend another day of your life hurting over that pathetic excuse of human space, because *three*, you are amazing."

Caroline let out a breath and slowly turned to look up at him. "What?"

He nodded, his eyes serious. I couldn't help it; I reached for Quinn's hand and bit my lip to keep from smiling as he squeezed my fingers in return.

"You are so amazing," Ten kept talking. "And I don't want to see something like what he did to you slow you down like it has. I want to watch you get over it and keep on living an amazing life that you *deserve.*"

"Oren," Caroline murmured, the awe in her voice making it obvious how much his words had affected her. Heck, they affected me and he hadn't even said them to me. She reached up slowly and cupped his cheek. He closed his eyes and she lifted her other hand to his other cheek.

I held my breath for that moment when their lips would touch, but Ten wrenched back and grabbed Caroline's wrists, tugging her hands from his face. Shaking his head, he said, "No. This isn't going to happen."

"But...but you left me all those drawings."

When Ten didn't deny it, Quinn glanced at me for confirmation. I nodded, and his eyes grew big with shock.

"Noel's been worried about you," Ten said. "He said you hid away in your room all summer, and he wasn't going to stop worrying until you finally started to live again. Those stupid pictures made you smile. They made you—"

"So...what? You made them to cheer me up just so *Noel* could feel better. It had nothing to do with me whatsoever?"

"Caroline." He groaned, closing his eyes. "I am sorry, but nothing—*nothing*—is ever going to happen between you and me."

"You got that right," she growled before spinning away and marching off. The fire and anger in her eyes made me smile, though. Their story was far from over.

I leaned up toward Quinn. "Is it just me, or is it kind of fun to watch them fight?" It felt like...foreplay.

When he didn't immediately answer, I lifted my gaze to him. The seriousness in his expression made my stomach drop. When he took my elbow and drew me into a quiet empty classroom, my heart started to pound hard.

"Is it just me, or did that feel...right?"

"Right?" I repeated slowly, not sure how to answer, because I wasn't too sure what he was even talking about.

"Spying on them together," he said. "You and I... we're watchers. We worry about our friends and keep silent tabs on them, waiting to step in when they need us. That's just...it's us. Doing that together felt right."

"I..." I shook my head, completely discombobulated because he was dead-on. It *had* felt right to stand there with him and listen in on Caroline and Ten's conversation.

He shifted closer to me, the closeness of his huge, hard body making my head spin with delicious memories. "You know I didn't use you for revenge, right? Cora had nothing to do with what happened between us."

Not expecting him to say that, I sniffed and shook my head. "Of course I know that. When Ten said that about you going after one of her friends for revenge, I just kind of classified it under the ninety percent of stupid stuff he says."

"Good." Quinn's lips tipped in a smile, but his face remained serious. "I can't stop thinking about it. About us. That night. It was just so...I want more." His pleading eyes lifted to mine. "Don't you?"

I was tempted. So tempted. But the obstacles in our path were so ginormous.

I groaned. "Quinn, you're still on the rebound from Cora."

He shook his head. "No, I'm not. I'm really not. I know that sounds insane since a week ago we were picking out a ring for her, but...there is something between you and me. You can't deny that. There's been something growing between us since the moment we met."

No, I couldn't deny it. But I clenched my teeth and closed my eyes. "If you have felt something for me this entire time, then why...why did you stay with her? Why buy her a ring? Why ask *me* to help you pick it out?"

When I opened my eyes, I could see on his face that he finally knew exactly what he'd put me through when he'd asked me help him choose that ring. Realization puffed from his breath as he took a step back.

"I...I...I'm so sorry, Zoey. I..." He shook his head. "I thought it was just me. I thought I could control it."

"Control what?" *His feelings*?

"M-m-my attraction to you. I thought I could ignore how much I wanted you, and we could just be friends. I *like* being your friend. But after Friday night, I realized I want both. From dating Cora, I didn't think being friends with my girlfriend was necessary. But Noel, and Mason, and Pick...they're *best* friends with their women. Maybe that's how it supposed to be. Friends *and* lovers."

"Quinn," I sobbed. "Stop putting me through this. We can't do this. You *know* why we can't do this."

His face fell, but he nodded compliantly. "I know. And I'm sorry for causing you more distress, but I had to try. You know I had to try, right?"

All I knew was that I ached so deep inside, I felt like my spirit was being ripped to shreds. Unable to say a thing in response, I spun away from him and fled. I just...I couldn't deal with this.

THIRTY-FOUR

⋘ ZOEY ⋙

CORA MARCHED into my bedroom where I was writing a new story on Wednesday evening, all dressed up in her party clothes. She tossed some kind of pink cloth on my bed.

"Put that on. I'm going out tonight, and you have to come."

I glanced at the pink...dress, I guess it was, and went back to writing. "I don't want to go out tonight." And I certainly didn't want to go out with *her*.

"Well, too bad. You have to. The girls are demanding I go out with them to help me get over my break-up. It wouldn't look right if you didn't come."

The urge to be nasty rose in my throat. I wanted to spit something like, "*Oh, you mean it'd look like I didn't support you and your faithless, cheating ways?*" But then I remembered what I'd done to her, and how I'd spent the entire evening with the guy she'd been in a serious relationship with for months on the very evening he broke up with her.

The guilt kept me quiet. I ducked my face. "I'm not going." If Quinn could tell Ten he wasn't going out with him to get over Cora, I could tell her the same thing. "I'm sure you'll have plenty of other girls with you to *support* you."

"But you're my *roommate*." She picked up the dress and shoved it in my face. "It's doubly important that you show *your* support."

I glanced up at her. "But I don't support what you did."

"And I don't give a flying fuck what you feel in your tender, little, self-righteous heart. Appearances are everything, Zoey. You're going, or I'll tell all my friends we broke up because he cheated on me...with you."

So, I WENT OUT with Cora and her friends, but I chose my own outfit, putting on skinny jeans, tall boots and a long top.

They decided to hit Forbidden first. Maybe they wanted Quinn to be working so they could flaunt Cora in front of him and make him miss her or something. I don't know, but he wasn't on duty, so whatever that plan had been fell through anyway. Ten and Asher were the two guys manning the bar. Cora's crew found a table near the front doors and a waitress took our order. I glanced toward the bar a few times, but both guys seemed too busy to notice us.

Cora wasn't as bad as I thought she'd be. She was so, *so* much worse, whining to her friends about her new single status, and they all—every single one of them—sympathized with her. Did they not even care that it was over between her and Quinn because of *her* actions?

Apparently not. And then I learned why. They didn't *know* it was because of her.

I had no idea what Cora had told them until Tamsen, I think her name was, said, "I can't believe he cheated on you. He always seemed like such a dedicated guy."

My eyes grew wide. *Say, what?*

"I know." Cora put on a sad face and fake wiped at her cheek, but all the while, her gaze lifted to mine. "It's always the quiet ones."

Or the liars, I wanted to spit back. My gaze narrowed. I couldn't believe she'd told them *he'd* been the cheater. They probably had no idea she'd slept around throughout her entire relationship with him.

"And he was the worst lay ever," she went on, making my blood pressure skyrocket.

I knew I'd only been with one person, but Quinn Hamilton was far and gone away from being the worst at anything he did in the bedroom. His merely looking at me could fry my hormones.

"Talk about vanilla lover. He never did anything but straight missionary, always skipped the foreplay, and he totally lacked sexy talk."

Quinn's voice from Friday night moved through my head.

After the touching and kissing comes the licking.

So pink and delicate.

God, yes. That's the flavor, right there. That's what would keep me coming back for more, every time.

Ready for another biology lesson?

I pushed to my feet, needing to escape before I blew a gasket.

Cora lifted her eyes. "Oh, are you headed to the bar? We need another round of strawberry daiquiris. Thanks."

I stared at her a moment, but then I glanced toward the bar...or rather toward the bartenders.

Maybe heading that way wouldn't be such a bad idea after all.

I marched to Asher and Ten. Asher grinned at me as he passed a fruity-looking drink to a waitress.

"Hey, Zoey. You look amazing tonight. What can I get you?"

Asher was too nice for my needs, so I bypassed him and planted myself in front of Ten, where he was busy plunking an olive with a toothpick and setting it just so into a martini glass.

Pointing in the direction of my roommate's table, I said, "Go destroy her."

Ten glanced up. He blinked at me for a moment before he arched an amused eyebrow. "Wow, Blondie. Do I really look like some kind of trained pet to you, who sits and fetches on command?"

I clenched my teeth. "She's talking smack about Quinn to all her friends. She told them he's the one who cheated on *her.*"

His eyebrows lifted. His gaze veered Cora's way before it narrowed on where she was surrounded by her skank posse. "Oh, bitch is going down."

Setting one hand on the bar, he hopped over it and

stalked off.

My chest filled with an eager excitement. I knew I should've felt bad for siccing Ten on her, but she deserved it. Guilt and joy blurred in my head. Curious to see what he did, I hurried after him.

"...and he refused to go down on me, the selfish prick," Cora was saying as Ten approached her from behind.

He startled her by snapping his fingers and saying, "Oh, damn. That was my bad, sorry." She spun a·round to gape up at him. Setting a hand against his heart as if he genuinely wanted to apologize, he sent Cora a wince. "You see, I told him how bad you stank down there. And the flavor..." He winced and shuddered. "It took me a fucking week to get that nasty aftertaste out of my mouth. It's my fault if he refused to eat you out."

My jaw dropped. I couldn't believe he'd said that. What was worse, I couldn't believe he'd actually been with Cora. Wha... *when* had that happened?

Glancing at her stunned friends, Cora started to shake her head. But the panic was getting to her. "You're such an asshole."

"Well, you're a fucking slut who had to beg me for weeks before I finally let you into my pants." He shrugged and lifted a hand to let her know he had no excuse for himself. "And everyone knows I usually need *no* encouragement before fucking a willing wo·man."

Tears filled Cora's eyes. As she pushed up from the table and fled toward the hall that led to the bath·rooms, everyone else at the table hurried after her, trying to comfort her.

Wow. Ten definitely knew how to clear a table. Note to self: never get on this guy's bad side.

He swung toward me and lifted his eyebrows, waiting for my response.

I cleared my throat and patted him on top of the head. "Good boy."

Ten threw his head back and laughed. "Damn, Blondie. Sometimes you crack me up." Throwing an arm around my shoulder, he led me up to the bar.

"Get her a Long Island," he told Asher as he showed me to a barstool.

I didn't really want a drink, but I didn't want to say no to Ten either, so I lifted my purse from my lap to get some money. Asher lifted a hand and waved my money away.

"It's on the house. Anyone who looks out for our Quinn need not pay."

"Damn straight," Ten agreed. He hopped back be-hind the counter and took an order from someone else as Asher set my drink in front of me.

I thanked him but didn't drink. I was running my fingernail up the condensation dripping down the side when Cora's voice from behind me made me lift my head and whirl around.

"I suppose I have *you* to thank for that attack." She scowled and crossed her arms over her chest.

I wasn't proud of sending Ten after her, but I wasn't sorry for it either. "You shouldn't have said all that about Quinn," was all I could think to answer.

Noticing her talking to me, Ten started our way, but I put up my hand to stop him, letting him know I could handle this. He paused, but kept watching us.

Cora snorted as she watched our silent byplay, only for a lightbulb look to enter her face as if she'd just then figured something out. She turned back to me slowly, her eyes narrowed. "Why, you dirty little slut."

My heart skipped a beat. I was so sure she'd just figured out what Quinn and I had done, I almost passed out from the shock. But then I wondered if she thought maybe *Ten* and I had been together. So, I said, "Excuse me?"

She leaned in close. I wanted to pull away, but I stiffened my back and met her glare for glare. "We're leaving," she snarled. "This pigsty stinks." Her gaze slid to Ten, letting me know he was the reason for her retreat.

Hooking her hand around my arm, she tried to pull me off my barstool, but I resisted.

"I don't think so. I'm not going anywhere else with you, and I refuse to listen to you spew more lies about people."

"Oh, you're going, or I'll tell all the girls you've had Ten, too."

I snorted and rolled my eyes. "Well, maybe I'll just do one better to you, Cora. I'll—*gasp*—actually tell the *truth* about you."

She frowned and shook her head. "What do you mean?"

"I'll tell your friends how sick you are. You didn't want them to know about your renal problems, right?" When her eyes widened, I clicked my tongue. "Or maybe I'll tell one of your doctors just how much you like to drink. That *is* one of the reasons they reject someone from getting a transplant, isn't it? Substance abuse?"

When she paled, I knew I'd won the battle. I would never tell on her, of course, but she didn't know that.

Straightening her back, she lifted her chin regally high. "Well, look who grew a backbone." Then she turned away as if giving me the cut direct and stormed off.

I stared after her, feeling...I don't know. Alive. Powerful. I wanted to...I just wanted to see Quinn. Liking my new backbone, as Cora had called it, I pressed my hand to my rapidly thumping heart. She had no idea what kind of man she'd let go when she'd decided to treat him like crap and then spout lies about him. But I knew, and I'd been an idiot for let·ting him slip through my fingers. If he was really a dull vanilla, then I didn't want any other flavor.

"Heading out?" Ten asked, taking my untouched drink away without commenting about it.

I smiled at him. "I have someone to see."

The approving grin that grew across his face only emboldened me more. "Go get him, baby."

So I did.

When I knocked on Quinn's door twenty minutes later, I was ready to get my man. He answered, wearing his sleep pants and a rumpled shirt. His hair stood up on one side as if he'd been lying on it. He looked good enough to tackle and devour.

So I did.

"I'm ready for another biology lesson," I said, grab·bing a handful of his shirt. Then I rose onto my toes and kissed him. Hard.

For someone who totally wasn't expecting it, Quinn reacted almost immediately, only stumbling back half a step before he caught himself and then crushed me against him. His large hands cupped my head. "Zoey," he gasped before his lips captured mine.

My mouth opened under his, and his tongue was eager to fill it. I climbed his big body, because I needed every part of me rubbing against every part of him. He dropped his grip from my face to catch my butt and hoist me up where I wanted to be the most.

My legs wrapped around his waist. He spun me to pin me against a wall and then he began to grind. Oh God, but feeling his thick, long erection through his pants caused this delicious, throbbing clench of muscles deep in my womb. It reminded me just how much I'd missed feeling him there. I needed him inside me, moving, pumping, thrusting.

"I did a little research after...you know, learning about flower anatomy," I panted out as he began to kiss his way down my throat.

"What?" He lifted his face, looking too dazed to remember the biology lesson he'd given me the last time we were together.

So aroused that my breaths wouldn't calm down, I nodded. "Did you know that an imperfect flower is one that has either all female parts or all male parts, but not both?"

He blinked, clearly confused about why I was telling him this. "Yes," he said. "I knew that."

Of course he knew that. But that so wasn't the point.

"So...so if you..." I bit my lip as I shifted my hips so I could ride his erection a little faster. "If you and I, male and female parts, came together, we'd make—"

"A perfect flower," he whispered, finishing the sentence for me as his eyes lit with realization.

I smiled. "You want to make the most perfect flower ever with me?"

Lust and awe filled his gaze. "Yes." He cupped my face, stared into my eyes, and then kissed me hard before repeating, "Yes," even stronger. Then he peeled me off the wall and began to carry me down the hall. "Condoms are in my room."

I nuzzled my nose up the side of his neck and nipped his earlobe with my teeth before saying, "I'm on the pill. Doctor's orders."

"In that case...the kitchen's closer." He veered left and then let go of me with one arm so he could shove everything off the top of the table. "I can't get inside you fast enough."

"I'll get my jeans, you get the top."

He agreed by swiping my shirt over my head. I fumbled with my jeans, zipping them down and then tugging them off my hips while Quinn whipped my bra off within seconds. Then he grabbed the heels of my boots and pulled them both off at the same time before helping me fling my pants over his shoulder.

"God, you are so perfect." His eyes gleamed as he had me lie down on my back with my legs hanging off the side of the table.

The chill against my butt and spine fled the moment he hooked one of my legs under his arm and then slid his hand in his pants only to come out with his thick cock ready to impale. "And look at these beautiful swollen petals." He slid the head of his shaft up along my folds. "You're already blooming, all wet and ready for me."

My breasts were so sensitive and hard as they heaved up and down from my chest. "I've been wet for you since last Friday."

He lifted his attention, his gaze intent on my expression. "Is that why you changed your mind about us? Because of this."

I shook my head. "No."

His face flooded with joy and he shoved inside me, making me cry out and bow my back off the table.

"Okay, maybe a little," I revised, panting when he paused half way in me.

One eyebrow lifted. "Only a little, you say?"

"Please," I begged. "Quinn, please. A lot, okay. A lot. *All* of it. I need all of it, in all of me. Deeper." I reached out for his hips, hoping to catch him and force him forward, but he just smiled and shook his head.

Then he closed his eyes, waited a beat, and whispered, "Okay. Now."

He opened his lashes just as he thrust forward, breaching the rest of me. My pussy clenched around him, so hungry for his presence it began to contract.

"Oh God. Oh God. Oh God."

He started moving, and that was it for me. I came all around him, screaming, and begging, and thrashing for more.

He stroked me through my orgasm, stretching me from the inside and massaging me with his thumb from the outside. It wasn't until I came down, panting and limp, that I realized he was still going. I opened my eyes. "You're still..."

He grinned, even though his eyes were glazed, and his forehead was damp. "I love watching you come. How many times do you think we can get you to come before we leave this table?"

"Uh..." I had no idea, but I think he wanted to find out.

After running his hands up the outsides of my thighs, he

clamped my legs together and bent them up until they were almost touching my chest. When he began to move again, the change in how he felt inside me from this new position made my eyes widen.

"Oh, that's... Oh, wow."

Quinn chuckled and leaned in a little against me so my body was supporting some of his. Then he cupped my breasts and finally gave them his attention.

"*Ohmigod!*" I jerked from the intense sensation and bumped my head back against the table as I panted through the pleasure.

"I love your breasts." His gaze was drawn to them as his hands massaged and his fingers plucked at the pearled nipples. "They fit my hands so perfectly. I want to fit one in my mouth."

He leaned in and sucked one tip into his mouth, which essentially made his large body press in closer and force my legs to stay where he'd put them, trapping me as he assaulted me with his cock and tongue. I gripped his hair, not able to do much else but feel and cry out my next orgasm when I came again.

"One more," Quinn whispered into my ear as soon as I began to wilt from the last high he'd given me. I shook my head, unable to believe I could last one more time, but he parted my legs so he could wedge his big body right up against mine. Then he pressed his forehead to mine so he could look into my eyes.

I think we shared everything in that moment. We breathed in the same air, intertwined our fingers so the sweat from our palms was the same, and we began to convulse together. Then we watched each other's stunned expressions while our orgasm flourished between us.

When it was over and the calm returned, I cupped his face in my hands. His lashes flickered open. We were eyeball to eyeball when I said, "This is why I came back." I brushed his hair across his forehead. "Because you're you, and I couldn't stay away from you."

He kissed me, softly and gently, nothing but lips on lips, then nose rubbing against nose. "I'm glad you did, because I wasn't sure how I was going to be able to stay away from you."

THIRTY-FIVE

ᴥ ZOEY ᴥ

I WOKE THE NEXT morning to Quinn's naked butt right in my face. And then he bent over.

I grinned, suddenly fully awake. Curled on my side in his bed, I faced his way as he pulled up a pair of pants, and—damn—covered his perfect tush from my view. With a frown, I reached out, stretching since he was standing a good two or three feet away from the mattress, and then I tugged his pants back down until I could see those taut, rounded globes of goodness again.

"Hey," he yelped and spun around.

I giggled sleepily up at him. "Hey, yourself. I was having fun looking at those. Why'd you have to go and cover them up?"

Pleasure spread across his face. "Oh, you want to play, huh?"

He crawled back onto the bed and pinned me to the mattress.

Since I had him right where I wanted him, I stretched and preened out my pleasure. "I definitely want to play. You have a problem with that?"

"Not at all." He nipped my lips and then angled his head to the side and urged them open with his tongue. The hot, open-mouthed kiss that followed left me weak and breathless.

"How do you always make me want you so easily?" I demanded, panting for him.

"Jedi mind trick," he panted back right before his breath fanned my neck.

Oh...*golly*. His lips barely pressed against the tender spot right behind my ear and I couldn't help it, I moaned and arched against him like a cat being scratched.

"On your belly," he instructed, rolling me over. "Time for paybacks, so I can enjoy *your* backside."

I immediately rolled over.

Since I was still naked from our night together, his fingers skimmed around to my front and found their way between my legs as his hips arched against my bottom, letting me feel just how very aroused he was. My breasts began to ache a split second before he cupped one.

A finger batted against my nipple while one finger on the other hand pushed inside me. My mouth opened in a silent scream.

Quinn groaned behind me. "You are so wet."

"For you, always. Oh...God. Don't stop," I commanded as my hips rolled with the thrust of his thick digit. "Don't stop. Please."

Quinn pressed another finger in and pinched my nipple at the same moment. The quick, crisp nip of pain sent my nerve endings haywire until I began to come, hard. The muscles contracting in my abdomen wrenched and twisted savagely enough that I cried out from the pressure. I squirmed against the hand between my legs, wanting to escape and latch on to such sweet torment at the same time.

His tongue slid up the back of my neck. Our bodies pressed together perfectly as I arched back into him. He was soft and yet hard all at the same time, his flesh all sleepy warm and smooth but the muscle under it hard and supportive. I so loved that about him and couldn't stop my fingers from reaching back and sinking into his hair. I almost wished I was facing him so my hands could be running up and down his back, marveling at how wonderful he felt. Even the bumps from his scars felt absolutely perfect under my fingers, making little paths of puckered skin to follow in a mazelike pattern.

"Quinn." I broke when he bit the back of my shoulder. "I

need you inside me. Please. It feels so empty without you there." My womb had nothing to clench around; it needed something right there.

Grasping my hips, he remained sitting upright as he drew my bottom back onto his lap and slid me up against his arousal. When the blunt tip of his penis pressed into my opening, I threw my head back and let out a relieved breath. He slid his hand up from between my legs, over my navel and to my breasts. When he cupped one, I choked out a whimper. Then he finally filled me completely.

I reached back and grabbed his thighs, my nails digging into his skin. "Harder."

He complied, nearly jarring my teeth as his next powerful thrust reverberated throughout me. I buried my face in my pillow and bit it to keep from screaming too loudly.

Quinn pressed forward, and I moaned from the comfort of his weight against me and the erotic pressure of his cock sliding deeper.

It was so naughty and wicked, and yet delicious and amazing. I never wanted it to stop.

"What are you turning me into, Quinn Hamilton?" I demanded.

He panted behind me and softly slid his hand up my spine and then up into my scalp to grip my hair. "I don't know. But I love it." He leaned forward to kiss the side of my jaw. "I am so addicted to you. I could do this forever. I love kissing you, and touching you, entering you. Fucking you."

His strokes became longer, slower, excruciatingly frustrating because I just wanted him to slam into me and pound us both into oblivion. This slow death was driving me crazy. I clutched his pillow. "Oh my God. *Please.*"

His breath tickled my ear. "Please what?"

"Make me come."

He chuckled, the jerk. He knew he had absolute control over me. "Yes, ma'am." Ten seconds later, he had me screaming into the pillow again as I contracted around his steely length.

TOO DROWSY TO move after Quinn has his way with me—or maybe I should say, after I coaxed him into having his way with me—I began to fall asleep as soon he pulled free from my body. Then he kissed my cheek tenderly and crawled off the bed.

"Can I finally take my shower now?" his voice teased as he lovingly laid his sheets over me and tucked them in around me. "Or does my beautiful, in-satiable girl need anything else this morning?"

"Breakfast," I mumbled with a smile, remembering how he'd always made Cora breakfast. Hoping I could get that same treatment, I opened one eye and asked, "With bacon?"

He winked. "You got it." Then he leaned in, sniffed my hair and kissed me one last time on the cheek before strolling from the room.

I tried to go back to sleep but thinking about him in the shower, all naked and clean, smearing slick soap over his hard, large body and down between his legs... I suddenly wondered what the heck I was doing in here, alone, while he was in there all wet and sexy.

Grinning goofily to myself, I popped out of bed and pulled on one of his large T-shirts. Bypassing a bra and panties, I shot out of his room and down the hall to where I heard a shower running. I took a breath before grasping the handle and pushing my way inside.

Steam had already filmed the mirrors and heated the room. I considered stripping naked before slipping in with him. But then I bit my lip, suddenly unsure. What if he didn't like company in the shower? What if my presence upset him instead of delighted him?

Testing the waters, I said, "Quinn?" and slipped the shower curtain aside just enough to see in.

"What the fuck?" Under a pounding stream of water, a fully naked Ten spun around to gape at me.

I screamed and lurched backward, tripping over the toilet and sprawling onto my butt onto the floor. The shower curtain flew the rest of the way open. I scurried upright, shoving Quinn's shirt down to cover as much of my bare legs as possible.

"*Blondie?*" he screeched, only to cover his dick with both of his hands as my wide-eyed gaze landed on it without my permission. I slammed my eyes closed. "Oh my God, oh my

God. I'm sorry. I'm so sorry."

Spinning away blindly, I fled, running smack into the door before I patted my hands around, found the doorknob, and yanked it open to dart into the hall, only to collide with a huge, hard body.

I screamed again, not expecting anyone. But then Quinn's smell reached me and instead of trying to escape him, I latched on and climbed up him, and clutched him gratefully.

"Wha...?" he started in confusion.

"I thought it was you," I babbled. "You said you were going to take a shower. You said you were going to take a shower. Why weren't you *in the shower?*"

He hugged me to him. "Ten was already in there, so I thought I'd start breakfast instead."

I buried my absolutely mortified face into his chest. "Oh my God. I'm never sneaking into a bath-room to shower with you again."

"You were...?" Before he could finish the question, the bathroom door slammed open behind me.

I clutched Quinn tighter and totally didn't mean to blurt out, "Something's wrong with his penis."

"What?" a clearly confused Quinn said as Ten choked out a horrified growl.

"I'm sorry," I said, still freaked out about every-thing that had just happened. "I didn't mean to say that out loud, but...oh my God. It doesn't look like yours. There's this big, blood bruise-looking thing on it."

"Blondie!" Ten cried in a strained voice. "*Shut... up.*"

I finally glanced back at him. He had a towel wrapped around his waist, but he was still streaming wet. As I looked at him, though, all I could see was that huge discoloration on his junk.

"I'm sorry," I said, genuinely remorseful for blurting what was probably something very private a-bout his privates. "I just couldn't keep it in. I tried. But...oh my God. What is it? Does it hurt?"

Quinn choked out a surprised laugh, while a blushing Ten slapped his palm against his forehead. "It's a *birthmark*," he gritted out. "Just a birthmark. Nothing is wrong with my dick. It doesn't *hurt.* I've had it since birth."

"It was big... I mean the bruise, not the penis." When Ten buried his face in his hands and groaned in misery, I winced. "Sorry. I'm so sorry."

He lifted his hand. "Just...shut up. Please, for the love of God...stop talking."

"I'm trying," I cried, "But it was just so—"

He growled again and pointed his finger in a threatening manner. "You are dead to me." He stalked toward his room, only to pause and glance back and point at me again. "You owe me breakfast for this. Eggs, toast, and bacon. Lots of fucking bacon." Spinning away, he stormed off to his room, calling over his shoulder, "And Sunny D too," right before he slammed his door, hard.

I looked up at Quinn. "I can't believe I couldn't stop talking. I feel so awful. I have to be the worst person ever. Did you see him blush? I can't believe I made Ten blush."

Instead of scolding me for my stupid, uncontrollable outburst, Quinn grinned. "You are so adorable." He kissed me on the tip of my nose. "I love that you were the first person I've ever seen make my roommate blush."

"It's not funny." I groaned. "I was completely insensitive and—"

"And you're weren't serious at all when you said you were never sneaking into my bathroom again to shower with me, right? Because honestly, as long as it's me in there, and not Ten, you could sneak in every morning and I'd be perfectly okay with that."

"Quinn!" My scold went unheeded though because he picked me up, tossed me over his shoulder and carried me into the bathroom, where we showered together.

After that, we finished breakfast together, making sure a mollified Ten got everything he'd ordered. When he finally emerged from his room, fully clothed, he cleared his throat, scowled at us and grumbled un-der his breath as he filled his plate and sat across from Quinn, pausing to glare at us every few bites. And he completely forgot to say thank you.

"It goes without saying that what she saw in the shower stays between the three of us...right?"

Quinn shook his head. "Why would I go around talking to anyone about your junk, man?"

Ten's shoulders loosened, but when he looked at me, he narrowed his eyes. I lifted my hands. "Of course, I'm not going to say anything." Why would I? I felt awful enough for the way I reacted; the least I could do was keep it private. "But I can't believe word hasn't gotten out before...what with all the girls you sleep with," I murmured more to myself.

Ten winked. "I have my ways of keeping it under wraps."

Literally, was my guess.

I shook my head. What a morning.

Mere months ago, I never would've guessed I'd be discussing a guy's birthmark on his penis so casually and without wanting to die from embarrassment twenty minutes after seeing it. Oh, how the times had changed...how *I'd* changed. But I just didn't feel so in·secure and timid about everything, not when Quinn was near. And I wasn't joking when I said near.

He didn't let me sit in my own chair. Instead, he'd pulled me onto his lap and together, we ate off the same plate.

Ten watched us for a second, scowling and chewing before he swallowed. Then he pointed his fork our way. "So...how long has this been going on? Last night was so not your first time together, because you wouldn't be this familiar with each other yet. And thanks for letting me know you were already getting some, *buddy*. Make me feel like an idiot for trying to find you pussy when you were already—"

"Shh." Quinn scowled at him and hugged me closer.

Ten rolled his eyes. "Seriously, man, you don't have to mark your territory like that just because your girl accidentally saw my awesome body all naked and wet. She ain't going to hop over here to ride the Ten Express." Then he leaned in and winked at me. "Even though the colorful peckers like mine do feel better in you."

"Cut it out," Quinn growled, pulling his arms even tighter around me.

Rolling his eyes, Ten scooped up another forkful of his omelet. "Jesus, man. You make no sense. This one is a million times more faithful than that last one, and yet you're already fifty times more possessive of her."

If anything, that only made Quinn's arms band tighter around me. "Don't make comparisons," he ordered softly.

"But they're so obvious," Ten argued. "This one is *sooo* much better." Ten gave a low whistle as he sent me an appreciative look. "I mean, she—"

"Ten," Quinn growled in warning.

His roommate sighed. "Just keep her out the bathroom when I'm showering, because too much more of that and I'll just invite her in with me."

"Oh my God." I whimpered in complete mortification—because okay, I wasn't totally cured from blushing just yet.

As I hid my scorching hot face in Quinn's chest, he roared, "Enough."

He surged to his feet, taking me with him.

Ten just grinned at us. "You guys are so fucking cute together. I love it. Congratulations by the way. You better name your firstborn after me."

I curled my arms around Quinn's neck as he carried me from the kitchen and back to his room.

"I'm sorry," he murmured regretfully in my ear and then kissed my cheek. "Do you want me to throw him out?"

"No." I pressed my mouth to his neck because he smelled so good there...and I just had to have my mouth on him. Plus, his caveman carrying kind of turned me on. "I actually liked hearing that someone likes me more than her."

He groaned and caught my face so he could mash his mouth against mine. "I like you more than her, too. I crave you so much it's all I can think about. All I want. Maybe all I need."

I didn't get a chance to respond because he pressed his tongue in and I grew too obsessed with craving him right back. We parted only long enough for him to lay me on the bed and crawl onto the mattress with me.

"Is it bad if I grew hard the moment he said pussy? I instantly envisioned yours, and then I wanted inside it."

I gulped, watching him rip off my jeans. "Only if it's bad that hearing you say that makes me wet."

With a grin, he hiked up the shirt I was wearing. Then he ripped off the panties I'd put on to make breakfast, tearing them to smithereens. "I don't mind being bad with you." Dipping his face between my legs, he slid his tongue inside me and showed me just how good bad could be.

THIRTY-SIX

◈ ZOEY ◈

I SNUCK OVER to Quinn's apartment on Sunday night after he texted to tell me Ten was working and he was home alone. It was my first booty call, I realized, and it made me giddy as I stole up the stairs to his apartment.

He looked similarly excited as he opened the door for me and let me in. His blue eyes sparkled with mischief and he bit his lip as he took my hand and pulled me inside and closed the door behind me.

"Did you have any problems getting here?" he asked, his voice hushed.

I shook my head. All he was doing was holding my hand and I wanted to attack him, but I only shifted a step closer. "I was home alone too, so no one noticed me leaving."

His grin spread and he tipped his head as if he was going to kiss me, but he didn't. "Good," he whispered.

I couldn't handle it. I lifted my fingers and touched his face, grazing my nails over his dimple. "Why're we whispering?" I had to ask, my voice just as quiet and conspiring as his. "I thought you said Ten was working tonight."

"He is." Quinn dipped in closer until our brows brushed.

"But it feels naughtier to talk like this, like we're sneaking around." His eyes fluttered as if he was going to close them, but he didn't. Then he glanced his cheek off mine and admitted in a soft, husky voice directly into my ear. "I like feeling naughty with you."

Lifting my second hand, I cupped his face in my palms before slipping them up his jaw and dipping my fingers into his hair and then grasping fistfuls. Then I whispered into his ear, "You can be as naughty as you want with me."

A growl rumbled from his chest as he crushed his mouth to mine. His tongue speared into me, and I whimpered as he picked me up by the bottom and spun me around to press my back against the wall and anchor me there while his lips attacked mine.

We couldn't get enough, grappling and tugging at each other's clothes, teeth nipping at the other's skin, hands unable to stop gripping and tearing.

"I want to do you right here against this wall," he rasped into my ear as he tugged my panties, the last of my clothes, down my legs.

I was in no condition to deny him anything, so I just nodded, staring down at him with wide, amazed eyes as he knelt in front of me to help me step out of my underwear. He lingered down there, and I squirmed a little inside, remembering how his tongue felt on me. I was so wet it was embarrassing. And yet thrilling.

A long breath escaped him as he looked up and met my gaze. "You are so beautiful," he murmured.

My heart fluttered in my chest and I didn't know how to answer. His gaze captured me as if he knew he possessed every freaking molecule of my being.

"When you look at me like that, I feel like a helpless little fly caught in your web."

His confession caused a laugh to blurt from me. *I* was the one caught and entranced under *his* spell.

"Do I hear another biology lesson coming?" I asked.

His grin exploded across his face. "The spider builds his web to catch his food."

I groaned and covered my face as if I hated his biology lessons, when actually I loved them.

He ran his fingers up the insides of my thighs. "As soon as his victim comes along and gets caught in his web, he *strikes.*"

I yelped when Quinn's arms snaked around my legs and wrapped around me. His naughty grin grew. "After he binds his silk around his little fly so she can't possibly escape, he bites her with his venom."

Quinn sank his teeth into me, right between my legs with a playful kind of nip. I groaned and buried my fingers in his hair, pulling taut at his scalp when his tongue licked across my clit. He killed me with his mouth, massaging that sensitive little bundle of nerves until I was squirming against him, so close to the brink that I didn't care how hard I was pulling his hair now, or that I might've hurt his back when I wrapped one leg around his shoulder and dug the heel of my foot into his spine. When he plunged two fingers into me, I lost it.

I was loud and unashamed by what a commotion I made, because the louder I got the more enthused and hungry he turned. I loved that. I wanted him ravenous.

When I finally breathed out a drained breath, he broke his mouth from my pussy and wiped the back of his hand across his red, swollen lips. His blue eyes were especially bright when they met mine. His gaze told me how amazing he thought I was, how much he loved being here with me like this, how precious this moment was to him. But he didn't verbalize any of that. He didn't have to. Instead, he said it in his own way...his geeked-out, biology-loving way.

"So after the spider injects his venom, he retreats a safe distance to let her die."

"Check," I murmured in a dazed voice as I remained collapsed against the wall. "I definitely feel limp enough to be half dead."

Quinn's smile was as deadly as it was smugly adorable when he glanced up from stepping out of his boxer shorts. My gaze went directly to his cock as it bobbed away from him, hard and long and so freaking thick. The droplet of pre-cum beading from the head made my mouth water.

"Did you know the French call an orgasm *la petite mort*, the little death? Because of that near state of unconsciousness after coming so hard?"

I shook my head, watching the flash of his white canines and remembering what they'd just done to me. "No," I said, "but it makes sense." I could die a happy girl right about now.

Setting one hand on the wall, he used the other to take

himself in hand and guide his cock to me. "But back to your lesson. Spider venom not only *kills* his victim, but it also liquefies all her organs because he can't process solid foods."

Oh, yeah. He'd definitely liquefied my insides. I felt like nothing but a gooey pile of mush. But I was so far past creepy, crawly spider talk. When Quinn Hamilton was touching himself, there was only one thing on my mind.

"Is it bad that I've become obsessed with this part of you?" I asked, reaching out so I could wrap my hand around his girth.

He clenched his teeth and a raspy sound exited his throat. "No," he said as he leaned in to press his lips against my forehead as he let me play. "I like your obsession with it."

I ran my fingers over him, intrigued by the thickest vein running down the entire length. I smiled, knowing that if I asked him, he'd probably know the scientific name of that vein.

His voice was strained as he squeezed his eyes closed. "Your touch is so gentle and soft."

I glanced up and studied his face as I gripped him again and slowly pumped him. "Is that bad?"

"No. But it's driving me insane. You can...you can be rougher...if you want."

"Rougher?" I repeated, very interested by the idea. I could tell by his expression that rougher was exactly what he wanted. "Why you naughty, naughty boy," I leaned in to whisper into his ear. "Show me how rough you want it."

He growled and instantly covered my hand, squeezing my fingers harder around his erection. Then he picked up the speed, helping me jerk him off.

"Oh God." I squeezed my legs together as I watched. "I think I'm going to come again."

"You better believe you are."

Abruptly letting go of my hand, he gripped my hips and lifted me higher against the wall. I squeaked in surprise and let go of his cock to grip his shoulders. As soon as he had me positioned where he wanted me, he thrust forward, impaling me at an angle that had me crying out and instantly constricting around him. It was rough and fast and utterly amazing.

Afterward, he gently carried my limp remains to the

couch, where he curled onto the cushions with me and cradled me into his arms. He was so tender and kind it made me melt against him and close my eyes with a satisfied sigh. The soft teddy bear had returned after taking me with an animalistic passion. I loved both extremes.

In the quiet aftermath, after we recovered from our near-death experience, he stroked my hair while I ran my fingernails up his back, following the grooves of his scars like I was working my way through a maze.

He shivered and hummed deep in his throat. "That feels so good. You will not believe how much they itch sometimes."

I opened my eyes, surprised he was actually bringing attention to his scars. "Do they really?" I made sure to keep doing exactly what I was doing. He re-warded me by relaxing deeper into me, his huge beautiful body growing deliciously heavy as his face nestled into my hair.

"How did you get them anyway?" I didn't change the speed or pressure of my administration, hoping to God I hadn't triggered anything bad by asking.

But he remained completely lax against me. "That actually came from one of my mom's men. Not her."

I couldn't contain a horrified gasp as I hugged him to me.

He hugged me back. "She liked to pick guys who could get as drunk mean as she did."

"Was it a belt?" I asked. When he nodded, I shuddered and tried not to gag. "It must've been awful. My dad took a belt to me a few times, but it only left a mark once when he used the wrong end."

Quinn's hand went to the back of my knee as if he remembered seeing that mark and knew where it had come from. "Yeah, well, this guy thought the wrong end was actually the right end to use on an eight-year-old boy."

Eight? I clutched him a little closer. "Why'd he go after you?"

"He was beating my mom. No idea why *they* were arguing, but I tried to stop him. I usually didn't intervene because my mom typically started it and gave back as good as she got. But she was no longer at a place where she could fight back." His sigh was heavy and full of dark memories. "I didn't do much damage to him, though. Probably didn't even leave a single bruise. My mom and I both ended up in the hospital that night."

"My God." I ran my fingers over his face, so relieved he'd survived all that. "I never ended up in the hospital from any of my experiences."

Quinn lifted his face and looked up at me, his eyes curious. "Not even once?"

I shook my head. "I was one of those extremely obedient children. I learned early which lines never to cross, I hid when he wanted me to be scarce, and I was there when I needed to be there, doing my duties."

His dark swirling eyes told me he didn't believe me. Then his fingers drifted over my shoulder to sweep across my old cigarette burns. "What about these?"

I sniffed out a sad laugh. "He found an opened, half-empty pack of cigarettes in his study one time. He thought they were mine. When I denied it, he lit one and held it against me until I cried out and started sobbing, begging him to stop. After he asked me again, I still denied it, insisting they weren't mine. So he lit another and burned me again. It took five times before I finally admitted they were mine. The next day, one of his friends asked him if he'd left his pack of cigarettes and favorite lighter at our house."

Quinn curled his lip as if he wanted to hunt my father down and hurt him. "Did he apologize?"

I let out a short, hard laugh. "My father? No way. He slapped me for lying to him by finally admitting they were mine."

"Bastard," he growled.

Loving how protective and fierce he looked, I kissed his cheek.

His lashes fluttered and he leaned in and pressed his forehead to mine. "It must've been hell for you."

I shrugged. "It was manageable. I knew my limits. Physical, fist-to-skin beatings were actually pretty rare. Maybe once a month."

"Once a month is not that rare." He ran the backs of his knuckles across my cheek. "But Cora made it sound as if you were always scared for your life and showed up to school every day freshly bruised."

With a roll of my eyes, I began to stroke his back again. "Cora has a way of overdramatizing things. At-tacks didn't really come because I'd disobeyed. Usually, it was something that set him off at work, and he'd need to vent on me, using me as his whip-ping post to relieve his stress." I shrugged. "I guess it was a good thing he was a powerful man at his bank. He usually got his way in his business dealings. So the abuse was limited. It was the psychological and emotional treatment I hated most."

Quinn nodded. "I know what you mean. I always preferred it when my mom would just whack me on the side of the head and walk away than when she called me worthless and told me how she wished I'd never been born."

"Oh, God. I hate that line. My father used it on me *all* the time. Or he'd tell me I was going to turn out a whore, just like my mother."

Growling deep in his throat, Quinn tightened his arms around me. "You are not—"

"I know." I kissed his chin, appreciating the vehemence in his voice. "But it still tears you down. It makes you feel weak."

"Worthless," he added softly.

"Alone," I said.

Quinn gazed in my eyes. "Unloved."

"Trapped," I whispered.

We gazed at each other for the longest time. I don't think I'd ever understood anyone the way I under-stood Quinn in that moment. He got me completely, and I got him. I felt shredded and bare, and yet completely liberated in my exposure.

"Thank God we're free of them," I managed to croak, feeling things for another person that I'd never felt for anyone.

"Yeah," he murmured. "Thank God."

"These last few months, away from him, have been an experience I'll never forget. And if he finds me and forces me to return home—"

"*Finds you?*" Quinn cut in, blinking away his con-fusion. Then his eyes filled with horror. "Oh God. He doesn't know you're here?" He gasped, guessing the truth.

I shook my head, realizing only Cora knew what it had taken for me to get here, and maybe she didn't even know the full extent of my escape. But I told Quinn, detailing how I'd transferred the money from my account and gotten my car and escaped in the night. At one point, he covered his mouth with his hands and just watched me from wide, blue eyes.

"But I had to leave. I had to come here," I started. My lips began to form Cora's name as I was on the brink of telling him how much she needed me. But then I remembered; I couldn't tell him that part. An ache formed in my chest. I hated keeping anything from him.

He nodded anyway, as if he understood everything. "Of course you did. He didn't treat you like a daughter. You were his slave. No one should live like that."

I licked my lips nervously. If Cora had never told me about her sickness, I never would've broken free. I probably would've remained my father's slave for the rest of my life.

"What do you think he'll do if he finds you?"

"Oh, he will," I said with total reassurance. "There's really no if about it. Eventually, he'll come. It's just a matter of time."

Quinn let out a harsh breath as if he were trying to brace himself for the inevitable. "What're you going to do when he does?"

I shivered; I couldn't stop myself. Quinn tightened his arms around me protectively. When I leaned my face against his shoulder, he kissed my hair.

"I don't know." And that was the honest truth. "Legally, he can't force me to go back with him. I'm an adult, and the money is mine; I inherited it from my mother after she died. He can't touch it. I just..." I squeezed my eyes closed. "I hope I have the willpower to tell him no if he tries to intimidate me into returning with him."

"You will," Quinn assured me. He leaned in to kiss me, and we didn't just share lips then, we shared souls. "You're strong. And besides, I'll be right there with you, standing by your side and holding your hand when you do it. If he tries to touch you, I'll—"

"Quinn," I rasped in reprimand. I didn't want to hear him say what he'd do to my father. He wasn't violent, and instinctively I knew he hated violence; it made him think of his mother, as if maybe he might become her. I didn't want him to go through that.

He nodded, remaining quiet, but the lethal intent remained in his gaze. "He'll never hurt you again. I promise it."

I nodded, and it was my turn to kiss him. His mouth latched onto mine eagerly.

Our lips stayed connected as we kissed deep into the night, chasing away all the haunting memories of our past and filling them with something light and beautiful and precious. I realized then that no matter what happened, I'd always have this—memories of him—to keep me warm for the rest of my life.

THIRTY-SEVEN

⊷ QUINN ⊶

EVERYTHING WAS different with Zoey.

I'd always been so unsure around Cora, nervous about finally having my first girlfriend and worried I'd do something wrong. I'd wanted to impress her and get her to like me so much I hadn't bothered with trying to figure out whether I really liked her in return.

With Zoey, we just...clicked. I *knew* I liked her. I never worried about needing to impress her because I had this sense I already did without really trying. I was usually too concerned about when I'd get to see her again to worry about that, anyway. I just wanted to be with her constantly. The urge to always find my way close to her was like an itch just under the skin that could never be relieved until she was back with me.

Even though I'd ordered Ten not to compare her with Cora, I did in my head, too. A lot. She always came out the victor. In looks, temperament, compatibility, likeability, even in the bedroom. When it came to sex...wow, there was no contest at all. Zoey lit up in my arms like a wildfire every time I touched her. Her eagerness for me was genuine, and I couldn't get enough of it.

With Cora, I'd been clueless, and she'd been the one with

all the experience. When we'd dated, I didn't think I had a problem with that. She taught me what she liked, and I was willing and ready to learn everything I could to please her. But she'd always led. I didn't think I had a problem with that, either.

Until Zoey.

Now, *I* was the teacher. And I was the one giving her her first experience with every new thing we did. There was something so hot and bonding about that, about knowing I was the only man who'd ever touched her there, or kissed her here. I wanted all her firsts, and I craved each one I took.

I felt closer to her because I knew every detail about her sexual past. That was probably wrong of me, but I still liked it. And I didn't just know all her secrets; I *was* her secret. It made me trust her implicitly. I told myself I should have some reservations. After the way Cora had lied and betrayed me and so absolutely hoodwinked me, I should've been wizened and hardened to the next girl who came along. But Zoey was so sweet and innocent I couldn't summon an iota of doubt over anything she said to me.

Six days after we started our secret relationship—secret because we didn't want Cora finding out and making a big deal about it—I went to school anxious and jittery. The last time I'd gotten a chance to see Zoey was yesterday morning in Art Appreciation. I'd had to work last night and I had to again tonight, which meant I wouldn't get to see her again until tomorrow, Wednesday morning

I walked to my next class, unable to concentrate on school or think about practice I would be attending later in the afternoon. Coach was finally going to officially label me as a second-string quarterback. I'd been working for this spot for a year now. I should be excited that today was finally the day. Instead, I was tempted to pull out my cell phone and fire off a text to Zoey, even though I'd had a ten-minute conversation with her earlier when I called to say good morning.

This constant craving for her was driving me nuts.

But even as my hand went to my back pocket while I strolled along the sidewalk, I spotted her up ahead, walking with Cora in my direction. Neither of them noticed my approach. Soon they would, though. It was inevitable; I was going to walk right by them. I frowned slightly, wondering why they looked so buddy, buddy. I didn't get a sense from Zoey that she and Cora were even remotely friendly any more.

But then I heard Cora saying, "You won't forget, right? This Saturday? It can't be rescheduled," and I figured it had to be something about their apartment.

"I won't forget." Zoey sounded a little irritated by the reminder.

She was the first to see me. My insides fired to life, and great...I instantly went hard. Remembering every single thing we'd done together, I stared at her a little too intently, and way too obviously. She began to look away, but did a double take before her eyes widened.

I couldn't help it. I smiled. When she blushed, I mouthed the word, "*Library*," without really thinking what I was doing. I was that desperate for her.

She darted a quick look at Cora, who was checking something on her phone and didn't notice me for another half a second.

"Oh," Cora said with genuine surprise when she finally looked up. She pushed her chest out and then tossed her hair over her shoulder. It was pathetic how hard she tried to preen in front of me. "Hey there, Quinn."

I sniffed, making a face at her, wondering why she thought there was anything friendly, or even civil between us.

Then my gaze returned to Zoey and my internal organs started burning. I held her stare until they passed and she was gone. I hoped she'd understood my message because I was already veering toward the library, and my mouth was watering to taste her.

ZOEY

"UMM...IS THAT all you needed from me?" Heart racing, I glanced at Cora and bit my lip, hoping she didn't notice my eagerness.

Quinn probably hadn't even said library. It'd just looked like the word his lips were forming. And heck, even if he had said it, that probably hadn't meant he wanted me to meet him there. But that's where I was going anyway.

Cora snapped her phone shut and sent me a bored glance. "Why would I need anything else from you?" She'd gone over doctors' appointments with me, and that was pretty much the only thing left between us.

"I'll see you then." I waved a half-hearted goodbye and darted back in the direction I'd just come from.

I couldn't get to the library fast enough. When I reached the front doors, I glanced behind me self-consciously just to make sure Cora hadn't followed me for any reason.

My heart leapt into my throat when I swear I saw the red top she was wearing and blond hair, but then whoever it was walked behind a building. I blew out a breath, telling myself I was paranoid.

As I swept inside the front doors, I started grinning. Even the possibility of getting to see him had my blood pounding with excitement. I didn't have to search; I went straight to our spot. But as I turned down the aisle of books that led there, I slowed to a stop. He wasn't there.

My shoulders slumped. But then a breath later, two arms slid around my waist, making me squeak in surprise. I was pulled back against a hard chest I'd recognize anywhere.

"You came." His voice was filled with wonder be-fore he spun me around.

His smile created a buzz that echoed through my entire body. I smiled back and touched his dimple; my lips hurt from stretching them so far. His own smile widened. And then he was pulling me up to his level and kissing me.

"God, Zoey. I can't resist you in a pair of jeans or even shorts. But a skirt—" He shook his head even as his palms caught my bare thighs and smoothed their way up the outsides, right under my skirt. "You want to kill me, don't you?"

I kissed him a little more desperately, my body coming alive as his heated touch branded my flesh. I climbed him and he pinned me to a wall of books. Then his fingers were skimming under my panties and cupping my bottom.

"This is so wrong," I panted out even as I wound my legs around his waist and pressed my forehead to his shoulder when he slid his longest finger over me to find out how wet I already was.

He bit my neck, right below my ear. "I lose all sense of right and wrong when you're in a skirt." With a tortured groan, his finger pushed inside me.

I choked on a gasp, and lifted my face to look over his shoulder. "What if someone catches us?"

"What?" His teeth nipped at my throat and his fingers pumped me faster.

"Quinn," I tried to resist, but I was too busy moving with him. I didn't want him to stop, so my warning came out sounding a little too much like a plea.

"I wish this was my cock," he whispered into my ear as he added another finger.

It was embarrassing how easily he could make me come, but a couple strokes later I was biting his shoulder and squirming against him as my release crashed through me.

"Shh," he whispered into my ear, and then chuck-led at his library pun.

"I think...I think I need to pass out now." I curled my arms around him and hid my face in his chest, embarrassed. "I can't believe we just did that."

"Me neither, but it was really hot."

I lifted my face, and he sent me a shy yet mischievous smile, making his dimple dip like crazy. Unable to help myself, I kissed his cheek and then whispered into his ear. "I want to finish you, too."

His body rippled, letting me know just how much he liked that suggestion, but he shook his head. "I don't have anything. It'd make a mess."

I took a breath and then said, "Not if I swallowed."

Quinn's body froze, his eyes widened, and his mouth dropped open. "Y-y-you..." Then he glanced around, "It'd be way more obvious what was going on if someone caught us doing *that*."

The idea excited and scared the crap out of me at the same time. I kind of wanted him to turn me down, but I also kind of wanted him to go for the idea.

I think he suffered from the same dilemma. Indecision warred across his face. So I said, "If you don't want me to—"

"No! I do," he was quick to correct me. "I really, really do. I just—"

"Then, I am," I decided.

So, I did!

QUINN

I WAS STILL IN A daze three days later, unable to forget what Zoey and I had done in the library together. It was the dirtiest thing I'd ever done and yet, I grinned and my entire body heated every time I remembered it. Even as we sat through art class beside each other on Friday, she blushed every time I stole a glance at her. Then I'd start grinning, unable to stop.

We were so obvious, Reese leaned toward us and winked, "It's about time you two finally figured it out."

I looked at Zoey. She looked up at me. And we just started smiling all over again.

I didn't want to leave her after first hour. But she had biology and I had history. I took history class with Cora, except she hadn't showed up to it since I'd bro·ken up with her, which was a godsend. Her friend Rachel still showed up, though. She approached me before the professor arrived.

I was completely suspicious.

"Hi, Quinn." She sat beside me, in the spot where Cora usually sat. When I sent her a guarded glance, she smiled and fluttered her lashes. "So, you and Cora are really over, huh?"

I gave a single, stony nod. "Yep."

"That's too bad. You were the best boyfriend she ever had." She set her hand on my desk, inches away from where I was resting my elbow. Then her smile widened. "The cutest, too."

I narrowed my eyes at her.

"I bet you're getting pretty lonely without her." When she leaned in, moving her hand to rest it on the back of my chair, I leaned away. "You know, I could help you with that," she said into my ear. "I've heard I keep pretty good company."

The look I sent her told her just how insane I thought she was. "No, thanks."

Rachel wasn't deterred. She flipped her hair and kept talking. "She said you were the biggest she'd ever seen. I'd like to find that out for myself."

"Well, you're just going to have to keep wondering, because it'll be a cold day in hell before I take on a carbon copy of *her*."

Shock ricocheted across her face before she sat back in her seat away from me. As a blush stole up her cheeks, I continued to stare dryly at her. Finally, she cleared her throat. "I guess you're still bitter."

"I guess," I said. "So you can go back to wherever you came from now and leave me alone."

She stood with a sniff and couldn't seem to get away from me fast enough. I watched her go and let out a shudder of relief. Then I smiled to myself. It'd felt kind of good to stand up for myself and send her away like that.

I reached behind me for my backpack to pull out my phone, so I could text Zoey. Feeling this good always made me want to talk to her. Plus, I wanted to wash my conversation with Rachel out of my head with a pure, sweet one with my girl. But I couldn't find my phone anywhere in my bag's front pocket where I usually kept it while I was in class.

I was still frowning and searching for it when the professor started class. Damn. I hoped I hadn't left it at home. I didn't want to suffer through an entire day without even being able to text Zoey.

After history, I had a free hour—an hour where I usually found Zoey in the library—so I hiked over there, hoping to catch her. I checked our spot first. My cock twitched when I stood in the place where she'd gone down on me between the book stacks. But Zoey wasn't there.

I had a couple papers to work on and tests to study for, so I found a table out in the front and pulled out my calculus book. I hadn't even studied for five minutes when a shadow fell over the page I was writing on. My breath caught in my chest, thinking it was Zoey. But when I looked up, Cora smiled at me.

"Hey, baby." She pulled out the chair next to me and sat down. "I heard Rachel hit on you in history class. I'm sorry about her. She has no control over her ovaries."

I smirked at her. "Must be why you two are so close."

Her eyebrows lifted in surprise before she murmured, "Well, look who's turned into a smart-ass," as if impressed with my verve.

I sighed and glanced away from her. "What're you doing here, Cora? You have to know you're not getting anything from me."

She slid her arm around the back of my seat, much the

same way Rachel had last hour. I glared at her, but she just smiled back, refusing to move away. "I just want to make amends between us, Quinn. You're the sweetest, most forgiving person I know. And I hate thinking you might hold a grudge."

A nasty flavor flooded my mouth. I shook my head. "You're just going to have to learn to adjust, then, because I am still holding a grudge against you, and I don't feel like getting over it any time soon." I glanced distastefully at her proximity. "Do you mind leaving me alone now? I really, honestly want nothing to do with you."

She drew in a breath and slid her arm off my chair as she straightened. "Well, I'm sorry you feel that way."

I wasn't. I kept giving her a hard stare until she stood up, lifted her chin and strode away. I blew out a breath, glad to be rid of her, even though I was pretty sure I wasn't done with her for good. People like Cora didn't just fade off into the woodwork. And her being Zoey's roommate was going to make it real ugly in the future when she found out about us. With a sigh, I buried my face in my hands and tried not the think about what would happen when all that went down.

A chime from my book bag had me lifting my face.

What the...?

I twisted and unzipped the pocket where I hadn't been able to find my phone earlier. After digging my hand inside, I jolted when my fingers almost immediately wrapped around it.

Pulling it free, I found a new text from Zoey. **I can't stop thinking about what we did in the library**.

All other thought flushed from my brain. My body responded immediately. I cursed the fact that I'd have to work tonight and couldn't spend it with her. But maybe...

I'm here now. Want a repeat?

I bit my lip waiting for her answer, hoping she was willing to be as wild and abandoned as we'd been on Tuesday.

I wish. But I'm stuck in the print lab waiting in the longest line ever to get a paper printed. Tonight?

Disappointment had my shoulders sagging. **I have to work, remember? Unless you want to come over after...** I ended my pleading with an emoticon to show her just how much I wanted her to say yes.

Sorry, my big man. I have a big paper to finish. I promise I'll make it up to you after you win your game tomorrow. K?

My stomach roiled. Her excuse sounded exactly like the million and one excuses Cora had always given me when we'd been together. A moment of fear clouded my brain. Was Zoey playing me, too? But then I reread the text, and something else odd triggered in my brain.

Big man. That was what Cora had always called me. Surely, Zoey hadn't been around her roommate enough to glean that nickname off her. But that could only mean...

I swallowed and glanced behind me at my back-pack. My phone had not been in that pocket after Rachel had talked to me—after she'd reached her arm around the back of my seat—and then it had miraculously reappeared after Cora had slunk by... and set *her* arm across the back of my seat.

Realizing I hadn't been texting Zoey just now, I stared in shock at the words Cora had written to me. I fisted my hand and set it against my mouth. She knew about what we'd done in the library...which meant she knew about us, period.

This couldn't be good. I started to text Ten to ask him for Zoey's number, since Cora had apparently cleared it from my phone and replaced it with her own, when I paused. What if she'd messed with more of my numbers? To test the waters, I typed: **What's the first thing you ever said to me?**

Ten answered almost immediately. **Man, seriously. What the fuck are you smoking?**

I blew out a relieved breath because I already knew without a doubt that I was communicating with my roommate. But I went ahead and explained every-thing. **Just answer the question. Cora hacked into my phone and changed numbers around. I need proof I'm actually talking to you. I'm ninety percent sure she knows about me and Zoey.**

Instead of texting back, he rang my number. "Shit," he muttered as soon as I answered. "I never trusted that fucking bitch."

"Well, I wish you'd clued me into her months ago. Now, give me Zoey's number. Cora cleared it off my phone. I need to warn her."

Ten obliged. But before he hung up, he said, "Oh, yeah, and the first thing I ever said to you was that steroids made your pecker shrink."

A grin lit my face as I hung up. That was exactly what he'd said to me on the first day of practice when he'd looked up at me and refused to believe I was just naturally this big.

Before I could text Zoey, Ten texted a selfie of him flipping off the camera. **It's still me!**

What a goofball. I shook my head and glanced at the time, only to curse under my breath. I had less than two minutes to get to my noon class. I typed in a warning to Zoey, anyway, gathering my things as I told her to be careful around Cora, that she'd been in my phone, tried to pass herself off as Zoey, and that she knew everything.

THIRTY-EIGHT

⚜ QUINN ⚜

ZOEY DIDN'T answer my text before I started calculus, and she hadn't responded by the time I got out. I had two more classes before I headed straight to practice, and then I had to hustle to work after that. When I'd heard nothing by the time I got off work at two Saturday morning, I began to panic. I would've gone to her apartment when I woke, but I had a noon game and the coach had wanted us in early. I didn't get another moment to check my phone until we'd been excused to the locker room where we were sup-posed to put on our game uniforms.

Still nothing from Zoey.

Needing answers, I texted Caroline. **Is Zoey going to the game with you?**

Sitting on the bench in front of my opened locker, with my leggings on but no shirt, I tapped my fingers on my knees waiting for a response.

"Who're you texting there, Hamilton?" Noel asked, coming up behind me and stealing the phone out of my hand before I could stop him. "You've been awfully guarded and yet a little too happy all week. You got yourself a new woman you don't want anyone to know about?"

Just then, my phone dinged. With a grin, Noel glanced

338

down at the screen. His smile died.

"Motherfucker." He dropped the phone and dove at me, tackling me off the bench and onto the floor.

"Wha...?" I lifted my hands over my face to protect myself after my head cracked against the floor and he pinned me by the chest. I could've bucked him off, but I was too surprised to see him so mad. Plus, I didn't want to hurt him.

"Hey, hey, hey!" Ten shouted, rushing over just as Noel wrapped his hands around my neck. "What the fuck, man?" He tried to pull Noel off me, but Noel wasn't budging.

"Are you fooling around with my sister behind my back?" he growled.

"*What!*" Ten cried. He picked up my fallen phone, read the message and let out a groan. Shoving it at Noel, he muttered, "Maybe you should've read the actual message, dumbass. He's fooling around with *Blondie*. He was just asking Caroline if she'd seen her to-day, which she hasn't, by the way," he finished with a concerned glance toward me.

I closed my eyes, more worried than ever while Noel let up pressure on my throat and rolled off me. "Sorry, man," he said before sitting up and running a rueful hand over his hair. "You were being so secretive about it, I didn't think it could be anyone else but Caroline."

I waved his apology away and told him it was okay. Ten wasn't so forgiving, though. Lifting his hands, he continued to gape at Noel. "Seriously? Not even holier than thou *Hamilton* is good enough for her in your eyes? Why don't you just ship her off to a fucking convent already?" With a final sniff and shake of his head, he muttered, "Ass," and stalked off.

Noel had the grace to appear contrite. "It's not that I think you're not good enough for her," he told me, keeping his tone low. "I just didn't like the idea of you sneaking her around behind my back. That douchebag who hurt her back home snuck her around like she was some kind of dirty little secret. I wouldn't be able to respect anyone who couldn't date her out in the open and be proud of being seen with her in public. She deserves at least that and more."

I nodded, totally understanding. Glancing after Ten, who was now on the other side of the room mood-ily jerking on his own clothes, I wished he'd been here to hear Noel say that, too.

The coach came in, shouting for us to hurry up. We had five minutes left to get changed.

THE NEXT TIME I had a moment to check my phone was after the game, after we'd won thirty-four to zero. Zoey had yet to respond to me, but Cora-pretending-to-be-Zoey had written again.

Sorry, I didn't get to see you on the field in those tight pants, lover. Cora forced me to go shopping with her. I'll see you at the after party, okay?

I typed in a quick affirmative, playing along, and wondering what her game was. Forgoing a text, I tried to ring Zoey. When it went to voice mail, I left a message, hoping she listened to it.

I had no idea what was going on, but I didn't like this. Cora had something planned, but she'd made it sound like Zoey was going to be at the after-party, so I was going to that party to find her.

"Hey, man. You hear from her yet?" Face full of smiles from our win, Ten bounded over to tackle me from behind and pat my back. But I couldn't smile back.

"Not yet." I glanced up. "Where's the after-party tonight?"

The question caught him off guard, but he answered with a smile spreading across his face. "Are you seriously going to it tonight? Fuck, yeah. We can ride together."

I shook my head "No...I want to stop by Zoey's apartment on the way. See if she's home first."

Ten's smile fell, but he nodded.

Zoey wasn't home. Henry informed me that she'd rushed out the door five minutes before I'd arrived. With no place left to look for her but the party, I headed that way.

The place was loud and packed, reminding me why I hated them as soon as I stepped through the front door. Hope sank in my chest as I skimmed the front room, looking for her. She could be anywhere, and there were so many people. I'd just turned to start into the next room when a hand caught my forearm.

I turned, but it was Cora. I started away again but did a double take at the last second. She had the beginnings of a black eye, and I swear her nose was swollen. "What happened to you?" I kind of wanted to high five the person who'd done that do her.

She fluttered her lashes. "Wouldn't you like to know?"

When she reached out to draw on my chest with her finger, I pushed her hand away. Then I shook my head and rolled my eyes toward the ceiling. "I don't know what you're trying to do, but it's not going to work. I know you took my phone and changed out her number for your own."

Her eyebrows lifted. "Wow. I'm impressed. I didn't realize you'd be so clever." Her eyes heated as she glanced down my chest. "My big, clever man." She reached for my shirt again. This time, I grabbed her wrist and held it hard.

"Where's Zoey?"

Drawing up into a huff, she glared at me and ripped her arm out of my grip. "You mean my whore roommate who betrayed me with my boyfriend?"

"I mean the beautiful, amazing girl I moved on with *after* you and I broke up. The only betrayal was yours, Cora. You may be in denial, but that's how it happened."

"Well, don't you sound all self-righteous? Tell me, how were you so pure, and innocent, and honest when you hooked up with her the very *night* you threw me away? Hmm? You can't tell me you didn't even *think* about her when we were still together."

Guilt crowded my throat. I guess I hadn't been all that faithful if she thought of it that way. I'd started developing feelings for Zoey long before Cora and I were over. I may have never strayed physically, and I never would've, but my grandmother had taught me that sinning in my heart was still sinning. And in my heart, I *had* been unfaithful to Cora, because I'd fallen for Zoey long before that first night we were together.

Looking smug, Cora began to laugh in my face. "You must really be a better teacher at sex than a student."

Frowning, I glared at her. "What're you talking about?"

She shrugged. "Oh, just that me showing you everything about pleasing a woman really wasn't that much fun. But apparently, Zoey liked the lessons you gave her. She'd been trying to get on every cock willing to take her since she arrived at this party to-night. So you must've taught her to appreciate *some-thing*."

I snorted, not even believing her for a second.

"Whatever. Just tell me where she is."

"Oh, honey. I don't need to tell you. I'll gladly *show* you. She went into that room, right over there." Leaning in closer, she whispered, "And you'll never guess who she was with."

Finally. An answer. Needing to see Zoey for myself, I started that way, but the door opened before I could reach it. Zoey stepped out. Her hair was a complete mess, her cheeks were flushed, and her lips were as swollen as they got whenever I'd been kissing her for too long. And her clothes...her clothes were in a complete disarray with the neckline ripped, showing off her creamy, beautiful shoulder.

Her dazed-looking green eyes found mine just as some guy slipped out of the room behind her. Too busy pulling his shirt on, Ten didn't see me. But I saw him. I saw him and Zoey together, leaving that room and looking as if they'd just fucked.

The blood drained from my face.

For the longest moment, I just stood there, afraid I was going to pass out. But Zoey? Zoey and *Ten*?

I shook my head. Not Zoey. Just...no. I stumbled a step back, and Zoey's eyes flashed wide. She shook her head madly and reached out in my direction as she stumbled toward me. I shook my head harder and spun away, tripping over a laughing Cora in my haste to escape.

ZOEY

I HADN'T HEARD from Quinn since leaving him Friday morning in art class. He'd sent me a longing glance and mouthed the word, "*Bye,*" before he'd started for his history class and I went to biology. But that was it.

I'd texted a few times but never received an answer back. When I tried to call, it went straight to voice mail. I knew he had to work that night, and I was tempted to stop by Forbidden, but I was worried that would look too clingy. We hadn't been together long enough for me to be sure if it was okay that I wanted to see him, like, all the time.

So, I stayed away. Frankly, I was too paranoid to leave the apartment. An unrecognizable number kept leaving messages and texts for me all day. Afraid my father had found me, I was too scared to even read them. So, I deleted them and blocked the number. On Saturday, Cora woke me early, a little too perkily happy for my taste.

"You have more testing today while I take my dialysis," she announced.

I groaned and rolled onto my back. "I remember," I muttered, wishing I could go anywhere but back to the renal center with her.

Quinn had a big game today. If he won this one, they were set for the playoffs for divisional champs. I'd wanted to be there so bad. Pulling up my phone, I texted him, letting him know I couldn't make his game, but I wanted to see him as soon as possible.

Finally—finally—he texted back, saying, **That's fine. We can meet up afterward. Love you**.

I stared at the last two words, my chest swelling with shock. He'd never said that to me before. I couldn't believe—

"Are you ready to go or not? I've got a kidney to flush out over here."

"Sorry." I shook my head, stuffed my phone into my purse and followed her from the room.

Her eyes sharpened with an evil glint, but I was getting used to those looks. It was best just to believe she had an ulterior motive behind everything she did.

She was quiet on the ride, tapping her fingers against the steering wheel as she flipped through stations and annoying the heck out of me when she'd change a channel just as I'd start to get into a song.

Once we arrived, I went through my regular tests, getting used to some of the routine of them taking my blood pressure, urine sample, and blood test. A lull came as I had to wait for Cora to finish, so I studied some homework until she was done. She was just concluding her treatment when the doctor who'd given me my exam approached me with a wince.

"We hit a snag on one of your tests."

Both Cora and I lifted our faces. "What do you mean a *snag*?" Cora demanded, arching him a glare.

The doctor fiddled nervously for a second before he glanced back and forth between us. "It seems you're beginning to develop a small urinary tract infection. We're going to have to put you on antibiotics so it doesn't move into your kidneys. If the kidneys get damaged, we'll have to delay, possibly even cancel the entire transplant."

"The fuck you say," Cora exploded. When she glanced at me, her eyes narrowed with hate, so much hatred I actually shied away from her.

I clutched my chest, wondering how this could have happened. "I...I don't understand. I've been following all my directions, drinking plenty of water, cranberry juices, keeping to the recommended diet, cleaning regularly."

The doctor shook his head, puzzled. "Your records don't show you have a history of getting them frequently, either."

"No," I agreed. "I've never had one before."

"Have you become sexually active recently?" he asked, scowling to himself, obviously perplexed, as he shuffled through his paperwork to recheck my results.

"What?" I uttered. My face drained and I glanced hastily toward Cora.

Her face turned a purplish red as her jaw hardened. "Yes," she growled to the doctor as she glared at me. "Yes, she has. Why?"

Oh God.

Panic gripped me. But she *knew*.

How did she know?

"Oh." The doctor looked up in surprise. "Well, that explains it then. I swear, the sexual education teachers these days really need to explain how important it is to you young girls to clean up directly after having relations."

Protectively wrapping my arms over my chest and wanting to die of mortification, I stood there and listened to him lecture me about how I needed to urinate after every "relation," or at least wipe the "area" so stuff from my partner didn't get up into my urethra and cause bacteria to grow.

Next to me, a stiff Cora nodded the entire time, agreeing with everything the doctor had to say. But as soon as he finished his lecture and sent me on my way with prescription for my UTI, the glance she sent me told me just how much she was seething under the surface.

We left the treatment center together, side by side. I didn't speak until we were outside. "How long have you known?" I finally asked.

She cracked off a low, hard laugh before searing me with a hateful glance. "How long have I known what? That you're the little slut who screwed my boy-friend's brains out the night he tried to ask me to marry him?"

Her voice was quiet and controlled but filled with enough fury to fuel a rocket. "I figured it out at the bar when sweet, innocent, *peaceful* Zoey Blakeland sent Oren Tenning after me to defend Quinn."

Shock reverberated through my system. I couldn't believe she'd known that long, and done nothing. I opened my mouth to ask why she'd said nothing.

But she suddenly fisted her hand and growled at me. "I swear to God, if I don't get your kidney because you were too busy fucking my boyfriend, I will *kill* you."

For the past five minutes, I'd been feeling like crap because of that very possibility. The last thing I wanted to do was to keep anyone from getting healthier, due to my own carelessness. Realizing my relation-ship with Quinn might've just harmed her entire life made me physically ill.

Before coming to Ellamore, I would've started apologizing right then and there. But in the past few months...no. I didn't apologize. I jerked to a stop and turned to glare right back at her.

"He is *not* your boyfriend. You fucked around on him, and he moved on, end of story. I never—*never*—would've touched him if you hadn't cheated on him and lost him first."

She slapped me. Hard. "You worthless cunt. I could *die* because of this, and you're worried about who was *faithful* and who wasn't? How fucking selfish can you get?"

Rage swelled. Angier than I'd ever felt in my life—for the way she'd treated me, for the way she'd treated Quinn— I balled my hand into a fist and lashed back. Forget slapping, I hit her right in the nose.

"You won't die," I growled. "Roaches always find a way to survive."

Pain sliced through my knuckles and my cheek stung like hell, but I felt good. So good. Almost as good as I felt when Quinn was inside me.

Until Cora whipped her hair out of her face, and I saw blood leaking through her fingers where she was holding her nose. She stared up at me with a mixture of fear, shock, and...was that respect?

"Oh shit." I covered my mouth with both hands and immediately started to shake, feeling awful. She'd just finished a round of dialysis and here I was, jacking her in the face. That was so wrong.

But it'd felt so good.

I opened my mouth to apologize, but then I shut it. I wasn't sorry, I decided. For what she'd done to Quinn, I should've hit her twice.

So I spun away from her and marched off.

She gasped in outrage. "Where the hell do you think you're going?"

"I'm finding another way home. I refuse to ride in a car with you ever again." Glancing at her shocked expression, I added, "From here on out, I'll get myself to all the tests and appointments. I'm moving out tonight. My kidney is the last thing you'll ever get from me."

I left her there to chew on that. After checking the time on my phone and realizing Quinn's game was probably just now ending, I prayed they were winning, and I typed him a quick text to let him know that Cora was onto us.

THIRTY-NINE

∾ ZOEY ∾

THANKFULLY, I found a bus stop not too far away, and I only had to wait half an hour to get a ride back to Ellamore. I started packing as soon as I made it to the apartment. I had no doubt that Quinn and Ten would let me stay with them until I found my own place. Maybe Caroline would be willing to rent some-thing with me. That could be fun.

Needing boxes, I borrowed a couple from Henry. I'd just put all my notebooks into one when my phone chimed with a text.

From Cora.

I don't know why I even read it, but I did.

If you want to keep your precious boyfriend, you better come to this party and fetch him. He's drunk and horny and I can't forget how good he feels inside me.

She'd attached an address. Quinn still hadn't res-ponded to my message. I shot off another to him. But the only thing I got back was: **Oops. Sorry. Quinn's busy right now...going down on me. Love ya. Cora.**

"Bitch," I muttered. I had no idea when she'd jacked with my phone, but I knew then, without a doubt, that Quinn had not been receiving my messages, and he was not doing any such thing with Cora.

I didn't like knowing he was at that same party with her, though. She couldn't be trusted, and she was mad enough tonight to try something even more devious. He was still unaware that she knew about us. I needed to warn him. Snagging my purse, I raced out the door.

The party was still going strong when I showed up. I waded through people until I spotted Ten challenging some guy to a drink-off.

"Ten!" I yelled, pushing through arms and shoulders to get to him.

Hearing his name, he glanced my way. When his eyes immediately flared with anger, unease stirred in my belly.

"Well, look who finally decided to grace us with her royal presence."

I had no idea what he was talking about, but I'd worry about that later, when I found Quinn. "Where's Quinn?"

"He's looking for *you*, princess."

Thinking he was too drunk to be of any help, I started away, but Ten wasn't finished talking to me. He grabbed my arm. "What the fuck, Blondie? Do you *enjoy* breaking his heart?"

I paused to send him an incredulous glance. "Excuse me?"

"He's been trying to get a hold of you for over a day. But you never fucking answered. And then you went and even ditched on him today...just like Whora always did. Why are you avoiding him? Why didn't you make it to the game?"

"I..." Flustered, I shook my head. "I'm not avoiding him. I've been trying to get *a hold* of him. But I just found out Cora's been messing with my phone. And I couldn't make the game, because I...I..."

Ten sighed and rolled his eyes. "Because you went with your fucking, lying roommate to one of her dialysis treatments?" he guessed.

My eyes flared with shock. "How...?" I shook my head, confused.

He moved in closer. "I made it a point to find out everything about her when she and Ham started bumping uglies on a regular basis. I know what's going on with her."

Mouth falling open, I gaped at him, unable to believe he knew. "Why didn't you ever say anything?"

With a roll of his eyes, he moved me into a quieter corner to talk with more ease. "She was trying so hard to keep it a secret, I decided to use it as blackmail against her."

"Wait. *What?*" I totally didn't understand.

"The night she found about Noel and Aspen being together, I knew she wouldn't be able to keep her big, gossiping mouth shut. So, when I saw her sitting alone in her car, waiting on you and Quinn and Caroline, I told her she'd better not go spreading rumors about them, or I'd go telling everyone about her worthless kidneys."

I just stared at him. "But...you didn't blackmail *me* to keep silent about Aspen and Noel," was all I could think to say.

A big grin spread across his face before he winked. "Because I didn't have to. You're actually a decent human being who knew better than to risk the future of two people who need to be left alone so they can live their happily ever after."

"I would never hurt Noel and Aspen like that," I agreed.

Ten nodded and glanced past me, scanning the room. "Right, so...Ham. Cora fucked with his phone too, but he figured it out and has been trying to call you anyway."

I frowned until I realized the unrecognizable number that had been showing up must've been from him...not my father. I closed my eyes and covered my face with my hands. "Is he here?"

"Yeah. He said he was going to stop by your place on the way over, so you must've just missed him. He's probably here by now, though. You go that way, and I'll go this way. One of us has to run across him."

I nodded, grateful I had Ten to help me search now. "Okay. Thank you."

I made it through two rooms, looking for Quinn before I bumped into Cora. Literally.

"Oh! Sorry—" I started before I looked up and realized it was her. She hadn't even tried to conceal her black eye, and I tried not to feel bad about giving it to her, but I still kind of did.

She grabbed my arm. I began to recoil in horror, but she just smirked and dug her fingers in harder. "This way," she called over her shoulder.

I resisted, but she tightened her grip. Not sure where she was trying to take me, I finally gave in. Both Quinn and I knew she was up to no good. She couldn't do anything to hurt us. And maybe, hopefully, she was taking me to him.

But the room she led me into was empty.

I sighed, tired of her games. "Cora—"

"Now, now," she chided pleasantly. "Don't start with me in that tone. Not when I have a present for you."

"I'm not interested," I said dryly.

Eyes lighting with devious inclination, she asked, "Are you *sure*? You were so eager to scoop up my leftovers when it came to Quinn. Don't you want to taste someone else I've already had?"

"No." I started to turn away, but a dark figure filled the doorway, blocking the exit. I backed up a step before the guy entered. It took me a second to recognize him. Cain Belcher, the guy Quinn had pushed against the wall the first night I met him, leered at me, taking me in from head to toe, as he stepped into the room.

"Cora told me you wanted to ride my cock, pretty girl. Well, here I am, willing and ready."

"What?" I spun to her, my eyes wide with horror. But she was already on the other side of the room, opening a door to a second exit.

She paused before leaving. "Don't worry, sweetie. I already told him how rough you like it, and how much acting like you're resisting turns you on." Then she slammed the door.

I raced to it only to find it locked. I pounded on it. "Cora! This isn't funny."

Her muffled laugh came back to me, telling me how much she disagreed.

A hand gripped my waist from behind. I yelped and whirled around, backing into the door.

"She lied," I rushed out, gaping up at him with wide eyes. "I don't want you. I don't want this at all."

But he looked too glassy-eyed and drunk to care.

"As long as I get some pussy, you can fight as much as you want, honey."

"What? No!" I pushed against him, but he didn't seem deterred. "Stop!"

He kissed me hard, smelling like garlic and sweat, and tasting like beer. I struggled against him, gagging and hitting him on the chest, then the side of his head.

He cursed and hit me back until I saw stars.

I checked out long enough for him to get his pants undone and try to stick his tongue down my throat. I bit it and he hit me again. The hitting I could take. My father had acclimated me well to that kind of pain. It was the added worry of being raped that freaked me out.

Fighting as hard as I could, I bit and scratched and tried to scream again until he clamped a hand over my mouth and kneed me in the stomach. When he began to rip open my jeans, I shook my head frantically, trying to beg him with my eyes. He had no mercy. He jammed his fingers down the inside of my pants and cupped me hard between the legs, making tears spill from my eyes.

I squeezed my lashes shut, trying to cope with reality. I couldn't believe this was happening. I couldn't believe Cora would—

"Blondie? You in here?"

The door opening across the room, letting in noise from the party raging outside, startled my attacker into taking his attention off me. I wiggled my leg free enough to hike my knee up and catch him as hard as I could in the nuts.

As he groaned and doubled over, I escaped from between him and the wall to launch myself as a dumbstruck Ten stood frozen in the doorway.

"*Ten*," I sobbed.

"Holy shit." He shook his head and caught me, dragging me behind him before he looked down at Belcher, who was curled up on the floor in the fetal position, cradling himself and gasping.

Grabbing him by the shirt, Ten dragged him back to his feet. "Oh, honey. You just roughed up the wrong girl." He fisted his hand and wound his arm back. But at the moment Belcher closed his eyes and braced for the impact, Ten paused and shook his head, dropping his hand. "No. You know what? I think I'll just save your pretty face until Blondie's boyfriend can get his hands on you."

"Boyfriend?" Belcher croaked, cracking open one eye to look up at Ten. "Who's her boyfriend?" He glanced at me, and I immediately hugged myself, backing away from him.

"Oh, you'll find out...soon," Ten promised him before shoving him toward the doorway. "Until then, you'd better run as fast and far as you can, because he's coming for you. I'll make sure of it."

Belcher stumbled out of the room, half limping, half running. As soon as he was gone and the door fell shut behind him, reality crashed down on me. Re-living in my head what had just happened, and even worse, what could've happened, I began to whim-per out these gasping sobs. Feeling his phantom touch everywhere, I tried to wipe it away, but it just kept clinging to my flesh, so I gave up and rocked back and forth for a moment before I remembered my pants were still undone. I fumbled to pull them together, but my hands wouldn't stop shaking, so I started breathing hard because I was so upset that my fingers wouldn't work right.

I was half a second from a hysterical, hyperventilating breakdown, when I heard Ten shout, "ZOEY!"

He'd never called me by my name before. It broke through my daze and made me realize this wasn't the first time he'd tried to get my attention. I blinked and looked up at him, gulping down my panic.

"Don't you fucking freak out on me," he warned, his voice stern. "I can't handle shit like that."

When he ripped off his shirt, I gaped in horror and started to back away from him toward the one door I knew had to be unlocked. "What're you doing?"

He paused at my cry. "Relax, I'm just giving you something to cover yourself. He practically shredded your shirt."

I glanced down to see that I was showing him half my bra. My fingers instantly went to straighten as much of my shirt as possible. My face ached where Belcher had hit me and my skin crawled where he'd pawed me.

I sniffed back tears when Ten tried to hand me his shirt. "I'm okay." I didn't want his shirt. I just wanted Quinn. I must've said that aloud, because he sighed.

"I'll call him. But first I'm calling the campus cops."

Cops, questions, having to tell someone what had just happened to me did not sound appealing at all. "No." I shook my head. "I just want Quinn."

I turned away from him and hurried toward the door. "Blondie!" Ten called after me, his voice irritated. "Damn it. *Wait.*"

I hurried out into the party, pausing when the noise and people assaulted my senses. Panic nearly took me under. So many people, no space. But through the horde, I spotted him. Quinn. My lifeline. My heart and soul. The relief of seeing his face nearly buckled me.

I gasped his name, but he lurched to a stop, staring at

me until his face drained of color. Next to him, Cora folded her arms over her chest and smiled as if proud of herself. Quinn looked past me to Ten, who was still struggling to get his shirt on. Then he began to shake his head.

"No," I said, when I realized what he thought. "*Quinn!*"

He backed away before taking off and escaping through the people. I needed him, no one else would do, so I raced after him, aching for him to hold me, to *understand*. To believe me.

FORTY

QUINN

HER VOICE TORE into me, slashed open my guts and left me bleeding. Even though she pleaded for me to stop, I kept going, picking up my pace. Things seemed to tilt sideways in my path and I wanted to reach out for the wall to catch my balance, but I didn't want her to see how much this had just devastated me. I would walk away from her without any kind of assistance.

Shoving my way outside, I hit the open night air and sucked in a clean breath. But I still felt nauseated. I wanted to rip out every horrible sensation bub·bling inside me and just throw it all away. When I reached the end of the block, I heard her again. "Quinn, *please*! Wait."

A half sob, half growl left my lips. I sounded like a wounded animal who'd just had a limb ripped off by a predator and was still trying to escape for its life, warning everyone away with a snarl and at the same time trying to lick its wounds.

As the park approached, I heard the heels of her sexy tall boots clacking against the sidewalk behind me as she hurried to catch up. The sound was so feminine and sweet, and Zoey, it made my heart wrench again.

Zoey. God, not Zoey.

"Quinn, you *know* me." She was crying.

The anguish in her voice hurt. My own eyes instantly filled with moisture, and I wanted to punch something.

"Please." She caught my arm. "Would you just stop and *look* at me."

I stopped and whirled around so fast she gasped and cringed away from me. I gnashed my teeth be·cause every instinct inside me wanted to reassure her and apologize for spooking her.

"Damn it," I muttered and spun away again, veering to the left so I could pace into the park. "Damn it." I clutched my hair and walked into a tight circle be·fore bending at the waist and trying to exhale all the pressure pent up in my chest.

"Quinn?" Her voice was timid as she slowly approached.

I dropped my hands to my sides and looked at her, suddenly numb and blank.

She stopped a few feet away and wiped the tears off her cheeks before hugging herself. "Why are you acting this way?" she finally asked, confusion and pain filling her expression. "You know I would never betray you, *could* never betray you."

"Y·y·you—" I wasn't going to be able to say anything right now without stuttering, so I growled out my frustration and spun away. When I spotted a bench nearby, I collapsed onto it and slumped my elbows onto my knees before burying my face into my hands.

A moment later, Zoey gingerly sat on the opposite end of the bench. I could feel her sitting so close and yet so far away. Everything in me that loved her strained her way, begging me to just reach out and gather her into my arms. But I stayed cold and hard and kept myself the entire length of the bench away from her.

She sniffed, letting me know she was still crying. "You don't believe me, do you?" Her voice trembled. "You think Ten and I..."

I swallowed and my throat felt like it was on fire. "I believe you," I finally said, my voice so hoarse, I'm surprised she heard me.

But she must've heard because she said, "Then why are you still all the way over there?"

I thought about it for a second longer, then I scrub·bed the heels of my hands over my face hard and sat up straight. When I turned to her, she looked a·bout as awful as I felt.

"It hurt when I found out Cora had cheated and lied about everything," I said, shaking my head. "But when you walked out of that room like that, with Ten, it...it destroyed me."

More tears filled her eyes. "But I didn't—"

I just kept shaking my head. "Doesn't matter. It doesn't matter if I believed it for five seconds or five months, it ripped me apart, and I don't ever want to feel like that again." I apologized to her with my eyes before admitting, "I'm not ready for this."

She whimpered and whispered my name. More tears slid down her cheeks.

"I thought I was okay after...after what she did. I thought I'd handled it and gotten over it. But...I think she did break something in me. I think I need time to heal. I think...I think it shouldn't scare me like this to realize how deeply I've let you in."

And I had let her in...completely. I hadn't even questioned it when she'd told me she was on the pill. I'd just believed, because she was Zoey. That made me twice the idiot since I should've learned my lesson after Cora.

I thought Zoey was going to crumble, but she straightened her shoulder and nodded before looking into my eyes and rasping, "I understand. I knew you needed time after her. I just...I should've made you take that time instead of convincing myself you were okay."

I think watching her stiffen her spine and bear this hurt more than if she'd kept on weeping and begging. I swallowed the lump in my throat, but it wouldn't go down.

"I'm sorry," I said. "I'm so sorry."

She laughed softly and wiped at the last of her tears. Pushing to her feet, she murmured, "I'm the one caught coming out of a bedroom with some guy and *you're* the one apologizing? You're something else, Quinn Hamilton."

"It feels as if I stole your innocence, and now I'm just shoving it right back in your face."

"You didn't steal anything." With a smile, she pushed to her feet. "You can't steal something that was given freely." After a regretful sigh, she leaned down and pressed a gentle kiss to my forehead. "Go and heal. Just...take care of yourself, Quinn."

I snaked my arms around and snagged her around the hips, drawing her against me so I could bury my face in her waist. Her smell enveloped me and con-soled me. I squeezed my eyes closed, knowing even as I was pushing her away, she was the only person who could comfort me at a time like this. Her fingers in my hair almost made me purr.

I was a split second away from changing my mind. What the heck did I think I was doing? I loved this girl. We clicked. She adored *Psych* just as much as I did, she got my love for biology even when she wasn't a fan herself, and she was the best lover and best friend I'd ever had, all rolled into one.

I would be miserable without her.

But she was the one who finally pulled back, brushing gently at my hair. I couldn't take any more of this, so I mumbled something about how I had to go. I surged to my feet and stumbled away. I had no idea where I was headed; I just started walking, hoping I could clear my head and decide I didn't want time or space away from her after all.

ZOEY

I WAS STILL SITTING on the bench where I collapsed after Quinn left me, numb and alone in the dark, when a panting Ten raced up.

"There you are." Breathless, he paused to rest his hands on his knees. "Where's Ham? Did he already go after Belcher?"

I shook my head. "No. I didn't tell him about Belcher."

"What?" Ten straightened and glanced around. "Then what the hell did you tell him? Where is he?"

"I didn't tell him anything except that he was wrong, that you and I didn't...that we didn't do anything."

Ten shook his head, confused. "I don't get it. Why the fuck didn't you tell him about Belcher?"

I wasn't too sure why myself. "I don't know. I wanted him to believe me without telling him everything." I looked up at Ten, feeling lost. "He said he believed me, but I don't think he really did. He broke up with me, saying he needed time, and then he left." Every-thing inside me felt as if it was crumbling. "Why didn't he believe me?"

"Jesus fucking Christ, Blondie." Ten groaned and covered his face. "Why do you *think* he couldn't believe you? Cora put him through such a mind fuck, he doesn't even know if he should believe his own bladder about whether he has to take a piss or not."

I shuddered and held myself a little harder. "May-be he was right then. Maybe he *does* need time and space. Maybe he needs to heal from her before he can move on with anyone else. You said yourself that he shouldn't rebound right back into a committed relationship."

"I said..." He shook his head as if boggled. Then he exploded, "I wasn't talking about *you* when I said that shit. I was talking about some other nameless-faceless stupid replica of Whora. I thought he was still respectfully staying away from you when I said that. Fuck, I never would've...not if I'd known you two were...shit, you two are meant to be together. I don't care if it happened at the worst time ever for you guys. You just...you're two halves of a whole. He comes alive when you're around, he gains confidence, grows happy. You just...damn it. You two weren't ever supposed to break up."

My shoulders heaving with pain, I started to cry again. I couldn't hold the tears in, no matter how hard I tried. I shook from head to toe and cried harder the more I tried to stop.

Ten sighed. "Come on," he murmured. When he grasped my arm, right at a tender spot that Belcher had bruised earlier, I gasped and wrenched away, cowering from him without meaning to.

"Shit. Sorry." He lifted his hands and took a step back. "Okay, fine. I'll just stay over here, then. Can you stand on your own and walk?"

With a nod, I pushed to my feet. My legs felt shaky, but I managed. Ten stayed at least five feet away at all times. If I wasn't such a mess, I'd probably think it was funny how much a person could hover from so far away. But he kept pace with me and sent me a worried glance every time I winced.

When we reached his truck, I faltered. I knew I could trust him, but I really didn't want to be enclosed alone with anyone. Not right now. "My car's over there," I started, but he shook his head.

"We'll get your car later. You're in no condition to drive.

Now get in."

My nerves wrenched with fear, but I followed his instruction. "I don't want to go back to my apartment."

"Well, good. I wasn't planning on taking you there."

I nodded. I didn't care where we went from there. I just wanted to get out of here.

𝒻ORTY-𝒪NE

❧ TEN ☙

BLONDIE WAS PASSED out in the passenger seat when I parked in front of my and Ham's building. I hoped like hell he was home so he could take over baby-sitting duty, because this shit was freaking me out.

She looked so scared and small, helplessness ripped through me. I hated not being able to do any-thing for her, and I wanted to be anywhere else in the world. Ham's woman already stirred up too many memories in me of someone else, someone precious, who'd been hurt, someone I had also been helpless to help.

I gulped and shook my head, shoving those memories down. I would've carried Blondie up to our place, but I didn't want to scare her in case she woke to me touching her. So I nudged her knee until she stirred.

"Can you still walk?"

She rubbed her bleary eyes and nodded. Without a word, she followed me up to my door. When I unlocked it and let her in ahead of me, she paused, looking worried before she entered.

"Hamilton?" I called as soon as we were inside.

No answer.

Shit.

I swear, Blondie looked relieved though. "C-can I use your shower?" Her voice was so small, making me wish I would've hit Belcher a few times before letting him go tonight after all.

Since she knew her way around, I just pointed her down the hall. "I'll get you something to change into."

After she hurried away, clutching her shirt to her chest, I went into Ham's room and found a shirt and sweatpants for her. The water was running when I inched open the door and laid the clothes on the edge of the sink's counter for her to find. Then I retreated to the front room to pace.

I texted Ham, telling him to get his ass home, but he didn't respond—fucker probably really did think I'd boned Blondie. The idiot.

No way was I equipped to deal with her in this state, so I shot off another SOS text. All this one said was, **I need you. My place. Now.**

Thirty second later, an answer came back: **Be there in five.**

I couldn't help it, I grinned. But, shit, it was nice to know she would come to me in the middle of the night, just like that, no questions asked.

True to her word, Caroline knocked on my door damn near five minutes later.

I craved seeing her so hard that I wondered if I had called her because she would be the best person for Blondie right now, or the best person for *me*. Oh, well. Too late to matter now. She was here, and both Blondie and I were going to get a nice, healthy dose of her.

I ripped the door open, and a relieved breath of air seeped from my lungs. Damn, why did it always feel as if I was holding my breath until I could see her again?

She'd come fresh from bed. She hadn't bothered to comb her hair or even pull it into a ponytail. It looked as if some fucker had been fisting his hands in it all night. Her T-shirt was huge and looked like some-thing she'd probably snagged from her brother, and definitely like something she would sleep in. And her pants were plaid flannel. My mouth watered. I wanted to just invite her to crawl back into bed—my bed—and cuddle with me. Okay, more than just cuddle, but I could live with the cuddling stage for a while and working our way up from there.

Jesus, why did she have to look so damn good?

"What the fuck are you wearing?" I demanded, making sure there was plenty of accusation in my voice. Couldn't let her know how much I loved her looking like this.

She scowled at me and stepped inside. "Pajamas. You know those clothes people wear in the middle of the night when they're *sleeping?*"

I snorted. "Never worn any."

She snorted right back, narrowing her eyes. "Figures."

"Seriously." I motioned to her clothes. "Where's the slinky, tight, slutty clothes? What if this had been a booty call? Please, God, at least tell me you have a matching bra and panty set under there."

"I don't even *own* a matching bra and panty set. And I *knew* this wasn't a booty call." She tossed me a dry glance. "There was no reason to bother dressing up."

I scratched my hair, confused. "Then why the hell did you think I was calling you?"

"I *assumed* you'd accidently strangled one of your whores to death, or something equally kinky and awful, and you needed help disposing of the body." She yawned and glanced around. "So, where is she?"

I stared at her, touched. "Would you really help me bury a body?" That was so fucking sweet. If Gamble ever gave me his blessing to bang his sister, I'd be all over her so fast. "There is no dead body, by the way."

She scowled, looking confused. "So, if there's no dead hooker for me to help bury, then why *did* you call me over?"

From down the hall, the bathroom door came open. Caroline lifted a curious eyebrow, so I tipped my head that way. "For her," was all I said.

Caroline moved to the opening of the hallway—God, I even liked watching the way she moved—and peered down it just as Blondie, decked out in Ham's baggy clothes, ducked her head hesitantly out at us. Her face was blanched of so much color it made the red bruise sprouting on her cheek really stand out.

I hissed a curse under my breath and balled my hand into a fist.

Caroline covered her mouth. "Oh my God. *Zoey?*"

The two girls rushed toward each other, hugging tightly. If it were under any other circumstances, I might've gotten a little excited about watching them come together so eagerly, and I totally would've crack-ed a threesome comment. But then Blondie ruined the possible eroticism of the moment by bursting into tears and sobbing all over Caroline.

Fuck. Poor kid.

Caroline lifted her face to sear me with a fierce stare. "Who did this?"

"Caine Fucking Belcher," I said. "He had his hand down her pants when I caught them together. He would've...you know, done that R-word to her if I hadn't stumbled across them."

Blondie shuddered and started gagging. I winced for making her relive that moment again by bringing it up. She burrowed deeper into Caroline, and Caro-line petted her hair and murmured soothingly into Blondie's ear before looking up again.

"Belcher," she repeated. "The same guy who was passing around naked pictures of Aspen?"

There had only been one naked picture, but I lifted my eyebrows, impressed. "Good memory."

"That bastard," she sneered, looking ready to find Belcher and murder him with her bare hands. Then she frowned and glanced around. "Where's Quinn?"

When Blondie cried even harder at the mention of his name, I scowled at Caroline before saying, "Good fucking question."

"I don't understand."

She frowned, confused, so I caught her up to speed on the part of the story where Quinn caught us coming out of the room, looking like we'd fucked.

"...and then he took off, so idiot Blondie here didn't race after him to tell him what had really happened; she just wanted him to *believe* her all on his own steam, so she raced after him to say pretty much no-thing, for which he dumped her and took off...again."

"Hey, don't call her an idiot," Caroline scolded, hugging Blondie to her tighter. "She was nearly raped. I think she's allowed to have a scrambled brain at the moment."

Okay, so she might have a point. I grumbled a little under my breath and ran my fingers through my hair.

Caroline sighed and pulled up her phone with one hand while she continued to hold Blondie with the other.

"Good idea," I said, snapping my fingers. "*You* try getting a hold of Ham. Maybe he'll answer for you. He's been ignoring all my attempts."

"I'm not calling Quinn. I'm calling Noel."

I frowned. I hated being around the both of them together. I had to behave myself when Gamble was present, overseeing every move I made near his sister.

"And Asher," she added after a moment, making me frown even harder.

"Hart? Why the fuck are you calling Hart?" Just how close had those two gotten? If he hadn't respected my request to stay away from her, I was breaking his face. That's all there was to it.

"You're going to need more than two people to contain Quinn when he finds out what really happened. He'll want to kill Belcher."

I laughed, when inside I really flinched with jealousy. "Oh, and you think *Hart* has the kind of muscle to help hold him down? He's a fucking *singer.*"

"He's a good talker. Maybe he can talk sense into Quinn before Quinn does too much damage."

In my opinion, Quinn *needed* to do some serious damage. I was going to be haunted for a good long while by the image of a crying Blondie trying to fight Belcher off her. I hoped Ham pounded his fucking face in.

But what I said to Caroline was, "Hey, I'm a good talker. I've talked *your* brother off the ledge more times than I can count."

She rolled her eyes and opened her mouth to res·pond, but Zoey lifted her face. "Can I stay at your place tonight?" she asked Caroline.

Caroline's shock over the request was pretty evident.

"I can't go back to Cora's. Not after what she did."

Caroline glanced at me. "Wait. What did *Cora* do?"

I frowned and shook my head, clueless. Stepping in a little closer and curious about that answer myself, I had a bad feeling there was more to Cora's involve·ment than just jacking with a couple phones.

"She..." Another tear trickled down Blondie's cheek. She wiped it away and sniffed. "She asked him to...she told him I wanted to be with him. That's why he was in that room, that's why he...he..."

"Wait a fucking second," I said a little more harsh·ly than I intended to because my voice made Blondie flinch. "Are you saying that fucking bitch *told* Belcher to rape you?"

She nodded, making me fume. "Yeah, or at least... something like that. She called him there, and she... she knew what he'd try to do to me."

I curled my hands into fists. "I'm going to kill her. I'm going to fucking—"

"You can't. She—"

"I don't care how fucking sick she is. No human being that cruel deserves to live. And you are not giving her your kidney. I absolutely refuse to allow it. Not after this."

"Wait, *what?*" Caroline broke in.

"Just..." I sighed and took her arm, urging her toward the door. "Take Blondie to your place, okay. We'll take care of Belcher and the fucking whore."

"But—"

After I nudged the two girls into the hall, I waved them good-bye. I had a roommate to find and worth-less people to destroy.

But Blondie paused and glanced back at me with her huge, green, frightened eyes. "You're going to tell him, aren't you? You're going to tell him everything."

"He needs to know." But I shrugged apologetically after I said it.

She nodded, and I kind of felt like shit for making her look so sad. "Just..." She looked up at me again, killing me with her sad eyes. "Please let him know I'm sorry. I'm so sorry for not telling him sooner."

ℱORTY-ℐWO

∽ QUINN ∾

NOEL, ASHER AND Ten were waiting for me when I unlocked my door and stepped inside my apartment.

Ten started in immediately. "Man, you seriously don't think I fucked her, do you?"

My shoulders slumped, and I collapsed my back against the door as soon as I shut it. Closing my eyes, I fisted my hands down at my sides. So that's what this was all about. A stupid intervention for our friends to make me forgive Ten...again.

"I told Zoey I believed her," I said, though seriously I didn't know what to believe anymore. I just knew I couldn't trust my own instincts.

I had thought Cora would be faithful, that she'd loved me and wanted me to ask her to marry me. But look how wrong that had been. Then I had thought Zoey had been innocent and incapable of such betrayal, except everything I'd seen tonight pointed in the opposite direction. I still didn't want to think anything bad of her, but...God. I honestly didn't know what to think.

"I know you two didn't do anything." I said, anyway.

Mostly, I said it because I wanted him to leave me alone. I already felt bad enough. I already missed Zoey. I'd already

366

debated with myself a million times over whether putting space between us had been the right move or not. Maybe if I'd just forced her to tell me why she'd been alone in that room with a shirtless Ten, and why she'd come out looking like someone had kissed her, we could've hashed it out and been over it by now. *Together* and over it. But I'd let Cora condition me into not asking questions, into respecting *privacy*.

"Well, it kind of sounds like you do think they hooked up," Noel said. "Otherwise, why'd you break up with Zoey?"

I opened my eyes and stared at them. How did they know about that? "I didn't break up with her," I instantly said, though...crap, maybe I kind of had. I only knew I'd needed space. I needed to straighten my head out, and I hadn't wanted Zoey to get caught up in any of my leftover hang-ups caused by Cora. But I *had* pushed her away, hadn't I? I had asked for time apart...right after seeing her and Ten together.

"Blondie sure as fuck thinks you broke up with her," Ten said.

"Your girl wasn't very forthright with details about what really happened tonight," Asher quietly added.

I glanced at him, frowning. What did *he* know a-bout tonight?

Noel arched an eyebrow. "You ready to hear what really happened?"

Yes.

But I shook my head no.

Ten growled and marched menacingly toward me. "Well, too bad. You're getting an earful, anyway. Fucking Whora, your fucking ex, found out about your fucking around with Blondie, and had fucking Belcher feel her up at the party tonight."

I blinked, not expecting to hear *that*. At all. I didn't even really process it at first. So, I shook my head to clear it. "What?"

"Yeah." Ten went on. "Whora said something about how Blondie was so eager to share all their men, she should try out Belcher too, except when she left Blondie alone with him, Belcher didn't want to stop 'scaring' Blondie, so he was trying to fucking rape her when I came across them."

"What?" I said a little louder this time. This time, his words just barely began to sink in, yet they didn't totally resonate in my brain. I stepped away from the door, ready to hurt him if he was joking with me.

"Her clothes were all messed up because *Caine Belcher* had just tried to rape her, and I was half dressed because I took off my shirt and offered it to her since hers was torn, but she was too intent on trying to find *you* to accept it."

"You..." Ten could've pulled out a knife and stab-bed me through the stomach and I don't think it would've surprised me or pulverized me as much as this did. Actually, I would've preferred it if he'd stab-bed me. That way, Zoey wouldn't be—

I saw red. Every vein in my body turned into one angry, throbbing heartbeat. I killed Belcher inside my head fifty times between one heartbeat and the next, and then I killed Cora another fifty times within the heartbeat after that.

"Where is she?" I heard myself breathing hard. I felt my hands balling into fists, but I was so disconnected from my own body, it seemed like I was more of an observer than an actual participant in what I did.

"Cora or Zoey?" Noel asked.

I'd meant Zoey, but I said, "Both."

"Caroline took Zoey home with her. Cora..." Ten shrugged. "Who knows?"

"I'll try her place first." I knew where she lived. After that, I'd find out where Belcher lived, and then I'd hunt him down, too. And after that...I didn't know. I wanted to go to Zoey, but I'd caused this. If she and I hadn't gotten together, this never would've happened to her.

She'd gotten hurt because of me, and then I'd hurt her more when I'd turned away from her.

Guilt dug its claws in a little deeper, irritating the anger, which nearly had me breathing fire as I started for the door. How dare they hurt Zoey because of me?

"Uh...before you go." Ten winced, lifting a hand to stall me.

I paused to send him a stony stare. "Don't even think about trying to stop me."

"Man, we're not going to stop you."

"We're going to help you," Asher added. "Zoey's too sweet to be treated this way."

I nodded, but Ten still had his hand in the air. "I swear, I'm not trying to talk you out of going after the whore, but, uh...there's something you might need to know about Cora before going over there."

Of course there was. Cora was layered with secret after secret. She probably had so many *she* didn't even know who the real Cora Wilder was.

"She's kind of sick." Ten winced again and shrugged. "Kind of *really* sick. Like...she's dying."

I kept staring at him, waiting for the punch line, but when he said nothing else, I blinked. "Excuse me?"

"Okay, so..." He lifted his hands, letting me know he had an entire story to explain. "I never really trusted her, right? Right. So, after we fucked that one time and I found out you were still hooking up with her, she told me she hadn't known then that you wanted to see her again, but I wasn't sure I could believe her. And I couldn't go and ask *you* about it, or you'd get suspicious and figure out the truth, so I started kind of, I don't know, *following* her, hoping I could catch her with some other dude. Then I could tell you about her being unfaithful with *him*, but she was always too crafty to get caught. She wasn't as sneaky about the treatment center she went to three times a week, though."

"Treatment center?" I shook my head, utterly confused.

"What? Like, she's a drug addict?" Noel asked, just as boggled as I was.

Ten glanced at both of us. "She has kidney failure."

I backed up a step, not expecting to hear that at all. Actually, it was probably one of the very last things I was imagining. I had known something was going on with her health-wise, but I'd been thinking more along the same lines as Noel, that she'd been doing something to herself to provoke an illness.

"But...she can't...*what?*" I backed up a couple more steps.

With a solemn nod, Ten kept talking. "She's bad enough along that she needs dialysis three times a week to keep going."

"End stage," I murmured. Shaking my head, I sank down until I was sitting on the sofa. "That's just... That's not even possible. I would know. How could I not know something like that? And w-w-why would she..."

But I *had* known something was going on with her, that she was keeping things from me. Covering my mouth with my hand, I looked up at my roommate.

"Why wouldn't she say anything?" I think the fact that she'd kept this from me was more of an insult than realizing she'd cheated on me.

Ten sighed and ran his hand through his hair. "I guess it takes a really selfish person to understand why she'd want to keep that silent, but I get it."

"Then, please," I barked, "Explain it to *me*." Be·cause I didn't get it at all. I didn't get any of this. The Cora Wilder I had started dating months ago was nothing at all like the Cora Wilder I was learning truly existed. How had she been able to hide this side of herself for so long? And *why*?

Sociopath, I reminded myself. But a sociopath with *kidney failure*?

I gripped my head with both hands, because oh yeah, my temples were throbbing like crazy.

"Sickness and disease is gross," Ten said. "Stupid, careless people like me, like *Whora*, look at people with cancer and terminal illness with revulsion. They're weak and repugnant and should be hidden away from society. To learn she's one of them..." He laughed and shook his head, "She's in denial, man. She doesn't want people to know she's not perfect. She wants to stay the fucking queen bee. She can't have a flaw, or no one will follow her. So she hides it."

"Even from *me*?" I had to ask. I felt sick to my stomach. Ten might've classified himself in that same category with her, but I knew he didn't belong. He didn't really see others that way, no matter how much he wanted us to think he did.

Sympathy filled his eyes, letting me know just how right I was. Cora wouldn't have been sympathetic right then. But Ten was. "Especially from you," he said.

I nodded and blew out a breath. "And Zoey?" I asked, my voice going hoarse because thinking about her keeping this from me hurt worse than knowing Cora had. And I knew she had to have known about it.

"She's going to donate one of her kidneys for the transplant," Ten answered quietly.

Closing my eyes, I bowed my head. "Of course she is." I wouldn't have expected anything less from her. And wow, now that I thought of it, that was why Cora had brought her here. I was sure Zoey had willingly volunteered the transplant; she probably thought it'd been her idea entirely. But Cora had orchestrated the whole thing because she knew Zoey, and she knew what Zoey would offer.

How had Cora phrased it? *Zoey will do anything for me,*

because I'm like, I don't know, her god, I guess.

Everything made so much sense now. All the times Zoey had been so guilty around me, unable to divulge Cora's secret, knowing it would probably impact my relationship with her, because let's face it...if I'd known Cora was going through what she was going through, I never would've dumped her, faithless whore or not. It just wasn't in my chemical makeup to be that cruel. And Zoey had known that, because she would've done the same exact thing if she'd been in my shoes.

Cora had been right; Zoey and I were the same.

I pushed to my feet.

All three guys watching me warily jumped as if they expected me to start raging and tearing the room apart or something.

"So, what're you going to do?" Noel asked.

"I'm going over there and getting Zoey's things out of that apartment. She might be donating Cora a kidney, but that doesn't mean she has to live with her another day. I'm getting her as far away from that crazy, lying bitch as possible."

"Man, you don't think she's *still* going to cough up a kidney, do you?" Ten asked incredulously. "Even after tonight?"

I nodded. "Yes. She will." Because I would if I were her. "You guys coming with me, or not? It'll probably take a couple trips to move all her things out."

ZOEY

"THAT WAS NOEL."

Aspen's voice in the other room made me sit up. Caroline had tucked me into her bed about half an hour ago. Then she settled in next to me and booted up a movie on her laptop. She was all about romantic comedies of the eighties. But tonight, I just didn't care if Baby had been left in a corner or not. I couldn't concentrate on anything except the ringing of the phone a couple minutes earlier, or Aspen when she appeared in the doorway to wave Caroline into the hall for a hushed conversation.

I shoved the sheet off me and hurried to the door to listen in on them.

"Did Quinn finally make it home?" Caroline asked.

Closing my eyes, I held my breath and waited to hear Aspen's response.

"Yeah. And they're headed over to Cora's apartment right now to—"

"No!" I yelled, leaping into the hall. "He can't."

Quinn couldn't hurt Cora, no matter what.

"Zoey!" Aspen covered her heart. "You scared me. I didn't think you were—"

"We have to stop him." I grabbed Caroline's arm and started tugging her away. "He can't touch Cora. He can't hurt her."

"Zo—" She tried to resist, but I was having none of it.

"We have to go."

So, we went. Aspen stayed home with Noel's sleeping younger brothers. But Caroline drove me to Cora's apartment.

"There's Oren's truck," she murmured when we pulled into the parking garage.

"And Quinn's," I uttered with dread. I wrung my hands, hoping he hadn't done anything he'd regret, because if he knew about Cora, he would definitely regret it. And here I had thought Ten was going to tell him about her condition.

As we raced toward the front door, Henry held it open for us. "Evening, Miss Blakeland," he said with his ever-present cheer. "Sure are lots of visitors in your place tonight."

I thought he meant Quinn and Ten, and possibly Noel and Asher too. I had no idea someone else was there until I blew through the front door, with Caro·line hot on my heels.

When the visitor I wasn't expecting turned to face me, I skidded to a halt. "*Mr. Wilder?*"

What was Cora's father doing here?

The room grew quiet, and he looked very grave. A scowling Cora had slumped herself against the opening of the hallway and moodily crossed her arms over her chest—wearing, hey, was that *my* nightshirt?—while Quinn sat on the couch with his face buried his hands. Asher, Noel and Ten seemed to stand guard around him. The three looked at me with sympathetic expressions.

"What's going on?" I asked, though I was sure Quinn knew the truth now. If Ten hadn't told him, Cora's father would've clued him in to her health.

He must hate me right now.

But when he lifted his face and looked at me, I didn't see hate. I just saw despair. "She doesn't know," he said, not talking to me but to the room at large. "Someone needs to tell her."

Wait. What? I already knew about Cora. He couldn't be talking about that; he had to know I was already aware of her defunct kidneys.

So what was he talking about?

I took a step backward and ran into Caroline, who instantly snagged my hand and gripped it hard.

Turning my attention to Cora and her father, I shook my head. "Tell me what?"

Cora sniffed and rolled her eyes. "I'm bored. I'm going to bed."

As she turned away, Quinn surged to his feet and stepped into her path. "You're not going anywhere."

His hard tone and piercing gaze made me jump. I'd never seen him so livid.

Apparently, neither had Cora. Because she actually heeded his command and reluctantly came back a-round.

"Tell. Her," Quinn commanded.

But Mr. Wilder lifted his hand, wincing. "Cor—"

Ignoring him, Cora glanced at me with a sneer. "Nine months before you were born, my dad fucked your mom."

FORTY-THREE

QUINN

HALF AN HOUR EARLIER

HENRY GREETED US at the entrance of Cora's building. I sent him a respectful nod, realizing this was probably the last time I'd ever see him, because once I got Zoey's things out of here, I never planned on going near this building again.

"Evening again, Mr. Hamilton. Did you ever find Miss Zoey?"

"Yeah," I murmured as I passed. And then I'd made the ultimate mistake of walking away and hurting her.

Henry glanced curiously over Noel, Asher, and Ten as they followed me inside, but he didn't say anything about their presence.

Once the four of us were packed into the elevator and waiting to reach the eighth floor, Noel glanced at me. "So, what're you going to say to her?"

I didn't want to say anything to Cora. I didn't even want to look at her, but I knew I wouldn't be able to get back to Zoey's room for her things without getting past her.

"I don't know," I admitted.

"Well, I know what *I* want to say to her," Ten started, but I held up a hand in warning and shot him a look.

"*I'll* take care of her. None of you say a goddamn word."

Ten opened his mouth to argue, but in the next instant, the elevator let out a ding and stopped, admit-ting us to the eighth floor. I ignored him and the other two as we marched to 8E. Then I had to pause in front of Cora's door and wipe my hands over my face to collect myself before knocking. I'd be winging this big time because I still had no idea what to say.

I still wanted to hurt her, to wrap my hands around her neck and never stop squeezing. But I was going to be civil. At least, I was going to *try* to be civil.

Cora opened the door, wearing Zoey's nightshirt, the one that liked to slip off one shoulder and expose her perfect creamy skin. I growled at her. And civil went right out the window. But seeing her in Zoey's clothes made me lose my temper all over again. Plus my skin crawled big-time over the creepy *Single White Female* thing she had going on. When she pushed out her chest as soon as she saw it was me, displaying the fact she wasn't wearing a bra, I snorted.

"You really are pathetic," I couldn't help but say.

She opened her eyes to respond, but a surprised Ten exploded from behind me. "What the fuck happened to your face?"

Cora glared past me toward him. "None of your damn business." Then she blinked up at me. "What're *you* doing here?"

She was embarrassed by the bruise. I suddenly realized how she'd gotten it. "Zoey gave it to you. Didn't she?"

When Cora glared in return, I knew it was true.

"Damn," Ten murmured as if impressed. Then he slugged me in the center of the back. "Blondie gives a better black eye than you do, Ham."

I ignored him. My icy gaze on Cora made her step back. I couldn't even imagine what she'd done to sweet, pacifistic Zoey to make her lash out as she had. "I'm getting her things," I said. "Now."

When I took a decisive step forward, she dodged out of my way with a squeak. But a second later as Noel, Ten and Asher filed in behind me, Cora sniffed at us as if unimpressed, even though I could see in her eyes that we spooked her. She wasn't sure how much she could push me tonight. Zoey must've really rattled her by fighting back; she wasn't sure if I would too.

"I should've known she'd give you a sob story about what happened so you'd feel all sympathetic toward *her*," she muttered.

"You mean, you should've known she'd give me the *truth*," I deadpanned before I strode past her down the hall.

"Hey!" She snagged my arm. "I didn't say you could go down there."

I shrugged her off. "So stop me."

She didn't. She merely sniffed as Ten, Noel and Asher followed me.

After seeing her in Zoey's clothes, I'd been fore-warned that she'd been in Zoey's room, but I still wasn't expecting what I saw. Shock made my jaw drop as I jerked to a stop in the opened doorway.

All of Zoey's clothes had been dragged out of her closet and drawers. They'd been slashed with scissors or a knife, something sharp. So had her bedding and pillows. But what dug into my gut the deepest was seeing the shelf above her bed bare. All the notebooks full of stories she'd written were now strewn across the room and torn to shreds, making the place look as if it was covered in confetti.

"No." I set my hand over my heart, feeling the loss of Zoey's precious words stabbing me through the chest.

"Holy shit," Noel breathed from behind him.

Ten stepped around me and entered the room. "What the fuck?" He picked up the metal ring from one notebook, the only thing left of it. When he glanced at me, I swallowed.

"Her stories," I said. "She wrote stories."

"Damn. What kind of fucked-up monster would do this?" The surprise in Asher's voice made me turn just in time to watch Cora straighten her shoulders in self-righteous indignation.

"Well, what do you expect a girl to do when her boyfriend and roommate *betray* her?"

"You...bitch." I started toward her without thinking. My hands raised to wrap around her throat, and she backed herself against a wall before I'd even realized what was happening. I stopped myself before making contact though. My rage scared me so much it made my hands shake as I balled them into fists and dropped them at my sides. I'd almost touched a woman...in anger.

My God, what was happening to me?

"*Why!*" I growled into her face. "How could you do this to her? She was here to save your worthless life!"

Though I'd already stopped myself, I still must've scared my friends. Hands grabbed me by the shoulders and yanked me back.

I let them pull me away, glad to know they would've stopped me, and then ashamed that they al·most had to. Cora whimpered and started crying as she sank to the floor and covered her mouth with shaking hands. I wanted to snort at her innocent, abused act, but guilt and fear assailed me for going as far as I had. I dug my hands into my hair, breathing hard.

"She deserved it," Cora cried out. "You were *mine*. How dare she touch what was mine?"

And here returned my rage. "No, I *wasn't*. We were over, not that I was ever really yours anyway, not when you had so many other guys on the side."

"But you bought me a ring. You wanted to *marry* me."

"You *what?*" Ten spat incredulously.

I ignored him. Shaking my head, I rolled my eyes. "Why did you throw out those proposal hints in the first place, when you weren't faithful, when you never planned on *being* faithful?"

From the floor, Cora looked up at me, but her wet eyes were filled with more hatred than fear. "Why do you think? I can tell you already know the truth. Precious *friend* that she is, Zoey told you she was here to save my life, so you already know I'm dying. I just wanted to experience everything I could. I wanted the wild, party college life as much as I wanted to know what it'd be like to plan my own perfect wedding."

I shook my head. Wow. She was completely serious. "And you really thought you could just have it both ways?"

She lifted one shoulder and slid up the wall, regaining her feet. "Why not? I have a right to live my life to the fullest while I still can."

"No," I disagreed. "Not when it hurts others the way you have."

"I guess that just shows how different you and I are. When I want something, I go after it."

"Actually, it just shows how lucky *I* was to break free of you."

She shook her head. "If you think Zoey could ever satisfy you as much as I did, you're delusional."

"Yeah, uh huh. *I'm* the delusional one. Whatever." I was so ready to be finished talking to her.

I turned away to find that my friends had already boxed up some of Zoey's ruined things. They were carrying them from her room, which made my chest ease a little. I was so glad they were here to keep me from losing my temper, to keep me on track with my mission.

I took the box Asher handed me and turned down the hall, striding past a red-faced, sputtering Cora, who couldn't seem to believe I was ignoring her.

Tucking the box under one arm, I reached for the front door and pulled it open, only to skid to a stop when I nearly barreled into a guy standing there with his hand raised to knock. In his mid to later forties, the sandy and gray-headed man was taller and slimmer, and he had green, green eyes...just like—

"Dude, is that Zoey's dad?" Asher asked from directly behind me.

I blinked. He did look a lot like Zoey. The shape of his chin, color of his eyes, even the slope of his cheek-bones.

What kind of providence was this? My blood was bubbling with the need to hurt, to maim, and here arrived the man who had tormented Zoey her entire life? It was destiny.

I glanced back at a wide-eyed Cora, who was hugging herself as if cold...or as if she knew all her lies were about to come back and bite her in the ass.

"Is he?" I asked.

But the visitor repeated, *"Zoey?"* as if in shock. He glanced around me until he spotted Cora. "Cora, what is he talking about?" His face immediately molted red with rage. "Oh God. Tell me you didn't."

"Didn't what?" I asked, utterly confused. Who *was* this guy?

But Cora was too busy staring at the man to answer me. "She volunteered!" she cried.

"How did she even know what was going on with you?" he boomed, stepping past me as if I wasn't there blocking his way, so he could enter the apartment as if he owned it. "Did I not strictly forbid you to have any more contact with her after you graduated from high school, after I sent you out here to get you away from her?"

Cora shrugged, looking only slightly repentant. "Oops," she said.

"Damn it, Cora. How could you disobey me like that? And don't tell me you were just curious what she was like. You had *three* years to get to know her. I know the only reason you brought her here was be·cause you knew she'd be a match as a donor, don't even pretend it's not. How *could* you? Your mother and I sent you here because it hosts the best renal treatment center in the county. I hired a nurse to help you. We even pulled strings to raise your name on the transplant list. Why did you have to go after Zoey and drag her into it? She's already been through *enough* because of us."

"Hey." I stepped between the two of them to get their attention. "What're you talking about?" I wasn't the type to butt in on a conversation, but tonight was just not my night to act like my usual self. "What is he talking about, Cora? And *who* is he?"

The man blinked at me as if remembering I was there. Then he noticed Asher, Noel, and Ten with an irritated scowl. Turning back to me because I'd been the one to talk, he said, "I think the better question is who are *you*? I'm her father, and if I learn you're the one who gave her that black eye, I assure you, you'll live to regret it."

"I didn't..." Wait. Huh? *Cora's* father? That wasn't what I was expecting him to say at all, though now that he'd said it, it made sense for him to speak to her in that authoritative way. But he looked way more like Zoey than he did Cora.

"I'm Quinn Hamilton," I said. I'd never met Cora's father before, I'd never even spoken to him on the phone, but after dating Cora for as long as I had, I was sure he'd at least recognize my name.

He didn't. Cora had never even bothered to tell her own father the name of the guy she was dating.

He turned toward Cora for an explanation, so I turned to her for the same thing.

She sneered, meeting my gaze. "Surprise. You fucked sisters."

"What?" Mr. Wilder and I said at the same time. We glanced at each other, both of our gazes full of accusation. Then we turned right back to her for clarification.

"Didn't Zoey tell you?" she asked me.

"Tell me *what?*" I growled, because there was no-thing to tell. There couldn't be. Because Zoey and Cora were not... They couldn't be...*sisters*.

No. Just...no.

"Dude, *sisters?*" Ten whispered to Noel, sounding awed. "I've never even had sisters."

Spinning to him, I yelled, "*They're not sisters!*"

"Oh, yes, we are." Cora's smirk turned my stomach. "Half sisters anyway. Dear old Dad over there could never keep it in his pants. And when Zoey's mom started prancing around him, in heat...well, you know what happens when you don't use protection."

"Cora," her father warned, his voice low.

"What?" She glared at him before turning back to taunt me. "I'm surprised Zoey never told you, Quinn. She seems like the type who can't keep a secret."

"Dear God," Mr. Wilder murmured, looking sick to his stomach as he backed toward the wall and leaned a hand against it. "She knows, then? How long has Zoey known?"

He asked Cora the question, but I was the one who answered. "She *doesn't* know." She couldn't.

Spotting the couch nearby, I sank down and dropped the box of Zoey's things on the floor by my feet. At least two people grabbed my shoulders for support as I buried my face into my hands.

But how the hell was this happening? Zoey and Cora were *sisters?*

When the front door opened, I didn't have to look up to know who entered. I could sense her presence tingling my skin. And then her voice came to me, trapping that lovely sound in my ears. A sigh of thanksgiving eased from me, knowing she was close, while at the same moment, my muscles tensed with dread. She had no idea what she'd just walked in on, and there was no way to warn her, no way to soften the blow.

"Mr. Wilder?" she said, clearly surprised by his presence. "What's going on?"

Just hearing her say his name in that way and in that tone told me everything I needed to know. I looked up at her, and I knew Cora had been lying yet again.

"She doesn't know," I said when her seeking gaze caught mine. "Someone needs to tell her."

I knew I couldn't. I closed my eyes, unable to look her in the eye without wanting to break down, or break something...or someone.

But I also wanted to yank her into my arms and carry her from this apartment, this place that was causing her so much misery. Then again, I was afraid to go near her, too. The violence in me was so close to the surface. What if I reminded her of her father—er, the man who'd raised her as her father—and scared her?

Cora tried to get out of telling her, so I growled, "*Tell* her."

Mr. Wilder's face paled with panic. He wasn't ready for his indiscretions to be made known, but Cora was already sighing and muttering, "Nine months be·fore you were born, my dad fucked your mom."

Surprise reined on Zoey's face, but I could tell she still didn't get it. Blinking repeatedly, she shook her head. "Excuse me?"

But then Caroline, whom I hadn't even known had come in with Zoey and was holding her hand, gasped. "Oh my God."

Zoey glanced at her, confused. "What?"

Caroline pointed at Mr. Wilder. "Cora's dad looks exactly like...*you.*"

Zoey turned back to look at Mr. Wilder, who backed up a space until he stumbled into a wall. Her face paled and she shook her head. "Wait. What?" She glanced around· the room, but when her gaze landed on me, I balled my hand and brought my fist to my mouth. I hated that lost expression on her face.

I still wanted to go to her, but I wasn't sure how she'd receive me. I'd broken up with her after she'd al·most been raped. She had every right in the world to hate me right now. Plus a vision of Cora's throat right before I'd almost tried to strangle her swept through me. I was too violent for Zoey. Too much like the man who'd raised her.

She shifted her focus away from me, flitting it be·tween Cora and her father. "That's...that's not possible. My father is... My father's Ernest K. Blake·land."

Mr. Wilder glanced down, but Cora sniffed. "No. Ernest K. Blakeland was simply *married* to your cheating whore of a mother. He knew her baby wasn't his, but he couldn't pin his anger on your mom be·cause she went and died giving birth to you, which left only you for him to take his anger out on."

"No," Zoey whispered, but I could tell from the horror on her face that she believed every word. She shook her head. "Why didn't you ever tell me this before?"

Cora threw her head back and laughed. "Tell you what? That our daddy was too chicken shit to claim you and risk losing all his money because his funds were tied up in Blakeland's bank? He'd be destroyed if anyone found out he was your sperm donor. It didn't even matter that I made sure he *knew* you were being beaten on a regular basis. He couldn't risk losing his investments. Now...be honest. If I'd told you about him, and you saw how he was more concerned with saving himself than saving you, you never would've agreed to give me your kidney. Would you?"

Zoey clutched her stomach and sank closer to Caro·line, who wrapped both arms around her in support. "But...but...why didn't you ever tell me before that? Before you knew about your sickness?"

Cora shrugged. "It never served my purpose. I kind of liked you being blind to the truth."

A half sob, half laugh left Zoey's lungs. She glanced at her biological father, who shook his head and held true regret in his eyes. "Zoey," he started, his voice full of apology.

But she held up a hand. "No, you don't have to say anything. I understand perfectly. You're just as egotistic and self·serving as *she* is. And you know what? I'm glad you never tried to claim me. I think I'd rather have been raised with manners *beaten* into me than raised to be like *her*."

Cora sniffed and crossed her arms over her chest. "I suppose this means you're not going to give me that kidney now, are you?"

This gut·clenching, defeated expression crossed Zoey's face. But despite the fact that each piece of news seemed to beat her down, she still straightened her back and lifted her chin. "Of course I'm going to give you one. I said I would. Unlike you, I'm actually honest about the things I say."

Her gaze met mine. I nodded my encouragement, more proud of her than I'd ever been. I wasn't sure if I could've been the bigger person in this moment and helped a person who'd wronged me as much as Cora had wronged us. But I loved her amazingly selfless heart, anyway.

Pain wrenched her face as she kept looking at me, though. She turned to Caroline. "I'm done here." She started for the door, but something in the box Asher held caught her attention.

She stopped and began to reach for one of her tattered notebooks.

"Don't—" I stepped toward her, but she'd already realized what the mess was. With a gasp, she curled her hand back to her chest. When tears filled her eyes, I couldn't handle her pain. "Zoey." I touched her shoulder, but she whirled away and rushed from the apartment with Caroline hot on her heels.

Feeling rejected, I panted out a breath before turning slowly toward the two Wilders who'd just destroyed my Zoey. Cora's father managed to look contrite, but Cora lifted her chin, daring me to say something.

"If you ever talk to her or me again—"

"You won't have to worry about that," her father cut me off, his gaze narrowing on Cora. "As soon as the transplant's complete, she'll be coming back home..." Cora opened her mouth to object, but he kept talking over her, "...unless she wants me to cut off her monthly stipend." When she gasped, he met her gaze. "Remember, Cora. You don't have any control over your trust fund until you're thirty."

"You bastard." Tears immediately filled her eyes. "Zoey was right. I think I'd rather have been raised by an abusive asshole too." Huffing out her anger, she spun around and stomped back to her room, where she slammed her door.

Her father glanced at us remaining men. I glared back, and he cleared his throat. "Do you boys need help carrying any of those boxes?" he asked.

FORTY-FOUR

QUINN

I DON'T KNOW how he did it, but Ten found out where Belcher was before the night was up. It was after two in the morning, but I didn't care. I wasn't get·ting any sleep until that bastard paid for what he'd done.

He'd left the after·party for the football players and was at a frat house. When we found him, he had his hand up some girl's skirt. Ten had filled me in on a few more details on the way over, only enraging me more when he mentioned where he'd seen Belcher putting his hands on Zoey.

That hand he pulled out of the girl's skirt when we barged into the room was the first thing I was going to break. The girl he was with now looked wasted but she was giggling, so at least he hadn't been forcing this one to do anything. Which only made me angrier. Why had he tried to force *Zoey*, then?

"Hey again, Belchie." Ten grinned cheerfully and waved a few fingers. "Guess what? I found that boy·friend you were looking for earlier. You remember Quinn Hamilton, right?"

Belcher's eyes widened as I advanced toward him. He tried to crawl off the bed but got tangled in the sheets and fell over backwards onto the floor. I helped him up, by the hair.

"I didn't know. I didn't know," he sobbed, lifting his hands in surrender. "I swear to God, I didn't know she was yours."

"So that made you think you had free reign to kiss her while she tried to fight you off, free reign to *hit* her, to put your fucking hand down her pants?" I grabbed his wrist. "*This* hand?"

He screamed when I slammed his hand into the wall, then he screamed even louder when I slammed his head into it next. I remembered seeing the bruise on Zoey's cheek at Cora's apartment, so I made sure Belcher had more than a few on *his* cheeks. Ten had told me Zoey had racked him between the legs, but I didn't think one hit to the junk was enough. Not nearly enough. So I kneed him there a few times be·fore I planted my fist in his gut. Just when his eyes rolled into the back of his head and he began to crumble, I hit him one last time in the jaw.

But that didn't satisfy me. I wanted to hit him more. I wanted to hurt him more. I stared down at his unconscious body I'd watched fall to my feet, and my knuckles cracked, thirsty for more blood, more crunching bone, more give of unwilling flesh.

Blood roaring through my system, I turned to Asher, Noel and Ten, who were simply standing back and watching the show with appreciation. "That wasn't enough," I growled.

Noel nodded his understanding.

They took me to the university athletics facility to work off some of my adrenaline rush and beat down some of my steam. I lifted weights, I ran laps, I took on a punching bag, but I was too fired up to stop, aching to hit something...someone.

For a while, Noel and Ten kept pace with me and worked out beside me without saying a word. Asher didn't even bother to try. He camped out on the floor, pulled out his phone, and started to play some game that beeped a lot.

I was still going hard when Noel held up his hands, begging me to stop. He flopped down on the in·door track, collapsing onto his back, and panted hard. Ten was curled up on a pile of floor mats, fast asleep, but Asher was still playing away on his phone.

"Man, you gotta stop or you're going to collapse."

I wasn't even close to collapsing. But I sat beside him anyway, wishing for...I don't know what. I wanted to see Zoey. The only thing I knew could calm me right now would be to pull her into my arms and bury my face in her hair. I need the smell of her hair, the warmth of her breath on my neck, the softness of her skin under my fingers.

But after what I'd done to Belcher and what I could've done to Cora, after knowing all that violence was still in me, yearning to get out, I was too afraid to go near her. What if I scared her? What if she thought I was just like Ernest K. Blakeland?

Besides, she had to hate me for walking away from her earlier? I was so ashamed; I didn't even know how to start to apologize to her for that.

"Why can't I stop wanting to hurt someone?" I didn't mean to mutter aloud.

I think Noel was still panting too hard to have heard me, but Asher lifted his face.

He finally put his phone away and hopped to his feet, looking wide awake. Then he strolled over to sit with us. "Hamilton," he said on a sigh, situating himself into a lazy sprawl. "You're not your dad."

I lifted my eyebrows. "What?"

He motioned to my bare torso where I'd taken off my shirt over an hour ago. "Your back. All those scars. You were beat a lot growing up, right? Well, my dad hit me too."

I wasn't expecting him to say that, but I shook my head. "No. My mom did that. I never knew my dad." My mom probably hadn't even known who he was.

Asher merely waved an unconcerned hand. "Mom, dad, whatever. My point's the same. You're not her. We're not them. Your mother's violence is not in-side you, and what you just went through tonight has nothing to do with her. You did all that shit to protect someone you love, to get justice for your girl, not be-cause you're an angry asshole who wants to strike out at the first person in your path."

Fear sprouted in my stomach. "But what if Zoey thinks I'm like that? Her dad hit her too. What if she hears what I did and thinks I'm like him?"

Asher shook his head. "She won't. Trust me. To Zoey, you hang the moon. She loves you, man."

I shuddered and about lost it. "I want to see her," I

admitted. I had been telling myself to stay away. Every awful thing that had happened to her was be-come of me. But I couldn't help it. I *had* to see her. "I know I shouldn't. She probably hates me, but I just...I gotta see her."

Noel nodded and clasped my back as he groaned and crawled to his feel. "I'll take you."

Asher ended up taking off then, but Ten and Noel came with me to Noel's house. We found Zoey curled up on Caroline's bed with her head in Caroline's lap, while a drowsy Caroline sat up against the headboard and stroked Zoey's long, blonde strands. I stood in the doorway, just watching her sleep in the fetal position as if trying to escape all the nightmares haunting her. Then she whimpered and began to cry in her sleep.

Tears slid down my own cheeks. My chest felt like it was on fire. Caroline murmured a few words to soothe her, and Zoey settled, but I didn't. I choked out a sob and glanced at Noel and Ten on either side of me.

Ten had been strong enough to stay away from Caroline even though he wanted her. He knew he was no good for her, just like I was no good for Zoey. With Cora being her sister, my past with my first girlfriend would always be there, between us. I didn't need to put that kind of drama in Zoey's life. I had caused this to happen to her.

But no matter how much I commanded myself to walk away and leave her in peace, I couldn't do it. Zoey had taught me what true love really was, and no way could I abandon that. Maybe I could get her to forgive me.

I went to her and crawled onto Caroline's bed to pull her into my arms.

Caroline sent me a tired, grateful smile and got off the bed to go give Noel a hug. Then all three of them moved out of the doorway.

Zoey stirred against me, burrowing into me and settling her ear against my heartbeat. "Quinn," she murmured sleepily.

I kissed her hair and stroked her back. "I'm here."

"Love you," she mumbled sleepily. I don't know if she was still too asleep to know what she was saying or if she honestly knew she was talking to me. But the words moved through me anyway.

"I love you too. With every beat of my heart, I am yours, Zoey Alaina Blakeland. And I'm so sorry for everything."

Her eyes fluttered open before she looked up at me. "You don't have anything to be sorry for."

"Yes, I do. I walked away tonight when I shouldn't have. I walked away without realizing something awful had happened to you."

"Did you beat up Belcher?" she asked.

I brushed my fingers delicately over the bruise on her cheek. "Yeah. Does that bother you?"

She shook her head. "No. I...I'm glad. Thank you. I don't...I don't like that guy."

I grinned and pressed my forehead to hers. "Neither do I."

"Is he going to be in a lot of pain for a while?"

"Yeah," I repeated. "He is."

She lifted her hand to my cheek. "Thank you."

I closed my eyes and breathed in her amazing smell. "Does this mean you'll take me back?"

"If you still want me."

I touched my lips to hers softly. "I've always wanted you, and I always will."

ZOEY

I WOKE ALONE IN Quinn's bed. The scent of him wafted up from his pillows and sheets and made me smile.

I'd almost been asleep in his arms on Caroline's bed last night when from somewhere Ten's voice said, "Well, pick her up and bring her with us, already. I'm tired as shit. Let's go home."

Quinn had sounded amused when his answer rumbled through his chest and into my ear. "You're not going to balk about her staying at our apartment?"

In return, Ten had sounded confused and a little insulted. "Why would I balk? She's your first real girl-friend. That'd be a pretty shitty, asshole move on my part to bar your woman from our place."

Quinn had merely laughed before he scooped me up. I closed my eyes, wrapped my arms around his neck, and burrowed in.

And now, here I was, where he'd deposited me on his

mattress before he'd crawled under the covers with me and held me all night long.

I stretched and glanced around, not really wanting to move, but wanting to find Quinn more than I wanted to stay still. I sat up and pushed the covers off my lap before patting Quinn's shirt I wore to sleep in down enough to cover the tops of my thighs. As soon as I went to stand, the bedroom door cracked open. Quinn peeked inside.

"Hi," I said, glowing from the inside out.

He stepped into the room, carrying a glass of juice. "Hey. You're awake."

When I nodded, he brought the cup to me. "Here. I brought you something to drink. Ten said he'd take care of breakfast."

I paused halfway through my first gulp to look up in surprise. "Ten cooks?"

Quinn's dimple appeared as he grinned at me. "No. But he buys. He'll be back with donuts."

"Oh." I drained the rest of my glass before setting it on the nightstand. "Donuts sound good." My hands went to my lap as I eyed him. Knowing how much we had to discuss, I was suddenly uncertain of where to start. "So..."

He sat beside me and set his hand on my bare knee. "How're you doing?" His voice moved through me, a prayer and thanksgiving.

I looked up at him. The concern in his eyes made me ache.

I shook my head. "I don't know," I answered honestly.

His lips twitched with amusement. "Yeah. I think I'm about the same."

He was driving me crazy, being so polite. I needed to know just how much he must still be mad about.

"Are you upset that I never told you?" I burst out, only to bite the corner of my lip. "About Cora, I mean."

He blew out a shaky breath and grazed his hand over my knee before he ran his fingers up my thigh, where he grasped my hands from my lap and gripped them snuggly.

His voice was soft, without a hint of malice when he murmured, "What was it you once said to me: It wasn't your secret to tell?"

I frowned and shook my head. "But this...this affected *us*. You and me. You wouldn't have ever dumped her that night if you'd just known she was sick, would you?"

His amazing blue eyes held apology when they met mine. "I don't know. Probably not. Then again, my feelings for you were pretty strong. I honestly don't know how long I could have kept denying them and stayed with her. Stayed away from you."

With a nod, I bolstered my shoulders wider. It felt good to hear him say that, but... "You would've denied them forever," I said with complete assurance. "Because you're just that kind of guy. Being a good, honorable man is worth more to you than your own happiness." I sent him a smile to help him know I respected that about him. "We never would've gotten together if I'd have just told you the truth a long time ago."

He didn't return my smile. Instead, he seemed to deflate. "Are you asking if I regret us?"

"No." I immediately shook my head, but then I squeezed my eyes shut and lowered my face. "I don't know. I don't think I could handle your answer if I asked that."

He moved closer. I felt the heat from his body soak into me, and the warmth of his breath as he lowered his face to talk into my ear. Then I heard him loud and clear when he whispered, "I don't. I don't regret being with you at all." He kissed my forehead gently.

Well, I had been right. I couldn't handle his answer, even though it was the one I wanted to hear. Guilt, and longing, and love tore through me. I curled my shoulders in and immediately started to cry.

"But I'm her sister. Her *sister*." I still couldn't believe that part.

Quinn's strong arms enveloped me, and he crushed me to his chest. "I don't care." His palm cupped my face and he led me to him, where I rested my chest over his heartbeat and listened to the rhythmic lub-dub inside him as silent tears streamed down my face.

I wrapped my arms around his waist and grab-bed handfuls of the back of his shirt as he cradled me and let me cry all over him. He was warm and familiar. I selfishly gobbled up the moment, inhaling his spicy scent, memorizing the cadence of his heart, soaking in as much of his heat as I could steal. I loved hugging this man.

He threaded his fingers through my hair and shifted stray strands out of my face. "Better yet?"

I nodded against him, unwilling to break contact just

yet. "Yes. Thank you." I looked up and smiled through wet lashes, knowing I didn't deserve such affection from him.

But he just kept on giving it, regardless.

"I have something for you." He shifted, and I watched him lean off the side of the bed to pick up something from the floor. When he pulled up a familiar, tattered old notebook, my mouth fell open.

"How...?"

"It's the one I borrowed from you, remember?" He handed me the only few short stories I had left in one thin notebook.

I took it reverently.

He sent me a sad smile. "And here..." He thrust a small thumb drive at me next. "It took me so long to get it back to you because I typed it all out. I wanted you to have an electronic file too. I kept worrying about fires and floods destroying them, but I never thought Hurricane Cora would the one to...well, any-way...I know it's not enough to make up for the ones you lost, but...here."

I couldn't even accept the thumb drive; I was too busy bursting into a fresh batch of tears. "Thank you," I sobbed.

The sweetest man on earth was sitting right here, letting me soak the shirt I'd borrowed from him to wear, and I'd done nothing but hurt him.

"I love you so, *so* much," I babbled as I bawled, hugging my notebook hard.

He chuckled softly. "I was just going to say that to *you*." Tugging me into his lap, he wrapped his large, warm arms around me. "Do you know how happy I am that you came into my life? It feels as if I didn't really start living until you."

I shook my head, confused. "But I..."

He kissed me, shutting me up. "I know there's a lot going against us right now, but I don't care. As long as you're at my side, willing to accept me, I'm willing to work through anything."

Love exploded inside me. "Then so am I."

His grin lit up his dimple. "That's all I need to hear. We can handle this, Zoey. You and I."

FORTY-FIVE

⚜ ZOEY ⚜

I STOOD IN THE stands of ESU's football stadium for Quinn's divisional championship game and shouted with the rest of the roaring fans as Ten caught a pass from Noel and went in for a touchdown, tying the score up with our opponents.

"We're going to win, we're going to win, we're going to *win!*" Caroline chanted, nearly squeezing my arm off as she jumped up and down beside me, screaming her excitement as well.

There was still nearly four minutes left in the game. Anything could happen. But yeah, I had a feeling we were going to win.

"Go, Ellamore," I called. Our voices were flooded out by the other seven thousand fans yelling around us, but we didn't care. It only made us scream louder.

"Wait? Why is Noel staying on the field?" a confused Aspen said from the other side of Caroline. "Shouldn't the kicker be coming out for the one-point field goal?"

"Oh, shit," a tense Mason muttered from behind us. "They're going for the two-point conversion."

"Is that bad?" Reese asked, clutching his arm as if she thought it had to be bad.

"Not bad. Just riskier," Pick answered her, rubbing his hands up and down Eva's shoulders like some kind of good-luck charm.

I glanced around at our group and just grinned, feeling elated and hopeful. It was nice being here with them. Since moving in with Ten and Quinn and openly dating Quinn, they'd accepted me with no qualms at all, even though they all knew who my sister was and what she'd done. For the first time in my life, I was genuinely liked and welcomed as one of them. I had friends.

Next to me, Asher leaned close and murmured into my ear, "What's a two-point conversion again?"

I laughed and started to point out the different players and explain it to him, but Noel had already snapped the ball and the play had begun. Forgetting my explanation, I watched as he hand-passed the pigskin to Quinn, and Quinn dove into a pile of defenders. I held my breath, waiting with seven thousand other people to see if he'd crossed the line for the two extra points.

When a referee swiped out his hands, indicating the points were no good, Caroline clutched her face and wailed, "*No!*"

On the other side of Aspen, her two younger brothers hollered their disappointment just as loudly.

"It's okay," I reassured them. "It's okay. We're still tied."

We still had time on the clock to make more points, even if it was time for the other team to take possession of the ball. We could just keep them from scoring and then go into overtime to win.

But we still had three and a half minutes left, so I wasn't worried. A lot could happen in three and a half minutes.

All the players, except one, stood and trotted off the field to switch teams.

"Someone's hurt," Eva announced. "Who's hurt?"

We could tell it was one of our players by the color of the jersey. I immediately scanned the field for Quinn's number. When I spotted him next to Ten, I blew out a relieved breath...until a frantic Aspen asked, "Where's Noel? I don't see Noel anywhere."

"He's the one who's hurt," Caroline uttered, suddenly pale.

I grabbed her hand and she squeezed back.

Aspen gasped and immediately covered her mouth with her hands. "Oh God. Oh God. Oh God."

Reese and Eva rubbed her shoulders supportively from behind while Noel's brother's pointed when Noel bent his knee and the coaches helped him sit upright.

"Oh, thank God," Aspen breathed out.

But I could tell Noel wasn't completely fine. His legs could work because he stood up and everyone clapped as he hobbled to the sidelines, but he carried his shoulder all wrong.

For the next couple of plays, the ESU defense held the other team back, but not enough to keep them from scoring a field goal, putting us three points behind. All the while, Quinn and Ten—strictly offensive players—huddled around Noel, where he sat on a bench and had trainers working all around him.

When it was time for the offence to take the field again, Noel, the leading quarterback, did not join them. A minute and forty-eight seconds remained on the clock, and their second-string backup had to step in for him. *Quinn* had to step in for him.

"Oh my God," I uttered, covering my mouth as my stomach instantly began to churn. The divisional championships now rested on my boyfriend's shoulders.

Aspen's phone chimed. She checked the text. "It's from Noel. Oh God. He says they think he broke his collarbone. They're going to take him to the hospital."

"Well, let's go then," Caroline announced. "We can meet him there."

Noel's family and even Eva, Pick, Mason and Reese all gathered their things to leave. "Zoey?" Caro-line asked, glancing at me to silently ask if I was coming.

But I shook my head. Quinn had just been thrust into the spot of quarterback at the most crucial time ever. I couldn't leave him now.

"I...I'm going to stay."

Asher took my hand. "I'll stick around with her and bring her over once the game's done."

Caroline nodded, and then she was gone, hurrying away to follow her family.

I glanced up at Asher. He sent me a bolstering smile. "So, I know squat about football, but I can tell your man just got put in the hot seat, right?"

"Right," I said.

The catcher who'd taken on the punt had tried to run for it, only getting us to the fifteen-yard line. I chewed my nails as a huddle formed around Quinn and he pointed out the next game plan to them.

"But he'll do just fine," I told Asher. "He'll do great." Because he was great at everything he did.

Asher squeezed my hand. "Yes, he will," he agreed.

I clamped my grip around his fingers, and the play began. The ball was hiked to Quinn. His lineman charged into the defensive line to keep them at bay, the clang of helmets and shoulder pads making me hold my breath. When a defensive linebacker broke free and charged him, I squeaked in fear, knowing he was about to be sacked. But Quinn spun from the tackle and dodged out of the pocket, looking down the field for a receiver to catch a pass.

Ten broke free of the safety following him. As soon as he was open, Quinn wound back his arm and launched the ball his way with a Hail Mary. When it landed in Ten's arms perfectly, I screamed and jumped up and down. Ten clutched the ball to his chest and ran a good ten more yards before he was tackled, but I kept jumping and screaming out my excitement. I sprang at Asher and hugged him before laughing and screaming some more. After such a huge play, we still weren't far enough down the field to try for a field goal, though. And now we only had thirty-eight seconds left in the game with the clock still ticking, and no timeouts left for our team.

Quinn had to down the ball to stop the clock, but that left us with only two tries to make it ten yards before we'd have to kick.

"You can do it. You can do it. You can do it," I chanted, watching him as he clapped his hands, breaking up the huddle. He would have to throw—there wasn't time to try to run the ball. And everyone knew it. So the defense covered all the receivers. Quinn looked toward Ten first. But Ten had two defensive players around him, keeping him from catching anything. So, Quinn checked out another receiver, but that guy tripped and fell.

No one was open.

The defense closed in around him. Quinn side-stepped one guy trying to tackle him and found an opening, where he began to run. Oh God, he was going for it.

Since he usually played as a tight end, he knew how to run with the ball. And that's what he did. He broke free of the main cluster, but a safety started for him and would've caught him if Ten hadn't appeared out of nowhere and blocked that guy, keeping him from reaching Quinn. From there on out, he had a free sprint to the goal line, where he made a touchdown and won us the divisional championship game.

This time, even Asher screamed and jumped with me, sharing my enthusiasm. We danced in a circle and roared with the rest of the ESU fans. Our team was going to play in the national championships for the second year in a row.

"Let's go see if we can intercept your man." Asher took my hand and we tried to weave through the crowd together, but there was no way to get out onto the field with Quinn.

So we waited just outside the gates where the team came through. More people gathered, waiting for them as well. When Ten and Quinn came through together, their helmets off, with their sweaty hair sticking to their foreheads while they grinned out their victory, a crowd erupted with cheers.

Some groupie grabbed Quinn by the face and stamped a kiss to his mouth, but he immediately pulled away and scowled at her. I couldn't even be out·raged; I didn't blame the girl at all for her enthusiasm and wanting a piece of him. And since he instantly wiped the back of his hand over his mouth and glanced around until he spotted me—only me—well... groupies could try to get at him all they wanted. I knew he wasn't interested in them.

This man was all mine.

His grin grew. He mouthed my name, or maybe he shouted it, and I just couldn't hear it through all the people. As he tried to make his way to me, the crowd parted for him and suddenly, there he was, his shoulder pads making him larger than ever.

He picked me up off my feet and spun me in a circle before kissing me hard on the mouth. "We won."

Laughing, I stroked his face and touched his dimple. "I saw."

"Blondie!" Ten yanked me out of my boyfriend's arms before engulfing me in a bone·crushing hug. "Did you see that shit? We're so fucking awesome."

He glanced around, looking for more people to hug, maybe. But when all he saw with me was Asher, his face fell. "Where's everyone else?"

"They all went to the hospital for Noel."

Quinn nodded and grasped my hand. "Give us a minute to change and we'll go over with you guys."

I stepped back to Asher's side, and Ten and Quinn let their team sweep them along to their locker room.

Half an hour later, the four of us entered Noel's hospital room, where everyone else was already gathered around Noel's bed. We lurched to a stop when we found him sobbing against Aspen's shoulder.

"I'm sorry," he kept telling her. "I'm so sorry."

"What are you sorry for, baby?" She smoothed his hair out his face. "You played an amazing game. I'm so proud of you."

"I lost us the game, a shot at nationals, and no way do I have a chance at going pro now. How the hell am I going to support you guys with no future?"

"You do too have a future," Aspen scolded. "You're a smart, amazing, talented man. You'll be able to do anything outside professional football that you want. And don't you dare even worry about money. If we have each other, we can always work around that. Besides..." She shrugged. "I was scared about you going pro, anyway. You'd be out of town on so many away games, having all kind of gorgeous woman, *nationwide*, trying to get into your pants."

"Are you insane?" he squawked. "I would never cheat on you."

As he pulled her in for a hug and kissed each one of her closed eyes before kissing her mouth, I cleared my throat. "And you didn't lose us the game today, either."

Caroline gasped, "What? We *won*?" just as Noel and Aspen broke apart in surprise to gape at us.

As Quinn, Ten, Asher and I entered the room, Ten hooked his thumb over his shoulder to point at Quinn. "Mr. Second-String Quarterback here broke free of the line and ran forty-five yards for a touch-down. We're going to nationals. Again."

"You're going to...holy shit," Noel breathed. A smile broke across his face before he nodded respect-fully at Quinn. "Way to go, Hamilton. I knew you could do it."

"I'm sorry," an authoritative voice broke in from behind

us, making Quinn and me part and turn a·round to see the man in a suit standing in the door·way. "Is this Noel Gamble's room?"

"Dr. Frenetti?" Aspen gasped. She moved away from Noel's bedside to frown curiously at the older gentlemen. "What're *you* doing here?"

He frowned in acute displeasure when he met her gaze. "Aspen," he bit out, even as his gaze shifted to Noel, who was lying pale and sweaty on the bed with his arm wrapped in a cast. "I came to see if it was true. Your collarbone's broken, then?"

Noel nodded. "Yeah." His eyes narrowed. "But somehow, I'm not sensing your concern."

Dr. Frenetti held his hands behind his back. "We had an understanding the last time we talked, Mr. Gamble."

With a scowl, Noel glanced around the room at everyone gathered inside. His confused frown clearly told us he had no idea what this Dr. Frenetti guy was talking about. He returned his attention to the older man. "And I did what I was supposed to do. I stayed on the team and got us this far."

Lips flattening in a thin, disappointed line, Dr. Frenetti shook his head. "I only agreed *not* to expose her," he paused to send Aspen a significant, distasteful glance, "if you *won* nationals. This..." He flashed out his hand to motion to Noel's injury, "...is no better than where we ended last year."

Noel shook his head. "No." He glanced at Aspen, his gaze desperate. She went to his side, and he immediately took her hand. "You can't do that. She... you've already fired her. She's been gone from there for *months*. How could you...it's not my fault some asshole broke my collarbone."

"And it's not my fault you broke your word. I'm sending your story to the tabloids in the morning."

"*What?*" Aspen and Noel cried together.

Caroline waved her hands. "Wait. What? You're going to punish her just because she fell in love with my brother? What kind of douchebag—"

The rest of her rant was muffled behind Ten's hand. "He's a very *powerful* douchebag, sweetness," he told her quietly enough that only Quinn, Caroline and I could hear him. "Aspen's old boss can still des·troy her with just a few words in the right ears."

"I'm *punishing* her," Dr. Frenetti stated, "because she broke university policy and slept with a—"

"Oh, would you look at the *time!*" Reese spoke up loudly as she slapped her hands over Colton's ears, while beside her, Eva was busy trying to plug Brandt's. "It's time for us to take these *minors* out of the room."

But Noel's brothers were having none of it. They smacked the hands aside. "I'm not going anywhere," Brandt said, glancing back and forth between Noel and Dr. Frenetti. "I want to know what's going on. What did Aspen do that was so bad?"

Worried for the entire Gamble family, I gulped and reached for Quinn's hand. I glanced up at him as he took my fingers. He met my gaze before stepping forward and holding up a hand to gain everyone's attention.

"Aspen did nothing wrong," he answered Brandt before he turned to Dr. Frenetti. "And this man here isn't going to do anything to hurt her, either, because Noel *is* going to keep his word. Nationals are still two weeks away, and we're *still* going to win that game, whether he plays or not."

"And who do you think you are?" Dr. Frenetti asked, eyeing Quinn with some serious censure.

Rooting myself at my man's side, I squeezed his hand and smiled up at him with proud admiration. "He's Quinn Hamilton."

Dr. Frenetti's eyes widened. "Q-Quinn Hamilton, the backup quarterback who just—"

"Won the divisional championships for us?" Ten spoke up with a smirk. "Yep, that would be him. And I'm Oren Tenning, by the way. And no fucking way are we letting you get the drop on our man Gamble. Nationals are in the bag, and we *will* win."

"You should go back to wherever you came from now," Quinn said, "Because Noel is going to keep his end of the bargain, which means you need to keep yours too."

Aspen's old boss didn't seem to know what to say to that. He stuttered for a moment, glancing between Ten, Quinn, and Noel before he said, "You better win at nationals, or I'm taking that whore down."

"*What* did you just call her?"

While Asher, Pick, Mason, and Quinn surged toward the bed to keep Noel from coming off it to charge Dr. Frenetti, Ten threw his arm around the older man's shoulder and sent him a stiff smile. "Good to know, but you should probably go now."

He forcibly steered Dr. Frenetti from the room, and the other guys started talking all at once to calm an enraged Noel. I moved toward a white-faced As-pen, but Caroline, Reese, and Eva were already surrounding her and trying to comfort her.

Ten strolled back into the room, sans the asshole. He looked completely unconcerned that his best friend was freaking out on a bed and Aspen was nearly in tears. Instead, he strolled up to Asher and wrapped a companionable arm around his shoulders. "Hart, for the love of God, just start singing or something."

Asher glanced at him as if he was insane. "*What?*"

"This is a good day. We just won our biggest game of the year, Gamble's not going to leave us for the big leagues after all, and his woman just avoided becoming a scandal. So, why's everyone so upset? We should be celebrating. Now, get the party started with that special voice of yours that seems to drop panties on command and sing something."

Asher shook his head, but after a moment, he did start singing. When Noel realized he was singing Bob Marley's "Everything's Gonna Be Alright," he snorted and threw his pillow at Asher.

"Asshole." But it was obvious that Ten had been right—the song was already calming Noel's temper.

Asher caught the pillow to his chest. Then he strolled to Aspen, knelt in front of her, and began to serenade her through the rest of the song, flinging the pillow around with a flourish.

When I glanced up at Ten, who'd stopped beside me, I smiled at him and bumped my elbow into his. "That was unconventional, but it worked."

He grinned back, proud of himself. Then he scowled and shook his finger threateningly. "If you pet my head again and call me a good boy, I'm kicking Ham in the nuts so he can't pleasure you for at least a week."

"Do it anyway, Zoey," Pick called with a grin. "Hamilton's still got a tongue to please you with."

I groaned and buried my scorching hot cheeks in my hands. This group had a dirtier mind than any I'd ever thought I'd be a part of, but I loved being one of them anyway.

"Hey, leave her be," Quinn chided as he came to me and wrapped his arms around my waist from be-hind. "No one is going to prevent me from pleasing her in every way possible."

"Aww. You two are just too cute together." Reese nudged Eva and continued bobbing her head and swaying back and forth to Asher's song. "Didn't I tell you they were going to end up together the first day I met her?"

Eva looped her arm with Reese and they swayed together. "You called it, sweetie. Way to go."

I looked up at Quinn and he looked down at me. We started grinning simultaneously because I think we both realized we'd known it somehow too. We were just meant to be together. As our friends kept being crazy and ridiculous around us, we leaned into each other and kissed.

ƐPILOGUE

৶ QUINN ৶

TIRED OF WAITING, worried out of my mind, and shifting in my seat because my butt had gone numb, I glanced at my forearm I had crossed over my chest. Fresh ink stared up at me, amazing me all over again that I had an honest to God tattoo.

I traced the National Championships emblem in awe just as Ten elbowed me from his seat at my right.

"I still think you're fucking crazy for getting that tattoo. You know that, right?"

With a grin, I shook my head. "I was just following tradition. All you guys got your tattoos the night before the big game last year, so I had to do it this year."

"Yeah, and if we would've *kept* following tradition, we would've lost the next day, too."

"But we didn't." We'd won the national championship title, and Dr. Frenetti had kept silent about Noel and Aspen's relationship.

Ten snorted. "Yeah, you're a lucky we didn't lose."

I shrugged. "We had a reason to win this year."

"Hell, we had a reason to win *last* year, but we couldn't pull it out of our asses then."

"We had a better reason to win this year."

Ten seemed to think that over before he nodded. "Yeah," he agreed. "Gamble and his woman didn't need to turn into a national scandal. That's for sure. And what are up with these damn waiting room chairs? Do they purposely want your ass to go dead while you're sitting in them?"

I smiled. "You didn't have to wait with me."

Ten glanced away and grumbled something un-der his breath. I bumped my knee into his as my way of telling him thanks for sticking around anyway. It was Christmas Eve and everyone else in our group was home with their families right now, celebrating the holidays.

I was sitting here, though, because this was the date Cora had chosen from a handful of options to receive her new kidney. Worry lanced through me anew. They'd already been in surgery for over two hours. How much more time did they need for Zoey's part of the whole ordeal to be over?

"You think everything's going okay?" I asked under my breath as I glanced across the room to where Mr. Wilder and his wife—Cora's mother—were seated, waiting for news about her.

"Blondie?" Ten asked with a snort. "Hell, yes, she'll be fine. God wouldn't let something bad happen to one of his angels."

I glanced at him in surprise, because what he'd said didn't sound like anything he would say, *ever*. But then I saw the anxious gleam in his eyes, and I realized he was worried too.

He and Zoey had grown close since she'd moved in with us two months ago. He always found a way to talk her into doing his laundry or cooking his favorite breakfast, and she not only tolerated his crude, foul mouth, but she seemed to adore it and liked to pamper him. They acted almost like...siblings.

I was just glad they got along as well as they did because to me, they were the closest thing to family I had. Zoey was my other, better half, and Ten had turned into a much better friend than I'd ever thought he'd be.

Before I could respond to Ten's uncharacteristically sweet comment, Zoey's surgeon appeared in the doorway of the waiting room. I'd met him before they'd put her under the anesthesia. Remembering me, he came straight over. "Her surgery went well."

Relief poured through me, and Ten patted my knee in

congratulations. Across the room, Cora's dad stood as if to stretch, but I could tell he wanted to listen in on Zoey's report. I narrowed my eyes at him and then kept listening to the surgeon's technical jargon until he said we could go wait in her room and be there when she was brought down from recovery.

We waited for a little over half an hour before they wheeled her in. Her eyes were drowsy and her face a little swollen and pale, but her smile was all for me.

"Hey, you." Her voice was hoarse and barely above a whisper, but I didn't care. She was alive and smiling.

"Hey, yourself." I took her hand and sat beside her. "How're you feeling?"

"Cold." Her teeth began to chatter, so Ten and I hunted up some blankets to cover her.

I tucked the last one gently over her shoulders. "Any better yet?"

She closed her eyes and nodded with a sigh. "Yes. Thank you."

I kissed her forehead and began to stroke her hair behind her ear. "The doctor said you did great. Hardly any bleeding and no complications."

"Any word on Cora yet?" she asked, her lashes fluttering open.

I shook my head. I didn't care what happened to Cora or how her end of the surgery worked out, but then...I guess I didn't want Zoey to part with a kidney, only for it to go to waste and be rejected by Cora's body. So maybe I did care a little.

"No. Haven't heard anything."

Zoey nodded her understanding, and her gaze shifted to the other side of her bed where our room-mate lingered with his hands stuffed in his pockets.

"Ten," she said and slowly reached out an IV-stuck hand his way.

He caught her fingers. "Hey, Blondie. Glad you didn't die. Ham probably would've become a pain in the ass to live with if you had."

Her chest shook as she laughed softly. "I imagine he would have." Her smile settled into a gaze of adoration. "You're seriously never going to call me Zoey, are you?"

Ten shrugged. "Probably not." His eyes filled with a pain I'd never seen in him before. Glancing away, he mumbled what sounded like, "That was my sister's name."

Zoey's smile died. "Was?" she repeated.

He cleared his throat and met her gaze before nodding. "Yeah. Was." With a wince, he shook his head. Then he leaned down swiftly and stamped a quick kiss to her forehead. "I better go. I've got a fucking family thing I should probably go suffer through before the holiday's over. Just...take care of yourself, will you? And make sure this asshole takes care of you, too."

"Okay." Zoey let go of his hand and watched him stride from the room. Then her concerned gaze found mine. "Did you know he had a sister named Zoey who died?"

I shook my head, in just as much shock as she was in. "I had no idea he'd even *had* a sister." *Much less that her name had been Zoey, or that she'd died.*

"Poor Ten. I wonder how he was ever able to talk to me at all."

A smile lit up my face. "Easy. How could anyone *not* talk to you? You're a freaking angel."

She snorted and rolled her eyes, but the smile that followed told me how much she loved the praise. "I love you," she whispered.

I kissed her knuckles. "Not as much as I love you. In a way, I'm glad you decided to come to Ellamore and give away one of your kidneys, because it brought you to me."

"You know what," she slurred, "So am I. Thank God my half-sister is an evil, conniving witch, or we never would've met."

Together, we laughed softly. We'd discovered that finding a way to laugh and make light of it was easier to handle than the cold, dark truth: Cora was evil, and Zoey would always be connected to her.

Zoey's eyelashes fluttered, and I knew she needed rest. I was about to tell her to get some sleep while I kept watch over her, but someone knocked softly on the opened doorframe.

It was Cora's father. I straightened and stiffened indignantly, but Zoey's grip on my fingers warned me to behave.

"Hi," she said simply, not welcoming him, but not giving him the cold shoulder either.

"Hey." His gaze softened as he glanced over at her and stepped hesitantly into her room. "So, I see you made it through okay."

Zoey nodded. "How's Cora?"

His mouth twitched into a half grimace, half smile. "She made it through surgery as well. So far her body is accepting your kidney."

Zoey's shoulders eased. "Good."

Her biological father glanced away and cleared his throat. "I just wanted to tell you how sorry I am...for everything." When his green gaze met hers, her fingers clamped even tighter around mine. "If I had known what Cora was doing earlier, I would've put a stop to it long ago. I can only assure you that she won't bother you again..." His gaze flickered my way. "She won't bother *either* of you. She's always had a strong will and wanted her own way. Just like her mother. It's been a challenge to keep her even moderately in line. And..." He sighed and glanced down at his hands, touched his wedding ring before he kept talking. "I probably shouldn't have allowed her so much contact with you when you started high school. I knew she'd end up trying to control you. She does that with everyone. But..." He gave a half shrug. "I guess I was curious about you, too. Please believe me when I say you don't have to worry about her again. If there's one thing she listens to and respects, it's money. And since I control hers, I can keep her away from you."

"Thank you," Zoey said.

"And about...about Ernest." Shaking his head, he glanced away in shame. "It's troubled me for years, knowing how he treated you. But my marriage and—"

"You don't have to explain anything," Zoey broke in, wincing when she probably tensed enough to pull something she shouldn't have. I moved to remove Mr. Wilder from her room, but she tightened her grip on my hand, stopping me.

"I'm not proud of myself. There are so many wrong decisions I've made." Emotion swamped his features. "But Cora was wrong when she told you your mother and I were just some casual fling. Your mother was...." When his eyes misted, he cleared his throat. "She was everything good and kind; she re·minds me so much of you. Maybe if she had lived..." With a shake of his head, he cleared his throat again. "I know it's too late to save you from what Ernest did to you for all those years, but I *can* help keep him away from here on out. I've gone to the private investigator he hired to find you, and I paid him double to make sure you're never found."

I glanced at Zoey just as tears filled her eyes. "I...I appreciate that."

Mr. Wilder nodded. He drew in a deep breath and glanced away. "Well...I'd tell you to call me if you every needed anything, but I understand if you never want any more contact with me." He turned his attention to me and rasped, "Take care of my little girl," be-fore he spun away and hurried from the room.

"Wow," Zoey said, her voice hoarse and eyes more watery than ever. "That was my dad. My real dad." She glanced up at me, and I knew she'd contact Mr. Wilder again. She wanted a relationship with her real father. "I think he might actually love me."

I leaned down and pressed my forehead to hers. "Of course he does. You're impossible not to love."

"Oh, you're just saying that because...because..." She frowned, trying to think up a reason.

I smiled. "Because I had a million and one rea-sons *not* to fall for you, but I did anyway?"

"You did, didn't you?" She gazed at me with appreciation before closing her eyes. "Merry Christ-mas Eve, Quinn. I don't know what's going to happen from here on out, but knowing I'll be sharing it all with you makes me eager to start it."

"Amen," I murmured. "With you in my life, I'm looking forward to everything."

THE END

*U*P *N*EXT

A PERFECT TEN
Ten's Story

Let your hair down, Caroline, they said.
It'll be fun, they said.

I know I've closed myself off in a major way in the past year, ever since "the incident" where I messed up my life completely. It's past time I try to live again or just give up completely. But this is quite possibly the craziest thing I've ever done. In a last ditch effort to invigorate myself, I'm standing outside Oren Tenning's bedroom, I just peeled off the sexiest pair of underwear I own, and my hand is already raised to knock. My brother would disown me for doing anything with his best friend, and he'd probably kill Oren. But if I play my cards right, no one will ever know about this. Not even Ten.

Maybe after tonight, I'll finally get over this stupid, irrational crush I hate having on the biggest jerk I've ever met. Or maybe I'll just end up falling for him even harder. Maybe I'll discover there's so much more to my crude, carefree hunk than meets the eye.

ACKNOWLEDGEMENTS

There are so many people to thank, so much support I don't deserve. But I appreciate it all anyway! To name just a few of you lovely individuals:

To my beta/early readers: Shi Ann Crumpacker, Alaina Martinie, Lindsay Brooks, Ana Kristina Rabacca, Patty Brehm, Chelcie Holguin, Eli Castro, Mary Rose Bermundo, Amanda at Beta Reading Bookshelf, Jennifer at Three Chicks and Book, Jawairya, Laurie at Just One More Page, and Michelle and Pepper at AllRomance Book Reviews. Thank you times a million! Your feedback was so awesome. I think I used most every suggestion for improvement you guys gave me. So many grateful hugs to you.

I can't thank my critique partner, Ada Frost, enough for being there at every phase of this project. This story really is for you!

Here's to my editor Stephanie Parent, proofreader Shelley at 2 Book Lovers Reviews, and then my niece Katie Cap for willing to give my story another final proofread! You're the people who make my messy crud shine and look like something people might actually be able to read. Such book magicians! Thank you.

I'd also like to thank my growing support from readers: people like Soha Khalil! Thank you for the ego boost and making me feel awesome by asking if I was the real Linda Kage writing back to you. I was! Then hugs and kisses to Jodi Bibliophile for a support I could never repay. Eva will gladly share Pick with you! To Sarah Turner for the sweetest letter anyone has ever written to me, trying to make me bawl! To others like Tiffany Choez and Audrey Thunder for tagging me so much when you mention some of my books on Facebook. Things like that totally thrill me. And thanks to reviewers like Jawairya, Jennifer Skewes, and Heather Carver who contact me right after I post about a new upcoming book, making me think people really want to read my stories! And thanks to others like Kari Matthes who contacted me on Goodreads just to gush. You have no idea how all your kind words chase away the doubts and keep me writing. Thank you.

To my entire, huge family. I love you guys. I love your support and story ideas, especially that one from Mark for a coon hunting romance! Thank you to Kurt and Lydia for putting up with me on the daily and for not yet dropping me off at a curb somewhere and speeding away as fast as you can. You're the best!

Finally, thanks to Jesus Christ for dying for my sins (whew!) because there's no way I'll get to Heaven someday on my own steam. Your love, mercy, and grace humbles me. Thank you.

ABOUT THE AUTHOR

Linda grew up on a dairy farm in the Midwest as the youngest of eight children. Now she lives in Kansas with her husband, daughter, and their nine cuckoo clocks. Her life's been blessed with lots of people to learn from and love. Writing's always been a major part her world, and she's so happy to finally share some of her stories with other romance lovers. Please visit her at her website

www.LindaKage.com

Made in the USA
Lexington, KY
20 October 2017